Tinted Chapstick

The San Francisco Mystery Series, Book 4

ALEXI VENICE

Published by Palmer Publishing

ISBN-13: 979-8842758012

Editor: Rob Bignell at Inventing Reality Editing Service.

Book Cover Design: Bo Bennett and Alexi Venice

Formatting: Bo Bennett at BookMarketingPro

Books by Alexi Venice

The San Francisco Mystery Series
Bourbon Chase, Book 1
Amanda's Dragonfly, Book 2
Stabscotch, Book 3
Tinted Chapstick, Book 4
Sativa Strain, Book 5
#SandyBottom, Book 6
Lady Hawthorne, Book 7

The Monica Spade Series
Conscious Bias
Standby Counsel
Graffiti Red Murder

Standalone
Hawaiian Paradise Surprise

Dedicated to My Creative Team for The San Francisco Mystery Series.

Contents

1

San Francisco

Jen looked through the peephole in Tommy's front door and her heart exploded with rage. Roxy MacNeil was standing on the other side.

That fucking bitch. How dare she show her face here after stealing Amanda!

With frantic fingers, Jen unbolted the door, an adrenaline surge coursing through her veins. She swung it wide and stood face-to-face with the faux-grunge Scottish savant.

"I'm sorry—" Roxy said, her trademark shock of blonde hair falling across her smoky blue eyes, tempting Jen to rip it out by the roots.

Jen's fury and hatred coalesced into an explosive force as she drove her shoulder into Roxy's slim chest, slamming her against the wall of the covered porch.

"Whoa!" A whoosh of air rushed from Roxy's lungs—a sound so satisfying to Jen.

"Fuck you!" Jen hissed, straightening to full height so she could pummel the evil pussy poacher who had seduced Amanda. Fueled by betrayal and humiliation, Jen landed a punch with her right fist into Roxy's rib cage.

Roxy doubled over in pain, gasping for air.

A fraction of the pain you caused me, Jen thought.

Jen's initial dominance indicated this might be a very quick fight, even though Roxy had bragged at Delores Park only a week ago that she was a *government spy. Ha! Laughable!*

"Stand up and fight like the secret agent you supposedly are!" Jen snarled, raising her fists. Something she had never done in her life.

Roxy held up a hand, signaling for mercy while gulping air. After several breaths, she straightened in time to see Jen's fist coming toward her face. At the last second, Roxy parried and ducked, resulting in Jen's fist slamming into the wall.

"Fuuuuuuck!" Jen screamed. White, hot pain shot up her arm. She felt the crackle of a broken knuckle, covering her right hand with her left. As she registered the extent of her injury, she felt the sharp blow of a sucker punch to her right lower back delivered by Roxy's right elbow.

Jen teetered then collapsed to her knees.

Roxy quickly scooted behind Jen to gain a tactical position. Roxy capitalized on Jen's position, clenching her arm around Jen's neck from behind and trapping her in a headlock. "Bloody hell, woman. If you'd just let me speak. I came here in peace with a message from Amanda."

God, I detest that Scottish accent. "That's *your* fucking problem." Jen pictured them together, laughing, kissing, making love, and her desire to rip Roxy apart returned.

"I don't want to fight you, and you don't want to engage me," Roxy warned. "I'm professionally trained."

Just hearing *professionally trained* from Roxy's lips made Jen want to puke. Even though her back was spasming from the sharp elbow—and she was on her knees—she channeled what she had learned in self-defense class, turning her head to the right and dropping her chin to weasel out of the headlock. She simultaneously delivered blows to Roxy's legs with her elbows, finally connecting with Roxy's knee. She heard the whack of bone on bone and Roxy hissed in pain.

Marshaling her athleticism and strength, Jen surged up like she was squatting 200 pounds and again turned on Roxy. Throwing a wide punch with her left fist, Jen connected with Roxy's nose. Jen both felt and heard the bridge crunch, the sound repulsing but, again satisfying. As a physician, she was sworn to help, not hurt. On the other hand, this wormy, lying bitch had stolen Amanda so deserved every bit of whoop-ass Jen could unleash on her.

Roxy raised her boot to kick Jen in the side but Jen grabbed it and flipped Roxy on her back, causing the trickle of blood from her nose to gush like a geyser.

Professionally trained my ass! As Roxy lay at her feet bleeding like a stuck pig, Jen heard a car door slam. She looked down at the street to see Tommy running up the steps.

"Jen, stop!" he yelled.

She was thinking the same thing—that she needed to stop before her revenge turned into cruelty. More importantly, she saw Kristin in the back seat of Tommy's unmarked cruiser, and there was no way Jen was going to fight in front of her daughter.

"Jen, what the fuck?!" Tommy asked when he landed on the top step, kneeling to assess Roxy.

"That lying snake showed up here, so I gave her a taste of how I felt when she stole Amanda," Jen said, catching her breath.

"You broke her nose?"

"Yeah, and it felt kinda good." She examined the back of her right hand, watching the broken pinky knuckle swell in front of her eyes. The pain was temporarily obscured by her endorphin release from the fight. "What are you doing back home, anyway?"

"I forgot my cell phone," he said. "Watch Kristin for a sec while I deal with Roxy."

Jen gingerly walked down the steps, babying her broken hand and sore back. She opened the back door of Tommy's car and slid into the seat next to Kristin, trying to come down from the adrenaline rush of pummeling Roxy. *Calming breaths. It's over. Refocus my mind. Let go.*

"Hi, Mama," Kristin said, reaching out her hand.

"Hi, baby," Jen said. The innocence of Kristin ripped open Jen's heart. She never wanted Kristin to see her this angry—unglued even—so she summoned her motherly love with a game face, willing herself to recalibrate.

Going from a jealous rage to an adoring mother, however, stretched her emotional ability, her instinctive fight mode still battling with her endearing motherly side. She was sure that Kristin's observant eyes saw, even though she might not comprehend, the war raging across Jen's face.

Sadly, Jen had actually *embraced* the satisfaction of hurting another human being, but seeing Kristin immediately restored her sanity. She suddenly felt shameful over breaking Roxy's nose. Even though she had enjoyed it—the sound, the feel—she told herself it was a once-in-a-lifetime loss of control that would never, ever happen again.

She turned and looked up the steps to see Tommy helping Roxy to her feet. Roxy staggered, crumpling despite Tommy's help, the blood from her nose running like Niagara Falls down her designer T-shirt. Tommy ran inside the house while Roxy leaned against the wall, pinching the bridge of her nose in an unsuccessful effort to stem the tide. A second later, he returned with his cell phone and a towel. Jen couldn't hear what he was saying but Roxy nodded. He helped her down the steps and around to the other side of his car, where he opened the front passenger door for her.

"What's going on?" Jen asked from the back seat.

"We're going to the hospital, that's what," Tommy said.

"You have to take Kristin to daycare. We can call an ambulance for Roxy," Jen said.

"Jen! Stop it! I'm taking her to the ER. You should come too. It looks like you busted up your hand pretty good." He pulled the seatbelt across Roxy and closed the door. On his way around the back of the car, he stopped at Jen's open door and looked at her hand. "You have a boxer's fracture," he said, eyeing the displaced bone above her pinky knuckle. He stretched the seatbelt across her and latched it, giving her a peck on the cheek as he closed her door.

"Shit," she muttered, not knowing how to extricate herself from the humiliation of going to the hospital with Roxy, knowing she would see her former colleagues there. She cradled her hand while they drove in silence to San Francisco Community Hospital, her old stomping ground. The only thing that tempered her pain was watching Roxy suffer in the front seat, her head tilted back against the headrest, blood oozing from her nose.

Tommy parked in a spot reserved for emergencies and removed Kristin from her car seat while the women got themselves out of the car. He made sure to walk between them as they entered the ER, even though the intense rage had been replaced by a temporary truce.

He correctly assumed that Jen would control herself in front of Kristin and her colleagues. The only female talking was Kristin, who was jabbering rapidly in 13-month-old-speak about the bloody towel Roxy was holding to her face.

Jen and Roxy registered at the front desk, and Roxy was immediately placed in a wheelchair and whisked away by a nurse. Tommy remained standing by Jen because he wasn't stupid. He was holding Kristin, loved Jen, and didn't want to incur her wrath.

"I'll swing in and check on you in a few minutes," he yelled after Roxy. She waved over her shoulder as she rolled through the double doors.

After Roxy disappeared, a nurse collected Jen, Tommy, and Kristin. He was delayed slightly by having to set aside his gun and show his I.D. when they went through the metal detector but caught up to Jen and the nurse as they entered a room.

Once they were settled, Tommy said, "I'll text the daycare and let them know Kristin will be late."

"Probably by a few hours," Jen said.

He busied himself on his phone while Jen sat stick straight, holding her throbbing hand, trying to maintain a pleasant expression for Kristin's sake. Kristin's big blue eyes scanned the room and every item in it.

After a few minutes, the ER physician came in, and he was none other than Dr. Lane Wallace, Jen's former colleague. "Hi, Jen. Tommy," he said, shaking Tommy's hand and hugging Jen.

"And this must be your daughter."

"Yes. This is Kristin," Tommy said.

"What a beautiful girl. She resembles both of you. Hi, Kristin. I'm Dr. Wallace."

"Hi," she said, then buried her face in Tommy's shoulder.

Lane smiled and sat on a stool, sliding over to Jen and sitting knee-to-knee with her. "What brings you in today?"

She held out her right hand.

"Ah. A boxer's fracture. Does this have anything to do with the broken nose in Room 20?" He tilted his head in the general direction of Roxy's room.

Jen nodded. It wasn't uncommon for the ER to see and treat both parties to a fight. Hence, the need for such stringent security measures in

7

the event the parties intended to finish at the hospital what had started on the street.

"You must have swung wide," he said.

"I connected, and that's all that counts."

"Next time, try to aim front-on with your index and middle finger, like a professional boxer. You're less likely to break your fifth metacarpal phalangeal joint that way," Lane said.

Tommy rolled his eyes. "Hopefully, there won't be a next time."

"I really just lost it in the heat of jealousy, Lane. Humiliation and revenge took over," Jen said, looking at the floor. "I felt the bridge of her nose crack when I landed my punch."

"Happens to the best of us. You're human. Sounds like a good story over a beer someday." Lane smiled, as he palpated the top and bottom of her hand. "I can feel the fracture on the top of your hand. I want to get an X-ray, so we know whether we can effectively splint it."

"I agree," she said, wincing as he pressed on her bone. "The last thing I want is an orthopedic surgery with a pin in my hand."

Lane muttered in a low voice to the nurse for a radiology technician to perform an X-ray. He smiled at Jen. "It's so good to see you. I've missed you."

"How are things? How is Angelina?" Jen asked, referring to his 10-year-old daughter.

"She's returning to a normal routine. Back at her private school here in town. We bought a new house."

"Good to hear. And, Susie? How long is she in for?" Jen asked, referring to Lane's ex-wife, who tried to kill Lane twice and successfully killed his lover. Tommy had arrested her, and she was now in prison.

"Chance of parole in 20 years."

Jen refrained from saying that wasn't long enough. "How is Angelina coping with the stigma of a mother in prison?"

"From my perspective, she's doing fine. Time will only tell." He shrugged.

"Are you still sailing?" she asked.

His expression brightened. "I just bought a new boat. She's supposed to be delivered to the yacht club next week. You should come out with me—all three of you."

"I'd like that," Jen said.

The radiology tech entered the room and swiveled the portable X-ray machine into position so she could take the appropriate views of Jen's hand. She quickly snapped the images and left the room. A few seconds later, Lane pulled up the digital images on the computer screen.

"Let's take a look." He moved the screen so Jen could see it too. "There's the fracture." He pointed with the tip of his pen above her pinky knuckle where there was a slim line of white indicating a hairline fracture.

"I think you should be able to reduce that when you apply the splint," Jen said.

"Might hurt a little. I can do a hematoma block for you," Lane said.

"Perfect."

The nurse brought in a tray of supplies with a pre-loaded syringe. She sat next to Lane and cleaned off the top of Jen's hand with Betadine solution.

9

Lane donned his latex gloves and steadied Jen's hand on the arm of her chair. "Here comes the poke for the Novocain, okay?"

"Yep." She clenched her jaw.

He inserted the needle and withdrew slightly, drawing blood from the hematoma surrounding her fracture, confirming he was in the right spot. He slowly injected the Novocain, which would be carried by the blood into the fracture, numbing it.

"God, that hurts worse than when I hit the wall," she groaned.

"You hit the wall with this hand?" Lane asked.

"Yeah, Roxy ducked. I actually broke her nose with a sharp left jab." She raised her left hand, which was red and puffy but not broken.

He set the syringe on the tray. "Well, the plot thickens. Let me inspect that hand."

She set it in his hand.

"No 'fight bite,'" he said, looking for broken skin from Roxy's teeth or cartilage.

"I already looked for that but thank you."

"I hope you had a good reason for breaking your right hand like this."

"I did. Roxy slept with Amanda," Jen said matter-of-factly.

He looked long and hard at her. "I'm sorry. I hope you don't intend on doing the same thing to Amanda."

"Nah, I think I got it out of my system."

"Your hands are too valuable to use for street fighting. You need them to make a living," Lane said.

"You're right. I should've used my head."

Lane laughed. "Let's apply the splint." He laid out the white fabric covering the fiberglass splint and placed her hand in it.

The nurse moistened the fabric and Lane conformed the fiberglass to Jen's hand, pressing on the metacarpal bone to straighten it as the splint hardened into place.

"Nice work," Jen said, admiring how the splint wrapped around her ring and pinky fingers, holding her broken bone in place.

"Thanks." Lane finished wrapping the splint and securing the fabric.

At that moment, they heard a scream from down the hallway, followed by a "Bloody hell!" in a Scottish accent.

Jen smiled at Tommy. "That's a satisfying sound."

"They must be packing her nose," Lane said. "It was bleeding pretty badly."

"I hope they shove a tampon or two up there," Jen said viciously.

"Down, girl. I'm sure she's in enough pain to make you happy," Lane said.

"There isn't enough pain for what she did to me."

"I understand, trust me. But forgiveness can be very healthy for the soul," Lane said.

She nodded, holding up her splinted hand and admiring his handiwork. "So noted. This looks awesome."

"You know the drill. Wear it for four-to-six weeks then start your exercises."

"Thank you. And, I'd love to go sailing with you sometime."

He stood. "Excellent. I'll call you. I should attend to my other patient now. Good seeing you." Tommy and Lane shook hands on Lane's way out the door.

"I need to check on Roxy before we leave," Tommy said.

"If you must. I'll watch Kristin," Jen said, nodding to her.

Tommy set Kristin down so she could toddle over to Jen. He was gone only a few minutes and returned with a message. "Roxy needs to talk to you."

Jen was stunned. "What? Out of the question."

"That's what I said, but she said you have to hear this directly from her, so I think you should."

"Great. Are you on her side now?"

"Of course not. You know how I feel about you, Jen. Just go listen to what she has to say." He spread his arms to pick up Kristin from where she was standing against Jen's legs.

"Fine." Jen reluctantly rose.

"No matter what she tells you, no more fighting."

Jen saluted in Tommy's direction and left the room. She trudged down the familiar corridor and entered Room 20 to see Roxy on the bed with a swollen nose, bloody gauze tails peeking out from her nostrils. From Jen's experience in treating broken noses, she knew the packing aggravated the fracture, resulting in pain that sometimes was worse than the initial break. "Hey. Tommy said you wanted to say something to me."

Roxy opened only one smoky blue. "Thanks for coming." With her plugged nose, her voice sounded like she was wearing a diving mask.

"What?"

"Amanda checked into the Sunnyvale Clinic for drug rehab. It's a 30-day inpatient program. She can't have a cell phone or access email, so she asked me to tell you where she was, and that she's committed to getting clean."

Jen did a mental inventory of the drug and alcohol rehab clinics she knew in San Francisco, but that one didn't pop into her mind. "Where is it?"

"South of Palo Alto. In Sunnyvale," Roxy said.

Jen processed the info then turned her attention back to Roxy. Not wanting to be in the same room with her longer than necessary, she asked, "Anything else?"

Roxy swallowed hard, resting her head back on the pillow to stop the room from spinning. "Yes. She told me she loves you, and there's no future between us. So, congratulations. You win."

Even though there was no sarcasm in Roxy's tone, Jen still balked at Roxy's word choice. "Fuck you," Jen said, moving toward the bed.

Lane stepped in front of her. "Not here, Jen. The police will arrest you."

"I didn't mean that sarcastically," Roxy said, the effort clearly painful. "She doesn't want anything to do with me. She only wants you and Kristin. I get the impression she'll do anything to win you back."

"Thanks for fucking up our lives," Jen seethed. Every time she looked at Roxy, she saw those lips on Amanda, the image like a rapier to her heart.

"I'm sorry. I didn't know Amanda was abusing valium and high in Cape Cod. Yesterday, she told me the doctor diagnosed her with PTSD from her war with the Mafia two years ago. She never went to counseling or properly healed from those battles. Getting shot on my patio in New York obviously traumatized her further. She needs therapy."

Jen listened, surprised that she hadn't noticed Amanda's abuse of valium. *When did she take it? Why didn't I notice a change in behavior?*

She pictured their busy life together at Amanda's house in Sea Cliff. There weren't any signs. Well, except for Amanda crying in the shower after her shootout on China Beach over Eddy Valentine. And drinking heavily and getting tattoos after the shootout in Hawaii. And taking the valium that Dr. Cohen had prescribed for her after the car bomb went off at Moffitt Field. Then becoming horribly agitated and sleepless after seeing Vhina shoot Nutini on her patio. He had almost shot Amanda that night, and her nightmares went on for days, reliving his sinister threats.

More recently, she had consumed half a bottle of wine on top of a valium on their date-night at Pacific Café. *Maybe the signs were there. Was I just too preoccupied to notice?* She felt a stab of guilt.

"I'm sorry," Roxy said, jolting Jen out of her troubled reverie.

Jen looked at Roxy's eyes, where she saw genuine concern. "Me too. Stay the hell out of our lives." She turned and left, hoping never to see Roxy again.

2

Sea Cliff
One month later

Amanda unlocked the kitchen door and walked into her empty kitchen, its previous loving glow obliterated by her betrayal and the sudden departure of Jen and Kristin.

She stood motionless, replaying her memories of feeding Kristin for breakfast at the table in front of the sliding door. Kissing Jen while eating a late-night snack at the counter, then slipping her hands under Jen's sweater. Lying with Jen on a blanket on the floor in front of the fireplace. She envisioned Jen's nude body, the firelight playing off her curves and dancing in her eyes. Only a month ago.

"Are you sure you want to live here instead of with us?" her mother, Chloe, asked, shattering Amanda's memory. Chloe set a bag of groceries on the counter and turned to look at Amanda, who had Chloe's almond-shaped eyes, slim nose and defined jawline.

"Yes, Mom. I've lived here for over a decade. I'll be fine." Amanda set the cat-carrier case on the floor. Zumba was screeching out a high C, demanding to inspect the backyard he had missed, having spent the last month at Jack and Chloe's.

"You could have the lower level to yourself at our house," Chloe said.

"Mom, I have to return to the DA's Office, and the commute from Hillsborough is brutal. Just let me try living here. If I get lonely, I'll call you." Amanda opened the carrier case and followed Zumba to the sliding door to let him out.

Concern furrowed Chloe's eyebrows but she let the subject drop.

Jack entered with Amanda's cello in its huge black carrying case. "Where do you want your instrument?"

"How about down in my yoga studio? No one will hear me down there."

"Nonsense. You were always very accomplished at the cello, dear," Chloe said.

Amanda laughed. "You wanted me to play chamber music in some little ensemble for the rest of my life, didn't you?"

"A little ensemble?" Chloe said. "If you'd stuck with it, you'd be playing with the San Francisco Symphony."

"Now we're really dreaming big. I didn't get grandma's musical genes, and you know it. And besides, I love being a prosecutor."

"I just worry about you in such a violent career," Chloe said into the fridge as she stocked the groceries.

"Lay off, Chloe. Amanda will be fine," Jack said then winked at Amanda.

"Will you at least play something for us today?" Chloe asked.

"Geez, Mom. Not right now. I'm moving back in, and I want to get settled. How about next time you're in town?"

"Just don't let your skills get rusty. I think it's destiny that you were able to pick up your music again while at the clinic."

"That might be a bit dramatic, but I promise to practice every day like a good girl."

"The music is in you, dear. I can see it on your face when you play," Chloe said.

Having had this conversation a thousand times in her life, Amanda had no patience for it today. She busied herself with letting out Zumba and storing the cat-carrier in the closet next to the pantry.

"You should have enough groceries for the week, and there are homemade dinners in the freezer," Jack said, steering the topic to safer ground while he folded the empty grocery bags.

"Thanks Daddy."

An awkwardness fell around them, Chloe and Jack questioning whether they should stay, and Amanda at a loss for how to ask them to leave.

"Want to go over some campaign details?" Jack asked. As the chair of her re-election campaign for District Attorney, he'd tentatively scheduled fundraisers and speaking engagements after limping along without her for a month. Amanda had to get back into the game.

"Sure," she said, going to the fridge. She was pleasantly surprised at her parents' choices. Her favorite yogurt. Apples. Cheese. It was all there. Out of habit, she looked at her wine fridge on the other side of the kitchen island. Jack had stocked it with bottles but not wine.

Jack followed Amanda's eyes. "I hope you don't mind. I removed the wine and replaced it with sparkling water."

"Thank you. I could dive into that right now."

"I'll join you," Jack said, hitching up his belt.

Amanda crossed the kitchen and opened the wine fridge like she had so many times, but she didn't feel reliant. Instead, she felt liberated from old thinking, back when she tried to control everyone and everything in her orbit. Her stated goal during rehab was to work on letting go. Giving up control to live a happier life.

She selected a Pellegrino and turned to Jack at the island, who had three glasses of ice and was cutting some lemon slices.

Chloe buzzed around the kitchen, turning on lights and the TV. "Shall we sit at the table?"

"Thanks Mom."

They all sat, and Jack opened his laptop. "Let me see. The first big fundraiser will be at the St. Francis Yacht Club next week. All our chums from the Peninsula are coming."

"That sounds intimidating." Amanda felt herself breaking out in a sweat at the prospect of socializing.

"You know all these people. I emailed you the guest list, and your mother and I will be by your side the entire time."

"I don't know. It's so soon." Her lips turned down into a moue.

Jack relaxed his gaze. "The time has come for making public appearances if you want to win this election. I've done as much as I could do while you were in the clinic, but I can't have an absentee candidate. You have to want this, dear. I mean, really want the job and dedicate yourself to campaigning for the last few weeks. People need to shake their candidate's hand and look her in the eye."

"I know." She blew out a raspberry. "I just need to get in the right mindset. It'll be fine." She sipped at her water and shook her long mane of black curls away from her face.

"Are you returning to work this week?" he asked.

"First thing tomorrow morning."

"What about Jeremy Jones?"

"He was a solid Interim DA, but now I'm back."

"Do you think he'll resist?" Jack asked.

"Jeremy? No. He's loyal to me," she said with a flick of her wrist, as if swooshing away a fly.

"Good to hear. Tomorrow after work, we meet with the marketing team about a TV commercial."

"Lovely."

"I'm not joking. You have to do one. Every candidate does these days and you're behind schedule."

"What am I going to say?"

"Our media relations man, Chance Greyson, has something in mind. He developed some talking points for you, and he's already shot the rest of the commercial."

"Is he the one you've been working with for the last month?"

"Yes. He's excellent. He's done so much, even without you present. He has a message and talking points for you about your rehab too."

"As long as he's not sappy."

"He's a professional." Jack's phone rang. "Excuse me. Hello?"

Amanda could hear a male voice on the other end.

"Hi, Kip. How are you?" Jack said in his silky-smooth lawyer voice. His unflappable demeanor had been one of his greatest assets during his successful career as a Silicon Valley attorney.

They sat in silence while Kip droned on in Jack's ear.

"I think I have the nature of your inquiry in mind, Kip. Let me call you back in five minutes, okay?" Jack said.

The men said goodbye, and Jack set his phone on the table. He rubbed his hands over his face and looked at Amanda.

"What?" she asked.

"Kip is outside in his van. He wants an impromptu interview."

Amanda shook her head. "Jesus. I just walked in the door. I'm not in the right headspace, I haven't done hair and makeup, and I'm wearing jeans."

"I know. He said he'll give you 30 minutes to get ready."

"Why the rush? What's so important?"

"Your opponent, Gavin Morales, gave an interview earlier today smearing your reputation by saying you were cloistered away in a drug rehab clinic in southern California." Jack placed his hand on her forearm.

"Going negative out of the gate, huh?" Amanda ground her teeth. "I'd hoped he wouldn't do that. Will we reciprocate?"

"We can if you give Chance and me permission."

"Let's see how my interview goes, then decide."

"I want to call Chance. Maybe he can come over and prep you for the interview. I can probably stall Kip for an hour."

"I like the sound of that. It's time for me to meet this Chance guy anyway."

Jack called Chance, who said he'd drop everything and come over right away. Jack told Kip to drive around for an hour and return.

"Let's do the interview in my living room," Amanda said. "Mom, will you turn on some lights and straighten up in there?"

"I'd be happy to," Chloe said.

"Might as well get this over with my first day back," Amanda said. "I have a pretty good idea of what I'd like to say, but I'd like to bounce it off Chance. I'm glad he's coming over." She rose from the table and disappeared up the stairway to apply makeup and change into a work suit.

Thirty minutes later, she came down the stairs and Jack introduced her to Chance, a slim and fit man in his mid-thirties. "Pleasure to meet you, Ms. Hawthorne."

"Please call me Amanda. Thanks for coming on such short notice. What do you think of Kip's request?"

"You look terrific, by the way." He cleared his throat. "I wasn't surprised when I heard Gavin Morales malign you in his interview this morning. In fact, I'm surprised he held off this long."

"Seriously?" Amanda asked, surprised that her opponent, a criminal defense attorney she'd known, and detested, for years would have that type of inside intel.

"Oh, yes. I know his campaign manager. Big-league nasty stuff. He travels across the nation working on campaigns. He's never worked San Francisco, though, so we have the home-field advantage," Chance said.

Amanda immediately warmed to Chance. He appeared knowledgeable, experienced, and confident—just what she needed.

"I've been working on some talking points for you over the last couple of weeks," he said, removing a paper from his briefcase. "Can we sit somewhere and review these?"

"The kitchen island," Amanda said. They sat side-by-side, furiously bantering over the points and polishing her phrases.

Thirty minutes later, Jack and Chloe greeted Kip at the front door, showing him and his cameraman to the living room. The cameraman set up in front of two winged-back chairs where Kip and Amanda would sit.

Amanda and Chance joined them. "Hi, Kip."

"Amanda Hawthorne! Don't you look fantastic!" Kip said, giving her a peck on each cheek.

"Thank you." She wasn't surprised that he was wearing more makeup than she was.

"I'm Chance Grayson, District Attorney Hawthorne's media relations manager. You'll be seeing more of me."

Kip studied Chance for a second, then extended his hand. "I'm Kip Moynihan. Have we met before?"

"I don't think so," Chance said, then quickly assessed Kip under a hooded glance, framed by long eyelashes.

Kip focused on Amanda. "Thanks for accepting my request for an interview. I didn't want to run a story without a comment from you. I'm not sure I've believed Gavin Morales' word on criminal cases all these years, so I'm less inclined to trust him during a campaign."

"Thanks for the courtesy," Amanda said. "You and I go way back, so you know you can always come to me, right?"

"With Jeremy Jones being Interim DA and all, I didn't know you were available," Kip said.

"Well, I am. I return to work tomorrow," she said.

"Here's my card," Chance said, pressing his card into Kip's palm, "For the duration of the campaign, call *me* before you reach out to Ms. Hawthorne."

Kip raised his eyebrows. "Will do." He pocketed the card and again turned back to Amanda, "Shall we get started, so we can talk about your absence, return to work, and campaign?"

"Looking forward to it." Amanda perched on the edge of a leather chair and gestured for Kip to sit in the other.

After introducing himself and Amanda for the camera, Kip dove into the juicy questions. "District Attorney Hawthorne, it's no surprise to our viewers that you're running for re-election."

"That's correct."

"Is it true that you've been out on a medical leave for the last four weeks?"

"Yes. My leave is complete, so I'm returning to work tomorrow."

"Do you mind telling the viewers *why* you were out on leave?"

"Not at all. I believe in transparency. The voters know me as an honest District Attorney and can count on me to be honest throughout this campaign. I was a patient at a clinic that addresses drug and alcohol abuse for people who find themselves abusing prescription medications."

"Are you addicted to pain meds?"

"No. I was *abusing* painkillers because I'd been shot. There's a difference between abuse and addiction. The point is that I completed the clinic program, so I no longer need pain meds to manage my gunshot wound pain or trauma from being shot by the Mafia."

"Are you referring to Nick Nutini's all-out war on the DA's Office?"

"Yes. I mistakenly thought I could return to work immediately after being in several shootouts with Nutini's mobsters, including having a car bomb go off next to me at Moffit Field. I thought I'd dealt with the physical pain and trauma, but a month ago, I was working on another case and found myself getting shot again in New York City. I took a bullet to my rib cage. The doctor removed the bullet—which was very painful—then prescribed pain meds for me."

"Is the doctor you're referring to your very public fiancée, Dr. Jen Dawson?"

"No. Jen has never been my doctor."

"Who *was* your doctor?"

"A government doctor who works on a certain extraction team."

"That sounds clandestine. Who shot you?"

"I can't talk about the confidential mission, but I can say the man wasn't a U.S. citizen and was in New York illegally."

"Why would a DA be on a mission in New York?"

"I was part of a team, and the bad guys didn't pay attention to state or city limits."

"Fair enough. When did you notice you had a problem with painkillers?"

"A few days after I was shot in New York. I took the painkillers the doctor prescribed and promptly decided that I couldn't cure my gunshot wounds or trauma with pills. I tried that the first time around and it didn't work. I wanted to learn how to deal with both the physical pain and mental trauma without drugs, so I checked into a clinic south of San Francisco."

"What did they teach you?"

"To address the trauma by learning new techniques for pain control and stress relief."

"Can you tell the viewers about those techniques?"

"Certainly. I like to do yoga for stress relief, because it requires me to focus my mind on breath and movement, pushing out other thoughts. I also play cello, which brings me great joy. Playing a musical instrument requires concentration, liberating my mind from pain, and it's a terrific way to wind down and relax."

"Are you pain-free now?"

"I don't know if I'll ever be pain free from the wounds, but I've learned to live with it."

"When are you returning to your position as the DA?"

"Tomorrow. Assistant DA Jeremy Jones acted as the Interim DA, and he did a marvelous job. We spoke earlier today, and he's ready for me to return. I look forward to it."

"How about Dr. Jen Dawson? I didn't see her here when I arrived."

Amanda squinted at Kip, wondering how much he knew. "That's correct. Dr. Dawson isn't here. I'd prefer not to go into detail about our personal relationship because she deserves her privacy."

"Understood. Are you in a relationship with anyone else?"

"No."

"Were you in a relationship with anyone else while engaged to Dr. Dawson?"

"As I said, I'm not going to discuss my personal life when it impacts someone else's privacy." She cast a warning look at Kip.

He paused a moment while he fished around in his satchel then produced two 8x10 photos. The first was of Amanda, Jen, Roxy, and Mayor Woo at the Dyke March. "Who is this woman in the photo with you at the Dyke March?"

"In addition to Dr. Dawson, a work acquaintance," Amanda said.

"Does she have a name?"

"I'm sure the viewers can understand that people who might do undercover police work don't want their names released."

He showed Amanda the second photo. It was a clear shot of Roxy and Amanda in the lobby of the Palace Hotel, walking alongside each other, but not touching. The fact that they were caught on camera jolted Amanda, but she regained her composure, recalling the only time she had visited Roxy's hotel room, and how she had rebuffed Roxy's advances. *So, Kip is playing dirty too. Right into Gavin Morales' hand.*

"This is a photo of you and the same woman leaving the Palace Hotel. Were you having an affair with her while you were engaged to Dr. Jen Dawson?"

"Kip, that's ridiculous. During an investigation—or undercover work—my job takes me to many places in the city with law enforcement. That was one such place."

"So you're denying that you had an affair?"

"Again, two people are in a relationship, so I'm not going to talk about it. Dr. Dawson deserves her privacy."

"Very well. Do you mind if we talk to her?"

Amanda's stomach clenched for Jen. "Feel free to request an interview."

"We will. Switching to another topic, the San Francisco Police Union endorsed your candidacy last week. Were you surprised by that?"

"Not at all. I've worked closely with the SFPD for over 15 years. I have a proven track record of charging and prosecuting crimes in this city, and I intend to continue that with their support."

"Thank you for your time, DA Hawthorne. Good luck on your campaign."

Amanda watched the red light on the camera turn off then stood.

"Do you have Dr. Dawson's contact info?" Kip asked.

"Of course. Here." She read Jen's phone number to him.

"You're sure you don't mind my reaching out to her?"

Amanda felt baited but she had no choice. "Feel free, Kip. I don't think she wants her privacy invaded—especially with our, her, baby girl in the picture—but you can try."

"I noticed you said, 'our' but then corrected yourself to 'her.' Care to comment on that?"

"As I've said in the past, I'm not going to talk about our child, so stop asking."

"Okay. Off limits, I get it," Kip said, raising his palms at her.

"Mind if I ask where you got those photos?" Chance interjected.

"Can't reveal my sources," Kip said.

"Again, call me or text me if you're handed something like that again. I can do the detective work for you," Chance said.

There was a pause while Kip regarded Chance's designer sweater, tailored taupe pants, and brown brogues. "I'll think about it."

"Thanks for coming over," Amanda said, shaking Kip's hand.

"Thanks for the access. I appreciate it," Kip said.

"Call Chance if you need anything else," she said, backing out of the room.

After shaking hands all the way around, Jack showed Kip and the cameraman out the door.

3

The next day, Jen felt her phone vibrate in the front pocket of her white doctor coat, but she was in an exam room with a patient, so she resisted the urge to remove it.

"I'm going to send a prescription for the cream to your pharmacy. Just apply it twice daily for a week, and I think your rash will clear up," she said to the male patient.

"Thanks Doc. You're a lifesaver," he said.

"Come back and see me if it doesn't clear up in 10 days."

Jen clicked the mouse to order the correct strength of cream from the patient's nearby pharmacy then concluded their visit. When she returned to her office to dictate her note, she looked at her phone. She didn't recognize the phone number of the caller, but there was a voicemail, so she listened to it.

"Hello, Dr. Dawson. This is Chance Greyson. I'm the Media Relations Manager for Amanda Hawthorne's re-election campaign. Amanda gave an interview to Kip Moynihan yesterday. I hope you saw it on the news last night. Kip requested an interview of you, too, so I was wondering if we could count on you to say something short and positive. We don't want the story about your relationship with Amanda to take on a life of its own. Can you call me back?"

Jen lowered her phone and stared at the wall, seeing only a wall. *Fuck me. Does she want me to tell the public she's a two-timing snatch hound? Because that's the truth. If she thinks I'm going to cover for her, that's not going to happen.*

Jen switched to her computer screen and searched the KPIX news website for Amanda's interview. She found it and clicked on the video, instantly recognizing the background as Amanda's living room.

She looks good. Her eyes are clear, and she doesn't have any dark circles. She's wearing her battle face—very confident. No contrition. Teflon all the way.

Jen listened as Amanda said, "I'd prefer not to go into detail about our personal relationship because Dr. Dawson deserves her privacy."

I can live with that, although she sounds a little defensive. And her lips are pursed.

Jen watched as Kip held up the photo at the Dyke March with Mayor Woo and Roxy. She couldn't suppress a mini-sneer when she noticed that Roxy's nose looked much straighter in that pic—pre-left hook. She recalled how furious she'd been at the time, watching Roxy cozy up to Amanda on the stage during her speech in the band shell. *God, it felt good to break her nose.*

What Kip produced next, however, made Jen's insides churn. Kip held up the photo of Amanda and Roxy walking through the lobby of the Palace Hotel. She paused the screen. *Was that photo taken before they went on their business trip to New York? Or more recently? Are they still a thing?*

The longer Jen stared at the image, the more she could feel the jealousy percolating through her bloodstream, reminding her of the shock and pain of Amanda's confession in their bedroom a month ago. The desire to unleash more wrath on Roxy, and maybe on Amanda, too, surfaced. She absent-mindedly rubbed her pinky knuckle, reminding herself that she wasn't a fighter. The bone was well on its way to healing, but her heart wasn't.

When she analyzed the photo, she noticed that Roxy and Amanda weren't arm-in-arm, instead walking a few feet apart. *Not acting lovey-dovey. Amanda said it was undercover business, and she even looks a little irritated, not her look of sexual satisfaction, that's for sure.*

When the interview finished, Jen sat back in her chair and blew out a long sigh. Having no desire to become part of the circus of Amanda's campaign, she decided she wouldn't return Chance's call. *You're on your own, Amanda. The most you'll get out of me is Switzerland. I'm not going to help or hurt your campaign. Just leave me alone.*

Her desk phone buzzed. The display told her it was Ginny, the clinic receptionist.

"Hello?"

"Hi, Dr. Dawson. There's a gentleman up here who says he needs to see you and only you."

"A patient?"

"No. He says he's a process server from Superior Court."

That can't be good. Jen pushed away from her desk and walked quickly to the front reception area where the waiting room was filled with patients.

"I'm Dr. Dawson. What can I do for you?"

"I'm a process server. Do you have someplace private where I can give you something? I'm pretty sure you don't want me to do it here," he said, glancing at the waiting patients.

Jen wasn't sure what the legal meaning and implications of a process server were, but she held the door for him to enter the back hallway. She led him around the corner into a small conference room.

"What's this about?" she asked.

"Dr. Dawson, I'm serving this Summons and Complaint on you. It's a civil lawsuit filed in the Superior Court of California. The caption says it's a medical malpractice case." He removed a sheaf of papers from a plastic folder.

"What the—?" She took the papers, and he wrote on the back of his copy that he had served her.

"I'm sorry, Doc. Just doing my job. You should contact your attorney right away. Don't let that sit on your desk, okay?" He nodded, turned, and left.

Jen dropped into one of the chairs and flipped through the pages until she landed on a paragraph that described a patient interaction. She read madly, racking her brain to recall the precise circumstances. The complaint stated that Jen had treated the patient in the ER at San Francisco Community Hospital two years ago. *Two years ago? How am I supposed to remember something that happened two years ago?*

The patient had been in an automobile accident and had broken her pelvis and both legs. She came in as a trauma, and Jen was part of the team that treated her. They saved her life that night, repairing her internal organs and broken bones, so she could walk again. Apparently, several weeks after she was discharged, her wrist still hurt, so she went to a doctor who diagnosed a wrist fracture. Since she now had some alleged mobility limitation in that wrist, she was suing all the physicians who saved her life that night for failing to diagnose and treat her wrist fracture.

What a scam. This isn't fair.

Jen crumpled the papers and threw the balled-up wad against the wall. It bounced off and tumbled onto the floor. Ginny peeked her head in. "Need help with something, Dr. Dawson?"

The heat of embarrassment crept up Jen's neck. "No. I have it under control. Thanks."

Ginny looked at the crumpled ball. "That's what I do with stuff I don't want to read too. Can I take this for you?" She knelt to pick it up.

"No, I've got it," Jen said, sliding out of her chair and holding out her hand for the ball. Ginny handed it to her, and Jen immediately returned to her office, where she smoothed out the crumpled papers on the top of her desk.

She opened her desk drawer and removed a folder containing a brochure for her professional liability carrier. She found the phone number and called. Unlike her car insurance company, the claims specialist was helpful and understanding.

"If you could scan and email over the Complaint, we'll assign it to an attorney right away," the specialist told her.

"It's sort of wrinkled, but I think my receptionist should be able to scan a decent image," Jen said, feeling guilty over her immature behavior.

"Once it's been assigned to a lawyer, I'll email you his name. You should expect a call from him in a few days."

"A few days? My imagination could run wild in a few days' time. Could he call me today or tomorrow?" Jen asked.

"I'll see what I can do."

"Okay. Thanks."

After they hung up, Jen returned to Ginny and asked her to scan and email the summons and complaint to the claims specialist. *Done.*

Jen was dying to read the patient's medical record, but that was stored on the computer system at the hospital, not at the Cohen Clinic where she currently worked. Unsure whether she was even allowed to access the patient's record now that she'd been sued, she resigned herself to waiting for her lawyer to call her. *What a shit day! First, Amanda's campaign. Now this!*

There was a knock on her door. "How's it going?" Melissa Cohen, the senior partner of the practice asked.

"Not so hot. I was just served with a malpractice lawsuit." Jen explained what she knew about it.

"I heard. Ginny told me you crumpled the papers and threw them against the wall, so I thought I'd better check on you. I'm sorry. It sucks to be sued."

"Word travels fast around here."

"Well, I'm the boss, and Ginny sees everything. She's supposed to tell me stuff. Besides, I've been there. I had a case about five years ago. The lawyer will tell you not to take it personally—that it's just about money—but it was a criticism of my care. The patient's family accused me of not diagnosing cancer in time, and they had the gall to tell me not to take it personally. It felt pretty fucking personal to me! Until my lawsuit was resolved, I obsessed about it day and night."

"I know the feeling. I just want to read the medical record, but my insurance company told me it might be a few days before I meet with the lawyer," Jen said.

"There's nothing you can do but compartmentalize and try to move on with your day. I'm sure your lawyer will explain everything to you. Trust the process," Melissa said, throwing up her hands.

"So far, 'the process' just interrupted my clinic with a lawsuit," Jen said.

"Come here," Melissa said, holding her arms wide. "Let me give you a hug."

Jen rose from her chair and received a comforting, mama-style hug. "Thank you."

"You're welcome. Now, chin up and shoulders back. We have a clinic to run." Melissa disappeared down the hallway.

Jen realized she was absent-mindedly rubbing her pinky knuckle again. While it felt good to massage it, she wondered if it was becoming her "go-to" reminder of pain. The pain of losing Amanda and now getting sued.

4

Hall of Justice

Amanda pushed through the glass doors of the District Attorney's Office. The previously routine motion now felt sentimental, as she had come to appreciate that she needed this place as much as the people of San Francisco needed her.

Her job defined who she was, giving her a sense of purpose, challenging her mind, and, most importantly, a way in which she could contribute to society. She truly cherished being a civil servant, tackling the distasteful crimes and atrocities that people of her wealth usually didn't want to be bothered with, much less dedicate themselves to solving.

She was met by the staff rising from their chairs and attorneys emerging from their offices, gathering to welcome her back. As she walked to her office, people smiled, patted her on the shoulder, and said, "We missed you" and "Welcome back."

Jeremy Jones watched and waited, resting his skeletal frame against the doorjamb of her corner office, his sharp analytical eyes sizing her up.

"Welcome back, Amanda," he said, when she was finally standing before him.

"Thanks."

They hugged briefly, his long arms wrapping around her petite frame. She turned and faced the eager staff assembled before her. "Thank you, everyone. Believe it or not, I really missed this place." She laughed and they joined. "I want to thank Jeremy for serving as Interim DA while I was out." She clapped, and everyone followed suit.

There was a silence during which everyone looked at her, expecting more.

"Thank you all for your hard work holding down the fort while I was gone. While in rehab, I had a lot of time to think and prioritize my life, and I want each of you to know that you, this place—" She gestured widely to encompass the office, "is my life's work and my top priority. What we do here is more important than any one person can do. Me or anyone else. So in my absence, I'm sure you carried on and were true professionals, doing the work that needed to be done every day. Without you—each one of you—the system would break down. Chaos and anarchy would surely follow. And I'm not just talking about a Friday afternoon."

A chuckle buzzed through the space.

"Seriously, we don't just serve a role in the justice system, we *are* the justice system. Through our values of honesty, hard work, integrity, and commitment, we *define* the system and its reputation. Whether I'm here or not, that reputation means something. We, as a collective, *mean* something," she gestured in a circular motion. "I'm honored to be a member of this team and stand side-by-side with you, fighting for what's right, what's just, and what's ours to do. I appreciate you and your support more than you know, and look forward to catching up on all the files. Thank you."

Everyone clapped. As the staff retreated to their offices, Jeremy held Amanda's office door open for her. "Have time to talk now?"

"I'd love to. Let me drop my things." She stowed her bag in the bottom desk drawer and turned on her Tiffany Dragonfly lamp while Jeremy situated himself on her sofa. She joined him, sitting in a comfortable club chair facing her picture window with a view of the Bay Bridge. "How did it feel to be boss for a month?"

"It certainly made me appreciate the masterful way you guide the Assistant DA's with their cases, coordinate with the Chief of Police, deflect Mayor Woo, and keep the media satisfied, but at arm's length," he said, idly removing a fleck of lint from the pocket of his sharp new suit.

"You're a quick study. I'm sure you settled in by the second day."

He bubbled like a rolling stream, his gaunt frame producing a rich baritone sound, which was one of his secret weapons when arguing a case to a jury. "The transition period would take a wee bit longer than one month, I'm afraid. I was in a basic holding-pattern, just making sure we didn't have any midair collisions."

She appreciated his overture of humility, considering that quality one of his most promising assets for a long, successful career. "How is the Federal Reserve Bank case going?"

"We got a solid confession from Tiffany Hendrix explaining how she and her husband, Rich, extorted $12 million from Jina Pak, in return for not ratting out Jina's conspiratorial role with the North Koreans."

"I'd love to watch Tiffany's confession if it was taped."

"It was. I'll email it to you. Tommy did a great job."

"What about Rich? Did he lawyer up and plead not guilty?"

"Initially, but he ultimately signed a plea agreement because we had so much evidence. Roxy MacNeil did a great job of finding the bank transactions and authorizations that incriminated him."

At the mention of Roxy's name, Amanda's insides churned—but not in a romantic way—as she considered their Cape Cod tryst the biggest mistake of her life. They hadn't spoken since Amanda's day of admission to Sunnyvale Clinic. Amanda had told her goodbye—and meant it—insisting that she was in love with Jen, intending to make amends with Jen once she was clean and sober. She wasn't surprised that Roxy had stayed in town, however, to complete their investigation and prosecution. Returning her attention to the topic at hand, she asked, "Did Judge Grady approve the plea agreement?"

"That hearing is set for tomorrow if you want to join. It should be quick. I think Rich will be there in person."

"I'd love to. What time?"

"Ten. It's on your calendar already, indicating that I'll take the lead, so you don't have to prepare anything."

"Thanks. And Tiffany?"

"Doing four years in a light security, all-female penitentiary."

"That was fast," Amanda said.

"Sometimes it all comes together if the parties are willing." His sardonic smile indicated that he had leveraged Rich and Tiffany.

"Loose ends?"

"A few. We have a meeting this morning with Tommy and Roxy. Frankly, I think she wanted to stay until you returned. Just my guess."

Amanda didn't reply because Jeremy didn't need to know the details. Facing Roxy would be the second emotional hurdle of the day. The first had been waking up to an empty house.

"They intend to update you on Clara Sandoval, the bank employee who Jina Pak entrusted with the jump drive, and some video of how the lead Korean hacker, known as HELLFIRE, got into the Fed building. It's unclear to me whether the *group* calls itself HELLFIRE, or whether that's the moniker of the *leader* of the group. Anyway, Tommy and Roxy were very insistent that they update you in person rather than have me do it."

"Will you be there?"

"If you want me to."

"Absolutely. You did the lion's share of work on this file." She paused a minute and gave him her soft eyes. "If you have time, that is."

"Happy to stay first chair," he said in a perfect deadpan voice.

"What else is new?"

From memory, Jeremy ran down the highlights of each big case in the office, preparing Amanda for meetings with ADAs about their files. Cataloging the salient facts of each file and remembering the procedural status of each case for her periodic meetings with the ADAs was one of her strengths. In the span of one month, progress had been made on key files, which was heartening, and underscored her remarks to the staff a few minutes earlier that this place could run without her. They finished in time for a fifteen-minute break before their meeting with Tommy and Roxy.

"I can't thank you enough for covering my leave, Jeremy. I sincerely hope I can return the favor someday—in some way. You might not take a leave *per se*, but if you decide to run for office, or need a recommendation for something, you know you have my full support."

He blushed for the first time she could remember. "Thanks Amanda. And likewise. I'll do anything in my power to get you re-elected, so please don't hesitate to ask."

"You've done so much already, but I'll tell Chance Greyson, my media relations manager, that you're on board. Thanks for your support."

They shook hands, and he left her office with the confidence of a young man who had reached a new career milestone as well as received the promise of a favor from a powerful, wealthy person. He had an extra spring in his step, anticipating that he would, indeed, ask for her support someday in the pursuit of his ambitious career goals.

Amanda entered her *en suite* bathroom to freshen up before meeting with Roxy and Tommy. She rested her hands on the cool counter and looked at her reflection—a helluva lot better than the last time Roxy had seen her. *Can I handle this? Can I face seeing someone who told me she was falling in love with me? What if she has the same charismatic impact on me? Tommy will be watching, and probably judging, and probably reporting back to Jen.*

She returned to her desk and fired up her computer. She had waded through emails over the last few days, almost all of which Jeremy had addressed. She had willingly given him access to her inbox, so he could assume her role while she was away. It was the only way to make sure nothing slipped through the cracks since she hadn't been allowed any electronic devices in rehab. She ended that today and changed her password.

She stared at the screen, not focusing on anything, considering how she would react to seeing Roxy. She had been abrupt and insensitive to Roxy when she had entered the clinic. Roxy had told Amanda that she loved her, but Amanda had never said it in return, knowing that she loved Jen and only Jen. Amanda had been shocked that Roxy had cried when Amanda told her she loved Jen. She had believed that, in Roxy's line of work, she was used to hookups with no emotional attachment. Apparently, Roxy had fallen, but that wasn't Amanda's problem.

At the time, Amanda considered Roxy to be a dangerous and momentary thrill, much like a drug, but Amanda didn't have the same chemistry with her as she did Jen—her soulmate. She was done with drugs and done with Roxy. They seemed intertwined in her mind to the point that shedding one made shedding the other easier.

Hell, Roxy wasn't even her type. Well, technically speaking, Roxy was slim, had blonde hair, and was blue-eyed, but those were just clit bait. Amanda needed more.

When Amanda compared Roxy to Jen, Roxy was too androgynous-looking. Too detached from real life. Too jaded. Too desensitized to killing. Amanda wondered if Roxy was even capable of feeling deep emotional attachment. Basically, the only thing they had in common was working on the case. They just didn't see the world the same way.

Jen, on the other hand, was perfect. She had the exact right mix of femininity and jock. She wasn't lipstick, as that was Amanda's domain, but wasn't butch either. She landed in the middle of the spectrum—maybe chapstick—her athletic body so tan and fit, her intense clinical eyes aware of everything, and her long blonde hair soft as silk. Perhaps her most attractive characteristic, though, was her mind. In stark contrast to Roxy, Jen didn't have any dark corners to her mind, instead maintaining a goodness that radiated into everything she did. The loving mother she was to Kristin. An outstanding doctor. Her commitment to her patients. Her Italian meals. Her compassion. Her healthy, outdoor scent. God, she missed her.

Back to reality. Even through her vicodin goggles, Amanda had known there wasn't a future with Roxy when they had slept together on the Cape. Had she been a bit cruel when unceremoniously ending their relationship? Sure, but she refused to string Roxy along, thereby prolonging the agony for all three women.

She prepared herself to meet the inevitable and left her office. Hesitating in Jeremy's doorway for him to join her, they made their way down the hall to the conference room. Whether he realized it or not, Jeremy was a calming force for her.

As they drew near the drab conference room, Amanda could feel Roxy's presence before she turned the corner. When she entered, everything was a blur except for Roxy's smoky blue eyes, their unvarnished inquisitiveness searching Amanda's face. Despite the churning in her stomach, Amanda conjured a mask and smiled pleasantly. "Hi, Tommy. Hi, Roxy."

Tommy stood. "Do I get a hug?"

"Of course," she said, taken aback by his warmth. As he embraced her, she felt the genuine friendship through his strong body, appreciating the gesture like she never had before. They had been through so much together that there was a bond there, albeit one where she had stolen his girlfriend, mothered his child, then broken Jen's heart, but nonetheless, a bond forged through protecting the people they loved as a result of their dangerous jobs. She knew he had every right to hate her, but she was relieved that he didn't. When they broke apart, her eyes misted.

Roxy remained seated, so Amanda didn't move to shake her hand, relieved to conceal that her palms were exploding with moisture. She folded them neatly in her lap after she sat. Thankful for Jeremy's presence, she turned to him to start the meeting.

Jeremy cleared his throat, studying the body language and expressions of the women. "Thanks for meeting this morning. I want to welcome Amanda back and catch her up on our bank investigation."

"Let me start," Tommy said with his usual enthusiasm. "We boxed Rich Hendrix into a corner where he had to plea. I hope you filed the agreement for Judge Grady to approve tomorrow, Jeremy."

Jeremy nodded. "Done."

"You heard that his wife, Tiffany, is in orange already?" Tommy asked Amanda.

"Yes," Amanda said. It felt good to focus on something other than how her nerve endings were on high alert in Roxy's presence. She could smell Roxy's subtle perfume from across the table—probably White Linen.

"That leaves one remaining bank employee and a million-dollar loose end," Tommy said.

Roxy jumped in. "Over the last month, we ran several audits at the bank, and we finally figured out what the third line of computer code on Jina's jump drive accomplished."

Eager to learn, Amanda gave Roxy her full attention. Roxy's eyes were clear and bright, her pale skin creamy and smooth, except over her nose. The bridge of her nose looked puffy and slightly angled. There was a jagged—albeit tiny—red scar across it. Had she taken a hit to the face? Amanda could swear it had been broken. Maybe it appeared crooked because of the slant of light coming in from the dirty window.

Not surprisingly, Roxy's protuberant lower lip, covered in a deep shade of cinnamon today, still looked sexy. She was as stunning as she had been a month ago, but there was something hopelessly flawed about her too.

Amanda had looked past her dark shadow during her initial infatuation, but now its presence was evident, like an alligator's eyes barely visible below the surface of calm water— once camouflaged, but now obvious.

Amanda again rebuked herself for not having been more observant before acquiescing to Roxy's seduction.

"Following the money trail took several days," Roxy was saying, "but we figured out that Jina skimmed small amounts from almost every account held at the Fed, posted the odd dollar amounts as a generic 'transfer fee,' and withdrew the money, depositing it in a bank account under an alias. She never let much money build up in the bank account, though, transferring it to a second account every few weeks. From the second account, she transferred about $20,000 per week to an account in Cayman—"

"—which is where Clara Sandoval is currently relaxing," Tommy said.

"When did Clara go to Cayman?" Amanda asked.

"A week ago," Tommy said.

"Have you asked Sadie why Clara went there?" Amanda asked.

"Yeah. She told me Clara hasn't violated any laws, so to lay off. I mean, don't get me wrong, Sadie and I are on good terms, but she insisted that Clara is just trying to 'find herself' after the trauma of being involved in such a bizarre work situation." He sighed. "I'm not sure if Sadie knows what Clara is up to."

"Sadie thinks Clara is on an *eat-pray-love* sabbatical?" Amanda asked, incredulous at Sadie's naiveté.

He nodded. "Funny thing. By pure coincidence, I ran into Clara at the Bowl'd Acai food truck a month ago, on the way to my credit union. The chef behind the counter gave her an envelope, and I watched her sit in the sun and open it. From where I was standing, it looked like a small slip of paper inside, but I was too far away to read it."

"I remember you said they stopped at that food truck on their walks," Amanda said. "Do you suppose that Jina left Clara the bank account info in the envelope as a 'thank you' for dealing with the jump drive situation?"

"Bingo," Tommy said, pointing at her.

"Sounds to me like you need to visit the Caymans," Amanda said.

"I'm taking the company plane if you'd care for a ride," Roxy offered to Tommy, then glanced at Amanda. When their eyes met, Amanda found herself mortified at the memory. What they had done on that plane a month earlier had been sinful. She felt the heat creeping up her neck and suffusing her complexion. *Fuck, how does this woman do this to me?*

Satisfied with Amanda's blush, Roxy turned her attention back to Tommy. "Are you in?"

"I'm sure the SFPD budget would appreciate free airfare," Tommy said. "I just have to clear it with Ryan."

"Leave tomorrow?" Roxy asked.

"Sounds good. We should tell Amanda about HELLFIRE too," Tommy said.

"The North Korean hacker who was the mastermind behind the codes?" Amanda asked.

"The one and only. We actually caught him on security video entering the Fed building with Jina Pak late one night," Tommy said, pulling up the video on the conference room computer screen. They all watched as Jina used her I.D. badge to scan them in the rear security door, then took him to her floor and into her office. They emerged an hour later.

"Those are some pretty clear images," Amanda observed.

"Yes. I updated the MI-6 and CIA databases accordingly. That intel was worth its weight in gold. Now we know what HELLFIRE looks like. I'm investigating whether he's still in the area or has left already," Roxy said.

"Making Roxy Enemy Number One of the North Korean regime," Tommy joked.

"Don't remind me," Roxy growled. "Those fuckers are tracking my every move. I swear they have a satellite dedicated to only me." Her trademark sneer returned.

Amanda didn't share their joke. Being shot on Roxy's patio had just about undone her career and personal life. It certainly had torpedoed her perfectly radiant career trajectory, sidelining her right before an election. More tragically, in the span of one night, she had lost Jen.

An empty, hollow feeling echoed in her heart like a bass drum, pulling the corners of her lips down. *If they don't have anything else, I'm ready to go.*

Jeremy inhaled and jumped in. "So, Amanda and I will take care of business in court tomorrow and you two will be off to Cayman to track down Clara Sandoval and hopefully recover the $1 million for the bank."

"Sounds like a plan," Tommy said, rolling back his chair and patting the table. "Good to have you back, Amanda."

"It's good to be back. Thank you, Tommy." She was about to ask him to greet Jen and Kristin for her, but that seemed inappropriate on too many levels.

"Goodbye, Amanda. Good to see you're back at it," Roxy said. She hung back as the men exited ahead of her.

Amanda felt obligated to do more than simply say goodbye, so she lingered as well. They hugged, and what could've been a tempting reunion instead felt perfunctory and stiff. Through her peripheral vision, Amanda could see Tommy in the hallway, waiting for Roxy to join him. To the extent he intended to relay any of this to Jen, Amanda wanted it to be a quick and clean break. "Thanks for carrying me out of battle in New York. I'll always be grateful. I wish you the best."

Roxy studied Amanda's uncompromising expression. Icy professionalism. "I'm sorry there isn't a future for us."

Amanda dropped her head and stared at the floor. She'd never been particularly empathetic during a breakup, and this exchange was no exception.

Roxy shuffled her feet, waiting for Amanda to say something. When Amanda didn't, Roxy finally stepped in front of her and joined Tommy in the hallway.

5

Amanda followed Tommy and Roxy down the hallway then peeled off at her office door as they continued to the reception area. She rounded her desk and fell into her leather chair with a whoosh. She knew it was going to be emotional returning to work, but the tidal wave washing over her was enormous, deafening, and thrashing her into the sand. She just needed a moment alone to process.

Her phone chimed with an incoming text from Roxy. *That wasn't enough for me. I want to see you when I return from Cayman.*

Amanda leaned her head back against the chair with a groan. *Shit, shit, shit. Of course, she wants more. How do I twist myself out of this? Not reply? Reply 'No?' There's no doubt she saved my life, but I don't want a relationship with her. Fuck.*

She stared at the message again, then typed: *I'd be happy to explain where I'm at over coffee. Good luck on your trip.*

She looked up to find Tommy standing in her doorway. "Have a minute?"

"Sure. I thought you left with Roxy."

"I did, but I circled back because I wanted to talk to you." He closed the door.

"I'd like that." She rose and walked around her desk to join him on her sofa under the window.

After they were situated, he asked, "How do you feel?"

"Aside from return-to-work jitters, better than I have in a long time."

"Are you and Roxy a thing?"

She scoffed. "No. We were never 'a thing.' I was just traumatized from being shot, very impaired, and allowed myself to be seduced by her."

"Laying it all on *her* doorstep, are you? Do you mean to tell me that she took advantage of you?"

Her short laugh was like icicles falling on pavement. "I've missed your refreshing honesty." She gathered herself. "You're right— it takes two to tango. She might have taken advantage but I was a willing participant, sort of. At least, a drugged one. Almost unconscious but, nevertheless. Can you be that high and consent? Anyway, in her defense, the next day I wasn't high, and we...Jesus, why am I telling you this?"

Removing any superficiality from his voice, he said, "I don't care about the details. You broke Jen's heart, you know. Just about killed her. I watched her cry every day for three weeks straight. For a while there, her only reason for getting up in the morning was Kristin. She seems like she turned a corner last week, so I hope you don't plan on ruining her life again."

Amanda blanched with surprise and raised her hand. "Ruin her life? Never my intention. I love Jen and Kristin and only want the best for them."

"Do you plan on trying to win her back?" he asked, assessing her like a buck assessing its competition.

"One step too far, Tommy." Her voice dove an octave lower. "I can appreciate that you came to Jen's rescue, and you feel the need to drive home how much I hurt her. Okay, I got it, and I own my mistakes. I'm willing to admit them to anyone who will listen, and I want to atone. Believe me, I *plan to atone*. But I don't think you have the right to inquire about my romantic intentions—especially not while posturing like a stud in a pasture." She sat up straighter, throwing her shoulders back.

He stared at her into the expanding silence. She thought he was going to leave but then he said, "If I tell you something, can you please keep it confidential?"

"Of course."

"I mean from Jen. I don't want her to know I told you this."

"Seeing as how we're not talking, I'm pretty sure I can keep it confidential from her."

"That might be temporary. For all I know, you two will get back together. From what I hear you saying, that sounds like your intent."

"I love Jen but getting back together—" She sighed and threw a hand up in the air, "depends on her and how she feels about me. The new me. And I need to get my life back on track—being DA, running for re-election. Our relationship is out of my control."

"I think you're right and I'm glad you recognize that. I can see that your time away tempered your usual headstrong determination to go after whatever you want, no matter what the cost."

Amanda regarded him, paying special attention to his last remark. "You're right. I've broken others' hearts in the pursuit of my own goals."

"Thanks for acknowledging that you've created a lot of collateral damage." They both knew they were talking about his heart in particular.

"I'm sorry for what I did to you, Tommy."

"For stealing Jen or for breaking her heart?"

She closed her eyes, and, over the lump in her throat, croaked, "Both."

"That was a little cruel. I'm sorry. I accept your apology."

They sat in silence, the air heavy with hurt and regret.

"I didn't come here looking for an apology," he said. "There was actually something I wanted to tell you."

"Hm?"

"When you were admitted to the clinic, Roxy showed up at my house, wanting to talk to Jen."

"Yes," Amanda said. "I asked her to tell Jen where I was—"

"Well, Roxy did, and they got in a huge fight. If I hadn't separated them, I think Jen would've killed her."

"What?"

"Seriously. Jen broke Roxy's nose and was going in for the kill when I got there."

"No wonder Roxy's nose looks sort of crooked but not really," Amanda said, absent-mindedly touching her own nose.

"Oh, yeah. A solid punch broke the bridge of her nose," he said, punching the air in slow motion.

Amanda covered her mouth with her hands. "Oh, dear."

"They'd been at it a while when I arrived. Jen's knuckles were bruised and broken. She even broke her pinky knuckle—from hitting the wall, though, not Roxy's nose."

"She broke her knuckle?"

"It gets worse. I had to peel Jen off Roxy, who was on her knees, blood pouring out of her nose. I made Jen get in my car while I attended to Roxy's nose then drove them both to the ER. Roxy in the front seat, and Jen in the back."

"Oh my God," Amanda said, picturing the chaos.

"The only thing that kept Jen from diving into the front seat to finish off Roxy was that Kristin was sitting in the back too."

"Kristin saw them fight?"

"No. When we pulled up, Jen stopped. She immediately checked herself when she saw Kristin was with me. You'll never guess who treated Jen in the ER, though."

"Who?"

"None other than Lane Wallace."

"He's back in town?"

"Yeah. Spent a year in San Diego and moved back. Angelina wanted to return to her old school, and Lane likes the Bay area."

"Did Jen need surgery?"

"No. Lane numbed up her hand and set the bone in place. She wore a splint for four weeks."

"What about Roxy? Did she need surgery?"

"Something. I don't know if they did an actual surgery to reset her nose, but she had lots of gauze packed in there. Looked really painful. That's when she asked me to send Jen in to see her, so she could tell Jen that you broke up with her, Roxy, I mean. Jen was pissed when she came out of Roxy's room."

"Really?"

"Yeah. Lane told her she'd be arrested if she started something in the ER, so she pulled it together and we left."

"Wow. I had no clue. Two strong women who aren't afraid to fight. I'm glad I wasn't in the middle of that." Amanda put her hands to her face.

"But you were. Squarely in the middle. To the extent you still are, I'd appreciate you not hurting Jen again."

"You have my word that I love her, so I'll do everything in my power not to hurt her."

"Good luck," he said, standing.

She could tell by the way he said it that he was a little disappointed. *He wants her back too. Well, so be it. I've competed with him before, and I'll do it again.*

"It's good to be back, Tommy. Thanks for being candid with me."

"Anytime. I know you'd do the same for me."

6

Later that day, Jen emerged from one of her patient exam rooms at the Cohen Clinic and walked down the hall toward her office. When she turned the corner, she found herself facing Amanda, who was standing 20 feet away but still uncomfortably close. Jen had entered Amanda's bubble…a force of nature.

Jen's office was at the edge of the family practice section—next to the Behavioral Health Department—so it wasn't out of the realm of possibility that she would see Amanda entering or exiting, but she was still surprised. Jen felt trapped. Too late to duck and run, too hurt to say hello.

Their eyes locked. Oh, how Jen remembered getting sucked into the vortex of Amanda's stare. The hazel eyes that saw everything. The eyes that Jen had looked into during the throws of passion—the gold flecks dancing. The eyes that had cried when she had admitted betrayal. They were sharp again, though. Scary sharp. And penetrating. But vulnerable. More sentimental than Jen had remembered.

She searched Amanda's face, thinking she looked healthier than she had a month ago when they broke up. Her makeup was scant and there were no longer dark circles under her eyes. Now that the dark circles were gone, Jen was surprised to realize they had once been there. She was reminded of how insidious drug abuse was, claiming its victim in clear sight of loved ones. She hadn't even noticed that Amanda was falling until it was too late, their relationship ruined by her infidelity.

Jen thought Amanda looked sophisticated in a navy dress, her stylish raincoat hanging over her arm. She hesitated mid-stride—long enough to register Jen's discomfort—then tipped up her chin in a silent greeting.

Jen took a deep breath, telling herself that it was *her* workplace, and she had every right to be standing where she was. If anyone should feel like an intruder, it should be Amanda. She mouthed, "Hi."

Amanda said with uncharacteristic humility, "I didn't mean to interrupt your day. I'm done with a therapy appointment and am just taking the back hallway…to avoid…people in the waiting room. You know…" She waved her arm toward the waiting room to finish her sentence.

Avoiding people. "No worries. Do what you need to." Jen didn't even know what she was saying. Her gut coiled like a spring, and her nerve endings felt raw. *How does she do this to me?*

"How are you? How is Kristin?" Amanda asked, her smile shaky.

Rather than carry on a conversation from 20 feet away, risking everyone in the neighboring offices eavesdropping, Jen glanced around and quickly closed the distance between them. "We're good. Thanks for asking. Kristin has asked about you."

"God, I miss her so much. I spent a month in rehab and am doing my outpatient work here. I really like my therapist. She's good. I'm…I'm sorry I hurt you and fucked up everything." Amanda reached out to touch Jen's arm but pulled back at the last second.

Jen wasn't prepared for such a spontaneous and unvarnished admission. She held up her hand. "Don't. Don't start this here. Now. I get that you're sorry but I'm at work, and I need to concentrate on seeing patients. Talking with you is…too emotional." She felt like her insides had just been ripped out and tossed on the floor.

"You're right. I've been talking about me and my drug use nonstop for over a month, so I'm comfortable with it. I already hurt you enough. I don't want to disrupt your busy day too."

"You already have—more than you realize."

"I'm sorry." Amanda's eyes roamed over Jen's hand to see if she could tell where the broken knuckle was. She couldn't.

When she found Jen's eyes again, she saw glaring spears of hateful thoughts.

Jen snarled in a heated whisper, "I can't believe you slept with her—Roxy MacNeil of all people. We were engaged, Amanda. You made promises. You said loving things. Were those just empty words?"

Tears sprang to Amanda's eyes, and she said with urgency, tripping over her tongue and her lower lip trembling. "No. They weren't just words. I meant every word I said. Someday, when you're not in the middle of a busy clinic, I'd like the chance to explain what happened. I can see that now isn't the time. I love you. You're the only woman I've ever loved."

Jen crossed her arms, shifted her weight onto her left leg and jutted out her hip. "Explain?

Really? You think you can go to rehab for a month to work on you, then just pop back into my life and explain yourself out of infidelity? That's rich—even for you. I don't mean to get all judgy on you, but you have quite the nerve."

Amanda cocked her head. "You? Judgmental?"

There was a long silence during which they held a fierce stare, two scorpions circling.

Jen's lips thinned into a straight line. "I have every right. While you were gone for a month finding yourself, I was raising my daughter, living at Tommy's, working my ass off, and mending a broken heart. I didn't have the luxury of unplugging from the world to go talk about myself. So congratulations that you did, and now you have some perspective. You be you, Amanda. That's what you do best."

Jen wanted to scream, pull Amanda's hair, scratch out her eyeballs, throw her on the floor, and dive on top of her to pound her. Instead, she pushed by her on a mission to get to her office before she burst into tears. She didn't look back as she slammed the door and bent over to rest her hands on her knees. The tears poured out like a firehose. *Is this some cruel, fucking joke? Why did I have to fall in love with such a self-absorbed bitch? Never again.*

There was a light tap on her door. Jen grabbed a few tissues to mop her eyes, before saying, "Yes?"

"It's Melissa. May I come in?"

"Sure." She stepped aside while Melissa opened the door and entered, her white coat on and her stethoscope hanging around her neck.

"I saw Amanda leave and you run into your office. I'm sorry. Come here." Melissa opened her arms and Jen accepted another hug from her boss, a busy woman who surely didn't have time to dole out this much personal attention to her physician staff.

Jen cried on her shoulder, broken and battered. "It just hurts so much. I loved her, you know?"

"I know. I'm sorry," Melissa said again. "You're having a really bad day, aren't you?"

Jen straightened and stepped back. "The worst but thank you. I needed that."

"Do you want me to see your patients?"

"No. I have only one left. I'll be fine."

"I have time. I can if you want."

"No. It's important that I redirect my attention and focus on work. Running into Amanda was bound to happen sooner or later."

"I'll tell her therapist to instruct her to leave by a different route. I don't know why she was back here."

"Avoiding the waiting room and prying eyes. She's running for re-election, you know."

"Ahh. Well, that might be important to *her*, but *you're* important to me. She needs to leave the same way as all the other therapy patients."

"Thank you."

"Never forget. You're a valued physician in this clinic as well as a good friend. Hang in there, okay?"

"I will."

There was a knock on the door.

"Yes?" Melissa asked.

The door opened a crack, and the office manager, Vicki, stuck her head in. "Sorry to interrupt, but there's a bat on the ceiling in the lab."

"What?" Melissa and Jen asked in unison.

"I'm not joking. A patient fainted after having her blood drawn, and they lowered her to the floor. When she woke up, she saw a bat on the ceiling and fainted again."

"Oh, fuck," Melissa muttered. "I have a tennis racket in my office. Let's go."

Melissa and Vicki left in a rush. Jen splashed some cold water on her face. As she was drying off, there was another knock on her door. "Yes?"

Vicki was back. "Melissa is wondering if you can kill the bat with her tennis racket. A state surveyor just showed up to inspect the clinic, and Melissa has to take him on the official tour to answer his questions."

"Shit! What else could possibly go wrong? I mean, sure. I'm pretty good with a racket. Someone has to tell my last patient that I'm running late, though."

"I already asked Shannon to. Follow me."

Jen followed Vicki down the hall and they entered the lab where the bat was hiding in a corner of the ceiling.

Jen looked at it, neatly tucked up high, its wings folded tightly. Her heart went out. How was she going to kill something that looked so peaceful? "Do we have any sheets or pillow cases around here?"

"I knew no one would be able to kill that thing," Vicki said. "Melissa is the biggest wimp on the face of the earth." She removed a white pillow case from behind her back. "Here."

Jen stood on a stepstool and held the opening of the pillow case up to the bat. She prodded it with the physician hammer she used to test reflexes and it dropped into the case. The bat freaked out and started flying, poking against the fabric like molecules flying in Brownian motion, so she quickly tied off the opening of the case, holding it away from her body while they ran out the back door and down three flights of steps to the sidewalk outside. Jen opened the case and turned it inside-out. The bat flew off at record speed.

"Niiiiice," Vicki said.

"Thanks. I'd like to think I have more than just clinical skills."

"I never doubted it for a second."

7

North Beach
That evening

"More wine?" Tommy asked, holding the bottle over Jen's glass.

"Why not?" Kristin was tucked in for the night, and Jen had endured the worst day of her life, aside from the day Amanda had told her she cheated on her, that is. Or, maybe the day that Eddy Valentine shot at her while she was swimming at China Beach. Of course, there *was* the night she was taken hostage in Hawaii, and Amanda shot and killed the wise guy who had the tip of his gun barrel resting against Jen's head. Or, equally high on the list of horrors, was the day her car had exploded two seconds after she got out to retrieve her purse from Amanda's car. It was all relative, and, coincidentally, all related to Amanda. *All Amanda's doing. What I went through for her. And she showed up in clinic today! The nerve!*

Tommy finished pouring and Jen smiled. He got up from the kitchen table and grabbed an Anchor Steam from the fridge for himself.

"I can't believe you're flying to Cayman tomorrow with *Roxy* of all people," she said.

"You know I've been working with her for a month. She's good at what she does."

"Stealing fiancées?"

"Hmph. Having been on the receiving end of that, I know how you feel." He rested his hand on her shoulder. "Sorry. I shouldn't go there, and we agreed not to discuss Roxy."

"I know. I brought her up. Just promise me you won't sleep with her too," Jen said.

"That'll be the day! Not my type." That was a white lie, but he'd never, ever admit that to Jen. Come to think of it, he'd hit on Amanda, Jen, and Roxy—in that order—all before they'd told him they were gay.

"Speaking of which, how are you and Sadie doing?" she asked.

He shrugged in disinterest. "That fizzled out. She didn't explicitly say so, but I think I'm a vivid reminder of shooting Sung-Soo Kim in her kitchen. Going through something like that can either strengthen a relationship or kill it."

"I get that. The shootout in Hawaii made me respect you even more. I've never been reminded of that trauma when spending time with you, though. Here I am, even living with you now." She swept her arms wide to encompass his kitchen.

Tommy raised an eyebrow, acutely aware that Jen had returned from Hawaii to live with *Amanda, not him.* He wisely decided not to point that out, instead saying, "Sadie got really pissed when I called her to ask her why Clara was in Cayman."

"What'd she say?"

"First, she accused me of spying on Clara. Then she said that Clara was only trying to find peace, blah, blah, blah…"

"And, you don't believe her?" Jen asked.

"A million dollars was transferred from Jina Pak's bank account to an account in Cayman, and I saw the guy at the food truck give Clara an envelope. I think Jina set her up with a golden parachute."

"Do you think Clara knew about it in advance? Like before Jina was killed?"

He took a drink of beer. "I never got that impression. She seemed so surprised and confused about the circumstances surrounding Jina's murder, but anything is possible. I'm sure we'll figure it out once we confront her on the beach."

"You'll shock the shit out of her when you appear on the sand, hovering over her bikini-clad body lying on a towel," Jen said over her wine glass.

"Sometimes, I love my job. Can we move to the living room? The game is on." The Giants were playing, and Tommy always kept track of the score, occasionally watching when the announcers' voices rose in reaction to a play. He led the way to the sofa that was facing the flat screen.

Jen cozied up next to a pillow on the sofa and pulled a soft blanket over her. "I got sued today."

"What?"

"Yeah. My first official malpractice case. The care was from two years ago in the ER for a big trauma. We saved the woman's life and now she's suing us. Can you believe that? From what I can tell, it looks pretty bogus but that doesn't make it any less upsetting."

"I'm sorry. What's she suing your for?"

"Undiagnosed wrist fracture."

"After you saved her life?"

"Yeah. We fixed her spleen, pelvis, and leg fractures, but didn't get an X-ray of her wrist because she never complained it hurt—even after her other fractures were fixed."

"Just greedy." He glanced at the game.

"Tell me about it. Not much different than your Fed case."

"Who's your lawyer?"

"Don't know yet. The insurance company said he'll contact me in the next few days. I just didn't need this bullshit in my life right now, you know?" She calmed herself with another sip of wine.

"Do you want me to come with you?" His face was turned to the game.

"No. I think I can handle meeting with my lawyer by myself but thanks for the offer."

A local news update caught their attention when the announcer mentioned the DA political race, so he turned up the volume. Gavin Morales, the lawyer challenging Amanda for District Attorney, was giving a speech at a fundraiser.

Morales was in full theatrical mode behind the podium, exclaiming, "There are quite a few differences between Amanda Hawthorne and me. I've been married to the same woman for 20 years and have raised two children with her. My wife and I both work in San Francisco, and our children go to school in the Bay Area. I've demonstrated commitment in both my personal and professional life, unlike my opponent, who can't seem to keep a commitment on either front. She recently spent a month in a rehab clinic for drug addiction after cheating on her fiancée with the woman in these pictures. Hawthorne isn't loyal to anyone but herself, so how can we expect her to adhere to the integrity, loyalty, and commitment that this very important position requires?" Morales held up the 8x10 photos with Roxy in them.

"Holy shit!" Jen blurted. "I can't believe he said that! I can't believe he's holding up photos! Who *does* that in a campaign speech? What an ass!"

The screen switched to Kip Moynihan. "The gloves have definitely come off in the race for DA, as Gavin Morales attacked incumbent Amanda Hawthorne tonight at a fundraiser."

"That's dirty politics if I've ever seen them," Tommy said, turning down the volume again.

"That low-life dirt bag! Amanda shouldn't be humiliated and punished for treating her abuse of painkillers. It will just discourage people from getting the help they need," she said.

"I agree, but you're not going to defend her, are you?"

"Her media guy, Chance, left a voicemail for me, giving me the heads up that Kip might contact me for an interview."

"You're not seriously considering giving an interview, are you?"

"What Morales just did is unfair. It mischaracterizes her."

"So? Life is unfair. Let Amanda clarify it."

"Yeah, but I could undercut his insults in two seconds if I gave an interview. She's more qualified than *he* is to be DA."

"What about answering the 'infidelity questions?'" he asked, using air quotes.

"Maybe this Chance guy can help me dodge those."

"Dodge them? Are you kidding me? Hair and Makeup Man will go in for the kill, not letting you off the hook until he gets what he wants—you admitting that Amanda cheated on you."

"Oh, I don't think it will be that bad, do you?"

"Hell yes!" Tommy exclaimed. "This is a political campaign. You just saw what Morales is capable of. My advice is not to get involved."

"That's good advice, and I'd say the same thing if it weren't so damn unfair. She went to rehab for shit's sake. Let's not flog her in the center of the village. She needs to remain in office as the DA. If she isn't re-elected, I fear what will become of her. She was made for that job..." Jen's voice trailed off, as she turned her attention to her cell phone.

Tommy returned to watching the game.

Jen typed, *Chance. This is Jen Dawson. Got your voicemail. Yes, I'd be happy to give a short statement in support of Amanda. Call me tmrw.*

"There," she said, setting down her phone. "I'm sure I can say something positive about her that demonstrates she's really good at her job and deserves to be re-elected—"

"Even though she cheated on you." He drank some beer.

"Yes, there's that, but I can suck it up for the camera. She *needs* that job, Tommy, and you know it. If she isn't re-elected, think about what it will do to her spirit. What if she starts drinking again? Taking valium again? What would she do?"

"She's an intelligent, accomplished woman. I'm sure she'll think of something. Please tell me you're not going to turn into the abused political wife who 'stands by her woman' even though she's a cheating dick."

"I think I have a tad more self-respect than that, and she's not a dick." She shoved him in the arm.

"Are you sure about that?"

"Do you know something I don't?" She focused her piercing blue eyes on him.

"No. Just based on her fooling around with Roxy is all."

"Okay, then. I'm taking that into account. I'm just planning to give a short statement, not kiss her for the camera."

"Good to hear, 'cause I'd have to kick you out if you became a doormat for her."

"I'm surprised you haven't kicked me out already. I need to start looking for my own place—maybe a nice two-bedroom in the Sunset District for Kristin and me."

"I was *joking*, not hinting. You don't have to go anywhere. I like all of us under one roof. We're just getting into a groove." He reached over and ran his knuckles under her chin.

"Thanks for being so generous, but I think it's time—"

"There's no rush." He sighed and let his hand drop. "I should probably pack for tomorrow."

"Need help?"

He laughed. "No. I'm just going to throw some stuff in a duffel."

"Do you mind if I change the channel to a movie?"

"Not at all. Watch whatever you want and I'll join you in a few." He got up and went to his bedroom, where Jen heard him unzip a bag and slide open a drawer.

She surfed through the movie guide until she found something with a mix of action, adventure, and romance. Pulling the soft blanket around her neck, she snuggled in and relaxed.

A while later, Tommy grabbed another beer and joined her. "Whatcha watchin'?"

"I forgot the title, but it's pretty good. I picked it up about a third of the way in. From what I can tell, he's trying to save humanity from a meteor that's on a course to crash into Earth, and she wants to study it from a scientific perspective, so they're fighting, but they're really hot for each other."

"The smoldering romance?"

"My favorite."

A while later, she cuddled into Tommy and he put his arm around her. They watched as the hero and heroine finally hooked up, frantically undressing each other. He pinned her against a wall. She panted heavily between deep, sultry kisses. He unbuttoned her blouse. She wrapped her leg around his hips. He unfastened his belt, so he could take her before the meteor hit Earth.

"Oh yeah, that's how the ladies like it—fast and against a cold, concrete wall," Jen said, finishing her wine.

"Has *that* been my problem? And here, all these years, I've been sneaking under warm blankets to caress and kiss."

Jen looked at him. Caresses and kisses under a warm blanket sounded really good. She was throbbing in the only spot that needed attention. *Don't send mixed messages to Tommy,* she reminded herself.

Surprising her, he leaned in and brushed his lips against hers.

Out of habit, she reacted with a small kiss, but her senses weren't set on fire like they were when she and Amanda had kissed. Even though Tommy *was* a gentle lover, and he always took care of her needs, she just couldn't go there with him. It would be unfair to him to lead him on…. She had turned a corner as a lesbian and simply wasn't attracted to him any longer.

He backed away slightly and looked at her, his warm breath only inches from her face. "I want to kiss you."

"I'm gathering that. I'm sorry if I sent the wrong signals, Tommy. I just can't…go there…with you."

"Why? I thought we were rekindling what we once had. You let me kiss you the last few weeks—"

"Those were pecks on the cheek." A surge of heat crept up her neck, but it was the wrong kind. She was starting to feel ill-at-ease.

"Come on, Jen. I've seen you in a tank and underwear, prancing around here," he said, his voice challenging.

Her mind went blank. *Prancing*? She might have scurried from her bedroom to the bathroom, but she couldn't recall walking around the house half nude. She scooted back on the sofa, putting some distance between them. "I'm sorry if I led you on. That wasn't my intention. I love you in so many ways, but sexually isn't one of them."

His expression changed from frustrated to empathetic, and she was immediately relieved.

There was no denying the thick, uncomfortable air between them, but he seemed to have his libido in check.

"You're right. You haven't led me on," he said. "I was seeing what I wanted to see. I love you, and not just because you're Kristin's mother. When you moved out of Amanda's and into my house, I hoped...we could...that you might come back. We didn't talk about it, but I wondered. I look at you and I want you. I can't help it. I want to give you everything I have, take everything you can give, then do it again. *Everything*. I can't control how I feel about you, Jen." He rubbed his face then suddenly stood.

"I've overstayed my welcome. I'm so sorry." Her eyes filled with tears.

He extended his hand and she took it. He pulled her up into a hug, their bodies colliding and compressing with anxious frustration. She was skeptical at first that he wanted only a hug, but she allowed him to wrap his arms around her. For reasons she didn't understand, she started crying. *God. How pathetic. Is this over Amanda? Over Tommy? Why am I crying again? I thought I was done crying.*

He patted her head. "You're gonna be okay. Time will help."

She hiccoughed into his shoulder. "We'll move out soon. I don't want to take advantage of you like this."

"Take your time. You're not taking advantage. I love you and Kristin."

"You need a woman who can give you everything you want," she moaned, barely above a whisper.

"So do you," he said but with less enthusiasm.

His thoughtfulness made her smile, but in a pyrrhic way because of the damage she had inflicted on him during their breakup, in addition to her recent gut-wrenching pain from Amanda's infidelity. All in front of Tommy. She almost questioned whether the cost of coming out had outweighed the benefits. In her heart-of-hearts, though, she knew it had, but the pain she had had inflicted on Tommy. It wasn't fair.

"Thank you for being so understanding." She gave him a final squeeze and broke away so she could retreat to her room. *Tommy has been too generous. He's watched me go through the pain of what I did to him and that has to be so humiliating. He obviously thought Amanda was an experiment and I'd come back to him. Shit. I need to stop misleading him and get my life back on track.*

After she changed and gave Kristin a kiss goodnight, she lay in bed, staring at the ceiling, feeling all the sexual tension that had built in her—not just tonight with Tommy but over the last month.

Self-help wasn't an option because she didn't have any privacy in the bedroom she shared with Kristin or the bathroom she shared with Tommy. Besides, she had left her Rabbit when she packed her things at Amanda's. It was too much of a reminder of what she and Amanda had enjoyed together. Their shared intimacy. Amanda's hands wrapped around Sir Rabbit, pleasuring Jen, telling her to come as she looked in her eyes then smothered Jen with deep kisses when Jen started moaning. *Fuck, I loved her.*

She needed to buy something new. Something that wouldn't bring up an image of Amanda every time she looked at it. *I need to get a new life and our own place. With separate bedrooms.*

8

The next morning

"Goodbye, my ladies. I'll text you while I'm in Cayman." Tommy kissed the tops of Jen and Kristin's heads then set his empty cup in the sink.

Jen and Kristin were spoon-deep in their breakfast routine, Jen eating yogurt and granola; and Kristin, a scrambled egg and toast that she mostly dropped over the edge of her tray to Zane.

"Good luck finding Clara and the money," Jen said, casting him an apologetic smile from their exchange last night.

"I'm confident we will." Tommy stood by the door, his hand on the knob.

"Just so you know, I might scout out a few apartments while you're away."

He inclined his head, registering that her message was about more than just housing. "No rush. You're welcome to stay as long as you like." He smiled, but his puppy dog eyes looked like he'd lost his best friend.

"Thanks for hosting us but you deserve more." She hoped he understood—once and for all—that she wouldn't be returning to him. To the extent she had led him on, she regretted it. He needed someone who wasn't her, and *she* needed a new woman in her life—soon.

"Love you," Kristin said to Tommy, as she banged her tray with her plastic spoon.

"You're so smart!" Jen said, high-fiving Kristin.

"Daddy loves you too." Tommy blew her a kiss then slipped out the door, his broad back covered in a blue blazer.

After dropping Kristin at daycare, Jen sat at her desk, reading the electronic medical record of her first patient of the day. Shannon, Jen's primary nurse, was currently rooming the patient, taking his vital signs and inquiring into his health status.

Jen's cell phone rang, interrupting her concentration. She sighed when she looked at the screen.

"This is Jen Dawson."

"Good morning, Dr. Dawson. Chance Greyson here. Thanks for your text last night. I take it you saw the inflammatory remarks by Gavin Morales at his fundraiser?"

"Yes. They made me sick."

"Would you be willing to give a short interview to Kip Moynihan today?"

"I have a full clinic until this afternoon, but I could do it after."

"Could I email you a few preliminary talking points to consider?"

"That would be helpful."

"I don't want to waste your time, so if you have two minutes right now, maybe I could toss some ideas out there for you to react to."

"Go for it."

"Okay. I'm *you* talking: 'Amanda and I are currently separated on friendly terms. We lived together for two years. I don't know what the future holds for our relationship, but I hold her in high regard.'" He paused, and when Jen didn't object, he continued. "'I'm not going to discuss my personal life because I'm not running for office, and I have my daughter's privacy to protect. I will say this, however, that I fully support Amanda for re-election to the District Attorney position. She's smart, dedicated, and works tirelessly for the people of San Francisco. I've never met anyone who's more committed to her work. During the time we were together, Amanda never wavered in her pursuit of justice.'"

"All good until the last few statements. I honestly can't picture myself saying those words."

"Okay...the 'more committed to her work' piece?"

"Yeah. Amanda is as committed as any professional I know. We're all committed to our work."

"Gotcha. I'll dial it back and email something to you. Shall I tell Kip that you could do an interview at 3 p.m. today?"

"Make it 3:30. We can do it here in a conference room, but I need to leave here by four to pick up my daughter, so you all need to be on time."

"Understood. Thank you for your courtesy."

"No problem. One thing though—"

"Yes?"

"This is the one and only interview I'm doing for Amanda. I'm not going to do this every week in response to some bullshit accusation by Morales. You get me this one time, then I'm out. Okay?"

"I understand your position. I can't make any promises about what will happen next, but I get where you're coming from. Trust me, Amanda doesn't want to hassle you, and she's deeply grateful for your time and understanding."

"I'll bet she is."

"I'm looking forward to meeting you this afternoon."

"Goodbye." *Dipshit. Does he know she's the one who cheated on me and got herself into this fucking mess? Does he appreciate her high-profile drama?*

Later that morning, Jen ducked into Melissa Cohen's office between patients. "Hey."

"How are you?" Melissa asked.

"Better than yesterday, that's for sure."

"Thanks for taking care of the bat. Fortunately, the surveyor didn't see it."

"I wonder how it got in here. We should call someone to inspect the ceiling."

"I think Vicki is doing that today." Melissa's soft features remained calm.

"Great," Jen said. "I have a question for you. Is it okay if I use the conference room for a short interview today at 3:30? Kip Moynihan wants a statement in response to Gavin Morales' attacks on Amanda."

"I saw those on the news. He's a real tool." Melissa stared at Jen for a minute, mulling over her request, her large brown eyes intelligent and compassionate.

When Jen first started at the clinic, she found Melissa's contemplative silences a bit disconcerting but now understood how Melissa processed information, considered the angles, then spoke diplomatically.

"I generally don't permit people to use the clinic conference room for personal business, but I'll make an exception just this once, given that Amanda is a valued patient of the clinic," Melissa said. "Tell Ginny to make sure there isn't anything in the conference room with the 'Cohen Clinic' name on it. I don't want the clinic on TV."

"Good catch," Jen said.

Melissa squinted at her, her thick, brown eyebrows knitting. "I'm kind of surprised. I didn't think you wanted anything to do with Amanda or her re-election campaign."

"I didn't. I don't. But Morales was totally out of line last night. He's painting her as some unstable druggy, and she's anything but. She went to rehab for painkillers, and she's getting the help she needs. She should be applauded for that."

"I agree and admire your ability to forgive." Melissa smiled, but her eyes still held caution.

"The fact that she cheated on me doesn't affect her ability to be the DA. That's one thing she's actually very good at."

"Cheating?"

Jen snorted. "That too, apparently, but I won't say that. Her media relations guy is emailing me some talking points."

Melissa exhaled the sigh of a boss who senses trouble ahead but generously allows an employee to chart her own course. "Be sure to keep Moynihan and his crew in the conference room. I don't want them wandering through the clinic. Tell Ginny too, so she can keep an eye on him." Melissa snapped her fingers. "And one more thing, ask Ginny to send an email to everyone in the office, so people know what's going on and to steer clear of the area."

"Good idea," Jen said, sensing Melissa's trepidation and the logistics involved. "If you don't want me to do this, just say so."

"No. It's not that. Go ahead. Just be careful. I don't want you to get hurt, and I don't want anything to splash back onto the clinic. Got it?"

"I appreciate your thinking of me and I assure you, I don't want the clinic to be a part of this either."

They paused for a second while their agreement gelled.

"Anything else?" Jen asked, giving Melissa the opportunity to add more conditions.

Satisfied with their plan, Melissa asked, "Have you heard from your malpractice defense lawyer yet?"

"No, but I haven't looked at all my emails yet today."

"Stay on top of that. There are strict timelines in a lawsuit."

"I will. Thanks for having my back."

"Anytime."

Later in the day, Jen checked her inbox, and there was, in fact, an email from the claims specialist at her insurance carrier introducing her by email to Rich Armstrong, her defense lawyer who was copied on the email.

Jen replied that she could meet the next day if he wanted to come to her office.

He thanked her and replied that he was looking forward to it.

That makes one of us, she thought.

***

Late afternoon

Jen was dictating a note on her last patient when Ginny peeked around the doorjamb, her long, auburn hair falling over her shoulder. "Chance Greyson is here to see you, and Kip Moynihan and his crew are setting up in the conference room."

"Perfect. Please show Chance back."

Jen quickly finished her last dictation. When she looked up, a man with curly black hair and a clean-shaven face stood in her doorway. He wore a cashmere V-neck sweater and tight jeans with the bottoms cuffed. "Dr. Dawson? I'm Chance."

She stood and walked around her desk to shake his hand. "Pleasure to meet you, Chance."

"Likewise." His handshake was pleasant and firm.

"I read your email and agree with all the talking points. I printed it, so we could discuss it quick." She sat in one of her guest chairs and gestured for him to sit across from her.

He sat and gently placed an overstuffed bag on the floor next to him. "Do you want to do a quick mock interview?"

"Please." As they reviewed a variety of scenarios, he coached her to keep circling back to her talking points, regardless of the question.

"You don't have to answer the specific question he asks. Just default to these bullet points. Repeat them a few times if you have to during the interview."

"I think I can do that," she said, folding the paper and setting it on her desk.

Allowing the prep portion to close with silence, he segued into a new topic. "Are you going to do your own hair and makeup?"

"What?" She self-consciously smoothed the top of her head where her long hair was drawn back into a simple pony. She thought she already had.

"You're a naturally beautiful woman—with those Nordic cheekbones and intense blue eyes—but the camera lighting will wash you out like a ghost. Mind if we touch you up a bit and add some color?"

"You travel with a makeup artist?"

"Yes. I'm it. One of my many talents." He removed a black box from his bag. Fascinated, Jen marveled as he opened the box, which contained two trays filled with tiny squares of powder—everything from eyeshadow to foundation.

"No wonder Amanda hired you. She looked really good in her last interview. I take it that was your handiwork?"

His eyes twinkled at Jen's confession. "Afraid not. She actually did her own hair and makeup for that interview. Now, come closer and face me."

Jen did as instructed, and within 10 minutes, she was wearing contouring makeup with eyeshadow, liner, and mascara that accentuated her natural beauty. He even carried a variety of lipstick shades. "I'm thinking bright red, how about you?"

"Ah, no. That's Amanda's color. I'm more of a soft-rose-barely-there kind of woman."

He laughed. "We call that 'tinted chapstick.'"

"Oh really? So, I have a label, huh?"

"Clearly. You're willing to go with a little makeup, but you're *oh-so-serious* in your collared shirt and white doctor coat. Chapstick all the way, but with a hint of rose. I can see why Amanda loves you."

Jen inclined her head. *He knows Amanda loves me?*

"Sorry. Probably shouldn't have said that, but the woman stops breathing every time your name comes up. At the mere mention of me coming over here today, she gave me a thousand instructions about what to say and how to act." He rolled his eyes theatrically. "Like I've never met an ex-lover before. Pfft." He flipped his wrist and waved his hand. "As far as I can tell, dear lady, you are her only Achilles' heel."

Jen was knocked off balance. The Amanda she knew wouldn't discuss her feelings with a new work acquaintance like Chance. "Perhaps she should've thought of that before she slept with Roxy," Jen snarled.

Chance leaned in with an earnest expression, not unlike the expressions Jen gave her patients. "She was high on painkillers but I'm not here to defend her. She's clean now and clearly loves you. That's all I'm saying. She's a hopeless romantic when talking about you.

Now, let's go out there and support her for re-election, huh beautiful?"

"I suppose," Jen said, momentarily at a loss for words. *Hopeless romantic?*

He escorted her to the conference room and she sat next to Kip, the camera pointed in her face.

"Hi, Dr. Dawson. How are you?" Kip asked.

"Very well, Kip. And yourself?"

"Can't complain. Just so you know, Chance and I had a conversation about not naming your daughter or bringing her up. So, rest assured, I'm not going there."

"Thanks for honoring our agreement," Jen said, referring to the standing agreement Amanda had with Kip—direct access in exchange for Kristin's privacy.

"Ready?" he asked.

"Yes. I only have a few minutes, so let's get started."

Kip introduced them for the camera, then explained the background and context by summarizing Gavin Morales' remarks at his fundraiser.

"Do you have a reaction to Attorney Morales' remarks?" Kip asked.

"They're offensive," Jen said.

"Why?"

"Amanda Hawthorne is eminently qualified to be District Attorney. I lived with her for two years and, during that time, she battled the Italian Mafia, protecting her witnesses for a trial. She's one of the strongest people I know, male or female."

"You're not living together now?" he asked.

"No. We're currently separated."

"Why?"

"We needed some space to define our lives and individual journeys. I think it's important for a person to know yourself before you can be a long-term partner with someone else."

"Are you referring to DA Hawthorne's abuse of painkillers?"

"I'm referring to both of our lives."

"Do you disagree that she was abusing painkillers?" he asked.

"I'm very proud of Amanda for paying attention to her own health and entering a rehab clinic to address her drug use issue. Reliance on painkillers is more common than you think. It's an insidious process that affects millions of people regardless of their profession, education, or socioeconomic background. Amanda looks much healthier now that she completed her clinical course."

"Did you notice anything when you lived with her?"

"Not at all."

"Did you encourage Amanda to enter a rehab clinic?"

"No. She did that on her own but with my full support."

"Are you still engaged?"

"No."

"Why not?"

"As I said, we're separated, so we can work on some individual goals before we work on goals as a couple."

"Do you plan on reuniting?"

"I don't know what the future holds but I respect and admire Amanda."

"Did she cheat on you with the woman in these photos?" Kip held up the two photos that already had been splashed all over the news—thanks to Kip and Morales.

"I don't know."

"Isn't it coincidental that you separated at the time she was photographed with this woman?"

Jen smiled politely. "First, I'm in the same photo with Amanda at the Dyke March. Second, as Amanda told you a few days ago, her position in law enforcement takes her to many places with many people. I don't know what's going on in that photo, and I'm not going to speculate on police business."

"Did the woman introduce herself to you at Delores Park?"

"Yes."

"Who is she?"

"She requested that I not mention her name because she does undercover work."

"I see. So, you don't have a problem with her?"

"No."

"Is Amanda currently in a relationship with her?"

"That's a question for Amanda, not me."

"Okay. Let's move in a different direction. Is Amanda committed to her job as DA?"

This was the softball that Chance coached Jen to hit out of the park.

"Very. She's a professional who's passionate about her work. She's brilliant, tough and dedicated. There are very few people who would do what she does in the interest of justice—protecting witnesses for a murder trial and fearlessly taking on a known mobster." Jen's eyes unexpectedly welled up with tears. "I have the utmost respect for Amanda and plan to vote for her."

The camera came in for a closeup as Jen let the tears spill over her lashes. "Can someone hand me a tissue?"

Chance produced one out of thin air and handed it to her, his hand barely visible in the picture frame. Kip paused while Jen dabbed at the tears.

"Sorry. I got a little emotional about describing Amanda's passion for her work and the love she has for the people of San Francisco."

"Understandable," Kip said. "Is there any doubt in your mind that Amanda can fulfill the responsibility that the DA position requires?"

"No doubt at all. She's more than qualified for the position."

"It's clear you're quite fond of her. When this election cycle is over, do you plan to get back together?"

"As I said, I don't know what the future holds, but I can assure you that I'll vote for her."

"Thank you for your time, Dr. Dawson. This is Kip Moynihan for KPIX news."

The camera clicked off.

"Thank you, Kip," Chance said.

Jen stood and Chance quickly guided her from the room so Kip wouldn't be able to ask any follow-up questions.

"Thank you for your time and support," Chance said, walking her back to her office.

"My pleasure. Thanks for the talking points. I'm glad we did the role play. That was harder than I thought it'd be."

"Best to be over rather than underprepared."

"Good luck on Amanda's campaign."

"Hope to see you soon." He gave her a light hug and left.

Jen entered her office, closed the door, and sank into her chair. She had a few minutes to catch her breath before she needed to pick up Kristin. *Damn. I didn't think I'd get emotional but when it comes to Amanda...*

9

The next morning, Jen and Kristin lingered over breakfast.

"Mama likes granola and you like eggs," Jen said, kissing the side of Kristin's head.

"Eggs!" Kristin said, flipping a spoonful into Zane's waiting mouth. He was so gentle with her, never snapping or jumping up.

Jen stifled a laugh. "The eggs are for you, honey, not Zane. He eats dog food, and he already had his breakfast."

Kristin's eyes lit up with trademark Vietti mischief. She dropped her spoon on Zane's head then grabbed a fistful full of egg and held it over the side of her chair, taunting Zane, a growly giggle bubbling up from her throat.

Jen was astonished. *Where is this new behavior coming from?* Before she could say or do anything, Zane's tongue wrapped around the eggs, and he slurped them out of Kristin's hand.

"Okay, that's enough of that. We're not going to feed everything to the dog."

In response, Kristin chortled heartily, slapping her tray her tray with delight.

"I guess breakfast is officially over," Jen said to no one in particular. She quickly rose and grabbed the dish towel while Kristin furiously scooped up eggs and toast and tossed them to Zane's waiting mouth like she was going for the gold in a contest.

Jen finally got Kristin's face, hands, and tray cleaned off, which was no small task with Kristin working against her. She set her down on the floor and Kristin chased Zane around the house, trying to grab his tail with one hand and holding her stuffed animal in the other.

At 45 pounds, Zane loved the attention, ducking and dodging around the coffee table and chairs, until he finally turned around and mouthed her toy, pretending like he was going to take it from her. She screamed, startling him, so he immediately released it, which excited her more. They started the game of chase all over again.

On the flat screen in the kitchen, the TV channel was turned to KPIX news. Jen was curious whether her interview with Kip would be broadcast today, so she kept one eye on the TV while she packed her workout bag. When she noticed Kip join the team at the news desk, a graphic of the DA's race over his shoulder—the DA emblem with photos of Amanda and Gavin—she turned up the volume. Kip gave an intro for his interview of her.

"Candidate Gavin Morales attacked Incumbent Amanda Hawthorne during a speech at a fundraiser, accusing her of being unfaithful to her longtime partner and ex-fiancée, Dr. Jen Dawson. I sat down with Dr. Dawson yesterday afternoon, and here's what she had to say on the topic of Amanda Hawthorne's character and bid for re-election."

The screen switched to Jen and Kip sitting in the conference room at the Cohen Clinic. Jen was surprised by her image. *Damn. Chance really did my makeup well for that lighting. I look professional in my white coat yet slightly glammed up. The eye shadow is more than what I'd usually wear, but he was right, it fades under the intense light.*

She listened to her answers as she started the dishwasher. When the interview concluded, Jen felt proud of her word choices. Well, some were Chance's word choices, but she strung them together and sold the message with grace and aplomb.

Kip's story continued past Jen's interview, however. "I contacted Gavin Morales for a comment, and we had a short phone call last night. Here's what he said."

The screen displayed text populating as Gavin Morales spoke over the phone. "Jen Dawson would say anything to support Amanda Hawthorne. She's a quack who left the San Francisco Community Hospital Emergency Room to work in a questionable clinic and is now neck-deep in a malpractice lawsuit. You figure it out." His voice was gravelly and full of sarcasm.

"How do you know that?" Kip asked.

"A lawyer in my firm represents her. I don't know anything about the file, but her case showed up on the firm docket. The lawsuit is a matter of public record. Google her. The quack doctor supporting her philandering ex-partner. Pathetic. Both of them—losers." He emphasized "losers" like a sloppy drunk.

Jen couldn't believe what she was hearing and seeing. *He outed my lawsuit? His partner is representing me? I haven't even met him! That motherfucker!*

She grabbed her phone and clicked open her work emails, scrolling through the endless list while she looked for one from her malpractice lawyer. There it was, an email from Rich Armstrong. She thumbed to the bottom of the page to see his signature block— Morales, Briggs & Sabelli. *How could this be happening to me? My dumb-shit lawyer works at Gavin Morales' law firm? I'm firing his ass.*

She replied to his email that he wasn't her lawyer any longer, then emailed the claims specialist at her malpractice carrier. She requested a new lawyer since Rich Armstrong's partner, Gavin Morales, just broadcast her lawsuit on TV, calling her a quack. How humiliating! She didn't appreciate her reputation being sullied by her supposed lawyer's partner on the morning news. *What a fucking nightmare.*

Next, she emailed Melissa Cohen and gave her the heads up about the malpractice case being reported on the morning news.

Melissa replied right away. *I saw it and I'm sorry. It doesn't change how I feel about you or your position at the clinic. See you at work.*

Jen replied, *Thanks for your support.*

She turned her attention to Kristin. "Well, baby. Mommy isn't having a very smooth week. It's a good thing I'm going to the gym this morning, so I can throw around some weights to burn off this stress."

"Yaner!" Kristin yelled, chasing Zane through the living room, still unable to pronounce the "Z" in Zaner.

As Jen zipped her bag, her phone chimed. It was a text from Amanda. *I'm so sorry this is happening to you. Your interview was stellar. Morales is a scumbag. Is there anything I can do to help you with your legal situation? PS - I think you need a new lawyer.*

Jen replied, *Ya think? There's nothing you can do to help. PS - I don't want to be involved in the asshattery of your campaign.*

She saw text bubbles forming over Amanda's side of the dialogue box, foreshadowing a reply, but they suddenly disappeared. She waited a minute, but Amanda still didn't reply.

Hmph. She must be off to bigger and better things, spinning her gossamer web, oblivious to collateral damage. "Well, Kristin, you and mommy are off to bigger and better things too."

Once outside, she buckled Kristin into her car seat and drove to the daycare. After giving Kristin a kiss and watching her walk into the colorful toddler room, Jen drove straight to her CrossFit box. She didn't have to be to work until ten on Wednesday mornings, so she had plenty of time to work out and hit the reset button on her roller coaster emotions.

A class was finishing its one-hour workout while she warmed up on the rowing machine. Her back straight, she made long pulls, letting the blood flow to her back and legs. She watched the class as she rowed, recognizing most of the 15 people, as she had been coming to this box for a few years.

She thought she'd seen one of the women before but couldn't be sure. The woman's back was to Jen, and she was working hard, pounding out the remaining combination of kettle bell swings, box jumps, and Russian twists. Jen noticed she was swinging a 35-pound kettle bell and jumping on a very high box. That weight was impressive for anyone, much less at the number of repetitions the woman was doing.

Jen's eyes floated from the woman's long, dark pony tail over her broad shoulders, showcased in a spaghetti-strap tank, and down the sinewy muscles that wrapped her shoulder blades. Her eyes continued their journey and rested on the black Lulus that conformed to the curved mounds of her solid ass. No amount of squatting could create that sweetly-formed shape. She had simply been blessed with ass genes. The woman was a prototype of female perfection.

Jen realized she'd been rowing for much longer than usual, all the while staring—no, lusting—after this woman's ass. *Stop it! I'm objectifying her. I'm no better than those Neanderthal men I find so disgusting.*

She shook her head, grateful that she was at the back of the class, so she wouldn't be caught in the act. Her shoulders and back were plenty warm, so she unstrapped her feet and returned the rower to its group of other machines.

Her overactive libido was shooting off like a bottle rocket but she was an amateur at the dating game. After all, she had been on the receiving end of Amanda's pursuit. Swept off her feet by Amanda's power and charisma, she'd barely had time to think. Now, she had to develop her own skills at flirting if she wanted to start a relationship. *Where to start? What to do? How do I know she's lesbian?*

She shook off her frustrated thoughts and carried her water bottle and phone to the opposite corner of the gym, setting them on the floor next to a rig where she could do squats and other heavy lifting. *Just concentrate on working out. I'm here to work out.* There was a rack of barbells standing lengthwise close by. She removed the 35-pound barbell and set it on the black mats in front of her rig. Next, she grabbed two 25-pound rubber plates and fastened one on each side of the barbell with a black, plastic collar.

After stretching, she knelt, grasping the bar in a wide grip. Sticking her butt out and squaring her chest, she was in the position her coach called "big-ass, big-boobs." Keeping her body tight, Jen picked up the bar and maneuvered it over her knees, then exploded up, lifting the bar, bringing her hips to the party, and pushing the bar overhead. She sank under the bar into a squat and locked the bar over her head, as she straightened her knees. She held the weight firmly over her head for a second before letting it drop to the floor, where it bounced on the rubber plates a few times

"Nice snatch!" she heard over her shoulder.

Jen smiled and turned to see who was complimenting her on the lift. She was thrilled to learn it was the dark-haired athletic beauty whose ass she'd been admiring. "Thanks."

"I've never been good at snatches," the woman said.

"I doubt that," Jen said, eyeing her from head to toe while she grabbed two 10-pound plates for her bar.

The young woman extended her hand for a plate and Jen handed it to her. They each added one to the ends of Jen's barbell.

"They're really good for you, though, and it feels so good when you nail them, that I keep coming back," she said.

"I agree," Jen said.

"Is this is your warm-up weight?" the woman asked in a honeyed patois.

Jen smiled but didn't say anything. She returned to her position in front of the bar, assuming a strong stance and wide grip, then did another snatch, hoisting the bar over her head and dropping under it into a squat that she pushed up. After full extension, she dropped the bar to the mats again. Feeling the rush of accomplishment, she smiled at her sexy companion. "I'm Jen."

"I'm Nicole. Good form. More weight?"

"Yeah." Jen grabbed two more plates and handed one to Nicole.

"What's your personal best?" Nicole asked.

"One hundred-fifty pounds." Jen secured her plate in place with the collar, attempting to mask her nervousness.

"Impressive." Nicole's deep brown eyes took a slow walk, starting at Jen's hands, traveling up her arms, lingering on her chest and shoulders, then strolling over her neck and finally coming to rest on her face. Considering that Jen had done the same to Nicole's entire backside while she was in class, Jen couldn't object. It was a bit unnerving, though. Judging by the fire in Nicole's eyes, Jen guessed Nicole liked what she saw.

"Thanks," Jen said. *I hope she didn't see me on the news this morning.*

"We should work out together some time," Nicole said.

"I'd like that."

"I'm usually here Monday, Wednesday and Friday mornings," Nicole said.

"What time?"

"Eight to nine."

"I'll try to make this Friday work."

Nicole smiled then walked away to grab a Bosu balance ball. She returned and set it a few feet away from Jen's barbell, the flat side up.

"Still working out?" Jen asked.

"Yeah. I like to do a few of my own exercises after class."

Curious what Nicole was planning, Jen watched. Truthfully, she just wanted an excuse to look at her body. *Is that such a horrible thing?* Nicole planted her feet on the Bosu ball then lifted her right foot and extended her leg in front of her, bending into a pistol squat. Jen watched Nicole's muscles synchronize, performing like musicians in a symphony, her sinewy legs straining against the smooth, black fabric, and her back, arms, and shoulders flexing simultaneously to create the perfect balance she needed.

"Impressive yourself," Jen said when Nicole stood up. She definitely felt chemistry between them.

Not one to show off, Jen did another snatch while Nicole watched.

"You look like you've done a few pistol squats in your life," Nicole said.

"Not on a Bosu ball," Jen said.

"I'm sure you could if you tried."

"I prefer doing them on a kettlebell," Jen said.

"A kettlebell?" Nicole laughed. "I don't believe you."

"It's true," Jen said.

"No way."

"Wanna bet?" Jen asked.

"What are we wagering?"

"Dinner?"

"If you can do a perfect pistol squat on a kettlebell, I'll buy. If you miss it at all, you're buying," Nicole said.

"Deal." They shook hands, their hands colliding in a firm grip.

Jen motioned for Nicole to follow her over to the stand of kettlebells, where she slid a 53-pound kettle out to the turf. Nicole watched while Jen did a pistol squat on the turf to warm up.

"You're really going to do this, aren't you?" Nicole asked.

"It's been a while, but I'm pretty sure I still can." Jen steadied her nerves and stepped on the handle of the large kettle bell. She floundered for a second then found her balance on her right foot. As her ankle initially shimmied, the kettle bell vibrated too. Very slowly and carefully, Jen extended her left leg in front of her, and bent her right knee, going into a squat, balancing with her arms out wide. She went all the way down into a squat, hesitated for a second, then slowly rose. Her entire body quivered as she rose, found her balance, and stood. After holding her pose, she hopped off.

Nicole smiled, revealing perfect white teeth against her dark skin. Even her smile was sexy. "I feel like I was suckered into that one. Guess I'm buying dinner, huh?"

"I won't hold you to it. A glass of wine would be fine," Jen said, sliding the kettle back over to the stand.

"Are you kidding me? That deserves dinner!" Nicole held out her fist for a bump.

They returned to the rig where Jen's barbell was resting and Nicole's Bosu ball was waiting for her to do more squats. Jen watched while she did one on each side. "Nice form."

"Thanks."

"Do you work around here?" Jen asked.

"I'm a graphic design artist for a company close by."

"That sounds cool." *Not a lawyer. Bonus.* Jen noticed that Nicole didn't ask what she did for a living, and she discovered she was relieved for once.

"Do you live in Pacific Heights?" Nicole asked.

"In North Beach. I'm currently looking for a place in the Sunset District."

"I love it over there," Nicole said.

"Me too." Jen did another set of snatches while Nicole watched.

"When can I take you to dinner?" Nicole asked.

"Fast mover, huh?"

"When I see something I want, I can be." Nicole waggled her eyebrows and her dark eyes simmered.

Jen felt that look all the way down to her toes. "Let me look at my calendar and arrange for a babysitter. I have an 18-month old daughter."

A genuine smile formed on Nicole's face. "Wonderful. In that case, maybe we should do a brunch date and you can bring her along. I'd love to meet her."

Jen smiled. *Score one for Nicole.* While the offer was noble, Jen wasn't prepared to introduce a *potential* girlfriend to Kristin.

"What's her name?" Nicole asked.

"Kristin." Jen couldn't help but smile.

"Beautiful. I bet she looks like you."

"A little."

"Do you know Rose's Café on Union Street?" Nicole asked.

"In Cow Hollow? I love that place."

"Me too. I think it's kid-friendly," Nicole said.

"I'd like to bring her there someday, but I don't think bringing her on a first date would be a good idea. She's had a lot of changes in her life recently, and I'm hesitant to introduce new people. Know what I mean?"

"I totally get that. Maybe I'll meet her some other time."

"Yeah."

"Let's text each other for a day that works," Nicole said.

Jen grabbed her phone off the floor and unlocked it. They traded phones and entered their contact information for the other.

"Ready for another set?" Jen asked.

"I'd love to but I have to run to work. It was nice meeting you."

"You too. See you soon."

"Count on it," Nicole threw over her shoulder in a flirtatious tone.

Jen watched Nicole return her Bosu ball to a pile on the opposite side of the gym then walk to the locker room. It was clear now that the Bosu ball routine had just been a pretext to meet Jen. She found herself admiring Nicole's well-rounded ass, again, as Nicole walked to the locker room. Jen had the overwhelming and undeniable urge to plant her hands there and squeeze. *Damn!*

When Nicole reached the locker room door, she glanced back and saw Jen still watching her. She tipped her chin up then opened the door and disappeared into the locker room.

"Brunch it is." A zing of excitement ran through Jen. She looked down at her phone and saw that Nicole had entered her contact information as "Nicole CrossFit Goddess." Jen smiled.

North Beach

That evening, Kristin fell asleep in Jen's arms as they relaxed on the sofa. Tired from socializing at daycare, Kristin ate a monster serving of spaghetti and meatballs for dinner while she jabbered on at length. After dinner, Jen gave her a bath and dressed her in a pink sleeper with footies. Kristin sipped a cup of warm chocolate milk, then Jen brushed her cute little teeth, and they cuddled on the sofa.

Kristin looked like an angel, sleeping soundly, her nose pointed in the air and her mouth open. While holding Kristin, Jen scrolled through apartment listings on her iPhone with her free hand until her arm fell asleep. Kristin was getting so big that Jen couldn't cradle her for as long as she used to.

She set her phone down and carried Kristin to their room where she lay her in the crib then gazed upon her sleeping girl with love, gave her a kiss, and tiptoed out of the room. She left the door ajar and smiled to herself that Zane had flopped down next to the crib.

"That's right, Zane. You keep watch."

No sooner had she sat down and pulled the soft blanket over her than her phone screen came alive with an incoming call from Tommy.

"Hey you. How's it going?" Jen asked.

"Not so great. How are you and Kristin?"

"Pretty good. Some drama with Amanda's campaign, but Kristin and I had a great day. She just went to sleep, or I'd put you on speakerphone."

"Give her a hug from me."

"I will."

"Listen, there's something I need to tell you." His tone was foreboding.

"What's wrong?"

"We found Clara Sandoval." He took a drag of his cigarette.

Is Tommy smoking again? Roxy's bad influence. "That's good news, right?"

"Not really. She was dead. Murdered in her hotel room." His voice was so low she had to strain to hear it.

"Oh, my God. How horrible." The hairs on the back of Jen's neck prickled, as she thought about the seemingly innocent young woman and the potential ramifications. "How?"

"Clean slit to the throat, just like Jina Pak. Must be the way the Koreans like to do it."

Jen heard talking in the background and assumed the female voice belonged to Roxy. "I'm scared, Tommy." She jumped up from the sofa and crossed the room to confirm the door was locked. Sliding the bolt lock into place didn't make her feel any more secure, though.

"You don't have to be. There's an unmarked cruiser on the street watching my house. It'll be there until I get home."

"Can I go to the window and look?"

"Sure. They should wave to you."

Tommy waited silently while she turned off the lights, walked to the window, peeled back the edge of the curtain and peeked out. She could see an officer in the driver's seat of a battered cruiser on the opposite side of the street. "Yep. I see them." She waved.

He wasn't looking in her direction, so he didn't wave back.

"Good. If you don't see them tomorrow, call Ryan Delmastro right away, okay?"

She groaned. "How am I supposed to sleep tonight?"

"You're pretty removed from the heart of this, but I called Pops, and he's ready to come sleep in my bed if you want him to."

"I'll think about that."

"He's excited to have a purpose. You know he likes helping us out."

"Okay. What about Kristin's daycare?" Jen asked.

"I spoke to the manager. There will be a uniform posted outside the door until we get this thing solved."

"Should Kristin and I leave town? Go back to Wisconsin for a month to visit my folks?" she asked, her pitch rising.

"I don't think that's necessary. You're not personally involved, and you don't work in law enforcement, so you're not a target."

She was quiet again, her mind racing as she paced the living room floor to the picture window, then to the kitchen counter, and back again. *But I'm living in your house, and you're a target.* "How widely known is this? Will it make the local news tonight?"

"Probably. Clara is from the Bay Area, and it's an international incident with the Korean government."

She took a deep breath. "Does Amanda know?"

"Yeah. I spoke to her earlier."

"Is she flying down there?" Jen's heart skipped a beat, picturing Amanda joining Roxy.

"No. There's no need for her. We'll stay here a few more days to work with the local police, but I should be home by the end of the week."

She found herself relieved that Amanda didn't have to go but pissed that she even cared. "Did you find the money?"

"Nope. It was all withdrawn by Clara, but the bank won't tell us how—whether she took it in cash or had it electronically transferred elsewhere. The trail has grown cold until we can file an action down here and get a local subpoena."

"Sounds like something for Amanda to work on," she said, again picturing Amanda meeting up with them.

"She can do that from San Francisco. Listen, I gotta run. Call me if you need anything. I miss you."

"I miss you too, Tommy. Please be careful."

"I will. Text me okay?"

"I will," she said.

She ended the call and paced around the kitchen then walked back into the living room. *Fuck. Why am I involved with these people? Tommy! Amanda! International spy games and murder! I should move back to Wisconsin. My parents would love to have Kristin and me nearby.* Unfortunately, her mind flashed to Amanda, picturing her rattling around alone in the house in Sea Cliff.

Acting on instinct, she texted Amanda. *I just heard from Tommy. Are we in danger?*

In sub second time, Amanda replied. *I don't think so. Do you want to come over here? You're welcome to stay here.*

Jen paused for an eternity. She set her phone down on the counter while she resumed pacing, running her hands through her hair. This was the moment of truth. Was she capable of facing danger on her own, or did she need Amanda's fortress and security detail? What would running back to Amanda say about her independence?

Besides, Cy was ready to help her, and she had the police outside. At the first sign of a challenge, Jen couldn't run back to Sea Cliff. She didn't want to live in that house again. She had been so happy there until she realized she was just a guest in Amanda's kingdom, under Amanda's control, vulnerable to Amanda's betrayal. She had to remember how her life was destroyed when Amanda had cheated on her. She had come a long way in a month and needed to continue on her own journey with Kristin.

She picked up her phone, and her thumbs hovered over the screen. Uncertain what to say, she set it back down and stretched her legs, making a path in the rug. She finally sat on the sofa, staring at her phone for inspiration, then typed a reply to Amanda. *No. We don't need to stay there, but thanks for the offer.*

Amanda replied, reading Jen's mind, as per usual. *Do you want me to come over there with my security detail?*

Jen replied, *No thanks. We're fine. There's an unmarked cruiser out front.*

She watched text bubbles form then Amanda's message populated. *Goodnight. Hug Kristin for me. I miss her terribly.*

A lump the size of a grapefruit formed in Jen's throat. There it was in type. Amanda missed Kristin. Jen suddenly felt horribly guilty for depriving Amanda, and Kristin, of the opportunity to be in each other's lives. *Why do I feel guilty? Shouldn't she be feeling guilty? How does she do this to me?*

She lay back on the sofa, wondering if she'd be able to sleep. Probably not, so she called Cy.

"Hello?" he yelled. Not only was he hard of hearing, but he also treated cell phones like they were walkie-talkies.

"Hi, Cy. It's Jen. Tommy said you'd be willing to come sleep over here tonight. Is that still an option?"

"I've been waiting for your call. I have a bag packed and I'm on my way."

"See you in a few minutes." She knew it would take him only five minutes to walk from his house, which was on the same block but down the hill.

In the meantime, she was determined to gather her wits. Pulling the blanket up to her chin, she focused on calming breaths and slowing her heart rate. *Relax. We're not targets. The police are outside. Think calming thoughts. What did I do today that made me happy?*

She ran through the day's events, and her mind rolled over each one, finally coming back to her flirtatious exchange with Nicole at the CrossFit box. At least it was something. A smidgeon of hope in her love life.

She forced herself to take deeper breaths, pushing the air out as far as she could and breathing in through her nose. She was jolted from her semi-meditation by a loud knock on the front door. Zane came running from Kristin's bedroom, barking.

"Shush, Zane. It's Cy. Don't wake up Kristin." She walked to the door. When she opened it, she was surprised to see an officer standing behind Cy.

"Everything all right Dr. Dawson?" the officer asked.

"Yes. Thank you for checking. Can I bring you some coffee or something?"

"No, ma'am. We have everything we need in the car."

"This is Cy Vietti, Tommy's father. He's going to stay the night," she said.

Cy turned and shook the young officer's hand. "I was on the force for 38 years. Thanks for your service."

"Impressive," the young man said. "I'm Officer Ortiz."

"Pleasure to meet you. Have a good night," Cy said then entered the house.

Jen closed and bolted the door. She hesitated briefly in the living room, feeling awkward in Cy's company when Tommy wasn't there.

"I'm going to drop my bag in Tommy's room," he said.

"Okay. Are you hungry? Can I fix you something?"

"No. Maybe a cup of coffee if you have some on."

"Sure. Coming right up." *Why does he think I have some on?* She marveled at how people of his generation could drink so much coffee, especially after dinner. *Does he plan on staying awake all night, keeping watch?*

They relaxed in the living room, he with his coffee and stretched out in Tommy's recliner, she with a large glass of ice water, stretched out on the sofa. Cy found a baseball game on TV, turned the volume twice as high as Tommy usually did, and settled in to watch. They made small talk during the commercials, then a comfortable silence settled in. That was one thing she appreciated about Cy—he was easy to be around. Like family.

Since watching baseball wasn't her thing, even though she enjoyed it as background noise, she searched her mind for what she could do to occupy herself. She scratched Zane's ears, but he wandered off in the direction of Kristin's room again, the TV probably too loud for him. Too amped to read a book, Jen decided to take a stab at writing poetry, which usually helped her sort her emotions and soothed her soul.

She situated herself under the blanket and clicked through the apps on her phone to notes. *What to write about? Fear? Love? Meeting someone new? Concentrate on my feelings around meeting Nicole. Combine them with the comfort that Cy has brought into the house. Let my feelings float onto the page. Follow a thread of thought, then let it go…*

She started typing—slowly at first—then allowed her feelings to take over, directing her fingers.

*Steeped in thoughts so dark to the core,
Hopeful emotions appear at the door.*

*Unwind my days of darkness and pain,
Unwind my heart to feel love again.*

*Lay down my arms, I will fight no more,
Let down my guard, as I'm not at war.*

*Floating outward, upward, and away,
Freeing the hurt that blocked my way.*

*Unwind my doubt, believe her words,
Accept the overtures that I heard.*

*Unwind my heart and open to her,
Allow the possibility of love to stir.*

God, does this poem suck, she thought. *Why did I ever think I could write poetry? How stupid. Actually, I take that back. I did write a good one about the narcissistic bitch who betrayed me.*

A pang of guilt spiraled through her. *I need to forgive and forget—move on. It will be good for my soul. Isn't that what Lane said in the ER? "Forgiveness can be liberating for the soul?"*

"He was safe!" Cy thundered, jolting Jen from her thoughts.

She almost flew off the sofa. "What?"

"Sorry, dear. Didn't mean to scare you, but he was safe at first. Stupid ump. Where do they find these guys?"

"Right."

"What? Did you say 'goodnight?'" he asked.

"No. I said, 'right.' I was agreeing with you about the ump."

"About Trump?" he asked.

"The *ump*," she said, pointing at the television.

"Trump is a buffoon!" Cy said for the hundredth time since he had become president.

"Right." She nodded and smiled.

"Goodnight," he said and returned to the game.

She shook her head and returned to her poem.

11

Pacific Heights

The next day, Jen entered the Cohen Clinic at her regular time, having dropped Kristin at daycare and introduced herself to the police officer stationed there. Fortunately, the other parents hadn't pieced together that the officer was necessitated by Tommy's job. To the extent parents were inclined to resent having a police officer's child in their daycare, however, the daycare staff protected Tommy and Jen by not disclosing that the officer was present at Tommy's request.

Jen had barely slept, electing to stay on the sofa rather than the bed in Kristin's room. She heard every little sound outside—including the ever-present running of the cables under the street—and couldn't get comfortable on the cushions, tossing and turning, periodically looking out the window to confirm the officers were still there, then pulling the blanket over her face. At one point, she considered inviting them inside, so she could retire to the bedroom and get some real sleep, but she dismissed that idea as too awkward. She was looking forward to Tommy's return at the end of the week.

She suspected she looked disheveled as she walked in the front entrance through the center of the waiting room. "Good morning, Ginny."

"Good morning, Dr. Dawson. I think Dr. Cohen wants to see you right away." Ginny tossed her long cinnamon mane over her shoulder, looking as though she was about to be photographed for an edgy album cover. She wore sapphire-colored lipstick that electrified her eyeshadow, giving an alien hue to her ever-curious eyes. In Jen's world, blue lips meant resuscitative measures, but in Ginny's case, the color was so dazzling that there was no mistaking her youthful vigor.

"About what?" Jen asked.

"Some computer stuff." Ginny twirled a strand of hair around her fingers.

"Computer stuff?" Jen paused before pushing through the door to the back.

"She'll tell you." Ginny picked up the phone to answer a call but motioned with her eyes for Jen to get moving.

Jen dumped her bag in her office and walked down the hall to Melissa's office.

The clinic IT guy, Brian, was seated in Melissa's chair, his hands hovering over her keyboard while Melissa stared over his shoulder at her computer screen.

"Hey, what's up?" Jen asked.

"Oh good. You're here. We've been hacked," Melissa said.

"Hacked? What do you mean?" Jen circled the desk so she could see the screen. What she saw when she got there sent radioactive shock waves through her. The third nuclear missile of the week had landed in her work world. There was an image of a skull and crossbones with the name HELLFIRE written over it in jagged red.

Her hand flew to her mouth as a cold shiver ran from her neck to her toes. "Fuck," she said under her breath.

"What? Do you recognize the name?" Melissa asked.

"Yes. It's...I think it's...a hacker who works for the North Korean government," Jen said. "Have you called the police? The FBI?"

"We called the police, just assuming it was a ransom case because we're a clinic." Melissa turned her full attention to Jen. "Why do you think it's the North Koreans? What would they want with the Cohen Clinic?"

"Because HELLFIRE is the hacker who stole $50 million from the Federal Reserve Bank. He works for the dictator of North Korea. At least, that's what Tommy told me. I'm not altogether sure whether HELLFIRE is one person or the name of a group of hackers."

"Are you kidding me? Why target *us*? We don't have $50 million at the clinic." Melissa's pitch was uncharacteristically high.

"I think I know why," Jen said, her mind processing.

Melissa rested a hand on her hip. "I'm all ears."

Jen glanced at Brian, who hung on her every word. "To get dirt on Amanda." Her voice was low and ominous. "Amanda is seeing a therapist here and she's campaigning for re-election. I'll bet you anything they're looking for her therapy notes."

"Isn't that a little farfetched?" Melissa asked. "I mean, why would North Korea care about the election for the DA in San Francisco?"

"Amanda is on the team investigating the North Korean bank heist at the Fed. The Fed already clawed back $50 million, and I imagine Yon Song-Muk is pretty pissed about that. Tommy and Roxy are in the Caymans right now, chasing down a bank employee who they think took a million dollars. Last night he called me..." Her voice quivered with emotion, "...to tell me that he and Roxy found the employee murdered in her hotel room."

Melissa's eyes widened and Brian's face went ashen. "If that's true, then we're fucked!"

"I have to text Tommy." Jen ran back to her office, her pulse quickening, and grabbed her phone out of her bag. She typed as she returned to Melissa's office. *I'm at work. HELLFIRE hacked into the clinic computer system and shut it down. What should we do?*

Her phone chimed with Tommy's reply, and she said, "I'm supposed to call Lieutenant Navarro at SFPD."

They watched as Jen dialed.

"Lieutenant Navarro," he answered.

"Hi. This is Dr. Jen Dawson, Tommy Vietti's...Tommy's...friend. He recommended I call you."

"Hi, Jen. I know who you are. What can I do for you?"

"I'm at my clinic. A hacker named HELLFIRE shut down our computer system."

"HELLFIRE?"

"That's what the screen says."

"Why?" he asked under his breath.

"Amanda is seeing a therapist here."

"Ahh. Amanda. The campaign. Her therapy notes will be plastered all over the Internet."

"That was my thought too."

"Do you want to warn her or should I?" he asked.

"I will," Jen said. "You can give her a report after you look at it."

"I'll be right there. Don't touch anything," he instructed.

"We won't." She looked at Brian's sweaty fingers resting on the keyboard as she gave Navarro the address.

"Lieutenant Navarro is on his way. He said not to touch anything."

"We already have, but it didn't help." Brian ran his hand through his shaggy hair.

"How are we supposed to see patients today?" Melissa asked.

"The old-fashioned way? With paper?" Jen suggested.

"You have no idea how difficult that will be," Melissa gritted.

"Don't you have a procedure to follow when the electronic medical record is down?"

"Sure, but we can't even open the electronic schedule to see what patient is seeing which doctor. Ginny will have to check people in, then ask the patient who they're seeing and when. Fucking disaster." Melissa threw her hands in the air.

While Melissa walked through the logistics, Jen texted Amanda. *Bad news. HELLFIRE hacked into our clinic computer system. Worst case scenario is that your therapy record will be made public on the Internet. I notified Tommy, and Lieutenant Navarro is on his way over.*

Amanda replied right away. *I'm going to call my therapist to find out what she put in my note so Chance can create some talking points for me. Thanks for the heads up. I'm so sorry this happened to you and Melissa. Pls give her my apologies.*

Jen typed, *Will do. I hope the therapy note doesn't embarrass you. A lot of people go to therapy, you know. The public should understand.*

Amanda replied, *I can only hope. I apologize in advance if your name is in there. I've only seen her once, but I talked about our relationship, and how much I want to get back together with you. I'm so sorry. If my therapist wrote all that down, the details will include you too.*

Jen took a deep breath and sighed, her heart doing a somersault at Amanda's confession. She wasn't necessarily surprised that Amanda wanted to get back together but seeing it in the text was sobering. She replied, *Thanks for the warning—on both accounts.*

When Navarro and his team arrived at the clinic, Ginny showed them back to Melissa's office.

"Hi, Jen," he said, shaking her hand.

"This is Dr. Melissa Cohen, the president of the clinic, and this is Brian, our technology guy," Jen said, introducing them.

Navarro sat down at Melissa's computer and looked at the screen. "Yep. That's the HELLFIRE signature from North Korea. He used the same trademark that he used for the Sony Pictures and Bangladesh attack at the Federal Reserve Bank a few years ago. We didn't see this signature for the recent Fed attack because he carried that out surreptitiously, stealing money behind the scenes with the aid of an insider. The fact that he froze your system and left a calling card indicates that he wants us to know it's him and that your data is already gone. When did you discover this?"

"This morning," Melissa said.

"Do you have patient information on your system?" Navarro asked.

"Of course," Melissa said.

"You should assume it's all been compromised. Call your insurance carrier and lawyer. I'm guessing you'll have to notify all your patients."

"Oh fuck." Melissa ran a frantic hand across her forehead. "First, I'm calling our bank. I'm sure there's an electronic trail to our retirement account."

"Good catch. Call the manager of the retirement accounts," Jen suggested.

"Have you disconnected your servers?" Navarro asked.

"No," Brian replied, his face turning the color of a ripe tomato.

"Let's go do that," Navarro said.

"We were supposed to unplug the servers? Melissa asked. "Who knew that? God. Could it get any worse?"

"With Amanda's enemies?" Jen asked. "You bet it could. I was shot at in the ocean, had a gun held to my head in Hawaii, and watched my car explode at Moffit Field during Amanda's mob war. This is *nothing* compared to that."

Melissa narrowed her eyes. "I think I met you for the first time when you were in the middle of that. I remember you came with Amanda to an appointment, and I checked her body for debris from the car bomb. You'd removed some shrapnel from her leg in the middle of a parking lot somewhere."

"At the hangar," Jen said.

"Now I'm in Amanda's circle?"

"Unfortunately, yes. She has a target on her back that spreads like a cancer to everyone who associates with her."

"I admire Amanda and all, but maybe we should revisit whether she can be seen here," Melissa said.

Jen swallowed hard. Turn Amanda away from the clinic at a time when she needed therapy the most? Melissa's point was valid, but Amanda was in desperate need of therapy. On the other hand, Amanda's presence was not only upsetting to Jen but also could impact thousands of patients. "Maybe," Jen said cautiously, but guilt exploded like a grenade in her chest.

"We need to call the staff together for a meeting," Melissa said. "I'm not even sure we can see patients today. Then again, how do we call them to cancel if we don't have access to our schedules?"

"We can run the clinic. If you want, I can see your patients while you work on the computer and business stuff," Jen offered.

"If you think you can handle it." Melissa sounded uncertain.

"Can I handle it? I used to work in the ER. Of course I can handle it."

Melissa smiled. "Thanks. Let's round up the troops and meet in the conference room."

Once the entire Cohen Clinic staff was assembled, Melissa addressed the five physicians, their nurses, three therapists, the receptionist, triage nurse, office manager and others. Brian was preoccupied with Navarro in the server room.

"I'm sorry to tell you this, but our computer system has been hacked by a well-known hacker to the SFPD and FBI—"

"and CIA," Jen added.

"This means that all of our patient records have been compromised. We're going to notify our insurance carrier and lawyer, so they can advise us about what to do next. Detective Navarro from the SFPD is here right now."

"What about our financial and retirement accounts?" Gregg, a young physician asked.

"Thanks for raising that, Gregg," Melissa said. "Vicki is working with our bank on payroll, and I called the manager of our retirement accounts. He assured me he's locking down our accounts."

"Are the hackers demanding that we pay a ransom to get our system running again?" Gregg asked.

"No. This isn't a ransom attack," Melissa said. "They believe it's a targeted attack against DA Amanda Hawthorne to obtain her drug rehab therapy notes to use against her in the re-election campaign."

There was a collective intake of breath and some "whoas" while Amanda's therapist, Susan, covered her mouth with her hand.

Jen looked at Susan. "I think Amanda is going to call you shortly to discuss what's in your note."

Susan nodded, her expression frozen while her mind processed what was in her notes. She cast Jen a sympathetic glance.

Great. She mentioned me by name in the notes.

"Can we see patients today?" another physician asked.

"We have to because we have no way of figuring out who to call to cancel," Melissa said. "We can't pull up the electronic schedule, so Ginny will get the patient name, ask which provider they're seeing, and their appointment time when they check in. We'll start a handwritten list, so I'm asking each nurse to keep track of the patients and their times, and keep the appointments moving. It's going to be a clusterfuck, but we owe it to our patients to see them."

"Are we supposed to tell them about the hack when we see them?" Gregg asked.

"Yes, but we should all say the same thing, so we need to work on messaging before we leave this meeting. Vicki," Melissa said, gesturing to the experienced office manager, "will be dealing with the insurance carrier and lawyers. Don't get her involved in seeing patients or troubleshooting those operational details until she's completed her other tasks."

"How am I supposed to know what meds my patient is on?" a physician asked.

"You'll have to ask your patient," Melissa said.

"What if the patient can't remember?" the physician asked.

"Then you'll have to deal with it and problem-solve with the patient. You're a smart person, use your brain," Melissa said, tapping her temple.

"When will we have the electronic medical record back online?" Gregg asked.

"I have no idea. I'll work with Brian and Lieutenant Navarro," Melissa said.

"How are we supposed to document our patient visits?" a physician asked.

"You'll have to handwrite all progress notes until we get our computer system back. At that time, someone will have to enter all the progress notes in the electronic medical record," Melissa said.

Gregg slouched in his chair. "How archaic! This really sucks. I'm not sure it's worth it to try to see patients if we have to write everything down. What a disaster."

"Get over the technology, Gregg. We're physicians. Talk to your patients, examine them, diagnose their problems, and make a plan," Melissa said.

"Easy for you to say. You're more experienced than I am."

"Oh, for God's sake. Help out in a crisis, will you?" Jen stared him down.

He glared at her like an insolent teenager but shut up.

"When you're in private practice like we are, it's not always easy," Melissa said. "When my grandmother and great aunt started the Cohen Clinic during World War II, look at what they were facing: Their husbands were in Europe, liberating France, which left them alone to raise the children in San Francisco. Grandma Cohen was one of the few female physicians in California and Great Aunt Margaret was a nurse. At first, they saw mostly women for free out of the house. They kept records with a pen and paper. When the line of patients extended around the block, they looked for office space and got a decent price on this building—in this very spot. The plaque that they hung over the door—"Patients Come First"—still hangs in my office today. Imagine the obstacles they faced, but they still saw one patient at a time, every day. That photo on the wall, hanging above Gregg, is Grandma Cohen and Great Aunt Margaret—the Cohen sisters."

They all turned to admire a grainy, black and white photo of two austere-looking women, one in a white doctor's coat, the other in a full nursing uniform, her starched nursing cap pinned to her hair. Melissa paused a second to admire them.

"All right everyone, as Grandma Cohen said, 'The challenges of yesterday must not cloud the horizons of today.' Let's make the Cohen sisters proud. We have 15 minutes before the clinic opens, so someone hand me a pen and paper, and we'll start writing our common message.

Once we finalize it, we can photocopy it for everyone."

Ginny, always astute, raised her hand.

"Yes?" Melissa asked.

"Did the Cohen husbands return okay from the war?"

"Thank you for asking, Ginny. Yes. When they returned, they were processed through the Presidio, only a mile from here, then went to work building row houses for the other veterans who got home loans under the G.I. Bill. Their construction business, Cohen Construction, grew exponentially and turned into one of the largest construction firms in California," Melissa explained.

"Cool story," Ginny said, a youthful optimism in her tone.

Ever the cynic, Gregg rolled his eyes and muttered, "Can the challenges of today cloud today's horizons?"

12

The next day, the Cohen Clinic ran the same drill. With great attention to patient recollection of appointment time and medical history, the physicians managed to see everyone without an electronic medical record. Having worked in the ER and treated many patients who weren't conscious for one reason or another, Jen was used to practicing medicine without relying on an updated medical record.

In the late afternoon, she found herself at her desk—jotting down handwritten notes of the daily patient visits—when she received a text from Tommy.

Roxy and I are back in town. We're on our way over to your clinic to review some computer stuff with Navarro.

Jen set down her pen and replied, *Just keep her out of my hair.*

I'll do my best. She's good at this stuff, though, he texted.

"Yeah, right," Jen muttered. She continued seeing patients all day, unaware of when Tommy and Roxy arrived. When she was tidying up her stack of notes after her last patient, she looked up to see Tommy standing in her doorway.

"Hey, beautiful."

"Tommy! I'm so glad you're back!" She jumped up and ran around her desk to hug him.

"It's good to be back. Did you miss me?"

"Terribly. I can't believe this nightmare we're involved in. The poor bank employee murdered in Cayman! Our computer system! And, now, just waiting for Amanda's therapy note to be splashed all over the news—probably mentioning me in it. You have to stop this nightmare."

"I wish I could, but we're dealing with a psychopathic dictator who will do anything to hurt us."

"But *we* didn't do anything to him." She motioned to herself and the clinic.

"Well, he can't put a name or face on 'the Feds,' so his intel has led him to Roxy, me, and Amanda."

She pushed back from him, noticing that he smelled strongly of smoke. "Poor Clara Sandoval. Why was she murdered?"

"We're pretty sure he thought she stole the $1 million. He doesn't realize that Jina Pak stole it and gave it to Clara. Such a fucked up, sad situation."

"I'm so sorry. You knew her, right?"

"Enough to know she was a good person who didn't deserve to get mixed up in something like this."

"Did you tell Sadie? How is she taking it?" Jen asked, stroking his arm with her hand.

"She's pretty broken up. We're gonna meet later at her house and talk to Clara's family together."

"I'm sorry. I'm sure that will be hard. If you need to stay overnight with her, feel free. I understand."

He stepped back and grasped her hands in his. "I want to sleep at home with you and Kristin. You're my first priority."

"Thank you. I feel like my life has been a nightmare since you left. I hope you can restore some sanity."

"I'll do my best."

"Did you help Brian fix our computer system?" she asked.

"I don't know the half of it, but Roxy and Navarro are with him right now. They're trying some recovery and mitigation techniques."

"Wonderful," she said sarcastically, the mere mention of Roxy's name bringing out the fighter in her.

"Relax. She's not a threat to you."

"You're right. She just stole my fiancée and ruined my personal life, that's all."

"It takes two to tango. Amanda was a willing participant—"

"—a drugged one," she cut in, anger rising. *Why are people attacking her so hard lately?*

He inclined his head. "Well, let me just say that I've spent a lot of time with Roxy over the last month. She's not as evil as you might think."

Jen's stomach churned. "I kind of feel like that's bullshit." She paused to steady her nerves. "Maybe we shouldn't discuss her."

Tommy's phone rang, saving him from having to reply. He looked at the screen and shook his head. "Excuse me. I have to take this."

He quickly disappeared down the hallway and went into the back stairwell, the phone to his ear.

Jen returned to her desk and her patient notes until a light knock on her open door caused her to look up. She stared into the smoky blues resting above the crooked nose of the bitch she had pummeled a month ago. "You again?"

Roxy's shock of blonde hair partially covered her left eye. "Hi, Jen. I'm here in peace. Actually, looking for Tommy. Have you seen him?"

Roxy's Scottish accent grated Jen's nerves. "He took a phone call and went that way." Jen tilted her head in the direction of the stairwell. *Sucks to be her with a slight hook to her royal nose.* Jen scanned Roxy's faded jeans, the sliver of exposed white T-shirt she wore, most of it covered by a designer grey hoodie with a chic, black leather jacket thrown over it. She looked like a grungy grad student on a pub crawl, but she had to be in her late 30's. *Who dresses like that?*

"You're staring," Roxy said.

"You're standing in my doorway."

"Fair enough. I was considering saying something else."

Roxy was a like a natural disaster about to unfold. Jen knew she was in danger of becoming engulfed but couldn't run. She felt like impending destruction was her destiny this week. "What could you possibly say?"

"That I'm sorry for what happened. I didn't know Amanda was as impaired as she turned out to be."

"Bullshit. You get paid to lie for a living, and you'll say anything to get what you want." Jen said, surprised at the ice in her own tone.

"I get paid to do a lot of things, but lying in my personal life isn't one of them. I'm not putting you on. I didn't know. If I had, I wouldn't have—" The right word seemed to escape Roxy's grasp.

"Seduced my fiancée?" Jen supplied.

"Yes. That." Roxy dug into her jacket pocket and removed a pack of Marlboro's. She tapped one out and ran it under nose, breathing in the scent.

"You know you can't smoke in here, right?"

"I assumed," Roxy said, closing her eyes for the briefest second.

"You're killing yourself by smoking those," Jen hissed, not disguising the disapproval in her tone.

"I'm not afraid of death. I have plenty of friends and family in Heaven," Roxy said casually, as if referring to a neighborhood in Edinburgh.

"And, see, I don't believe you. Your tone is a little too casual. I'm not buying it."

"Do you mind?" Roxy asked, gesturing for herself to enter Jen's office.

"Please, have a seat. I don't have any more patients today, so I'd love to hear why you're so fucking cavalier about adultery, death, almost getting Amanda killed...the entirety of it." *This woman doesn't even flirt with convention, she's so beyond the pale of normal behavior.*

Roxy sat, slouching against the back of the chair as if sinking into a sofa—a symptom of exhaustion rather than disrespect. She crossed her legs—finding a rhythm with her vintage boot—kicking the air and smelling her cigarette.

138

"I'm only telling you this because you've formed an unfair opinion of me. In a sense, I can't blame you, but I'm not the person you think I am."

"Do tell." Jen impatiently rolled her hand in the air.

Roxy continued despite Jen's hostility, averting her eyes. "I had a child and she died. That's why I do what I do, and I am who I am. I'm hopelessly flawed." Roxy stared at her swinging boot going to and fro.

Jen's hand flew to her mouth, hot embarrassment flushing her face. "I'm so sorry. I didn't know."

"Very few people know because I never talk about my past. In my profession, showing emotion is a weakness that could be used to hurt me and my country. I'm only telling you this because I have a moral obligation to set the record straight with you. I'm not a cold-hearted agent who doesn't value relationships and people. Quite the contrary. I'm so broken—" She patted her heart, "—deep down in here that I had to remake myself from the ground up, becoming a different person. I chose this line of work because I could hide behind an alias on each assignment, totally immerse myself, and run from the pain."

Jen gulped. "How old was your child when she died?"

"She was little. Only a few months. She had a congenital heart defect that was inoperable so was never going to make it. There was nothing they could do." Roxy stopped abruptly, her voice growing small and quiet. Her eyes took on an absent stare.

139

"What was her name?"

"Gracie," Roxy croaked.

"That's a beautiful name. I'm sure she was a beautiful girl."

"She was. So tiny. So fragile. Such a perfect human being in every respect—except her heart." Roxy covered her face with her hands.

Jen couldn't stand it any longer, feeling the pain Roxy had endured, envisioning her own daughter.

She rose and rounded her desk. Surprising Roxy, she bent down on a knee and hugged her as best she could while Roxy sat in her chair, crying silent sobs. Finally, Jen took the initiative to remove Roxy's hands from her face. Roxy's admission had wiped away the sardonic expression that usually resided there. What lay beneath was only sadness without any bitterness. Jen hugged Roxy tighter, which resulted in her scooting forward to cry openly on Jen's shoulder.

When she was out of tears, Roxy gently pushed away from Jen and sat back. "I didn't mean to lose control in front of you. I really didn't come here looking for pity. It's been ages since I cried like that."

"I know, but you found sympathy from me. Better?"

"A good cry can ease the pain even though it never goes away."

Jen remained on her knees, her hands on Roxy's legs. "How long ago?"

"Seven years."

"I'm sure it feels like yesterday sometimes."

"Time is elastic for me now. If you told me Gracie died yesterday, I'd believe you. If you told me that she died 20 years ago, I'd believe that too. I have no measurement for how long she's been gone because my love for her is eternal. She'll always be with me and I with her—" Roxy stopped, hiccoughing through another sob.

"I've never thought of time as exactly linear myself," Jen said. "Life is more of a stream for me that continues into afterlife. We move along, sometimes drifting, sometimes battling the rapids, our friends and family in the stream with us, moving through space and time together at a pace that may or may not be relevant to how we measure time in hours, days, weeks, or years." Jen searched Roxy's eyes.

"You just articulated how I feel. All I know is that I want to reunite with my baby someday, and I'll be broken on earth until I do."

"I understand your pain but I have a question for you."

"What?"

"Would Gracie want you to deprive yourself of the love and joy life has to offer because she went to Heaven? Wouldn't she want you to live a loving, joyous life in her memory until you reunite?"

"I try not to think about what she would think of me now."

Jen nodded. "Have you tried seeing a grief counselor?"

"I didn't know therapists could specialize in grief. Besides, I've changed, added too many layers for anyone to peel back to the innocence

141

I once had. I'm not sure I know that person any longer, or even want to return to her. That young woman allowed me to get blindsided by pain, so I'm not about to become her again. If that makes any sense."

"Reasonable position in light of your experience, but what if you felt better about yourself and your destiny if you went to a couple of sessions? Would you do that for me? For Gracie?"

There was a long silence while Roxy stared at Jen, her eyes puffy from crying. "I'll think about it."

"That's a start. I'd love to see some mending take place in your heart. It's too fragile to cover up, Roxy. Accept some help and love again. Let someone in."

"I'll try." Roxy didn't add that she had been prepared to let Amanda in until she entered the rehab clinic and told Roxy there was no future for them.

Jen squeezed Roxy's knees and stood. "Stay here. I'll be right back." She left the room and went to the drug supply closet. She found what she was looking for and returned to her office. "Take off your jacket."

"Why?" Roxy asked.

"Just do it." Jen waited while Roxy removed her jacket and hoodie, revealing slim, white arms.

Jen opened the small box she was carrying and removed a patch. She carefully peeled off the back layer and stuck the adhesive side to Roxy's deltoid, if you could call it that. Jen was shocked at how little muscle mass Roxy had.

"There. This is a NicoDerm patch. Toss the cigarettes and use this patch. Do you smoke more than 10 cigarettes a day?"

"Yes," Roxy admitted, shrugging her hoodie and jacket back on.

"Wear this patch for six weeks, then move to a lower dose patch for a few weeks, and so on. Here's the box. Read the back cover for directions on how long to leave each patch on. These really work. They're better for you than all that smoke and chemical in your lungs from cigarettes, but I suspect you know this already."

"As I said, I don't mind dying."

"How would you like to live with COPD, tethered to an oxygen tank, sitting in a nursing home? Does that sound like fun?"

"No."

"Hand me your cigarettes," Jen ordered.

Roxy reluctantly dug in her jacket pocket and removed the pack. She looked at it longingly, but dutifully turned it over to Jen, keeping the solo stick clutched in her other hand.

"That's the first step. You have to *want* to quit. I say, 'stop killing yourself and start living life for Gracie's sake.'"

Roxy's lower lip twitched. "No one's ever said that to me before."

"I'm sure they've wanted to, but you're an intelligent, powerful woman. Very intimidating. Just don't forget that you also have a heart. Open it, and you'll be rewarded beyond your expectations."

Roxy pushed up from the chair and wobbled a little like she was standing on a rocking boat.

Jen was taller and thicker from her muscle mass. In fact, Jen was surprised that Amanda found Roxy's stringy body attractive. She certainly wasn't Jen's type.

"Thank you," Roxy said, lurching forward and hugging Jen.

Jen reluctantly hugged her back, not too tightly for fear of crushing her skeletal frame. She patted her back. *I still hate you for stealing Amanda and hope you leave town soon.*

They separated. "So I'm supposed to look for a grief counselor, huh?"

"Yes. Most clinics that specialize in behavioral health will have one. We have one here, but I understand you're in the city on only a temporary basis, so you really need to establish with someone in your own town."

"That's New York for the foreseeable future. I'll look into it. Promise." Roxy patted Jen on the shoulder. "Impressive muscles. Quite solid actually. No wonder you kicked my arse."

Jen flushed. "Sorry about that. I was crazed with rage."

"No apologies necessary. I would've done the same thing."

"Take care of yourself," Jen said, genuinely meaning it.

"Bye." Roxy turned and left.

Jen circled her desk and sat back down to her notes. *That poor woman is so broken. Amanda must have felt the need to rescue her. I sort of did too. I can see how Amanda would feel attracted to her—to the darkness. Mysterious but vulnerable. Whatever. Not healthy for me to analyze their attraction. Time for me to get the hell out of here and pick up my baby at daycare.*

13

When Jen and Kristin entered Tommy's modest house, they were met by the aroma of spaghetti meat sauce in the slow cooker that Jen had prepped that morning. *There's nothing better than returning home to the smell of dinner,* Jen thought. She went to their room, Kristin toddling along behind her, and changed into a pair of joggers and a T-shirt.

"Should we take Zane for a walk?"

"Yaner! Walk!" Kristin said, throwing her arms into the air.

"Yes. Walk," Jen repeated for the benefit of Zane, who did circles around Kristin. She didn't know who was more excited, Zane or Kristin. She was amazed at Zane's expansive comprehension, which was similar to Kristin's at this stage. In a matter of weeks, however, Kristin would surpass him not only in comprehension but also in cognition. The growth rate of her daughter astonished her.

Jen poured a cup of food into Zane's bowl and busied herself in the kitchen, making last minute dinner preparations before they left on their walk. Suddenly, Kristin was at her legs with her mouth full. Jen looked down to see dog food protruding from Kristin's overstuffed mouth.

"Oh, no!" Jen said, leaning down.

Kristin smiled, and several pieces of dog food spilled out.

"Gross, honey. We don't eat Yaner's food. That's for him. It's not safe for you to eat." Jen wiped out Kristin's mouth with her finger then picked her up and set her on the counter.

Kristin started spitting, so Jen showed her how to spit into the sink. "Here. Drink some water and spit it out."

Kristin thought the water-spitting game was even more fun than eating Zane's food. After she had rinsed and spit several times, Jen placed Kristin in her high-tech stroller.

Once she clasped the leash to Zane's collar, they set off on a short walk around the neighborhood. Jen loved walking around North Beach, greeting Tommy's neighbors, who were friendly and adoring of Kristin. On the way back, she knocked on Cy's front door.

"Hello, my beauties!" he said.

"Hi, Cy! Are you still planning to join us for dinner tonight?"

"Of course," he said. "I bought a bottle of Chianti at Molinari's. Do you want me to come now?"

"That'd be terrific. We're just on our way back," she said.

Cy grabbed his well-worn tweed jacket with suede elbow patches then donned his matching wool flat cap. "How is my granddaughter today?"

"Bumpa!" Kristin said, smiling and squirming to get out of her stroller.

Bumpa lifted Kristin out so they could walk together. She held onto his finger as they walked up the hill. The pace was slow, but Jen relished the opportunity for Kristin and Cy to hang out together.

When they entered Tommy's house, Cy followed Kristin into the living room and sat on the sofa while she grabbed some toys that she wanted to show him.

"I can't believe how much she's walking now," Cy said.

"She's really got her game on," Jen said. "Was Tommy an early walker?"

He scratched his chin and thought a minute. "You know, I can't really remember. I was so busy at work when the kids were little, and the five kids sort of blur together."

"I can see how that would be the case," she said. "Speaking of which, have you seen Tina this week? Tommy has a bag full of empty plastic containers for her. It was so nice of her to send food home for him before I moved back."

"I can take it. I'm meeting the guys for lunch at Mama Mia's tomorrow," he said, referring to Tina's Italian restaurant in North Beach. Cy and his buddies ate lunch or dinner there several times per week.

"Good. I'll set the bag by the door. Just take it when you leave tonight."

Turning her attention to dinner, Jen filled a pot of water and put it on the stove for the pasta. She removed a sourdough baguette from a shopping bag and sliced it horizontally, adding butter and garlic, then wrapped it in foil and placed it in the oven.

"Hungry!" Kristin said from the living room.

"Come over here, sweetie. Mommy will give you a sippy cup of milk and some string cheese to tide you over before dinner."

"Yaner food!" Kristin yelled.

"No. You're not eating anymore dog food."

"She's eating dog food now?" Cy asked.

"Yes. She got into it today. Can you believe that?"

"I've seen kids eat worse. Tommy used to eat dirt."

Kristin came bolting into the kitchen and clung to Jen's legs, holding her hand up in the air. Hoping to stave off the hangries, Jen quickly poured milk and tore off a strand of string cheese. Sippy cup in one hand and string cheese in the other, Kristin held the cheese high in the air, just inches above Zane's drooling mouth. One false move and the string cheese would be his.

"Zane, come here," Jen said from the kitchen. She opened the cupboard where his food was stored and opened a bag of dog treats, hoping to give Kristin the chance to enjoy her cheese in peace. Making a quick canine calculation, Zane decided that a treat was worth more than begging for string cheese.

Kristin stood at the coffee table, jabbering at Bumpa and eating her cheese. Bumpa jabbered back, imitating her.

Jen dropped the pasta in the boiling water and picked up her phone to set the timer. She noticed she had missed a text from Nicole, her sexy new friend at the CrossFit box.

Hey Jen, looking forward to seeing you for our workout tmrw morning. Hope you can still make it.

Jen replied, *Planning on it. Better bring your A game.*

Some text bubbles formed, paused forever, then Nicole's reply appeared: *Anything for you.*

A surge of excitement sizzled through Jen. She questioned whether she should reply with something flirtatious too but didn't know what to say. Besides, sappy flirting felt a little premature. She didn't want to come off as desperate. Even though she was. Going without sex for over a month was driving her libido to a fever pitch. The sad truth was that she needed some, and she needed some *now*. She had to set those thoughts on the back burner, however, and return her attention to a family dinner with Cy.

Later, as they were midway through their bowls of spaghetti and warm garlic bread—red sauce outlining Kristin's lips—Tommy walked through the door. "Hey! How are my girls? Hiya, Pops!"

Kristin went full throttle with excitement, banging her fork and spoon, splashing tiny drops of red sauce in every direction. Jen quickly grabbed her bowl, so she didn't knock it over.

"Dadda home!" Kristin yelled.

Without regard for Kristin's sticky fingers and saucy face, Tommy gave her kisses on the forehead and cheeks. Her little fingers marked his neck with sauce as she hung onto him.

"Let me wash her hands and face, then you can take her out of her chair," Jen said, laughing.

"Yum, the sauce tastes terrific," he said, as he wiped the red streaks from his neck.

"I'll prepare a bowl for you." Jen washed Kristin and the tray.

Tommy pulled out the tray and removed Kristin, so he could hug her properly. "Just give me a couple of minutes on the living room floor with her. I haven't seen her for a few days, and we need to drive some of these big trucks." He growled, making low engine noises, as he pushed a plastic dump truck. Kristin was full of grins and belly laughs.

Jen returned to the kitchen and glanced at the flat screen where KPIX news was on. Kip Moynihan was sitting at the news desk again, and Amanda's face was in a box over his right shoulder with the caption, "DA Hawthorne's therapy records made public."

"Oh no, here we go," Jen said under her breath as she turned up the volume.

"A short time ago, Amanda Hawthorne's therapy notes from the Cohen Clinic in Pacific Heights were published on a website called, 'Truth for Election.' It's not clear who's behind the site, but some are speculating that supporters of Hawthorne's opponent, Gavin Morales, created it."

The screen switched to black type on a white background—quotes lifted from therapy notes.

Kip said, "Excerpts from the medical record of Hawthorne's drug rehab therapist state: '...Amanda successfully completed her four-week inpatient program and now wishes to establish with me for after-care. Her goals are to continue her sobriety and restore her personal relationship with her ex-fiancée, Dr. Jen Dawson. We spoke at length about steps she will take on a daily basis to reach her goals. I did, however, caution her that when there are two people involved in a relationship, we can't control what the other person says or does. Amanda indicated understanding...We discussed the stress of a re-election campaign, but Amanda insisted that campaigning isn't stressful for her in terms of triggering a desire for drugs or alcohol...We will plan to see her weekly for the next six weeks...'"

Kip provided his own commentary. "As you can see, the therapist note clearly indicates that DA Hawthorne isn't stressed out by the re-election campaign, so this leaked note isn't going to impact her willingness to continue campaigning."

"Did she have a comment in reaction to the leak?" the news anchor asked.

"Yes. We contacted her campaign, and they released this statement," Kip said, reading it aloud. "DA Hawthorne is disappointed that her therapy note for rehab has been made public, but she doesn't dispute the content or the truth of the statements made in it. She stands by it 100% and believes in the value of prescription drug treatment. As she said in her live interview, she over-relied on painkillers after being shot twice and having a car bomb go off next to her. Neither her job, nor the campaign, is stressful compared to being shot. She looks forward to this campaign and won't be slowed down by malicious, underhanded tactics like these from her opponent."

"So, she's doubling down on drug rehab therapy during the pursuit of public office," the news anchor observed.

"She's a strong person," Kip said. "Having interviewed her many times over the years myself—most recently last weekend—I can tell you that she has nerves of steel."

"Well, you'd have to in that line of work—putting criminals behind bars. Thanks, Kip," the news anchor said, and they switched to a new story.

Jen grabbed her phone and texted Amanda. *Your therapy note wasn't bad at all. It reflected what you've already said publicly. If anything, it should reassure voters that you say the same thing in private as you do in public.*

Amanda replied right away. *I agree. I'm not embarrassed by my therapist's note. I'm so sorry for dragging you into this. Thanks for being understanding.*

Jen started to type, *no worries*, but thought better of it. She didn't need this drama while trying her damnedest to start a new relationship. She had wanted a clean break from Amanda, but now that it wasn't happening, maybe she could hope for a gradual breakaway.

To make her desires clear, she replied, *Could you tell your therapist not to mention me in her notes? I don't want to be involved.*

I'll try my best, Amanda replied.

Something about the exchange made Jen feel hollow inside. She thought she wanted to leave Amanda, but typing what she just had felt a little cruel. She shook off the feeling as being overly-empathetic. *She's the one who fooled around on me.*

Tommy entered the kitchen with Kristin. "I heard the news. How do you feel about the therapy note?"

She shrugged. "It sucks, but to tell you the truth, it's not as bad as being sued."

"Right. Did you meet with your lawyer while I was gone?" he asked, sitting down to the bowl of spaghetti she set on the table.

"What? You've been sued?" Cy asked.

Jen spoke louder, so his 74-year-old ears could hear. "Yes. A woman sued all the providers who saved her life in the hospital ER after she was in an automobile accident. A few weeks after she was discharged from the hospital, she was diagnosed with a wrist fracture. She's alleging that we missed it."

"Lawyers!" he said. "They'll take any case nowadays."

"It gets worse," Jen said. "The lawyer hired by the insurance company to defend me is a partner with Gavin Morales at his firm. So, Morales learned I'd been sued, and said in reaction to my interview with Kip that I was a quack who was being sued for malpractice, so people shouldn't listen to my opinion about Amanda. Can you believe that? What a peckerhead. I told my insurance company, so they fired him and assigned a new lawyer."

"You've got to be shitting me," Tommy said between bites. "Oops. Sorry for swearing."

Cy snorted. "Those lawyers are incestuous. They're all in cahoots!"

Jen and Tommy smiled. "I agree with you, Cy. Not only did I get sued, but then my own lawyer's firm slandered me on TV!"

"You should sue him for defamation!" Cy spat.

"Trust me. I'm going to talk to my new lawyer about it," she said.

"What's his name?" Tommy asked.

"Let me look." Jen scrolled through her personal emails on her iPhone until she found her new lawyer's initial contact. "His name is Guy Deluca. Do you know him?"

"The name doesn't ring a bell, so he must not do any criminal work. What firm is he with?"

"Not Morales, Briggs and Sabelli, and that's all that matters, right?"

He nodded, his mouth full of spaghetti. "Want me to come with you for your first meeting with him?"

"No. It's business, not emotional. In fact, I think it's tomorrow at the clinic."

"Good. You want to get on top of that suit right away."

"Just what I need—another distraction in my life."

"We're here to support you," he said, opening his arms wide. She hugged him and Kristin joined.

"She loves it when we hug," Jen said.

"I can see why. Such a perfect couple…meant for each other," Cy said, waving his hand toward them.

Jen broke away. *Shit. Now I'm misleading Cy as well as Tommy. I need to move out of here before they think I'm going to marry him.*

"I never liked Amanda. I think she's arrogant," Cy continued, surprising both Jen and Tommy.

"Now, Pops—" Tommy began, but Jen spoke over him.

"If she comes across as arrogant, it's because she's extremely confident in her abilities as a trial attorney. She has to be tough to prosecute criminals—just as tough as the men."

"She has an air about her, though—" Cy said. "Inherited money will do that to a person."

"Be careful, Pops," Tommy said.

"Like she owns the world. That's it. She acted like she owned you, Jen, and no one owns someone else. You're better off without her."

"And, see—" Jen started, but Tommy put his hand on her arm.

"We're both friends with Amanda, Pops," Tommy said. "I'm pretty sure she knows she doesn't own Jen. Let's drop the subject."

"Fine with me," Cy said. "I'm just saying that Tommy is better for you, Jen. Never could get used to two women raising a child."

And, there it is—the real reason Cy doesn't like Amanda, Jen thought. She could feel white heat creeping up her neck. She was about to set Cy straight when Tommy signaled to let it go.

He leaned over and whispered, "Don't listen to him. I don't agree. I'll keep him busy after dinner."

She attempted to erase the livid look on her face, but her jaw was set like granite. "Thanks."

Tommy finished his last bites. "Come on, Pops. The game is on. Let's watch it."

Cy seemed oblivious to offending Jen and happily rose from the table to follow Tommy.

"That was a great meal, Jen. Thanks," Tommy said, throwing a puppy dog look at her over his shoulder.

She mumbled something incoherent in response and glared at their backs. Hanging back to tidy up the kitchen and cool off, Jen simmered over Cy's harsh observations of Amanda. *Why do people keep attacking her this week? She never acted like she owned me. She isn't as manipulative as people make her out to be. Can't they see that she's going through an incredibly rough time in her personal life while trying to run for re-election? Geez, cut her some slack, will you?*

14

The next morning, Jen stumbled out to the kitchen for coffee where she found Tommy sitting at the table and scrolling through emails on his phone while watching the morning news.

"Good morning, beautiful," he said.

"Ugh," she groaned.

"I made coffee."

"Thanks."

"You've been a good influence on me. I don't run down to Café Trieste every morning like I used to."

"Maybe I'll leave my coffee pot for you and buy myself a new one when I move out," she said, mixing her brew with the proportions of cream and sugar that promised to improve her mood.

"Still thinking about moving out, huh?"

"I have to, Tommy. We're not married, and sooner or later, you'll realize I'm cramping your style."

He cocked his head. "Or, maybe the reverse is true. Look, if it's about what Cy said last night, you know I don't agree with him. If you can't love me, I'd rather you loved another woman than another guy."

Her square jaw unclenched. "I never thought of it that way. And, for the record, I *do* love you— just not in that way. God, this is so uncomfortable. Do we have to discuss this right now?"

"No. I didn't mean to go there. Sorry."

"No need to apologize. You've hosted us for more than a month and I'm grateful. I saw some promising apartments online that I'm planning to check out." She rested her hips against the counter and cradled her cup to her chest.

"Want me to come with you?"

"No thanks. I'd sort of like to do it myself."

"Let me know if you need my help."

"Maybe with the actual move." She smiled over her cup.

He raised his arms and flexed his biceps.

"Can you still take Kristin to daycare this morning? I scheduled an early workout." She left out that it was with Nicole.

"No sweat." His crooked grin appeared.

"Nice pun, but I plan to," she said.

Suddenly, they heard Jen's name on the morning news, so they looked at the flat screen and saw Kip Moynihan reporting at the news desk. "Last night, more documents from the Cohen Clinic were released on the 'Truth for Election' website. The Cohen Clinic is where Dr. Jen Dawson, Amanda Hawthorne's ex-fiancée works, and where Hawthorne herself is going for drug rehab therapy. In this latest round of leaks, there was an email from Hawthorne's media relations manager, Chance Greyson, to Dr. Dawson, outlining talking points for her to use in my interview of her earlier this week."

Chance's email was displayed on the screen while Kip played excerpts of Jen's interview. She said, almost verbatim, the same phrases used in Chance's email.

"What the fuck?" Jen growled. "You can't tell me the North Koreans are going to this extent to get revenge on Amanda?!"

Tommy shook his head. "Partly, but I think it goes deeper. I think they found a buyer for their documents—Gavin Morales' cronies who are behind the 'Truth for Election' website. Morales is probably colluding with the North Koreans. Navarro is looking into it."

"Well, you need to arrest those motherfuckers for trespassing and theft!" she whisper-yelled so as not to wake up Kristin.

"Trust me. We're looking into it."

"I tried to do one nice thing for Amanda by giving an interview, and now I'm being lampooned. First, Morales outs my lawsuit, then HELLFIRE attacks our clinic computers, and now they're trying to make it look like Chance scripted my remarks. The reverse is true, you know. I told him what I wanted to say, and he summarized my thoughts in bullet points. For fuck sake! Why am I explaining this to you? I need to work out."

She set down her coffee and marched to her bedroom.

While she was changing into her workout clothes, her phone vibrated with a call. Chance Greyson's name appeared on the screen. "Hello?" she asked in a frosty whisper, tiptoeing out of the bedroom, because Kristin was still asleep.

"This is Chance. Is this Jen?"

"Yes."

"I take it you saw the morning news?"

"Yes."

"I'm so sorry, Jen."

"I'm sure."

"You know you told me what you wanted to say, and I summarized your points in an email back to you," he said.

"I remember."

"Would you be willing to give an interview clarifying that point?" he asked.

"I'll think about it. I'm on my way to the gym right now, and I don't want to be late."

"Got it. Text me later?" he asked.

"Yes. Bye."

She brushed her teeth and pulled her thick blonde hair into a pony. Quietly tiptoeing out of the bedroom with her gym bag, she blew a kiss to a sleeping Kristin, then paused in the hall outside the kitchen. "You're still good to take Kristin?"

"We'll have breakfast together and I'll take her to daycare. Enjoy your workout. You deserve it."

She smiled and blew him a kiss.

***

Nicole was already stretching on a black yoga mat when Jen entered the CrossFit box. Class was scheduled to begin in 10 minutes, so Jen grabbed a foam roller and dropped down next to Nicole.

"Hey." While doing a Superman stretch, Nicole winked at Jen.

"Hey, yourself," Jen said with a smile, her eyes automatically drawn to Nicole's sumptuous bootie, which was on display while Nicole's feet and hands were on the mat.

"I see what you're looking at," Nicole said, a smirk on her face.

Jen rolled her quad over the black foam, sliding back and forth next to Nicole

"You're totally blushing. Could you get any hotter?" Nicole asked, switching positions to pull her opposite knee up to her chin.

Pretty flirtatious early in the morning, Jen thought, then flipped onto her back and used the roller on her butt and hamstrings. Nicole watched from the corner of her eye but didn't say anything.

After moving through a few more stretches, they found themselves sitting next to each other, ready for class to begin.

"How have you been?" Nicole asked.

"Okay," Jen said.

"Saw you on the news. I wasn't sure if it was you at first, but when they said your name, I knew," Nicole said.

"Ah. Sorry you had to see that. My life is kind of complex right now. It's not always like this."

"Amanda Hawthorne is your ex?"

"Yes."

"So, I'm not going to make an enemy out of the DA if I go on a date with you?"

Jen laughed and touched Nicole's arm. "Of course not. I just gave an interview because the Morales campaign is lying. Amanda and I aren't together anymore, but it doesn't mean I wish her ill will."

"Nice of you to stick your neck out for her like that," Nicole said.

"Thanks. I'd like to think she'd do the same for me."

"I'm sure she would." Nicole glanced up. "Class is starting."

They stood and joined the group of a dozen others in the warmup stretches across the black rubber floor. Jen and Nicole partnered for the workout, trading off for the assigned exercises. While Jen did rowing machine, Nicole did the Turkish kettlebell get-up, and vice versa, for a variety of exercises.

They hit the locker room afterward to shower and dress for work. Jen was more modest, wearing her towel to and from the showers. Nicole, like many others, simply walked around nude. Jen cast several hooded glances in Nicole's direction and wasn't surprised to confirm that her athletic body, now nude, was straight out of Greek mythology—immortal material by any measure.

As they toweled off and dressed, Nicole said, "Judging by the way you're looking at me, we need to go on a date soon."

Jen looked at her sheepishly, and whispered, "I can't help myself. Your body is one for the history books."

Nicole laughed. "You're not so bad yourself, you know."

"Thanks. How about brunch at Rose's tomorrow?" Jen asked.

"That'd be great. What time?" Nicole asked.

"Ten?"

"Perfect. Meet you there." Nicole, fully dressed now, leaned down to Jen, who was sitting on the bench in front of the lockers. She guided Jen's chin up with her index finger and brushed a feathery soft kiss over Jen's lips. "Give you something to think about between now and then."

Jen was surprised that Nicole was so bold in front of the other women. Her tummy fluttered, making her lips yearn for more. "Mmm."

"Try to stay out of the news," Nicole whispered, then turned and left.

Jen watched Nicole's ass all the way to the door. *Stay out of the news….* She remembered her phone call with Chance this morning and texted him. *I'll be at the clinic in 30 minutes. Want to meet there?*

He replied right away. *Yes. I'll be there with my makeup kit. Plan to do an interview this morning. It will only take 15 minutes. I'll notify Kip Moynihan.*

As long as it doesn't interfere with my patient schedule, Jen typed, knowing there wasn't a schedule, technically speaking. The computer system was still down, so they were at the mercy of patients simply appearing. Only the patients knew the day and time, not the clinic. A circus.

Later, when Jen entered the clinic, she paused at Ginny's desk to get the scoop for the day. "How's it going?"

Ginny lowered her voice, so the waiting patients wouldn't hear. "It's a cluster. The computer system is still down. I told Dr. Cohen that we should just buy a new one."

"What did she say?" Jen asked.

"She agreed. I think the vendor is coming today."

"Good. Anything else?" Jen asked.

"Gregg is in her office, giving her a hard time about his retirement account. He thinks it's been hacked."

"Oh, no."

"He's got everyone worried about our accounts. He's going around saying that the 'care of the patient comes first, but the retirement account comes second.'"

Jen rolled her eyes. "Don't repeat that. I'm sure our accounts will be just fine. Let me go talk to her."

"Please do. You seem to have a calming effect on her," Ginny said.

Jen dropped her stuff in her office and went straight to Melissa's office. Gregg was standing in Melissa's doorway, agitated, his voice shaking. Jen couldn't hear everything he said as she approached, but she did hear, "If there's nothing left in my retirement account, you're going to pay for this." When he saw Jen, he stormed off in a huff.

"Good morning, Gregg," Jen said to his back as he walked down the hallway.

He didn't bother replying.

"How's it going?" Jen asked Melissa.

"Never better. You?" Melissa asked with a heavy dose of sarcasm.

"Heads up that I'm giving another interview to Kip this morning from the conference room."

Melissa tilted her head, studied Jen, then said, "I don't think that's a good idea, at least not at the Cohen Clinic. Thanks to Amanda, our computer system has ground to a halt. I'm afraid you'll make us a target for something worse by giving an interview from within these walls. If you want to give one outside on the sidewalk, fine. Just don't stand in front of the clinic and don't mention it by name."

Jen blanched. Was Melissa just being protective of her clinic's security or was there more to her directive? "I'm sorry. If you don't want me to give the interview, I won't. We just wanted to clarify that Chance sent me talking points that I verbalized to him, that's all."

"You're paying a very high price for coming to Amanda's defense every time there's a blip in the news. Have you considered not 'setting the record straight' and just letting the issue blow over?"

"I guess I was relying on Chance's expertise in handling media affairs," Jen said, her upper lip turning into a thin line at Melissa's suggestion that Jen abandon support of Amanda.

Melissa shook her head, but kept her gaze level with Jen's. "Let me state it another way. Your continued involvement in Amanda's campaign is jeopardizing our image and already has trashed our computer system. Do what you want in your free time, but if you intentionally bring trouble into these walls, I would have no choice but to let you go."

Jen stiffened. "Are you saying you'll fire me if I give an interview today?"

"Not at all. If your interview results in another attack on the clinic, however, then I'll have no choice but to fire you." Melissa closed her mouth, her jaw muscles dancing and her brown eyes unwavering.

Jen felt her world tilting off its axis. *Fired? Over helping clarify an email for Amanda's campaign? Who is this woman and what did she do with the Melissa who gave me a hug when I was sued? Is she being hypocritical, or am I expecting too much?* "Well then, the decision's been made. I'll tell Chance I can't do the interview."

"I think that's a good idea. I'm also going to call Amanda today and tell her she can't come to therapy here. Not until the campaign is over. I can't allow my clinic to get caught up in her international war with the North Koreans. I'm responsible for the livelihood of too many people."

"Are you going to give her the names of other therapists?"

"Yes. I have a list of reputable therapists she could see," Melissa said in a businesslike tone, leaving no room for negotiation.

"Okay, then. Talk to you later." Jen wanted to get the hell out of Melissa's office before she said something that would get her fired on the spot. Just when she considered Melissa a friend, she had pulled rank, reminding Jen who really owned the clinic. She quickly texted Chance that she couldn't do the interview.

After she sent the text, her nurse, Shannon, informed her that her first patient was roomed, a gentleman in his mid-40's whom she had seen last week for a complaint about a sore on his penis. She had sent his blood and urine to a reference lab for STD screening and it had come back positive for herpes, so she had told him a few days ago by phone then advised him to tell his wife. Jen further advised that his wife should come in for testing and treatment too.

He told her he intended to do just that. She felt sorry for his wife, knowing that his infidelity would need to be disclosed in their conversation. Which was worse? The infidelity or the STD that accompanied it?

Unfortunately, he was back today to receive more bad news from Jen. She entered the exam room. They shook hands, and she sat at the desk facing him. "I'm sorry Mr. Winter. I have bad news."

"What could be worse than what I just went through?" he asked.

"Did you tell your wife about the herpes? And to come in for treatment?"

"Yeah. She was mad as hell. I had to admit that I fooled around on her last year," he said, looking at the floor and shaking his head. "I don't know if we're going to make it."

"I'm sorry. That had to be rough. What I have to tell you today will unfortunately compound that situation."

"What now?" he asked, still staring at his shoes.

She paused, knowing the information was going to bring more chaos to his life. "The good news is that you don't have herpes. The reference lab contacted us late yesterday and informed us they made an error."

"What?" he asked in disbelief, his head snapping up.

"You don't have herpes. The bad news is that you already told your wife about your affair. I'm sorry."

"What the hell? Are you serious? Who is this reference lab?"

"Pro Medical Labs. It's a well-known, reputable lab. We've been using them for years. Unfortunately, mistakes of this nature sometimes happen. Not very often, but when they do, they're devastating. All I can say is that I'm sorry."

"I know it's not your fault, Doc, but I'm pissed. You and Pro Bullshit Labs are going to hear from my lawyer."

"Do what you feel is best, Mr. Winter. I'm very sorry this happened to you." She got up and left.

She closed the exam room door and returned to her office. *Sue for damages for telling his wife he had an affair? He'll never recover a dime. Moral of that story—never confess infidelity. Maybe the moral was never to have an affair in the first place.*

She immediately thought of Amanda and how she had told Jen only a month ago that she had slept with Roxy. *I have to respect her for telling me.*

When she grabbed a fresh sheet of paper to make a note of her visit with Mr. Winter, she saw she had a text from Chance wanting to talk to her about why she changed her mind about not giving an interview to Kip.

She replied: *My boss told me I couldn't continue the involvement in the campaign because it's harming the clinic.*

That's her prerogative, Chance replied.

She was surprised he didn't try to convince her. Relieved, she refocused on work.

15

Later, when Jen was in her office, handwriting the umpteenth physician progress note from a patient visit, her phone buzzed with a text from Amanda.

Chance told me that Melissa won't allow you to give a statement to Kip. I'm sorry that my campaign drama affected your work. No worries, we'll take care of it.

Jen stared at the message, considering what it took for Amanda to swallow her pride during the campaign, not clarifying to the media that the words Jen used were her own rather than scripted by Chance. She knew how obsessive Amanda was about controlling communications, especially something of this magnitude.

Score one for Amanda. Life would really suck if she lost this election because people thought I lied. I don't want the responsibility or blame for a loss. She needs to win for her mental health, or God only knows what could happen to her. She has to be DA.

Jen typed a reply to Amanda, careful not to contradict her earlier message to Chance that she wouldn't do the interview at the clinic. *Melissa didn't forbid me from giving a statement. She just said I couldn't do the interview from the clinic. And—this is important—she'll fire me if my interview results in more attacks on the clinic. I respect her decision. I'd do the same thing if I were in her shoes.*

Jen watched her screen, text bubbles forming over Amanda's side of the conversation. They hovered for an eternity before her message populated.

Me too.

Jen was surprised, and impressed, at Amanda's restraint. For once, Amanda wasn't making an argument to convince Jen that her, Amanda's, interests were elevated above everyone else's. Instead, she was letting Jen off the hook. Melissa too. Jen considered her options, weighing the pros and cons of helping Amanda but jeopardizing her relationship with Melissa. She replied, *I could do the interview over the lunch hour on the street as long as it isn't in front of the clinic.*

Amanda's reply was immediate. *I won't let you. Too risky. You love your job at Melissa's clinic.*

Jen smirked, wondering if Amanda was using reverse psychology on her. *I'm texting Chance right now.*

Amanda didn't reply to that, but Jen envisioned her sitting next to Chance, showing him the message.

Making good on her promise, Jen texted Chance, agreeing to meet on the sidewalk around the corner at noon.

He replied, *I'll meet you at your office at noon to do your hair and makeup. Then, we'll go downstairs to meet Kip.*

She replied, *Fine. I like the way you do my makeup.*

He replied with a smiley face.

Jen considered Amanda's conciliatory responses, and how she had said she missed Kristin. *Would she be interested in babysitting Kristin while I go out for brunch with Nicole tomorrow? Should I even ask? Would she view it as some sort of favor, expecting that I somehow return a favor? What am I thinking? She owes me for the interviews.*

As if reading Jen's mind, Amanda sent her a text. *I was wondering if there was a way I could see Kristin. I hate to ask, but I miss her so much. Could we get together?*

Jen dropped her phone on her desk like it was a hot coal. *Have you somehow bugged my phone? My life? My mind?* Even though Amanda's offer was well-timed, Jen decided she still needed to think about it. She just couldn't reply so soon.

As she was mulling over the pros and cons of Amanda babysitting Kristin, Jen's phone rang, surprising her. She didn't recognize the number but answered it. "Hello?"

"This is Attorney Guy Deluca. I'm calling for Dr. Jennifer Dawson."

"I'm Dr. Dawson."

"Good morning. Your insurance company hired me to represent you in the lawsuit filed by your former patient."

"I recognize your name from the email. It's good to hear from you."

"I'd like to meet with you today if you're available."

"I am. How about late afternoon—like four?"

"That will work for me. Shall I come to your clinic?"

"Yes. See you then. Thanks."

Jen ended the call and buzzed Ginny to ask her to reserve the conference room for her meeting with Guy.

Shannon, Jen's nurse, appeared in her doorway to tell her the next patient was in an exam room, ready to be seen. Since Jen couldn't look up the patient on the electronic medical record to review his health history, she and Shannon traded the scant information they could remember from his history.

"Holding 'mystery clinic' every day isn't a fun way to practice medicine, especially when our concierge patients expect us to remember everything about them," Jen said. "It reminds me of working in the ER, but patients didn't expect me to know their histories there and half the time, they were unconscious anyway."

Shannon nodded. "Tell me about it. I'm tired of writing everything down by hand and calling pharmacies to order scripts."

After seeing two more patients, Jen had a noon break. Chance texted that he was in the lobby, ready to apply her makeup. She scurried out, and they used the restroom next to the elevator so as not to enter the clinic and violate Melissa's rules. Ginny saw them go, so Jen knew she'd give Melissa a report.

A light rain was falling, so Chance held an umbrella for Jen as they walked to meet Kip, who had an assistant holding an umbrella over his head. Jen wondered if his hair color and makeup would wash off in the rain.

"Hello, Dr. Dawson," Kip said, shaking her hand.

"Hi, Kip. Good to see you."

"Is there a place we can do this out of the rain?" he asked.

"Not really," she said.

"How about your clinic?"

"Nope. Too busy with patients who can't be seen on camera. Need to protect their privacy."

"Is that the only reason?"

"Do you want to do the interview or not?" Chance asked.

"Fine. We can do it in the rain," Kip said to Chance, then turned to Jen. "Are you ready to roll?"

"Fire away," she said.

Kip introduced the interview and set the scene, then asked, "Dr. Dawson, an email from Chance Greyson, the media relations manager for DA Hawthorne's campaign, was recently leaked. In it, Mr. Greyson set forth talking points that you used—pretty much verbatim—in my interview of you earlier this week. Care to comment?"

"Thanks for the opportunity to clarify, Kip. Prior to the email, I had a phone call with Mr. Greyson and verbalized what I wanted to say about Amanda and her campaign. Mr. Greyson then summarized our conversation and emailed it to me in the form of bullet points. The thoughts, words, and phrases were all mine."

"So, to be clear, you aren't retracting that you said you supported DA Hawthorne for re-election and that, despite your breakup, you're still on friendly terms?"

"Correct. I stand by those statements as my own. I support Amanda and wish her the best in her campaign. I think she's eminently qualified for this office."

"Thank you. I have a related question for you. In addition to the email from Chance Greyson to you, I've heard that the medical record system of the Cohen Clinic—where you practice medicine and Amanda Hawthorne sees a therapist—is compromised due to a hack by people associated with Gavin Morales. Is this true?"

Where does he get his intel? Jen stammered for a millisecond, not having prepared anything in response to this question. She pictured Melissa telling her that she'd be fired if she dragged the clinic into Amanda's campaign again. "I'm not a spokesperson for the clinic. You'll have to work through appropriate channels at the clinic to ask questions of that nature."

"Can you at least confirm the electronic medical record is no longer functional?"

"I'm sorry, I'm not authorized to comment," Jen said, her smile polite, but firm.

"Okay. I get it. We can contact the clinic. I have another question for you. With respect to your daughter, are you and DA Hawthorne sharing custody?" Kip asked.

Keeping her expression inscrutable, Jen looked at Kip, seething that he again violated their long-standing agreement not to bring up Kristin on the air. Nevertheless, he had, so she had to say something that didn't sound angry or bitchy. "As I've said in the past, Kip, my daughter's privacy is paramount, so I'm not going to discuss her."

"I noticed you said, 'my daughter' and not 'our daughter.' Does that mean DA Hawthorne doesn't have any parental rights?" he persisted.

"Again, Kip, I'm not going to comment on that topic other than to say I respect and admire Amanda's parenting abilities. She's a terrific mother."

"Will she continue in the role as a mother?" he asked.

Chance jumped in. "Okay. That's enough, Kip. The doctor has to return to a busy clinic. Time is up. Come on, Dr. Dawson." Chance grabbed Jen by the arm and led her away. They walked around the corner to Jen's clinic entrance.

"Goddammit. Kip violated our agreement again. He just can't stop himself from bringing up Kristin every time we talk. Why?"

"Because it makes for a better story than the boring clarification of my email to you."

"Never again, Chance. Never again. I'm done doing interviews. I don't care what issues come up next in the campaign. Count me out. As it is, I'll probably have hell to pay with Melissa about the medical record question."

"Hopefully, she'll understand. Thanks for coming down today." He hugged her and turned to walk back toward Kip.

Jen returned to her office and plopped down in her desk chair. She needed a few minutes to gather herself before jumping back into clinic. The last thing she wanted while seeing patients was to be distracted by Kip Moynihan's bullshit interviews. *I have to extricate myself from this stupid campaign. No more interviews, no matter what happens next.*

Jen was jarred out of her thoughts by her nurse, Shannon, knocking on her door. "Mr. Torres is in Room 8. He's ready to be seen."

"What's he here for?" Jen asked.

"He has a sliver in his thigh," Shannon said, sneezing, then blowing her nose. "Sorry. I have a cold. My head is so congested."

"I'm sorry. Maybe you should sit down and rest for a few minutes. So, he has a sliver? How big?"

"He was fully dressed, so I gave him a gown and asked him to remove his pants so we could see it." Shannon dropped an Airborne tablet into a cup of water and watched it fizz.

"Do you think he's changed yet?"

"He should be," Shannon said.

Jen went to the exam room door, knocked twice and entered. "Are you ready for me, Mr. Torres?"

"Yeah."

She entered to see him fully clothed, sitting on the side of the exam table.

"I'm Dr. Dawson. I understand you have a sliver in your thigh?" She looked at his thighs, still fully clad in his jeans.

"Not my *thigh*, my *eye*," he said. "No wonder the nurse told me to take off my pants and put on a gown. I was wondering what kind of operation you ran here."

"Oh, dear," Jen said, briefly covering her mouth. "I apologize for the miscommunication. Shannon's head is congested from a cold. She probably didn't hear you. How did you get a sliver in your eye?"

"I'm renovating my basement, and something flew into it while I was ripping out some rotted wood."

"Let me take a look." She moved closer and shined her pen light on his eye. There was, indeed, a foreign object there. "I'm going to put a little drop of anesthetic on your eye, so I can remove the small particle, okay?"

"That sounds good."

Since Shannon hadn't understood there was something in his eye, there wasn't an eye kit in the room.

Jen opened the exam room door and looked for her. "Pssst, Shannon. Can you bring the eye kit in here?"

Shannon left the nurse's station and walked over. "Eye kit?"

"Yes. Sliver in the *eye*, not thigh."

"Ohhh. Sorry. My ears are so plugged, I guess I didn't hear him. I'll get it."

Shannon grabbed the kit off a cart and entered the exam room. While Jen looked for the anesthetic, Shannon apologized to Mr. Torres.

"Okay, I'm going to give you a drop of anesthetic. This won't hurt. Just relax." Jen held the small dropper above Mr. Torres' eye and let a drop of liquid fall onto his eye. He flinched but settled quickly.

After waiting a few seconds, Jen brought the Q-tip up to the corner of his eye and gently dabbed at the debris, removing it. Mr. Torres didn't even flinch.

"This is what was in there," Jen said, holding the Q-tip for him to see the small fiber on it.

"Wow. Amazing that something that small could cause so much pain," he said.

"It is, isn't it? Shannon will irrigate your eye with a little saline now," Jen said.

"If you don't mind, I'd like you to do it, considering she asked me to take my pants off."

Both Shannon and Jen smiled but didn't laugh. "I'm happy to."

"Sorry, Mr. Torres," Shannon said and left.

***

The afternoon flew by with a variety of patients and before Jen realized it was time, Ginny buzzed her from reception. "Your lawyer, Guy Deluca, is here. I put him in the conference room and got him a bottle of water."

"Thank you Ginny," Jen said.

Jen pushed away from her desk, which now boasted a mountain of paper scribblings that roughly resembled patient notes. She felt sorry for whoever had to transcribe her handwritten notes into the electronic medical record when it was back up and running.

The electronic medical record. Shit. Should I tell Melissa that Kip asked about it or just hope that he let it go? What if he calls her directly? She'll haul my ass into her office and fire me, that's what. I better warn her. Later. After I meet with my new lawyer.

Jen reoriented her thoughts as she entered the conference room to meet with her second lawyer. A middle-aged man in a pinstriped suit and Jerry Garcia tie turned and offered his hand.

"Hello, Dr. Dawson. I'm Guy Deluca."

"Please call me Jen."

"Likewise, call me Guy."

They sat and Guy provided an overview of the situation in which she found herself. She took an immediate liking to his affable nature and experienced delivery. He had enough gray hair to make him credible but was still energetic about her case. There was no lack of enthusiasm for defending her medical care, which she needed and appreciated.

When he paused, encouraging her to ask questions, she jumped right in. "As far as I'm concerned, this is a frivolous lawsuit. We saved this woman's life, and now she's accusing us of overlooking a hairline fracture of a tiny bone in her wrist. The treatment for that is immobilization, and with her other injuries, she was pretty much immobilized for several weeks anyway. It's not like she was out doing handstands and cartwheels on a broken pelvis and two broken femurs."

"I appreciate your logic, Doctor. However, I'm sure her lawyer will be able to find a doctor qualified in emergency medicine to give an opinion that you should have diagnosed the tiny wrist fracture. It will be our job to counter that with a physician who will defend your care."

"That sounds like a drawn-out process. Can't we just end this with an objective physician report or something?"

"I wish I could, but the process for making a motion to dismiss will take months. And I'm guessing this patient and her lawyer won't go away until they get money or lose in court."

"What are her damages?"

"She's alleging severe disability in her right wrist, impacting her career because one of her job requirements is typing. She alleges she can type for only a few hours before her wrist gets sore. She also alleges that she can no longer enjoy various leisure activities like biking and flying kites. She's demanding six figures in damages."

Stunned, Jen reached for the ends of her stethoscope that was usually draped around her neck but she didn't find them there. She cursed herself for leaving it in her office because having it around her neck was something akin to a security blanket while at work. She lay her fidgety hands in her lap. "Will the insurance company pay money even if I think we did everything right?"

"Probably not. The insurance company has the right to settle but it always takes the physician's preference into consideration." His message was tempered with a cordial tone but no guarantee.

"What are the other physicians saying?" she asked.

"You're the first with whom I've met. I'm scheduled to meet with the other ER physician, a general surgeon, and an orthopedist next week."

"I'll be interested to hear what they have to say."

"I'll report the prevailing sentiment back to you."

"What am I supposed to do in the meantime?"

"Nothing. There's no need for you to do any literature searches or any other type of homework. I'll get a copy of the medical record for you to review, but until then, please don't discuss the care with anyone."

"I think I can compartmentalize this, but I'll be really anxious about it until I have a chance to read the medical record."

"I understand. That's normal. And just so you know, I tasked my private investigator, Rick Spinelli, with getting some video of the patient doing her normal life activities. We want to verify that her disability claims are true. My team is also looking at social media to see what she's been up to."

"Oh. That's reassuring. You actually conduct surveillance?"

"Where the alleged loss doesn't fit with the mechanism of injury, and the patient has demanded a lot of money, yes."

"So you already have a plan." *Finally, someone in my life has his shit together and is looking out for my best interests.*

"Not my first case," he said, giving her a crooked smile laced with confidence.

"You're not going to discuss this in the media, are you?"

His expression immediately sobered. "I'm very sorry that happened to you. Morales was out of line. And, no, I won't discuss this in the media."

"That's good. Morales airing my lawsuit was devastating."

"We would never do that. Morales is a jerk. Trust me, I'll be voting for Amanda Hawthorne, as will most of the bar, I suspect."

"The bar doesn't like Morales?"

"He's got a bit of a reputation for being a snake. More importantly, Amanda has a great reputation among her peers."

"Good to know." Jen appreciated him verbalizing the sentiment. She faintly wondered if he knew their history. *Finally, someone who supports Amanda.*

"Is there anything else I can do for you?" he asked.

"No. I can't think of anything at the moment." As long as Guy had a plan, she was satisfied.

"I can give you updates, but I'm hesitant to use the Cohen Clinic email address since it was hacked. Do you have something more secure?"

"Let me give you my personal email account."

He wrote it down. "Great. I'll send updates to you on that email account, okay?"

"Thanks for your time, Guy."

They concluded their meeting, and Jen walked him out to the lobby where they shook hands and said goodbye.

Before she could leave to pick up Kristin at daycare, she had one last task. She dragged herself to Melissa's office and told her about the interview she gave to Kip.

"Thanks for being honest and giving me the heads up," Melissa said, shaking her head in defeat.

"I'm sorry, Melissa. It's just that...well, I'd feel awful if Amanda didn't get re-elected
184

because of an inaccuracy reported in the media that I easily could have corrected."

The hard edges that had defined Melissa's expression that morning had faded, replaced with softer lines and understanding eyes. "Perhaps I was too hard on you this morning. You understand where I'm coming from, though, right?"

Jen jumped at the new warmth. "Absolutely. You're being very reasonable about all of this. To be honest, I see your side of things as the person who employs everyone here. You can't jeopardize this clinic over Amanda's campaign."

Melissa held up her hand. "I like and respect Amanda too. Don't get me wrong. But I need to support her from a distance right now."

"I wish I could too," Jen said, resting the palm of her hand on Melissa's door frame.

Melissa studied Jen's face to the point of making Jen feel like an awkward adolescent.

"I respect your love and compassion for people, Jen. I just have one piece of advice: Make sure someone like Amanda doesn't take advantage."

Jen considered Melissa's warning. "Thanks for looking out for my best interests. Have a good night." She turned and left. *Why does everyone think Amanda is taking advantage of me?*

She returned to her desk and put the mountain of written progress notes in a box that Shannon had found for her. She thought more about allowing Amanda to see Kristin, and maybe her brunch date with Nicole was an opportune time for that.

She texted Amanda: *Do you want to babysit Kristin for a few hours tmrw morning? I have some errands and business.*

Simply making the offer to Amanda made Jen feel better, as if extending an olive branch chipped off some of the ice encasing her heart.

Moreover, Kristin had asked about Amanda practically every day since they'd broken up, so Jen was on the verge of feeling like she was depriving Kristin of an important relationship. No matter what anyone thought of Amanda, she'd always been good to Kristin, and Jen knew she always would be. She hoped Amanda was available.

16

North Beach
The next morning

By the time Jen awoke, Tommy had already left for work. He didn't know that Jen had offered, and Amanda had accepted, to babysit Kristin. Jen assumed he'd approve.

In preparation, Jen packed two of everything—from diapers to toys—for Amanda's house. She didn't know how well stocked Amanda would be since she was so busy with her campaign in addition to her heavy work schedule.

She loaded the overstuffed diaper bag into the car, followed by Kristin's collapsible stroller, then buckled Kristin into her car seat.

"You remember Mama Amanda, right?" Jen asked Kristin once they were on their way.

"Mama Man!" Kristin yelled from the back seat, unable to pronounce Amanda's full name.

Jen laughed. "We're going to visit Mama Amanda this morning, and she's very excited to see you."

"Toy cat!" Kristin said.

"Yes. Good memory, honey. Amanda has a cat named Zumba. I'm sure he'll be excited to see you too."

"Umba Cat," Kristin repeated, working hard to pronounce Zumba's name, which unfortunately, started with a "Z," like Zane.

"That's right. Zumba cat."

As Jen pulled into Amanda's driveway, insecurity rose in her chest, causing second thoughts. *Am I doing the right thing? Do I trust Amanda with Kristin? Am I sending the wrong signals to Amanda?*

She put the car in park and sat for a sec, slowing her racing mind and willing the Mexican jumping beans in her stomach to settle. There was no time to renege on the deal because the garage door opened and Amanda came bounding out to the car, followed by Zumba, his tail pointing straight into the air. Amanda was smiling from ear-to-ear, stopping expectantly by Jen's door then glancing through the tinted glass in the back seat at Kristin.

Jen noticed her own hand was trembling as she grasped the door handle and opened her door to an enthusiastic Amanda. The things Amanda did to Jen without even speaking. Just the sight of her—freshly showered and wearing a cozy sweater—caused Jen's nerve endings to crackle.

"Hi, Jen. Hi, baby," Amanda said.

"Good morning. Thanks for doing this," Jen said, opening the back door and unbuckling Kristin. She was going to set Kristin on the concrete to stand on her own, but Kristin was having none of that. She lurched forward, kicking Jen in the ribs and flying into Amanda's waiting arms.

"Whoa! I'm happy to see you too!" Amanda exclaimed, kissing the side of Kristin's head as she caught her.

Jen saw tears well in Amanda's eyes and immediately knew she had done the right thing.

Kristin was thrilled, laughing and hugging Amanda so tightly that Jen thought Kristin was going to strangle her. She knew Kristin had missed Amanda, but she hadn't realized how much. The truth was that Jen had been subconsciously hoping that Kristin would be as angry at Amanda as she was, even though that didn't make any sense, and she knew it. Instead, she embraced the love Kristin showed Amanda, so innocent and pure.

"Let me look at you." Amanda leaned her head back and took in every detail of Kristin. "So grown up now."

"Love you!" Kristin said, smiling while she touched Amanda's face.

"I love you too," Amanda said, kissing her on her forehead. "I've missed you so much."

Kristin babbled incoherently in rapid fire while hugging Amanda again.

Jen knew that Kristin had missed Amanda, frequently asking about her, but seeing how happy she was in Amanda's arms, Jen realized she'd been wrong to consider denying Amanda contact with Kristin. Kristin's elation and Amanda's tears reinforced how much they loved each other. Amanda had been good to Kristin when they had lived together. Incredibly good. There was no reason that Amanda wouldn't be equally good to her now. Falling into emotional quicksand, Jen watched the two of them reunite.

"Did you say you have some errands to run?" Amanda asked pleasantly.

Hearing Amanda say, "errands to run" was like a knife to Jen's heart. They had used that line on Tommy when they wanted to spend time alone—making love. *Did she remember?*

Jen blinked, blushing a little and realizing that Amanda was still waiting for an answer. "Ah, yeah. I'm meeting someone for brunch then looking at an apartment in the Sunset District."

If Amanda was surprised or curious, she didn't show it. "Sounds like fun. I'm happy for you. We'll plan to go for a stroll in the neighborhood then eat lunch. Are you thinking a couple of hours?"

Jen watched Kristin trace the outline of Amanda's face with her chubby little finger, making Jen's heart ping around in her chest like a pinball in a machine. Her mind was full of the dinging bells and whistles. "I don't know—"

"Take as long as you need. I don't have anything planned this morning. We'll just be here, hanging out." Tears spilled over Amanda's long, dark lashes, but she was smiling. She quickly wiped them away with the back of her hand, but the incongruency struck Jen.

Tears of joy or of regret? Does she feel as torn as I do? Jen turned back to the car. "Let me get her bag out of the back."

"Thank you." Amanda nodded and returned her attention to Kristin.

Jen set the bag on the driveway, not wanting to enter the house. "Do you need the stroller?"

"Ah, no. I bought one," Amanda said.

"Of course, you did."

"All good?"

"Yeah." Jen's eyes raked over Amanda holding Kristin and her heart burst into flame.

"I'll take good care of her. You know that," Amanda said, resting her hand on Jen's forearm.

As soon as Amanda's hand landed on her skin, Jen couldn't think straight. That touch. Those eyes that were shedding tears like Niagara Falls. "I know. I'm sorry if I gave you the impression—"

"You didn't. We're good," Amanda said, removing her hand.

Jen's throat clenched. She forced herself to transmit needed information about Kristin. "She just ate, so she won't be hungry for a while. Do you have diapers?"

"Oh, yes. I went shopping."

Jen leaned down to give Kristin a kiss on the head, bringing her face so close to Amanda's. "Bye, bye, honey. You're going to stay with Mama Amanda for a while, okay?"

"Mama Man," Kristin said cheerfully, looking at Amanda's face.

Amanda laughed. "Nice name. Did you teach her that?"

"Hardly. She has a tough time with three-syllable words and names that start with "Z.""

"Too funny. I won't take it personally." Amanda smiled. "Take your time. We'll have a good time—just the two of us." There was no venom or irritation. Just sincerity.

"I won't be long. It's a just a brunch date." *Oops. I shouldn't have said that. Why did I say that?*

Jen covered her mouth and her eyes flashed with embarrassment.

Amanda's hand was back on her forearm. "It's all right. Enjoy yourself. We'll be fine."

Jen sputtered, "I'm sorry. I know you will. I'm being silly. I should go." She got in the car and checked her feelings. Was she going to experience this cascade of emotions every time she saw Amanda, or was it because she was leaving Kristin with her? Or because she was on her way to a date with Nicole? *God, what am I feeling?*

Sensing Jen's trepidation, Amanda and Kristin stood in the driveway and waved as Jen started the car and backed out.

As she drove away, she kept telling herself that Kristin was going to be fine. More than fine. She would enjoy herself. They could make the two-mommy thing work even if she and Amanda started relationships with new people. *I won't be as emotional in the future as I was today. This was just the first time.*

***

She turned the corner onto Union Street in Cow Hollow and spotted Nicole pacing the sidewalk outside Rose's Café. She never dreamed her first date with a woman would be for brunch. She had pictured a romantic dinner, but that might be uncomfortable if they didn't hit it off. Brunch was a good start.

She found a spot on the street in the trendy fashionable neighborhood and parked her car. Nicole spotted her as soon as Jen crossed the street. Paying little regard for passersby, Nicole brushed a spontaneous kiss across Jen's cheek.

It was light and quick, but Jen leaned in, staying a second longer than she needed to. She savored the tiny buzz that hit her nerve center, elevating her mood.

Nicole's dark eyes took in Jen. "You look nice today."

"Thanks. So do you," Jen said, admiring Nicole's shapely body, clad in leggings and a hoodie covering something Jen couldn't see.

"Are you hungry?" Nicole asked.

"Sure." The truth was that Jen was so emotional over leaving Kristin with Amanda, in addition to being nervous about their first date, that she wasn't sure she could eat anything.

"Let's get a table." Nicole looped her hand through Jen's arm and escorted her inside.

Jen loved Rose's décor—the yellow-trimmed façade, white and blue awning, and blue-checkered chairs. It looked straight out of a children's storybook.

Once they were settled, they ordered cappuccinos and brunch dishes. Nicole decided to carbo-load on French bread pudding, but Jen went lean with scrambled eggs, spinach and prosciutto.

"So, how've you been?" Nicole asked, her curious eyes as sultry as they had been in the locker room.

"A little busy. You?" Jen said, understating her crazed day at the clinic yesterday, wanting to keep the conversation light.

"I thought I told you to stay out of the news," Nicole joked.

"You saw?"

"How could I not? KPIX keeps analyzing the DA campaign to death. The footage of you saying something about an email from the Hawthorne campaign has been repeated a thousand times."

"Ridiculous, right?" Jen rolled her blue eyes, letting the initial stress of the meeting flow off her.

"Do you need to blow off some steam? Wanna work out later?" Nicole sipped the cappuccino that the server set in front of her.

"I'm afraid I probably won't be able to today."

"Why not?"

"After brunch, I'm going to look at an apartment in the Sunset District."

"I love the Sunset. Where?"

"There's a remodeled place between Noriega and Ortega, on the Highway facing the beach."

"It's so quaint over there now that they redesigned Highway 1, making it veer away from the houses."

"I agree. Kristin, our dog, Zane, and I could walk the beach for miles."

"I'll bet there are great views of the beach from those houses."

"If you're on the second story, yes. I used to live over there, and I loved it."

"Why'd you move?"

"Ah…Amanda had a bigger place and really wanted me—us—to move in with her." Jen silently chastised herself for mentioning Amanda's name on the first date with another woman.

"Where?" Nicole unzipped her hoodie, showing off her defined sternal muscles lying under the spaghetti straps of her tank.

Jen found Nicole's smooth, dark skin and ripped body so distracting that she had to concentrate on moving her eyes north again to meet Nicole's gaze. "In Sea Cliff." The name of the neighborhood spoke for itself—in a nutshell, wealth.

"Oh." Nicole raised her eyebrows. Even though it was no secret that Amanda was independently wealthy, the fact that she lived in Sea Cliff usually surprised people.

"Anyway, I want to return to the neighborhood that makes me happy, you know? And that's the Sunset." Jen's eyes had slipped back down to admire Nicole's shoulders.

Nicole smirked her rose-colored lips as she watched Jen's eyes. "And, you should. With all the crap we have to face every day, why not live where you want to? If I could afford to live on the beach, I would."

The server delivered their plates, and Jen picked up her fork and knife but lacked any real enthusiasm for food. "What are you doing today?"

"I was going to see what you wanted to do. Maybe hang out. But if you're on a mission to find a place, then I'll think of something else. I could always do legs and butt at the gym."

"Wish I could join you. It's been forever since I squatted or did dead lifts." Jen could tell Nicole was hinting for an invite to join her apartment hunt, but she wasn't sure if she wanted someone so new in her life helping her with this decision.

Nicole smiled and chewed. She was sexy with her mouth full and her eyes sated. Even though she was into weightlifting, her long hair and sparkling brown eyes screamed femininity. Jen also noticed quite a bit of eyeshadow and mascara.

Jen's impression was that Nicole was a tad more girly than herself. More into glam, which was fine. Jen didn't feel the need to be the princess in a relationship but could envision Nicole occupying that space. Since her only lesbian relationship had been with Amanda, and Amanda was clearly a princess, Jen hadn't fully discovered her own spot on the spectrum from lipstick to butch. Chance had said she was "tinted chapstick." Maybe he was right because she couldn't help that she was attracted to pretty women, but she occasionally liked to wear makeup and high heels herself. *I wonder what Nicole thinks of me?*

"You're staring," Nicole said.

"Sorry. Lost in thought." Jen flipped a wave of blonde hair over her shoulder.

Nicole seemed simple—not as high maintenance as Amanda. Well, who was? No one even came close. *Why am I thinking about Amanda again?* She drank some cappuccino while she tried to shove her mental image of Amanda aside.

"There's a lot going on behind those blue eyes. Care to share?" Nicole asked between bites.

"That obvious, huh?"

Nicole nodded but didn't say anything.

Jen found Nicole's ability to wait for her to answer very attractive. If Jen hadn't spoken up immediately to Amanda, Amanda would sometimes answer her own question by supplying dialogue for Jen. Nicole, on the other hand, came off as content to eat, waiting for Jen to say what she wanted to, *when* she wanted to.

"I was just thinking about how pretty you are. Dating is sort of new to me," Jen admitted.

"Oh. Was Amanda your first serious relationship?"

"Yes."

"Like you're not pretty yourself...those cheekbones!" Nicole said, taking a drink of her cappuccino.

Jen smiled and blushed.

"You know you turn me on when you blush like that?"

Jen's face turned a deeper shade of red as she self-consciously busied herself by cutting some egg with her fork. When she looked up, Nicole was staring at her with one eyebrow raised.

"I heard you. I want to hang out with you today too, but my life is so complicated right now. I have to move, but Tommy doesn't want me to." She had to figure out how to describe Tommy without giving the wrong impression that she might be struggling with her sexuality. "He's Kristin's father and he loves me, but he knows I don't love him that way. The sooner we move out of his house, the better. It was supposed to be just a temporary living arrangement. He's really sweet and

198

understanding, but we can't continue living there."

"Were you married?" Again, simple and to the point without a hint of judgment.

"No. I was just breaking up with him when I got pregnant, which I don't regret for obvious reasons," Jen said, smiling. "Then I moved into Amanda's and had Kristin. When Amanda cheated on me, I moved out of her house in a rush. I didn't have my own place lined up, so Tommy offered his. Unfortunately, we've been there for six weeks, and it's getting awkward."

"Is he cramping your style?"

"I didn't realize it at first. Then I met you." Jen raised an eyebrow at Nicole. "So, yes. I believe he is."

"We can always go to my place." Nicole took a monster bite of French bread pudding. After she washed it down with coffee, she said, "God, this is heavenly. Want a bite?"

"Sure." Jen leaned in and Nicole fed her a bite. There was something so intimate about sharing food, then looking in Nicole's eyes as Jen savored the taste. Pleasure of the senses.

"See what I'm sayin'?" Nicole asked.

"I think I'm having a foodgasm." Jen's heart beat faster as she chewed, holding Nicole's eyes.

"That's a good start," Nicole said, maintaining eye contact.

A jolt of heat landed between Jen's legs. Swimming in Nicole's hot stare, Jen rethought her position on the apartment search. "Would you like to join me while I look at the apartment? I could use another opinion."

"I'd love to." Nicole sparkled with anticipation.

Jen smiled and dug into her food, finally able to set aside her anxiety and eat. Her mood noticeably lightened over brunch. "Did you have a busy week at work?"

"Yeah. One of our major clients is under a deadline to redesign their logo, and I'm the lead on the account, so we submitted design after design this week until we hit on the one they liked. High maintenance."

"So, you mostly design logos for businesses?"

"That, and signs, and advertising copy…"

"Sounds interesting."

"I love it."

"It shows."

Nicole was so easy-going and pleasant, eating her food and drinking her cappuccino. A refreshing change.

"Where do you live?" Jen asked.

"In Pacific Heights. Not too far from here."

"What street?"

"Steiner and Jackson, across from Alta Plaza Park."

"That isn't very far from where we work out."

"Now you know why I work out there. It's a quick walk from my place."

"I'd like to see your place sometime."

"Anytime. We could drop by today if you like."

"Maybe after we look at the apartment."

"When does it become available?"

"It's empty, so they really want someone now."

200

"Are you prepared to move that fast?"
"Oh yes. Most of our stuff is still in boxes."

17

While they lingered over brunch, Jen increasingly appreciated Nicole's chill attitude, and the way she waited for Jen to gather her thoughts before speaking. Nicole didn't rush the pace, giving Jen the impression that Nicole had all the time in the world and was interested in only Jen and whatever Jen had to say.

"Do you have any pics of Kristin on your phone?" Nicole asked.

"I don't want to bore you. There's nothing worse than parents showing people endless photos of their children."

"Don't be silly. She's the most important person in your life, and I'd like to see her, if you're comfortable, that is."

"Well, you're right about her being the most important person in my life. I won't argue with you there. I can show you a few." Jen removed her phone from her pocket and quickly scrolled through her pics. She found a closeup and turned her phone to Nicole.

A broad smile claimed Nicole's lips. "She looks just like you, and I can already tell that she's going to be a smart, strong lady, just like her mother."

Jen smiled. "The world's next triathlete, no doubt."

"I can see the love on your face for her. I'd like to have a child someday too. I haven't decided how I'm going to approach that, but I'll figure out a way."

Jen returned her phone to her pocket. "There are so many options now."

The server set the check on the table and Nicole scooped it up.

"No way," Jen said. "You don't have to buy."

"A bet's a bet," Nicole said. "Fair and square."

"Seriously. Let's split it then." Jen regarded her.

"Fine, if you're going to look at me like that," Nicole said. "I guess I know your business look now."

After they settled the bill, Jen went to the restroom. She joined Nicole outside, who was standing with her face turned up to the sun, her eyes closed.

"The weather is always so perfect in Cow Hollow." Jen stood beside her and turned her face up to the sun too.

"Yeah. Hardly any fog here." Nicole opened her eyes and turned to Jen. "Come here. You have some syrup on your cheek."

Jen leaned in and Nicole swept her fingers across Jen's cheek, guiding her closer. Nicole kissed her gently on the lips then retreated as fast as she had advanced, the fleeting graze lasting only a second.

If it hadn't been for the surge in her heart rate, Jen would've questioned whether the mini-kiss had even happened. "Mmm. I'm going to have to stay on my toes around you, aren't I?"

"I was just thinking the same thing," Nicole said.

"That's the third time you've barely kissed me. I'm looking forward to more."

"As in?"

"This." Jen leaned in and pressed her lips to Nicole's, immediately tasting syrup. They didn't take the kiss any further than their lips, but Jen let Nicole know she wanted more than just a few pecks here and there.

When they broke apart, Nicole said, "I like your style."

Jen's hormones donned party hats and blew noisemakers. She hadn't enjoyed the touch of a woman for too long and, despite her heartbreak, she was ecstatic that she was ready for more than just stepping on first base again. Just the realization that she could be hot for someone other than Amanda made her want to skip down the street singing.

"I need more of you," she whispered, her face only an inch from Nicole's.

"Likewise," Nicole said, taking Jen's hand in hers.

They turned and walked up the street.

"I'm parked over there," Jen indicated with a nod.

They strolled along in comfortable silence, window-shopping, Jen preoccupied with wondering when their next kiss would be. Nicole seemed content to walk slowly, her hand firmly holding Jen's.

"When is your appointment to see the apartment?" Nicole asked.

"In 40 minutes. We can take our time."

They paused to look at some workout clothes in a store window.

"That's cute," Nicole said, pointing to a hoodie on a mannequin.

"Very. I like how the gun metal-grey morphs into black. I love Sweaty Betty's, but it's so expensive." While they gazed at the hoodie, Nicole released Jen's hand and moved it to Jen's lower back then glided down to her ass, where she ran over the contour of Jen's shapely cheek before sliding her way back up to rest in the small of Jen's back. Delicious tingles ran through Jen, spreading a warmth that she had missed so much.

Jen's shoulders relaxed and she realized that she had been squeezing them tight since dropping Kristin at Amanda's. Her mind involuntarily conjured an image of Amanda and Kristin strolling around the Sea Cliff neighborhood. She fought off a vague feeling that she should be with *them* rather than enjoying her time with Nicole, so she turned away from the window and walked toward her car.

Nicole followed, reaching for Jen's hand again.

"Are you uncomfortable with PDA?" Nicole asked.

"No. It's not that. I've enjoyed everything we've been doing. I'm sort of a jumble of nerves today because I left Kristin with Amanda for the first time since we broke up."

"Oh."

"Yeah. I know. It's weird but Kristin loves her, and she's really missed her over the last month. She asks about her practically every day. That didn't make it any easier to leave her with Amanda, though, because I have all these angry feelings toward her. I'm not going to talk

205

about her, but you know what I mean. She cheated on me." *Fuck. I'm talking about her again.*

"I know exactly what you mean. I'd be conflicted too. Not all of my relationships have ended amicably—some my fault, others not. But, I've never had a child to worry about, so you're entitled to be emotional over it."

"I'm sorry. I'm violating the cardinal rule— never talk about your ex when you're on a date."

"Whoever invented that rule was clueless. That isn't how life really works, is it?"

"Not for me. Here's my car." Jen clicked the fob and the doors unlocked.

They got in and Jen started the engine. "Thanks for being so understanding. I'll try to get my shit together for the rest of our date. You've been very patient and I appreciate it."

"You 'appreciate' me? I was sort of hoping you were attracted to me."

Jen blushed. "Ha. That too."

Nicole reached over and covered Jen's hand. She gave it a quick squeeze then let go.

Jen put the car in gear, and they were off. "Enough about my fucked-up life. What else do you like to do besides work out?"

"I get together with my friends. Go out. Go hiking. You know."

"Where do you hike?"

"Mostly the Marin Headlands."

"I love it over there. We should go some time."

"That'd be fun. So, how do you like being a doctor?" Nicole asked.

"I love my job."

"In the ER, right?"

"No. I switched to a clinic. The pace is more relaxed, and I get to know my patients and their families."

"I could never do that. The sight of blood makes me faint. And touching all those people. Yuck."

Jen smiled. As they drove over to the Sunset District, Jen told Nicole about removing the bat from the building in the pillow case. A few minutes before her appointment with the real estate agent, Jen parked on the street in front of the apartment building. "This is it."

"Wait a minute before we go in." Nicole unbuckled her seat belt and twisted her body to face Jen.

"What?"

"I've been dying to do this all morning." Nicole reached over and placed her hand behind Jen's head. She gently brought Jen to her lips and kissed her. Not a peck, but not a French kiss either. Jen again tasted Nicole's soft, full lips and felt the spark of promise. Just what she needed to jumpstart her new life in her own apartment. Neither woman took the kiss deeper, enjoying it for what it was—their first *private* kiss.

One of Jen's favorite songs—*Heal Over* by KT Tungstall—was playing on her Pandora station: *"Come over here lady. Let me wipe your tears away. Come a little nearer baby. 'Cause you'll heal over. Heal over. Heal over someday."*

Jen certainly hoped so.

After a few seconds, Nicole backed away. "Thanks for trusting me enough to share your life with me."

"Thanks for bringing me back to earth."

"Funny, because I want to light you off like a rocket."

Fireworks exploded behind Jen's belly button. She hadn't had someone talk naughty to her in a while, and it felt good. Really good. "Want to see this apartment?"

"Anything you want." Nicole turned and reached for the door handle.

The real estate agent met them in the lobby. "I'm Gabrielle. Which one of you is Jen?"

"I am," Jen said, offering her hand. "This is my friend, Nicole."

"Nice to meet you. Shall we go up?" Gabrielle brought them to the second level where the two-bedroom apartment was located. As soon as they walked into the newly remodeled space, Jen fell in love. The living room ceiling was vaulted and had huge picture windows overlooking Ocean Beach. Well, the Great Highway was between the apartment and the beach, but the view of the ocean was unparalleled.

Jen so wanted to return to running on the beach. She envisioned pushing Kristin in the jogger, Zane by her side, running along the shore.

"Are you thinking about how much time you'll spend on the beach?" Nicole asked, coming to Jen's side.

"Uh-huh."

"Let me show you the rest of the unit," Gabrielle said.

Jen got the feeling the realtor was on a tight schedule. She guided them through the white kitchen, the single bathroom and both bedrooms. The master bedroom had a view of the beach as well.

Jen loved the entire place, forgetting to ask any practical questions about laundry facilities, the utilities, heat, or water. Fortunately, Nicole had her wits about her and covered the details, including getting a copy of the rental agreement for Jen to review.

"I'll let you two spend a few minutes alone, thinking it over, while I wait outside," Gabrielle said.

As soon as Jen heard the door close, she raised her arms in the air and whispered, "I love it!"

Nicole smiled. "It's in a great location. I'll give you that, but the rent is astronomical!" She held up the fact sheet for Jen to see.

"I'll find a way to make it work. I soooo need this space and a fresh start for Kristin and me. I feel happier than I've felt in a month!" Jen spontaneously flicked the paper out of Nicole's hands and pulled her in for a kiss. She found Nicole's full lips and kissed them with the same enthusiasm she had felt from Nicole in the car, except brazenly exploring this time.

Unprepared for Nicole's reaction or strength, Jen lost her breath when Nicole wrapped her arms around her back and pulled her closer, moving her hand to the back of Jen's head and taking control of the kiss. Nicole wasted no time in parting her lips, accepting Jen in her mouth, and giving her the warm, deep kiss she longed for. As first French kisses went, Nicole's was up there, making the room spin as she held Jen in a firm embrace.

Jen wasn't used to such strength in a woman, but shouldn't have been surprised since she'd seen Nicole lift weights. She let herself relax against Nicole's solid body and marveled at her ripped muscles as her hands glided over Nicole's shoulders and lower back, falling to rest on her butt. She pulled Nicole's hips into her own.

Jen couldn't believe she was finally holding the sweetest ass at the gym. Every bit as firm as it was round, the orbs filled her hands. As Jen drowned in Nicole's mouth, her hands caressed Nicole's ass, making Jen so wet that she would've taken it further if Gabrielle-the-realtor hadn't opened the front door and interrupted them.

"Excuse me, ladies. Sorry to disturb, but I have another appointment I need to run to. So, if you're finished seeing the apartment, then—" She held the door open and raised her eyebrows.

They broke apart, not embarrassed in the least. Jen smiled while Nicole bent down and grabbed the papers from the floor.

"We're done. Sorry for making you wait. I was just so excited," Jen said, wiping her lips.

"Good to hear. Are you serious about a down payment?" Gabrielle asked, eyebrow still cocked in skepticism.

"Absolutely. I just need my lawyer to review the lease. I'll call you tomorrow."

"Looking forward to it." Gabrielle locked the door after they walked out, and they all took the stairway down to the front door. Everyone shook hands and walked to their cars.

Jen and Nicole watched Gabrielle speed off. "You don't think she had a problem with us kissing, do you?" Nicole asked.

"I didn't get that vibe. I think she was just in a hurry. I'll see if she's frosty tomorrow when I call her."

"Hope I didn't kill your apartment deal by making out."

"It was worth it." While still on the sidewalk, Jen slipped her hand under Nicole's hair and grabbed her neck, bringing her back to her body.

They fell into another hot, steamy kiss while the realities of time and place drifted away. Jen was so horny she thought she was going to jump out of her skin. She didn't give a damn that they were on the sidewalk. She just allowed her hands to explore, first Nicole's ass, then her ribs, then between their bodies to find Nicole's breasts. Jen held both, admiring Nicole's strong pecks under her breasts. Her thumbs skated across Nicole's nipples, feeling them grow taught. Nicole's tremor made Jen even hotter.

Nicole leaned her head back, her breath hot and voice husky. "My place isn't very far from here. Wanna see it?"

Without hesitation, Jen breathed, "Yeah."

Nicole smiled and pulled Jen in for another full kiss, saying against her lips when they came up for air, "Let's get out of here."

"Right." They stumbled into the car, kissed again, and Jen managed to follow Nicole's directions to her place in Pacific Heights despite being lightheaded and flustered. What seemed to take forever was only twenty minutes, but Jen was burning with anticipation as they drove.

Nicole's left hand found its way to Jen's thigh and caressed at just the right pressure as Jen tried to concentrate on driving. She thought her pussy was going to jump out of her leggings into Nicole's hand.

"Be careful what you do to me. I can barely drive."

"You're fucking hot as hell." Nicole massaged closer to Jen's hotspot.

They found a parking spot on the street, and Nicole led the way up the stairs to her Victorian, holding Jen's hand even while she unlocked the door. Neither spoke as they walked up to the third level and Nicole unlocked her apartment door. Jen didn't see much by way of her apartment as they fell into each other's arms. Nicole kicked the door closed and tossed her keys somewhere with a clang.

They found each other in a collision of playful groping and hungry hands. With her body feverishly pressed up against Nicole's, Jen was another step closer to fulfilling her pent-up needs. Her hands found Nicole's ass again as Nicole maneuvered a hand between them to find Jen's breast.

"I take it you're into my ass," Nicole whispered, as she kissed a trail down Jen's neck, on her way to her breasts.

"You know you have a perfect ass, right?" Jen glided her hands under Nicole's tank to find her muscular back.

Nicole moaned, covering Jen's breast with her warm mouth. She unclasped Jen's bra, and had Jen's nipple in her mouth in seconds.

Jen's legs threatened to buckle, the swirling warmth of Nicole's tongue so overpowering on her nipple she felt like she was going to unravel in an orgasm. Gasping for air and writhing under Nicole's touch, Jen offered her other breast.

Nicole's pursuit of her breasts was so different than Tommy's had been when they were together a lifetime ago. He had approached her breasts like they were his toys, for *his* sexual enjoyment.

Both Amanda and Nicole, on the other hand, treated her breasts as erogenous zones to pleasure *her*, pulling sweet moans from her. Where Tommy took, her female partners *gave*.

Nicole laughed softly and moved to the other breast while massaging the wet one with her hand. When Nicole moved down Jen's lean abs, Jen put her hands on Nicole's shoulders. *What are we doing? We're like crazed animals.*

Nicole hooked her fingers in Jen's leggings and started sliding them down, but when Jen looked down, seeing Nicole's lips pressed to her tummy, she suddenly felt guilty. Her mind struggled for rational thought. *We're going to have sex. Now. In her living room. On our first date?*

As Nicole slid Jen's leggings lower, Jen pictured Amanda pushing Kristin in her stroller on a long walk around her neighborhood, and her libido came to a crashing halt.

She covered Nicole's hands. "Wait a sec. I don't think I can do this right now. It feels a little soon."

Nicole lifted her face from kissing the top of Jen's thong. She was on her knees. "What?"

"I can't go all the way with you. It's only our first date," Jen said, panting as Nicole put her palms on Jen's hips, staying where she was.

"If it's STD's you're worried about, I'm clean." Nicole blew hot air on Jen's pussy then kissed her through the thin fabric of her thong.

Jen sucked in air as her insides rushed like a river toward her pussy. When Jen didn't recant, Nicole kissed her way back up to Jen's breasts and stood, taking a breast in her mouth again, her tongue dancing around Jen's nipple. She sucked so hard that Jen arched into Nicole's face, wrapping her arms around Nicole's neck. "Ohhh…God."

Her body briefly left her mind, focusing only on the pleasure Nicole delivered.

Nicole leaned back, covered Jen's breasts with her bra, and neatly clasped it together again. "I understand your hesitation. Your life is complicated right now and I don't want to add to that."

"That's true," she groaned. "When I have sex with you, I want it to mean more than just a quick hookup." Jen watched Nicole pull her tank down over her bra, putting her back together. Even though her body wanted sex, her heart and mind wanted a relationship.

"I feel the same way," Nicole whispered. "I thought I'd be cool being your revenge fuck but I have a little more pride than that. I'm at a point in my life where I want a relationship too." She pulled Jen's T-shirt down and hiked the waistband of her leggings back up.

Nicole held Jen in a bear hug, savoring the warmth and full-on body touch.

Jen could feel her hips involuntarily swaying into Nicole's, her pussy springing forth like a wet summer morning. *Damn I want you. Why'd you have to be so honorable?*

"Would you like a cup of tea?" Nicole whispered into Jen's ear.

Jen moaned. "Tea instead of sex?"

"I didn't mean as a substitute. Nothing could sub for sex."

They parted enough for Jen to trace her finger from Nicole's ear to her neck. "How about a raincheck? I should pick up Kristin. I'm not entirely comfortable with her being at Amanda's this long."

"I can see you're distracted by that entire situation today. Would you like to come over for dinner next week?" Nicole asked.

"I'd love that. Maybe Tommy can babysit."

Nicole's eyes lit up. "I make a mean lasagna."

"I'll bring the wine."

"It's a date. I'll text you."

They kissed again, and Nicole walked Jen to the door. She kissed her lightly and said goodbye.

When Jen returned to her car, she laughed at her catawampus parking job. The right, front tire was on the curb, the car parked at an angle.

"Someone was in a hurry to get laid," she muttered to herself. *Desperate much?* She was sure Nicole was physical in bed and she looked forward to having all that energy focused on her, but Nicole was right. Jen didn't know if she was just using Nicole for a revenge fuck or wanted something more. She had to take the time to get to know her—and herself.

Get yourself together, girl.

18

Sea Cliff

The previously rote action of turning her key in the lock now twisted Jen's heart as she opened the kitchen door to Amanda's house. Once experiencing the thrill of anticipation at being with her lover, today she felt uncomfortable—like she was intruding. Zumba welcomed her, though, meowing and twining in and out of her legs.

"Hey, tomcat," she said, scratching his head.

She stood motionless, assessing the mood in the space before her. The kitchen and living room seemed hollow, not for lack of furnishings, but in spirit. The house lacked warmth and life.

As Zumba carefully smelled her shoes, visions of her previous life here danced through Jen's mind like a tragic ballet. Late nights spent on the floor in front of the fire with Amanda, experiencing her intense passion. Their morning breakfast routine with Kristin at the white table overlooking the patio, the sunshine bathing them in happiness. Zumba and Zane racing around playing. The memories dissipated like fog, the trappings of betrayal subverting their once-joyous mood.

Expecting to see Amanda and Kristin on the floor in the living room, disappointment mingled with curiosity as Jen wondered where they could be. Toys lay scattered about, but no one was in sight. Were they out on a stroll?

Then she heard it. Cello music. *Live* cello music. The rich sound floated up from the lower level, low and pure, a haunting melody beckoning to her. Like a sailor lured by a siren, Jen followed the music, Zumba prancing in front of her, his tail twitching as he led the way. He reminded Jen of the first time she had stayed overnight at Amanda's—when he had shown her the path to Amanda's yoga studio—where Jen had found Amanda on a mat that was perfect for making love.

Back to reality. She wasn't in Amanda's life any longer. Amanda had seen to that. The pain came out of nowhere and stabbed her in the chest as the cello music grew louder.

Does Amanda have a musical guest visiting while she's spending time with Kristin? Is Amanda sleeping with a cellist now? Did she have the gall to bring a new girlfriend over while Kristin is here? If she did, this is the last time…

Jen and Zumba quietly padded down the stairway to Amanda's yoga studio. Zumba entered, but Jen lingered by the doorjamb, listening. She peered in and saw the large instrument anchored between Amanda's thighs as she sat on a sturdy chair facing Kristin, who was sitting on a yoga mat, wrapped in a pink blanket, her pacifier in her mouth. Jen couldn't see Kristin's eyes, but her straight back indicated she was rapt with attention.

Jen was captivated too. Amanda? Cello? Not an expert at classical music, Jen thought she recognized the piece as *Clair de Lune,* but she wasn't sure. Amanda's eyes were closed as she swayed, trance-like, playing the ethereal tune, the bow working its magic across the strings. Her notes were clear and smooth, washing over Jen like a warm waterfall, filling her soul. Never had Jen imagined that Amanda played. To see her lost in the music was to see a different person. She seemed elegant and soft, not the hard-charging prosecutor Jen had known for the last two years.

Jen leaned against the door frame for support, mouth agape, marveling at the tranquility of the scene before her. Her eyes filled with tears as she watched her daughter enjoying the music made beautiful by Amanda's talented hands. What a transformative experience for Kristin—to experience the rich melody emanating from the belly of the cello as it reverberated through them. Amanda played the last note, elongating it for a ghost-like ending.

When Amanda opened her eyes, they found Jen, as if she'd been staring at her the entire time. In that moment, Jen saw raw vulnerability deep in Amanda's soul. Simultaneously, she saw peace. *Vulnerable? Peaceful? Not the Amanda I knew.*

Her own guard down, Jen was sure that Amanda saw the love and admiration Jen felt for her. To deny it would have been to throw away the value of her own emotions, and she wasn't about to do that. She was passionate, caring, and loving, and proud of it. She wouldn't let Amanda's betrayal rob her of her best qualities.

Jen could feel Amanda studying her, reading her, wanting to play her like the piece of music she'd just brought to life. Rather than being annoyed by Amanda's hungry assessment, however, Jen felt relieved to show Amanda her real feelings. Even though Amanda didn't deserve to know anything about how Jen felt, Jen didn't try to conceal her admiration.

She wasn't sure how long they held each other in their optical embrace, but she was jolted out of it when she heard Kristin yell, "More, Mama Man! More!"

Amanda broke eye contact with Jen to reply to Kristin. "Did you like *Clair de Lune*?"

"Yes! Cat da Moon!" Kristin squealed, clapping. She stood, her pink blankie falling like a cape around her, and toddled to Amanda's thigh. She reached out and tentatively touched the cello strings, so Amanda showed Kristin how to pluck them as Jen watched in silence, not wanting to interrupt Kristin's lesson. Kristin plucked then whooped each time a note sounded. Watching Amanda patiently teach, Jen realized she could never deprive Kristin of Amanda's company. Kristin loved her and received unconditional love in return. Jen was witnessing that.

After a few minutes, Amanda pointed at Jen with the bow, saying, "Look who's here."

Kristin turned and ran across the studio to Jen, throwing herself around Jen's leg. "Mommy!"

Jen patted Kristin's little back as she clung to her. "Hi, baby. That was beautiful, Amanda. Why didn't I know you played?"

"It isn't something I advertise, but I took it up again while I was in the clinic. We had a lot of time on our hands since they confiscated our cell phones. No TV or electronics. Just time to meditate, exercise, and play an instrument if you had one."

"Well, you brought tears to my eyes. And, thanks for introducing Kristin to the cello."

Amanda smiled, more content than Jen had ever seen her. "Thanks for allowing me. I love her dearly and hope my stupidity won't result in my not seeing her."

She definitely gets an A for atonement. Jen was speechless, finding herself staring into Amanda's deep brown eyes again, the gold flecks subdued, pacified by the experience of playing such a forlorn tune. Their attraction still ran deep, its pull so strong that Jen felt it all the way across the room.

Amanda broke the spell by sliding her chair back and rising, setting her cello in a handsome wooden stand then hanging the bow next to it. Dressed in her yoga pants and the hoodie Jen had admired in the window at Sweaty Betty's, Amanda joined Jen and Kristin. Two months ago, Amanda's approach would have culminated in a loving hug, but now they stood apart, Kristin still clinging to Jen's leg.

"Care for a cup of tea?" Amanda asked, her smile tentative but warm.

Second offer today. No sex but lots of tea. "Sure."

Amanda smiled and brushed past her, leading the way. They walked up to the kitchen, Kristin sucking on her pacifier and nuzzling into Jen's neck as she carried her. Jen pulled Kristin's blankie around her, holding her tight. "I think you lulled Kristin into nap time."

"I'm not surprised. My playing has put countless adults to sleep."

"I doubt that. You play beautifully."

"Thank you." Amanda filled a teapot with water and set it on the stove.

The pause in conversation seemed magnified by the absence of Amanda's playing, the silence seeping into the space around them. Amanda must have felt it too because she picked up her phone and touched the screen, bringing music to life over the speaker system in the kitchen. Jen noticed it was classical music for children. She smiled while rocking Kristin in her arms, swaying to the beat, soothing Kristin to sleep.

Amanda's eyes crinkled in amusement as she returned Jen's smile. She turned to prepare their mugs, warming some milk in the micro and frothing it with a little appliance Jen hadn't seen before.

"What's that?" Jen asked in a whisper.

"My new milk frother. My parents gave it to me as a welcome home present," she said, showing Jen. While waiting for the water to come to a boil, Amanda finished frothing the milk in the bottom of each mug.

"Fancy. A cellist *and* a barista now." *A little different from the gun-toting, controlling prosecutor.* Jen walked to the living room and lay Kristin on a large blanket in the center of the room. The floor felt a little cool to her bare feet, so she flipped the switch for the gas fireplace to warm Kristin as she drifted off.

Amanda poured the boiling water into a ceramic teapot and steeped their brew. She

222

watched Jen tuck in Kristin on the floor, smiling. "She's beautiful when she sleeps, isn't she?"

"Uh-huh," Jen whispered, pulling the blankie around Kristin's shoulders. She lowered herself next to Kristin, her hand on her small back, rubbing circles. She grabbed a few pillows that were strewn in front of the sofa and wedged them behind her own back as she leaned against the hearth. When she had lived here, if she wasn't at Amanda's premier stove in the kitchen, she was next to the fireplace, especially as the fog moved in and the temperature dropped. *This part of my life is over...*

A few minutes later, Amanda joined them and handed Jen a mug. She gracefully lowered herself to the floor a few feet across from Jen, leaning her back against the sofa. "To Kristin."

"Cheers," Jen said.

They both drank.

Amanda unzipped her new hoodie, revealing a lowcut tank. It wasn't racy by any means. In fact, it looked like soft, ribbed cotton, but was lowcut enough to be mildly revealing. Jen immediately appreciated the stark contrast between Amanda and Nicole. Where Nicole's skin was dark and overlay thick, well-defined muscles, Amanda's skin was creamy white, covering her toned body, healthy from yoga and playing cello. There was a delicate side to Amanda today that Jen hadn't noticed before.

The person before her wasn't a ruthless prosecutor, but a tender, passionate woman. Amanda reminded Jen of a black-eyed Susan, her beauty undeniable, and scrappy existence a testament to survival. Jen dragged her eyes from Amanda's décolletage to her contented eyes. Eyes that followed Jen's.

"I still can't believe you play the cello like a professional."

Amanda sighed. "I thought it was in my past. I didn't really intend to pick it up again until I realized I was abusing drugs, so I needed something to fulfill…" Her sentiment lingered unfinished in the air.

"I hope you keep it up. I'd like to hear more."

Amanda's lips curved into a sad smile. "Anytime."

They drank their tea.

"How is living with Tommy going?" Amanda asked.

"Okay, but I found a place today. That's where I went on my errand. I hope to sign the rental agreement tomorrow and move in next week."

"Really? Congratulations."

"Thanks. We've overstayed our welcome at Tommy's."

"I doubt that, but you still have a lot of things here if you want them." Amanda swept her arm to include Jen's bits and pieces scattered throughout the house.

"I know. I appreciate your leaving them in place. Once I make the move, I'd like to come by and get them."

Amanda nodded. "Where's your new place?"

"Between Noriega and Ortega in the Sunset District."

"Close to the beach?"

"Across from it."

"Your old stomping grounds. You like that neighborhood, don't you?"

"Guess I'm a sucker for the beach. There's so much for Kristin and me to see and do there."

"She loves picking up sand dollars and splashing in the water, that's for sure," Amanda whispered, gazing lovingly at Kristin sleeping. They both watched her fall into a steady breathing rhythm, resting comfortably. "If you need someone to look at your rental agreement, I'd be happy to."

"You'd do that for me?" Jen asked.

"Sure. Do you have it?"

"It's in my bag," Jen nodded toward the kitchen counter. She was so comfortable where she was, though, she didn't feel compelled to hop up and retrieve it.

"I'll do it tonight."

"Thanks." Jen sipped her tea. "How's your program going?"

Amanda's eyes moved to the floor, then glanced back up at Jen. "Good. I won't lie. It's hard work, and I was a bit unsettled to discover some things about myself."

"Like what?" Jen asked, her intense blue eyes assessing Amanda over the rim of her mug.

"If I tell you, I might start crying. Will that make you uncomfortable?"

"Not in the least. I value honesty. You know that."

Amanda nodded then sipped. "I'm in a 12-step program, and a few of the steps were pretty harsh."

"Ah, yes. I remember. Which one is the step about 'admitting the nature of your wrongs to God and another person?'"

"Five. I see you're familiar with it."

"I learned about it in an addictions class during medical school."

"Then you know how painful it can be to voice your indiscretions and wrongdoings to another person."

"More from personal experience than from a class, but yes."

Amanda squinted at her, temporarily thrown that Jen might have actually engaged in any indiscretions or wrongdoings. She couldn't picture it. "Anyway, now is as good a time as any to apologize to you for what I did. Here goes: I had a problem with sexual fidelity. When I fell in love, and I've only been in love once— with you—I felt vulnerable and naked. Unfortunately, falling in love coincided with the Nutini mob war, so I dove into the alcohol and drugs for liquid courage. I was rattled to my core but didn't want to admit it. Valium helped that. Getting shot in New York, however, scared the shit out of me and triggered my untreated PTSD from the mob war. I was in the hands of the CIA physician and Roxy. It was a fucking nightmare, and he gave me vicodin. Then I drank wine. I stumbled way off course and got tangled up with Roxy—the mistake of a lifetime. I was trying to cover up my insecurities and failings by accepting an invitation from her, which I wouldn't have done if I hadn't been drunk and high. I betrayed you, and I'm sorry. I'll never do it again." She took a deep breath. "And now I'm rambling."

Jen's defenses were melting away, one by one. "You're not rambling. You're sharing, which means a lot to me. I...I...never knew. I was just so hurt that I assumed. Well, I sort of made some stuff up in my own head. I couldn't think straight and I cried a lot. For a long time."

Jen tried not to escalate over the mention of Amanda and Roxy together, but her emotions were an extreme mix of love and hate, her pinky knuckle throbbing, and her body itching for a fight. Or something. She noticed her mug was trembling like the beginning of an earthquake, so she lowered it to her lap for stability.

Amanda continued. "At the rehab clinic, we had to work through all the gunshot trauma before unearthing my utter failure at intimacy and loyalty."

"I'm sorry. I just attributed it to...well...I don't know." Jen looked into Amanda's misty eyes.

Amanda held up her hand, patting at the air. "No need to apologize. None of it had anything to do with you. You didn't create my situation or even aggravate it. Instead, you were an incredible partner—always supportive." She finally lost her composure, the tears streaming down her face. She didn't turn away or break eye contact, though. She didn't even attempt to wipe them away. "Always there when I needed you, loving me. And, the sex—" She waved her hand to finish that thought, unable to talk.

"The sex was unparalleled," Jen muttered, the words leaping from her mouth before she could stop them. *What is it about Amanda that makes me blurt out shit?* She wanted to wrap her arms around her and console her, but that would send the wrong message—that she had forgiven her and was ready to start over. While she was working on forgiveness, she wasn't anywhere close to starting over. She had already led Tommy down a primrose path and would be damned if she'd create more confusion in her love life by giving Amanda the wrong impression too.

She needed some space so she stood, walked a few steps toward the kitchen, suddenly had a change of heart, then turned and lowered herself to the floor beside Amanda. Jen felt so fucking sorry for her. *Showing compassion is okay, right?* She sat next to Amanda and wrapped her arms around her. Amanda collapsed into Jen's lap and cried quietly.

Jen found herself stroking Amanda's thick, curly hair, soothing her. "It's okay. You're being harder on yourself than—" Jen paused, struggling for the right words, her hand resting on Amanda's shoulder. "Well, I've been pretty hard on you too."

Amanda continued sobbing, but Jen could feel a smile in response to her humor.

Here she was, holding Amanda and liking it. Jen had hated her, but maybe that was a disproportionate reaction. She needed to find empathy. As she struggled with her own emotions, her hand caressed Amanda's shoulder, moving in circles, running over her shoulder blade, then up to her collarbone, the warmth of Amanda traveling through Jen's arm. Electricity sparked. Not necessarily the sexual kind. The loving—this feels so right—kind. Jen realized her hand was under Amanda's hoodie on her bare shoulder. So soft. So warm. So perfect. Her body was like no other.

How does she do this to me? She quickly removed her hand and placed it on Amanda's hip, where she involuntarily started rubbing in circles there too. Round and round her protruding hip bone, pulling a few sighs from Amanda. Her hand was so close to the intimate parts of Amanda, but far enough away, so she could control her impulse to start something.

"Thanks for being honest," Jen said.

Amanda nodded, nervously rubbing her eyes. "I promise honesty from here on out. I'm so sorry for dragging you into my campaign. Into yet another mess. Your lawsuit outed by Morales. Your work computers hacked by Hellfire. It's like I'm a fucking—" She came up short again.

"Curse," Jen supplied.

"Yeah. Curse." Amanda convulsed in a silent sob.

"But the good kind. None of this is your fault, Amanda. You just happen to work in law enforcement. You're the DA for crying out loud. I don't blame you." Jen lowered herself to kiss the side of Amanda's head, breathing in the intoxicating smell of her hair, so feminine, so sexy. Her scent was as unique as her aura, infiltrating Jen's lungs then moving to her heart, her head, and down to her toes, drawing her back to the familiar—and erotic—home she had once relished. She draped her arm around

Amanda and cradled her, readjusting, so she could rest her chin on Amanda's head.

The center of Jen's being settled into place like a newly sprouted flower in a field of wild color. The rest of the world could move along without her while she held Amanda, Kristin sleeping soundly beside them. Jen's universe was temporarily righted, the previous jealousy and rage pushed aside. *Why was I holding onto all that hate? Forgiveness can be liberating for the soul.*

Soon, Amanda drifted off, her breathing becoming deep and low. Jen grabbed an ultra-soft throw blanket from the sofa and draped it over them while she readjusted, lying down beside Amanda and spooning into her back. She fell asleep too, holding on tight, their bodies and souls reacquainting. Jen felt more content than she had in a month, entering a deep, dreamless sleep.

19

Jen hadn't moved an inch from being spooned to Amanda's back when she was awakened by Kristin's little body draping over her side, her sleepy little head falling between Jen and Amanda.

Jen opened her eyes to see Kristin's loving blue eyes staring at her as she blinked away sleep and registered where she was. Jen quietly rolled onto her back, so Kristin could crawl onto her torso and cuddle. This was cherished time together, transitioning from a sleepy head to the life of the party. For Kristin anyway. Jen never wanted to be the life of the party.

"Good morning, honey. Did you have a good nap?" Jen asked, hugging Kristin.

Amanda moaned and rolled onto her back too, then surprised Jen by rolling onto her side, so she could face both Jen and Kristin. Amanda rubbed Kristin's back, and Kristin turned her head to face her, staring at her and smiling behind her pacifier.

"I love you," Amanda said.

"Lub you," Kristin said around her pacifier.

Happiness crinkled Amanda's eyes, pulling up her lips into a loving smile.

Just hearing those words from Amanda made Jen's insides melt. She knew they were meant for Kristin, but to be so close, so intimate, feeling like a family again, filled her with hope that they could once again create what they had. If only she could trust Amanda.

Of its own volition, her hand felt for Amanda's on the floor, and when she found it, she twined their fingers. The simple intimacy of holding hands, waking next to Amanda, with Kristin resting on top of her, filled her with joy and contentment. She wanted to remain in this moment forever, not dwelling on the past and not anticipating the future. If only she could bottle the peace she felt at this moment—the simplicity, the warmth, the love.

They heard a cell phone ring on the kitchen counter. Neither Jen nor Amanda moved.

"Must be yours," Jen said.

"The world can wait. I haven't felt this happy in months," Amanda said.

Did she say, "months?" She must've been struggling for longer than I realized. I was so caught up in pregnancy and a baby, I didn't realize.

Jen disentangled her fingers from Amanda's and instead squeezed her hand in a loving grasp. Oh, how she wanted to plant a kiss on her forehead, but she was scared. Scared of falling again. Scared of giving the impression she was a doormat, being the weak one in a controlling relationship with a powerful narcissist. Make no mistake, just because Amanda had gone through rehab didn't mean she had undergone a personality transplant. Jen assumed she was still *Amanda* at her core. But, at least the new Amanda was being honest about her failings.

Sensing Jen's ambivalence, Amanda moved her hand from Kristin's back to the side of Jen's face. She firmly, but gently, turned Jen's head

233

so she was facing her. Only inches apart, they considered each other.

Terrified, Jen held her breath. Looking into those deep brown eyes, the gold flecks dancing with love and warmth, she got lost so easily. She had fallen hard for Amanda before, and lately vowed not to fall so hard and fast—with anyone—again. But the love that was washing over her was so comforting and warm. Her heart stopped beating.

"I love you." Amanda whispered the phrase so softly, her breath barely touching Jen's face, her smile tentative.

"I love you too," fell out of Jen's mouth, her heart acting without consulting her brain. Jen's emotions, disobedient and floundering, reacted to Amanda in ways Jen didn't understand, much less have control over.

"Can you forgive me?" Amanda rasped.

Jen touched a curl framing Amanda's face then ran her hand down her arm. "I'm open to it. Just give me some time." As soon as she said the words, the sun thawed her cold heart, inviting it to play in the warmth of a spring day.

"I lub you," Kristin said again, smiling, as she looked from one mommy to the other.

"And we love you too," Amanda said, rubbing Kristin's back.

What would have been followed by a kiss a few months ago now remained only a tender declaration, like an unfinished song whose melody lingered in the air. Only time would tell whether they could make it happen.

Rejuvenated and ready for the day, Kristin squirmed, pushed off Jen, and toddled off in the direction of the kitchen. Amanda and Jen raised their heads to watch her walk away, disappearing behind the island. She was so proud of herself when she emerged on the other side that she came running to them, landing squarely on top of Amanda, practically knocking the wind out of her.

"Look at you! Running around the island!" Amanda exclaimed.

Kristin pushed away from Amanda and took off running again. Jen and Amanda propped themselves up on their elbows and waited for Kristin to round the corner, picking up speed until she launched herself, flying through the air to land on them.

"Whoa!" Jen said, barely catching Kristin. "We better slow down, little girl. You almost flew over us like a missile!"

Kristin looked up and chortled, a mischievous belly laugh that made both Amanda and Jen laugh too. When Kristin pushed off to do it again, Amanda jumped up and crouched, waiting for Kristin to come around the island. When she did, Amanda opened her arms wide and screamed, "Gotcha!"

Kristin screeched, blew out her pacifier, then ran the other direction, coming around the island to fly into Jen's arms. They hugged and rolled until Kristin yelled, "Juice!"

"How about we say, 'please?'" Jen asked. "Amanda, do you have any juice, please?"

"Plenty. I'll pour some in a sippy cup."

Amanda poured, and Jen pulled Kristin off the floor into a big hug, carrying her to the kitchen. Amanda handed the cup to Kristin and rested her other hand on the small of Jen's back. She stayed close, ostensibly helping Kristin hold the cup, but Jen suspected Amanda simply wanted to touch her body just like Jen yearned to touch Amanda.

Even through Jen's shirt, Amanda's hand felt like a hot stone resting on her spine during a massage. Hot and welcoming. Aware of all things Amanda, Jen was dialed into her sensuality, the electricity prickling her spine. Amanda could set Jen on fire with a mere touch, hotter than Nicole had been with her tongue a few hours earlier. A needle of guilt pricked her. *Damn. Why do I feel guilty about being with Nicole? And we didn't even have sex!*

"Hungry!" Kristin said, patting her chest.

"Do you have something to eat, please?" Jen asked, her face only inches from Amanda's. She saw a flash of lust in Amanda's eyes, making her own heart skip a beat.

"Do I?" Amanda mocked. "Of course. Just give me a few minutes, and I'll whip up some scrambled eggs with ham and cheese."

"That sounds delicious. What should we give Kristin?" Jen teased.

"Are you hungry too?" Amanda paused, looking at her.

Jen found Amanda's eyes. "Very."

They smiled at each other. *Well then, that's settled.*

"Does she want some cereal while I make the eggs?" Amanda asked.

"Maybe. Still in the same place?" Jen asked.

"Yeah," Amanda said, nodding toward the cupboard. "Want a cup of coffee if I make some?"

"I'd love some," Jen said. "I can make it while you make the eggs."

They worked together, easy-going and coordinated in the kitchen. In the past, Jen would've taken the lead with the eggs, but she was content to play second fiddle while she helped Kristin with her juice and cereal.

After they finished eating, Jen took Kristin upstairs to change her diaper. She paused briefly at the door to their old bedroom. Little had changed, other than the mood.

When they returned, Amanda had straightened up and loaded the dishwasher.

"We should probably get going. Thanks for the lunch. And nap. And babysitting Kristin. And...saying you loved me." Her expression was filled with raw emotion, making her feel exposed.

"I loved every minute and meant what I said." Amanda lingered over the words, and Jen saw a hint of sadness flicker in Amanda's eyes.

"Me too. Give me some time." Part of Jen wanted to go to her. To kiss away the uncertainty. To rekindle the passion. But that would be unfair to both Amanda and herself. She wasn't ready. They had come a long way today but she couldn't fall back into Amanda's world so quickly. She needed her independence, despite what her romantic inklings wanted. Her body wasn't under control when she was with Amanda. She needed some space to process, and they both needed time to recalibrate.

"If you leave your rental agreement, I'll review it," Amanda said.

"Thank you. It's all Greek to me, but I'm really excited about this place."

"I'm excited for you."

Jen gathered Kristin's things and stuffed them in her bag. "I'll talk to you in the next few days, huh?"

"How about I text you tomorrow?" Amanda asked.

"That'd be great." They found themselves at the door, Jen resting Kristin on her hip.

"How about a kiss?" Amanda asked.

Jen momentarily thought Amanda was asking her, then realized she was talking to Kristin.

Kristin leaned down, and Amanda kissed her forehead. "Love you."

That left Jen and Amanda to figure out how to say goodbye.

"Just to clarify, I meant that I'm *in love* with you, not just that I love you like a friend," Amanda said, her tone soft.

When did she start verbalizing and clarifying her feelings? She's more talkative sober than she ever was with a few glasses of wine on board.

"You know I feel the same way. I just need...I need...time. And independence. Can you give me that?" Jen asked.

"As much as you need," Amanda said, but there was an unmistakable hunger in her eyes.

Jen knew that look, having been seduced by it many times. She hesitated, holding Amanda's stare, but didn't move in to kiss her. Instead, the desire and sexual tension remained unfulfilled. It was just too soon. Too much in one day. She had taken a huge step toward emotional forgiveness but a physical reconciliation was inchoate. Once she started, she wasn't sure if she could stop herself, and she needed more time to heal.

Jen reached for the door knob, so Amanda stepped back and watched them go out to Jen's car. She waved as they later backed out of her driveway.

After Jen was safely ensconced in her car, and several blocks away, she blew out a sigh. Leaving Amanda today had been harder than she thought it would be. She actually found herself wiping away tears. Tears of uncertainty and happiness and relief. She never would've imagined that she would want to get back together with Amanda but this afternoon held such promise. She hadn't realized how much she yearned for her, as if Amanda owned her, heart and soul. She had been going through the motions of her life, taking care of Kristin, family dinners at Tommy's, practicing medicine, working out, all with a hollow feeling inside her chest. But today, being with Amanda—not Nicole—had colored in the outlines of her life.

I love her. She loves me. We could start over. We might start over, but not in that house. And not right now. I need my own space. I need to do this on my own terms and in my own time.

Damn. I want her. So bad. What am I going to do about Nicole? About Tommy?

20

North Beach

Together, Jen and Kristin walked in the front door of Tommy's house to Tommy and Cy watching college football in the living room.

"Hey, guys!" Jen said.

"Daddy! Bumpa!" Kristin ran to them.

Tommy caught her mid-air, as she leapt from the floor into his waiting arms, knocking him back against the sofa. "Whoa! When did you learn how to scale small buildings in a single leap?"

Jen laughed. "The running leap is a new thing— just started today."

"She's a mini football player. I'm not sure my body will survive this stage."

"You might have to get down on the floor and wrestle with her. She has a lot of energy right now."

"How was the apartment?" Tommy asked, already sliding to the floor with Kristin in his arms, Zane nuzzling them.

Jen set her bag down and filled a glass of ice water. She rested her buns against the counter. "I really liked it. I hope to put a deposit on it and start moving in next week."

"Wow. That was fast. Want me to look over the lease?"

"Ahh. No need. Amanda is doing that for me." She tried to sound nonchalant, but Tommy quirked an eyebrow at her.

"Amanda?"

"Um. Yeah. She babysat Kristin while I looked at the apartment, then she offered to review the lease." Jen conveniently left out that Nicole looked at the apartment with her, and they went to Nicole's afterward, where they kissed, but Jen froze and couldn't go all the way, and that she later spooned with Amanda, and they said they loved each other, and she was horny as hell, but drank tea instead of getting laid. All in one day. With two different women.

"You left Kristin with Amanda?" He sounded surprised but not accusatory.

She refocused her mind on Tommy. "Yes. I had to see the apartment and you were at work. She offered, so I took her up on it. You're okay with Amanda babysitting, aren't you?"

"Definitely. I just didn't expect *you* to be."

"She loves Kristin and Kristin was ecstatic to see her. I didn't realize..." Jen's voice unexpectedly hitched.

"How they could be a mother-daughter duo too?"

Her throat relaxed as she nodded in agreement. "You should've seen how excited Kristin was when Amanda played the cello for her. Witnessing them together sort of clinched it for me. No matter how I feel about Amanda, she's good for Kristin."

"The cello? Amanda? I never knew she played."

"Neither did I. She's really good." Jen recalled how the music had flowed.

"The decision is yours to make, but I support Kristin spending time with Amanda. I've known her for a decade, and I believe she's a good parent."

Jen was in a daze, reliving the sight of Amanda playing beautiful, rich notes then being pressed up to her back for a nap. So much was stirring to life inside her that she felt like her emotions were bubbling over like popcorn in a machine at the movie theatre. "Thanks. We'll continue…then…seeing Amanda…for Kristin."

"You're not talking about Amanda Hawthorne again, are you?" Cy yelled, turning from the game.

"Yes, Pops. She's part of our lives."

"Will she win this election?" Cy asked.

"I hope so because Gavin Morales is a criminal. If he's elected, it will be a short stint before he gets arrested," Tommy said.

"For what?" Cy asked.

"For colluding with the North Korean government to break into the Cohen Clinic computer system to steal Amanda's therapy note and Jen's email from Chance Greyson," Tommy said.

"How can you pin that on Morales?" Cy asked.

"We have our ways. Lieutenant Navarro and Agent Roxy MacNeil are investigating it. They found an electronic evidence trail, but they want to gather more financial information before we make an arrest. We don't want it to look like the SFPD is trying to influence the election."

"You're not going to let politics get in the way of actually making the arrest, are you?" Jen asked. She was firmly in Amanda's corner, her own credibility also on the line.

"No. We just want a solid case, so Morales' legal team and the media don't accuse us of trumping up flimsy evidence right before an election."

"But the public deserves to know if he's engaging in criminal behavior before they vote, don't they?"

"Yes, but Ryan wants our case to be air tight before we arrest Morales and his cronies. If we arrest and he successfully defends, then we'll look like we were supporting Amanda," Tommy explained.

"Roxy is staying in town to work on the case?"

"Yes. She's very good at this sort of thing, and it's an international situation, so both MI-6 and the CIA want an agent involved."

"Or she wants to stay in touch with Amanda." Jen still wasn't sure whether she could believe anything Roxy said.

"I don't know about that. She's been in a battle with HELLFIRE and the North Korean government for quite a while. After all, a Korean tried to assassinate her at her New York apartment."

"Don't remind me. That's where Amanda was shot and went off the rails," Jen groaned.

"All I'm saying is that she'd be involved whether Amanda worked here or not. North Korea is Roxy's specialty."

"Are they working together? Like, seeing each other every day?" Jen asked, unable to let go of images of Roxy and Amanda together.

Tommy sighed. "Please don't put me in the middle, but no, they aren't working together. I got the impression from Amanda that she didn't want to be in the same room with Roxy. *I'm working with Roxy.*"

Jen studied him, wondering if he was telling the truth or just what she wanted to hear. The photo of Roxy and Amanda at the Palace Hotel burned in her mind, making her hot with rage. "Will Roxy have to stay in town and spend a lot of time with Amanda *after* the arrest is made? Like, testifying in court?"

"I doubt it. Due to her covert status, she never testifies, you know." He cocked his head and looked at her, suddenly realizing this was more than a casual inquiry.

Jen didn't know Roxy even though she had seen a sad side of her in her office. She couldn't help but wonder whether she was being played—as in blatantly lied to. She desperately wanted to cross-check Roxy's baby story with Tommy but felt obligated to maintain Roxy's patient privacy—if Jen could call her a patient. Technically, they were just chatting in Jen's office, but she still felt an ethical obligation. "Has Roxy ever told you anything about her past?"

"Yes," he replied cautiously, glancing from Kristin to Jen and back.

"What?" she asked, trying not to look overly eager.

"A lot of stuff. Stuff that caused her a lot of pain and was the reason she got into the agency."

"Like what?"

"Why do you want to know?" he asked.

"Because she told me some stuff too, and I want to see if it's the same story."

He stopped wrestling with Kristin for a second. "When?"

"Yesterday. At the clinic."

"You talked to her?"

"For quite a while in my office. It's doctor-patient privileged, but I want to know if she was telling me the truth."

"About losing her baby?" he asked.

"Tell me more."

"She lost her infant then broke up with her girlfriend then joined MI-6. She talked almost the entire flight down to Cayman. I think she needed to unload."

"Oh." *At least she wasn't lying to me about that. However, she appears to be coming to terms with her past, and her story humanizes her more than the cocky punk she initially appeared to be. Does Amanda know about the baby? Would hearing that story change the way she feels about Roxy? The Roxy I saw in my office was pretty vulnerable, and Amanda has a strong protective gene, so she might get sucked into Roxy's emotions. Would she remember she told me she loved me? Could Amanda resist that type of emotional connection after sleeping with her? Fuck. I can't think straight.*

She caught Tommy staring at her, so she pretended like she was thinking about work. "How about our clinic computers? When will they be up and running again?"

"I have no idea. We took the hard drives for evidence, so it's up to Dr. Cohen to replace what she needs. She'll have to work with a private vendor for that."

"Good to know." Jen's phone chirped with an incoming text. Surprisingly, it was from her old colleague, Lane Wallace.

Hey, Jen. Want to get together this week? My new sailboat arrived, and I'm taking her out on a maiden voyage on Wednesday. Just a short trip outside the harbor to make sure everything is working right.

Jen replied, *What time?*

How about 3pm?

"Tommy, can you pick up Kristin from daycare on Wednesday afternoon, so I can see Lane Wallace's new sailboat?" Jen asked.

"Sure."

"He says it's a short maiden voyage in the Bay."

"That sounds great. Tell him hello from me," Tommy said.

Jen replied to Lane. *That works for me. Where do I meet you?*

Come to slip 23 at the St. Francis Yacht Club.

What can I bring? she asked.

Nothing. Just wear layers because it's warm in the harbor but cold on the Bay.

Got it.

Jen set her phone down. "What should I bring to a boat christening?" she asked Cy and Tommy.

"Bottle of champagne and a foghorn," Cy said.

"What?"

"Every vessel is required to have one. Bring one in case he hasn't bought one yet," Cy said.

"Champagne?" she asked.

"Fog horn!" he yelled then returned to watching the USC football game.

"What do you guys want for dinner tonight?" Jen asked, opening the fridge but not seeing anything. Her emotions were swirling inside, jumbling her brains.

"How about Mama Mia's?" Tommy suggested.

"That sounds perfect. I haven't seen Tina in forever," she said, referring to Tommy's twin sister.

Jen's phone chirped again. Amanda's name appeared, and Jen's heart skipped as she clicked open the text.

Thank you for this afternoon. You and Kristin righted my world.

Amanda had always had uncanny timing, as if she could sense when Jen was anxious. Jen's universe had been righted too, napping so close. Touching. If only Jen trusted her. Trusted herself not to be taken advantage of again. It was just too soon in Amanda's recovery to bank on her being faithful. Jen knew that Amanda, and only Amanda, had to be the reason she got, and stayed sober. The reason couldn't be Jen. She'd seen that scenario too many times— where the recovering person did it for a spouse, then resented the spouse later as a fun-wrecker. The sneaking and lying would start, thrusting the spouse into a policing role. Jen would *not* put herself in that position.

She texted Amanda back. *Me too. Let's take our time...make sure we're both healthy...before we start anything.*

She knew she was giving Amanda hope while simultaneously putting her at arm's length, but she had to. Amanda was going to be faced with some monumental temptations over the next few weeks—a stressful campaign and Roxy's presence at the Hall of Justice—so Jen had to see how Amanda handled those stressors independent of her.

Amanda didn't reply, which left Jen wondering if she had been too harsh. She amended her last message. *Kristin had a blast. I hope you two can get together again soon!*

Amanda replied with a smiley face containing red hearts for the eyes.

Jen's heart squeezed. She wanted to continue the conversation, but that would be misleading. Instead, she'd give it a day then ask about her lease.

When Jen looked up from her phone, Tommy was studying her. *Fuck, he probably knows exactly what's going through my mind. I have to get out of here.* "I'd like to take Zane for a walk if it's okay with you," Jen said.

"That sounds nice," Tommy said. "Want us to come?"

"Nah. You stay and enjoy the game."

Tommy rolled his eyes. She knew he preferred watching baseball over football, but it was something to do with Cy.

"Okay. Kristin and I will play. Won't we, sweetie?"

Jen changed into some joggers and tennis shoes then clasped Zane's leash to his collar. She desperately needed private time to think about the cluster her life had become.

She and Zane said goodbye, then walked up to Kearny Street and headed toward Telegraph Hill to see some greenery—the beautiful flowers on the Filbert Street stairs over the hill.

As she walked, she considered her two romantic experiences of the day, kissing Nicole versus napping with Amanda.

Nicole was youthful and vibrant, very sexy, and a fantastic kisser. There was no denying her physical beauty and sexual prowess.

Amanda, on the other hand, was in a league all her own. Charismatic. Beautiful. Smart. Powerful. Sexy in a more refined and understated way. And now, musical. And loving with Kristin. She was so much more than any other woman could ever be in Jen's eyes. Amanda was nuanced and deep. Brooding at times, but introspective and willing to confront her demons. She was a narcissist. So what? It drove her success. She was scary perceptive, knowing what made Jen tick.

The reality was that they had chemistry. It just worked. Except for when it didn't work—when Amanda took too many drugs and slept with Roxy. *Fuck if that didn't throw a wrench in our destiny. I have to let things cool. Too much happened too fast today. Space. Time. I need to let her prove—to herself—that she can make it through this stressful election, still working on a case with Roxy, without painkillers. When Roxy leaves town, I'll still be here. We'll see where we stand then.*

She made a loop down to Sansome Street then back up the Greenwich steps to Coit Tower, finally turning back down Kearny Street toward Tommy's. Her sexual need was still unsatisfied, but she felt a lot better.

21

Pacific Heights

Chance Greyson walked into his neighborhood bar on the corner of Fillmore and Clay Streets. Palmer's Tavern was an eclectic mix of diner in the front and toney country club in the back. He preferred the back, where he chose a red leather booth and ordered a Manhattan.

His eyes floated upward to the wood-paneled wall where they rested on a deer mount with a huge rack of antlers. Even though he'd looked at the mount many times, he still admired the strength in the thick neck, beauty in the face, and majesty in the antlers.

Being an outdoor enthusiast himself, he was scheduled to go on a hike in the Rocky Mountains after he got Amanda re-elected. A six-day hike at high elevation was his reward for slogging through, then winning, a muddy battle like this campaign was shaping up to be. Then again, nowadays, when was a campaign not a slug fest?

His eyes drifted to the swordfish mounted on the wall opposite the deer head. Of these two animals, which had the better weapon—the deer or the swordfish? The rack on the deer was as big as a bush, but the sword on the fish was awfully long.

Evolution had honed the buck's ability to spar, clashing antlers and retreating until the weaker buck, stunned and dazed, yielded. The swordfish, on the other hand, used its weapon to stun prey so it could eat them. Equally dangerous weapons, but used for different purposes, which reminded Chance that he had to choose the right weapon to inflict the maximum amount of damage on Amanda's opponent, Gavin Morales. Chance had many weapons at his disposal, but he wanted to tailor the strike to retaliate against Morales for condemning Amanda's relationship with Jen and for stealing her therapy note from the Cohen Clinic.

Through the years, Chance had learned that pompous blowhards like Morales were usually hypocrites. Chance had become successful in his field by turning over stones to look for dirt of the very nature the political opponent was throwing. When he had applied this method to Morales, he hadn't been surprised by the results. That wasn't even the fun part, though. The fun was just beginning.

His thoughts were interrupted by Kip Moynihan's presence. "Hi, Chance."

Chance rose and shook Kip's hand. "Thanks for agreeing to meet. Is a booth okay?"

"It's fine. Nice place. I've never been here before," Kip said, his assessing eyes scanning the clientele for familiar faces.

"My go-to bar," Chance said.

The server delivered Chance's drink. "Can I get you anything, sir?"

"What are you having?" Kip asked Chance.

"Manhattan."

"High octane. I'll have one of those too."

Chance's cocktail sat untouched while they waited for Kip's to arrive.

"How's the campaign going?" Kip asked.

"Very well, thanks. Amanda is as formidable as they come. If she were any less qualified, Morales' dirty tactics might work on her, but with a candidate like Amanda, they bounce off the Teflon."

"The release of her drug rehab therapy note was particularly cruel. Do you think Morales' campaign staff had anything to do with that?" Kip asked.

"I do. In fact, I have evidence proving they did."

The server delivered Kip's drink.

Chance raised his glass. "To uncovering the truth."

Kip smiled and clinked glasses. After a healthy swallow that left Kip whistling, he said, "That's quite the lead-in. I assume we're talking on the record."

"Always," Chance said.

"Do tell."

Chance removed a folded piece of paper from his inner suit coat pocket and set it on the table, smoothing it out and rotating it to face Kip.

"What am I looking at?" Kip asked.

"The legal record for a Cayman Corporation called, 'Truth for Election.'"

"Do you mean the website that's sponsoring Morales?"

"The one and only. I think it would behoove you to do a little investigative reporting on who formed this corporate entity."

"What does it say here?" he asked.

"Two corporations are the stockholders of Truth for Election—California Vintners and Pacific Rim."

"And, who is behind those corporations?" Kip asked.

"A few mouse clicks will tell you that Herb Whitehead is the sole stockholder of California Vintners and that the North Korean government, through another shell corporation, is the sole stockholder of Pacific Rim."

"You have to be shitting me," Kip whispered with the enthusiasm of a hunter pulling back the string on his bow. "The treasurer of Morales' campaign teamed up with the North Korean government to take down Amanda Hawthorne in a District Attorney election? What's the connection?"

"The North Koreans just had $50 million taken from their accounts around the world to hit 'em back for stealing $50 million from the Federal Reserve Bank in San Francisco."

"Please elaborate," Kip said over the rim of his cocktail.

"I can't make this stuff up. Let me connect the dots. Jina Pak's murder on Muir Beach was by North Korean operatives to eliminate her for her role in helping North Korea steal $50 million from the Federal Reserve Bank. Amanda was intimately involved in that investigation, so the North Koreans wrongly assumed that she was equally involved in clawing back the money."

"Holy shit," Kip said. "Truth for Election is all about revenge on Amanda?"

"She, Detective Vietti, and an MI-6 agent are the only visible manifestations of justice—

American-style. Amanda's re-election is an easy target, so they're going after her. The reality is that Detective Vietti and the MI-6 agent—who will remain unnamed—are far more involved in the North Korean claw-back project. However, short of killing Vietti and the agent—which they've tried to do, by the way—North Korea can't figure out the right way to retaliate."

"Do you mean that hot blonde who was photographed with Amanda at the Dyke March and again at the Palace Hotel a month ago?" Kip asked.

"I don't know who you're talking about," Chance said, his delivery belying his words. He used the opportunity to savor his drink.

"Is that why Tommy Vietti was poisoned and in the hospital?" Kip asked.

"Again, I don't know anything about that. I'm just here to talk about Amanda's campaign."

"Holy fuck. This is big," Kip whispered. "If Morales knew about this, he could be arrested for colluding with a foreign government to break into the Cohen Clinic medical record system to get dirt on Amanda!"

"And you have the scoop," Chance said, tilting his glass toward Kip.

Kip sat back and squinted at Chance. "Why me?"

"For a couple of reasons. Amanda likes you—"

"Yeah, right!"

Chance smirked as he rolled an ice cube around in his cheek. "Seriously. Like any public figure, she's not that fond of the media, but you've grown on her. Except when you ask her or Dr. Dawson about their daughter. You have to stop doing that."

"I'll try. In return for this scoop, I'll try," Kip said, waving down the server for another round.

Kip returned his attention to the paper before him, spinning it around with his index finger as he mulled over the information. "What about the negative Facebook and Twitter ads? Do you think Truth for Election purchased those?"

"I don't know, but I'm assuming you'll find out," Chance said.

They suspended their talk while the server took their drink orders and asked them if they wanted food. "Not right now," Kip said.

After she left, Chance said, "There's more."

"More? Are you kidding me? How could there be more?" Kip asked.

"Remember when Morales derided Amanda for supposedly having an affair?" Chance asked.

"Of course. Those 8x10 photos just landed on my desk one day, you know. I didn't go out looking for them."

Chance nodded patiently. "Remember when Morales bragged about being married to the same woman for 20 years and raising their children in the city?"

"Yes. He was definitely pandering to righteous voters," Kip said.

"Well, he's a hypocrite, and I have something better than an 8x10 photo to prove it."

Kip's eyes lit up as he drank his cocktail then popped the cherry in his mouth.

Chance removed a cell phone, not his own, from his suitcoat pocket. He opened it to a video and set it on the table for Kip to watch. "Hit play when you're ready."

Kip picked it up and tapped play. He watched a clear, daytime video of Gavin Morales kissing a woman—not his wife— outside a building on a sidewalk. "This is gold. Who is she?"

"No idea, but obviously not his wife. That's a full-on French kiss. It's hard to see who she is from the side angle, but I'd guess she's in her late 30's or early 40's. What do you think?"

"Could be, judging by her body shape. She's full-figured and quite a bit younger than him. The video ends right after their kiss. What happened next?"

"Exit out of the video and look at the photos on the phone," Chance indicated with a nod.

Kip clicked through a dozen photos of Morales and his paramour entering a residential building then later exiting the same building, holding hands. "These pics look like they were taken over the course of several days because they're not wearing the same clothes."

"Very observant," Chance said.

"Whose building? Hers?" Kip asked.

"You should do your own investigation—and soon," Chance said.

"What's the address of the building?" Kip asked.

"There's a pic in there of the street signs at the corner."

Kip clicked on the photo and nodded. "Who gave you the pics and video?"

"Confidential."

"They weren't altered in any way?"

"Hell, no."

"I assume Amanda Hawthorne has seen them?"

"Absolutely not," Chance said.

"Waiting for me to put the story together first?"

"You got it."

"Will she make herself available for a comment after I put the story together?" Kip asked.

"As long as it's before the voters go to the polls, sure."

"Nicely played," Kip said, holding up his glass in a salute to Chance.

"All in a day's work," Chance said, clinking Kip's glass.

"Want to stay and eat dinner?"

"I'd love to."

22

Marina District

Jen drove to the St. Francis Yacht Club and parked in the small lot. She grabbed her soft-sided cooler from the back seat and walked across the expansive lawn toward the boat slips. There was a large, white tent set up behind the club house, servers dressed in black scurrying to set up a bar inside. She chalked it up to a hoity-toity work function.

The clear sky and brisk wind promised excellent conditions for her sailing excursion with Lane. Dressed in a T-shirt and capris, Jen looked forward to getting some sunshine on the water. As she walked along the wooden docks looking for slip 23, she admired the sleek sailboats and yachts moored at their costly spots, some of their owners present and performing the never-ending chores of maintaining a boat.

When she arrived at Lane's slip, she was amazed at the sheer size of his new Beneteau, which had more hull above the waterline than the neighboring sailboats, giving the impression that it was massive. It was black with "Sense" written in cursive on the starboard side. The "S" had a long tail that ran the length of the boat.

Lane was in the cockpit, focusing on the large dashboard of electronics. "Hey, Lane. What a beautiful boat!"

He looked up, his vintage San Francisco Giants ballcap perched on his head. "Jen! I'm so glad you could make it."

He stood, favoring his right leg, which was burdened with scar tissue from the damage caused by his ex-wife, Susie, shooting him. "Please, come aboard. Forgive me if I don't jump up and help you, but the leg is a little stiff today."

"No worries," Jen said, removing her sandals and hopping on the deck. She carefully closed the gate on the railing behind her then dropped down into the cockpit to give Lane a hug. "So good to see you. Thanks for inviting me."

He returned the hug with equal force and grabbed her right hand in his when they separated. "Let's see the knuckle. How does it feel?"

"It's almost healed, but if I overdo it at the gym, it reminds me that it was broken."

He held her hand in his, palpating above her pinky knuckle, checking the metacarpal alignment. "Well, we're only six weeks out from the injury, so give it a few more weeks. It might be prone to stiffness in the future. Are you doing the exercises?"

"Oh, yes. Religiously," she said on a wink.

He released her hand. "Well, you certainly came out on top of that fight. I hope there haven't been any brawls since then."

"No. That was heat-of-the-moment rage and hopefully a once-in-a-lifetime event. I was wounded from Amanda telling me she had fooled around with Roxy."

"I'm sorry."

"Thanks. We're on better terms now. Working through some stuff, you know?"

He raised his palms. "Trust me. I get it. I'm the king of messy relationships."

She smiled. "So tell me about this beautiful boat! Did you name it 'Sense?'"

"No. That's the model that Beneteau wrote on the side. Her name is *Angelina*, which is written on the stern."

"Of course. How does Angelina feel about that?" Jen asked, referring to Lane's daughter.

"She's embarrassed, but now that she's a tweenager, she's embarrassed by just about everything I say and do, so I didn't have anything to lose."

"I remember the days myself. She'll come around in a few years." Jen patted his arm.

"Let me give you a tour below before we set sail." He walked to the companionway connecting the cockpit to the narrow stairway that spilled into the galley. Three wide steps and a sturdy railing helped Lane navigate with his stiff leg.

Down below, they were met by honey-stained wood cupboards and a dining table. The white countertops matched the wraparound fiberglass walls with multiple windows allowing sunlight in from above-deck. The sink and appliances were stainless. "This is gorgeous. It's bigger than some of the apartments I've lived in."

Lane's chuckle was like a pocket full of coins. "Me too. She's a beaut, isn't she? There's nothing like the look and smell of a new boat. She's 20 feet longer than my last Beneteau."

"You must've spent a fortune."

"I did. The insurance payment for my previous boat was substantial, and I dipped into my retirement account to cover the balance."

Her eyes widened, but she blinked away her surprise. *He used his retirement account to buy a new boat? Melissa would never approve of that.* "I brought you a bottle of champagne to christen her. Maybe we can pop the cork when we get back." She removed it from her bag and handed it to him.

He admired the label. "Thank you. This looks fantastic. I'll stow it in the fridge for later."

He showed her the two bedrooms and head, which was as spacious as any bathroom she'd been in, except for the narrow countertops running alongside the shape of the hull. She followed him back up the companionway to the cockpit.

"What do you like me to do?" she asked. "I'm at your disposal."

"If you could hop back onto the pier and untie the lines while I power up the engine, that'd be great."

In a matter of minutes, they motored out of the harbor, the sun hanging low for a short sail. Jen sat across from Lane at the second wheel on the opposite side of the cockpit.

"Why does your boat have two steering wheels?" she asked.

"Sailboats over 35 feet in length usually have two wheels, so the person at the helm can move to the high side of the boat when under sail— for better visibility," he said.

"Oh. It's kind of fun. I feel like I'm driving."

He smiled and secured his cap in anticipation of the wind they'd hit when they exited the harbor. "Can you hand me my pullover?" He pointed to a blue windbreaker on the seat and tugged it on over his Grateful Dead T-shirt. "You might want a jacket too."

As they neared the port exit, he raised the giant sails and as soon as they entered the Bay, the wind snapped the sheets taut, grabbing hold of the entire boat and energizing her.

He asked Jen to help refine the sails, but he was surprisingly self-sufficient, which was no small task on a 50-foot boat.

Jen reclined against the seat and let her head fall back, enjoying the feel of the sun, the smell of the sea, and the peaceful sounds of the boat slicing through the small swells.

"How does she drive?" Jen asked.

"Really smooth. Much nicer than my last boat." He charted a course in the general direction of Angel Island. The last time he had been on the Bay, he was being held at gunpoint by two mobsters who tried to kill him. The confrontation ended with him almost drowning, and his old boat being scuttled. What a contrast to sailing with Jen. Unbeknownst to Jen, part of today's voyage was Lane successfully overcoming the memory of that disaster.

"How is Angelina these days?" Jen asked.

"As well as can be expected. Like her daddy, she prefers San Francisco to San Diego, so she's happy we returned. I can see she misses her mom, though. It's so confusing for her. She wants to love her mother, but is conflicted because Susie tried to kill me. I scheduled an appointment for us to see a family therapist."

"Where?" Jen asked.

"None other than the Cohen Clinic."

Jen rolled her eyes behind her sunglasses. *I hope his medical record isn't hacked and his therapy notes plastered all over the internet.* "There are several good therapists there. I'm sure you'll be in good hands."

"How are you and Kristin doing with the breakup? Does she miss Amanda?" he asked.

"Tons. She asked about her every day for a month then got to see her last weekend. Amanda babysat her Saturday morning."

"How'd that go?"

"Better than I expected. They adore each other, and Amanda is really good with her. She was teaching her how to play the cello when I arrived."

"The cello? I didn't know Amanda was musical."

"Neither did I! She has so many unexpected facets to her...probably would take a lifetime to figure out," she mumbled.

"Did I hear you say she'll take a lifetime to figure out?"

"Yeah. She's a fucking riddle."

"Aren't all women?" he mused.

She laughed. "Would you like something? I brought some Pellegrino and salami and cheese from Molinari's Deli."

"I'd love some," he said, keeping his eye on the shipping and ferry lanes they had to cross.

She returned with a plate of snacks and plastic glasses full of ice and sparkling water.

He announced they had to tack, so Jen secured the food and drink while Lane talked her through the steps she had to take with the sail. She was reminded of what a good workout sailing was as she wound the sail tightly after they tacked. Back on course, they had a quick opportunity to eat and drink.

"How do you like being an outpatient doctor at the prestigious Cohen Clinic?" he asked.

"It's lower key than the ER, so there's no adrenaline rush. Melissa runs a concierge practice, and the patients' expectations are high. We treat entire families, so you get to know the parents and their children over time. I really respect the way she manages her clinic and I like the work I'm doing."

"Sounds to me like you're a little bored."

She considered that observation. "I wouldn't call it boredom. It just isn't the same intensity level as working in a trauma center. There are tradeoffs, though, because I don't miss the exhaustion and drama that went on in the ER. Also, my hours are really flexible, which frees me up to spend more time with Kristin."

"That alone is worth it."

"Exactly." She stuffed a bite of cracker, meat and cheese into her mouth.

"Was that true what Gavin Morales said on the news about you being sued?" he asked.

"God, yes. Can you believe it?" she hissed. She told him the entire story, including the care and treatment the patient received.

"That sounds like bullshit to me. I hope your lawyer gets it thrown out. I had to go through a malpractice case once. Totally sucked. All I can tell you is that it helps to talk to someone about it. Call me anytime to vent about the dickhead lawyers."

She laughed. "Touché. I can't believe that loser, Gavin Morales, outed me on the news."

"Isn't that an ethics violation?"

"Disclosing the existence of the lawsuit wasn't since it's a matter of public record. But you'd think slandering me on TV would be."

"He should be disbarred. Asshole."

"And to think Morales' name means 'morals' in Spanish. How ironic is that?"

"I hadn't thought of that," he said, chuckling.

"Changing topics, we haven't talked about *your* love life. Dating anyone?" she asked.

"I've been on a few, but I'm a helluva lot more cautious now that I'm a single dad with Angelina at home."

"I hear you. It's not just about *me* falling in love, it's about finding a woman who wants to be a parent to Kristin too. We come as a package. I have to really know someone—and trust her—before introducing my daughter to her. How have you handled that?"

"Probably not well. I haven't introduced any women to Angelina even though I've mentioned her while out on a date. If there isn't long term potential, why bother?"

"I couldn't agree more."

"Any prospects, or is it too soon since you broke up with Amanda?" he asked, keeping his eyes straight ahead.

"Ugh. Relationships are so confusing. I met someone I'm interested in, but Amanda and I still have feelings for each other, sooo—"

He nodded, his five o'clock shadow covering the lines around his mouth.

"Suffice it to say I don't know where either relationship is going. Too early to predict, I guess. Plus, we live with Tommy right now—platonically—but I'm still under his roof, so it's not conducive to entertaining, shall we say. On the bright side, I think I just found an apartment for Kristin and me so hopefully, we can move in soon."

"That does sound a wee bit complicated. I always thought you and Amanda had a pretty strong bond, though."

"Oh, we did. Do," she said.

"We need to tack again," he said. "Can you let out the main sail and get ready?"

"Aye, aye, Captain." She scooted over and released the metal clamp to let out more sail. This tack went much more smoothly than the last. When they finished, she picked up where she had left off. "Amanda is bound and determined to win me back. She told me she loves me."

"But you can't forgive her?"

"I think I'm capable of forgiveness, but I haven't really tried. I've just been holding the anger and resentment so close that it didn't occur to me to forgive and forget, like you advised me a while back."

"And?" he asked.

"And, well...we sort of took a nap together, and I really felt the connection again. There's something about us when we're together. Chemistry beyond anything I've felt for anyone else. It's like...we're soulmates. You know, she was high on painkillers and drunk when she fooled around with Roxy. After rehab, she seems disciplined about recovering and staying clean. I don't know. My mind and heart are battling with each other. My mind says take it slow, or even stay away. My heart, on the other hand…well, my heart beats faster every time I see her. I don't know what to do."

"When I feel that way, I go sailing."

She laughed. "You're a smart man. I knew you'd have good advice for me."

They sailed in silence for a time, only commenting on a passing boat or the beautiful view of Angel Island as they drew near. The trip back to the harbor flew by, and by the time they lowered the sails and motored back into Lane's slip, Jen felt more relaxed than she had in a month. The excursion had proven to be a relaxing diversion, giving her some perspective. She learned that Lane was onto something by solving his problems through sailing.

When they had the *Angelina* safely secured to the dock, Jen went down to the galley and opened the bottle of champagne. She reemerged on deck with two plastic cups full of champagne, and they relaxed in the aft cabin, enjoying the sights and sounds in the harbor and the ambient sounds of San Francisco.

"Cheers to your new boat," she said, holding up her cup.

"May she provide us many days of sailing adventure."

They clinked and drank.

"Those mobsters tried to kill me out there, but I'm back," he snorted. "They didn't know who the fuck they were dealing with. I'm unsinkable." He pounded himself on the chest.

"Like the infamous Molly Brown. Was that your first time on the Bay since that day?"

"Yep. And we did it." He patted her on the knee.

"Those stupid wise guys never met anyone like you and me," she said. "One of them shot at me in the ocean too, but he never got me. Then Amanda shot and killed him. Ugh."

"Can you believe what we went through?" He asked, his voice gravelly now. "Two physicians caught up in a fucking mob war?"

Laughter overtook them, the kind that bordered on insane.

Jen shook her head, smiling at his good mood. The absurdity of the situation they had found themselves in two years ago seemed surreal in retrospect. "How'd you survive being thrown into the Bay anyway?"

"I treaded water for as long as I could, but my bad leg was dragging me down. I was just starting to take on water when Ivanov's man picked me up in his boat." He took a healthy drink of his champagne.

"Amazing," she said.

"How'd you survive getting shot at while swimming?"

"He didn't hit me because I quickly unclipped my swimming buoy and dove to the bottom, under the waves, then swam as fast as I could at an angle down and away from the beach. It was terrifying." She tossed back the rest of the bubbly in her glass.

He waited while she ducked below and grabbed the bottle from the fridge. She returned and poured the rest into each of their red cups.

"Guess we killed that bottle of champagne," she said.

"What happened after you swam out, away from the shooter?"

She swallowed hard and grew serious. "Amanda and her bodyguard, George Banks, ran down the beach and shot the wise guy. Amanda was the last man standing in that gun battle." Jen's throat constricted on the last word, and she found herself thinking how devastated she would have been if Amanda had been killed during the shootout. A surge of love spread through her, clenching her throat.

"Then she...ahem..." Jen held up her finger for a second while she regained control. "She came running into the ocean looking for me. She was swimming between the waves, screaming my name. When I finally saw her, I knew something was wrong. She'd been shot in the arm." Jen had to stop because she was on the verge of crying— again—her brain flooded with the buzz of alcohol and the fatal sentiment she had experienced that day.

"Sounds to me like you still have feelings for her," Lane said, throwing his arm around her shoulders and hugging her.

"Very perceptive of you, Dr. Wallace. Maybe I didn't realize how much I loved her until now. She just hurt me so fucking bad." She leaned her head onto his shoulder and watched some seagulls fighting over a scrap of food on the pier.

"Yup," he said in a low, gentle tone.

They sat for a time in comfortable silence, Lane being one of the few people she could truly relax with. Maybe it was because they'd been through so much together in their ER days. Two warriors who had fought side-by-side. She had always respected and admired him as a doctor.

"Would you like to grab some dinner in the club?" he asked.

"I'd love to but am I dressed okay?"

"Oh yeah. People dine after a day on the water all the time. I'm a member, so no worries."

After locking down the *Angelina*, they entered the restaurant and Lane inquired about a table. The hostess said she'd have something in 20 minutes so they proceeded to the bar.

Jen removed her windbreaker and draped it over the back of a barstool. She grabbed the back of the stool for a second, balancing herself. The champagne, combined with the rocking motion from the boat, made her a little unsteady. "I'll be right back. Order me a glass of water, will you?"

"Will do." Lane slid onto the adjoining stool and rested his elbows on the bar.

On her way down the hall, Jen shook out her hair and pulled it back into a pony. *What a fantastic day! Lane's right. Sailing is so relaxing. That champagne wasn't bad, either. Yowzah, that went straight to my head.*

23

Marina District
Earlier

The hot sun beating down on her back, Amanda scanned the crowd as she exited the St. Francis Yacht Club onto the expansive lawn where a white tent was teeming with affluent people. Her kind of people. She forced calm upon her trembling hand that was wrapped around a cold glass of sparkling water, reminding herself there was no reason to be nervous.

These were longtime family friends, supportive and enthusiastic, here to contribute money to their favorite candidate. There were just so many of them. So many hands to shake, hugs to receive, idle chit chat to be made, smiles to be plastered on her nervous face.

Campaigning had been so much easier with Jen by her side and a glass of wine in her hand. Not having Jen with her was still painful, but she was beginning to appreciate that not being buzzed on wine was liberating, making her sharper. *God, please grant me the serenity to accept the things I cannot change; the courage to change the things I can; and the wisdom to know the difference.* She took a deep breath. *I can do this.*

Her father, Jack, saw her and emerged from the white tent, crossing the lawn to her. He was dressed informally in khakis and a blue blazer.

"Hey sweetie, how are you?" he asked, pecking her on the cheek.

"Fine. Just surveying the crowd." She forced calm into her voice.

"They're all friends you've known for decades."

"Is everything okay, Daddy? You look a little pale yourself."

He rocked his mane of gray hair. "Just got some bad news today."

"What?"

"I don't want to bother you with it right now. Maybe later."

She lowered her chin. "Out with it, or I'm turning around and walking out of here."

"Fine. My broker called and said that our account has been hacked. HELLFIRE left his signature calling card."

"Oh. Dear. God. How much?" She covered her mouth with her hand.

"Not that much— a little over $2 million. It's our personal account so we just keep some money on hand in case we want to put a down payment on real estate or something. The real money is hidden in a trust fund for you, Nate, and the grandchildren. We also have a few off-shore corporations with accounts. None of those assets have been hacked, so I put all the managers on notice. They employed extra security measures."

"I'm so sorry. I haven't been briefed on it yet by anyone at work."

"I asked Lieutenant Navarro not to bother you with it today. He's working with a senior detective by the name of Frank Degrugilliers. I told them I wanted to tell you in person."

"I know both of them fairly well."

"I'm disappointed but not worried. So don't you worry either. Navarro is working with the CIA and MI-6 to help me get it back." His smile and confidence weren't those of a man who had just lost a substantial amount of money.

"I know who that is too and she's good." His strength in the face of adversity was one of the characteristics she loved about her father.

"I'm sorry for my career splashing back on you." She adjusted his lapels.

"Small price to pay for my heroic daughter. Just get that bastard."

"That's the problem. I don't think it's just one guy. Or if it is, he has a small army at his command."

"Probably."

"And even if you get the lead guy, there will be more behind him. He's the product of a ruthless dictator with a lot of resources." She blinked a few times. "Out of our control. Come on, time to make the rounds."

Jack offered his arm and she gratefully slipped her hand through.

From that moment on, she was settled, even calm, as she and Jack worked the crowd, making promises and addressing concerns about criminal sentencing. He had been right. The partygoers were genuinely supportive and reassuring, promising not only to vote for her, but also to champion her candidacy to others.

She saw Chance across the space, cozying up to big donors. He waved her over, and she and Jack joined his group, pressing the flesh, smiling for the professional photographer Chance had hired. The photos would go on her re-election website.

To her right, Amanda heard an annoying cackle of laughter and turned. The unmistakable Mayor Woo was sidling up to a group of business leaders, laughing at their jokes, making promises he couldn't keep, and listening to their demands with an empathetic ear.

The ferret. Amanda seriously doubted whether he understood the complexities of what they were saying, much less had the power to deliver the favors they requested. However, his term of office ran simultaneous to hers so he, too, was in full campaign-mode for re-election.

"Why is Woo here?" she asked Chance. She was concerned he'd compete for her campaign dollars.

"I made a deal with him," Chance said.

"What?" She cocked her head, eyeing Chance suspiciously.

"In return for access to our shindig, he agreed to publicly endorse you, which he never has in the past."

Amanda nodded, agreeing with the horse trade. "Want to get a pic of us together?"

"Thought you'd never ask," Chance said. "Let's go over to him."

"No way," she said, maintaining her ground. "Bring him to me. I'm not groveling like a school girl for a pic with him. This is *my* party, and these are *my* people."

"I respect you more every day." Chance patted her arm then snaked his way over to Woo.

A few minutes later, he returned with Woo, who stood dutifully by Amanda's side for a pic. "Thank you, Mayor Woo."

"And, thank you, Ms. Hawthorne. I wish you the best."

"Likewise."

They shook hands for the photographer and after that, Woo was off to suck up to more of Amanda's friends.

After a few more hours of campaigning, Amanda said, "Excuse me, Chance, I'm going to the ladies' room in the clubhouse."

"Want me to escort you?"

"Actually, yes. That would be nice."

He offered an arm and they quickly made their away across the lawn to the back door of the club. "Thanks. I can find my way back on my own." Hoping to avoid a ton of women in the public restroom by the bar and restaurant, Amanda slipped into the women's locker room—used for showering and changing after a day of sailing.

She walked past the shower area and went into a stall. After washing her hands and toweling off, she rounded the wall and assessed her reflection in the large mirror overlooking the changing area.

At least my eyes are clear and my skin looks healthy.

She found a tube of lipstick in her small bag and applied the shimmering rose to her lower lip. As she outlined her upper lip, the door opened behind her and Jen entered. Amanda's hand lurched, creating a small line from her lips to her nose.

Their eyes met in the mirror, and Jen put on the brakes only a few steps into the room.

Amanda's heart skidded to a stop. Seeing Jen's intense blue eyes, full of surprise, rearranged the atoms in her body. She watched Jen assess her, her keen clinical skills cataloging Amanda's stress level and sobriety, she was sure. There were times when she felt as though Jen could see her soul, her innermost thoughts, and all of her insecurities.

"Hey. What brings you here?" Amanda asked, trying to sound casual.

"I went sailing with Lane Wallace. He bought a new boat. And you?"

"Fundraiser out back with Jack and Chloe's friends." Amanda nodded toward the back lawn.

Jen's posture relaxed and she fully entered. "I saw them setting up earlier. How's it going?"

Amanda turned from the mirror to face her. "I never knew that something so boring could be so anxiety-provoking. Jack and Chloe are helpful, though. Look at you. Sailing becomes you. Did you have fun?"

"Yeah." Jen pointed to her own lip and tapped. "You have lipstick on your upper lip."

Amanda was torn. She wanted to fix the smear but feared Jen would walk past her once she turned her back. *You're not getting away from me again.* Over the last few days, Amanda had daydreamed about getting together with Jen again. Another nap. Making a meal. Walking the beach. Anything. She yearned for more contact. Longed for it. Played over and over in her mind how their next interaction would go, her daydream always ending in a kiss. Here she stood, not having the courage or imagination to say anything. *Ask her how Kristin is. Don't let her walk away.* Amanda's mouth filled with cotton balls, and when she opened it, nothing came out.

"Need help?" Jen asked, a flash of compassion running across her face.

"Maybe. I seem to be tongue-tied. Must be campaign nerves."

A small smile formed on Jen's lips as she advanced on Amanda. She brushed against her while grabbing a tissue from the box on the counter and the brief contact further confused Amanda.

Jen carefully dabbed at the errant lipstick under Amanda's nose and, when that didn't remove it completely, she used her thumb, anchoring her fingers on Amanda's cheek.

Amanda's desire sprang into a gallop under Jen's confident touch. She breathed in Jen's healthy scent—a mixture of sunblock and sea—and absorbed the heat from her tanned body. Having no control over how she reacted to Jen, and not being ashamed of her vulnerability in the least, she leaned into Jen's touch, allowing her eyes to convey what she felt.

"Better," Jen said, still focusing on Amanda's lips. She brushed her knuckles across Amanda's cheek, then let her hand fall. She didn't step back though, which Amanda interpreted as a positive development.

Amanda wanted to grab Jen's hand, maybe guide it back over her cheek and kiss her palm. She glanced down, assuming it was the hand Jen had broken in her fight with Roxy.

"That feels better." Summoning her courage, Amanda grasped Jen's hand, running her thumb across Jen's knuckles. "I'm so sorry."

They looked at each other and Amanda saw tenderness in Jen's eyes, reducing her to a puddle. Was there forgiveness too? She couldn't tell. Maybe she was imagining what she *wanted* to see.

"I have to go. They'll be wondering where I am," Jen said, nodding toward the door. She could feel Amanda's charisma like a gravitational pull. So composed and powerful. Passionate and sensual. She looked healthy and self-assured. Jen also saw unvarnished contrition there too. She could feel herself going weak at the knees, the alcohol buzz enhancing her craving to touch. *I shouldn't keep Lane waiting. Not equipped to deal with this right now. Too tipsy. Too dangerous.*

"Yes. Of course. Is Kristin with you?" Amanda asked, her eyes lighting up at the possibility.

"No. She's too little to sail," Jen said, her voice hoarse. "I meant, Lane will be wondering where I am."

"Right," Amanda said, picking up on the subtle shift in mood. Trying to recapture Jen's tender side, she delicately played with the back of Jen's hand.

Jen felt Amanda's thumb gently rub her knuckle again, clearly signaling that she knew about the boxer's fracture. *How did she know which one?*

"I really enjoyed our nap together," Amanda said flirtatiously as she swooned toward Jen.

"Me too," Jen rasped, Amanda's caresses setting her hand on fire.

"I know the value of what we had. Once-in-a-lifetime love. I'm so sorry for screwing it up." Amanda didn't know what more to say, but she felt that being honest was all she could do. Even though she'd said all this before, she felt like she needed to say it again. Maybe a hundred more times.

Jen pierced Amanda with her eyes, full of liquid courage from the champagne. "I'm still working on forgiveness. Please give me time. You need time too, to finish the investigation and win your election. I hear Roxy is staying in town and working on the case."

Ah, the source of hesitation. She thinks I'm tempted by Roxy. Let me clear that up right now. "She's working with *Tommy*. There is no Roxy, or anyone else, in my life. There never really was."

"Let's not rewrite history," Jen warned. Her terse correction came out a little harsh, but just hearing Amanda say Roxy's name made her furious.

"You're right." Amanda moved her hand to Jen's shoulder, resting it on the front, impressed with how solid Jen's muscles had become. "I didn't mean to downplay what I did. I just meant that…well…there's no comparison. I love you and always will. You own me."

Jen stood for an eternity, allowing Amanda's warm hand to embrace her shoulder

Amanda searched Jen's face, looking for a sign of encouragement. *Please give me a second chance.*

Tears welled in Jen's champagne eyes. Angry at herself for losing control, she resisted with every ounce of energy she had. *I'm not going to cry. I'm not going to cry.* She lost the battle and a few drops trickled down her cheeks. She immediately cursed herself for being a wimp. A tipsy wimp.

Risking Jen's temper—or worse, rejection— Amanda reached up and gently thumbed away the first tears. When Jen didn't flick her hand away, Amanda moved to Jen's hair and smoothed back a few windswept strands, hooking them behind Jen's ear like she had so many times.

"I love you," Amanda said, whispering it this time, her voice breaking and lower lip trembling.

As Amanda's breath washed over Jen, a crushing weight suddenly lifted from her shoulders. She had denied their inevitable attraction—at least her side—wishing their destinies weren't intertwined. But here they were, both powerless over what flamed between them. Jen broke into a silent sob, lowering her head. *Oh fuck, I'm crying for real now.*

Amanda immediately cupped Jen's face. She raised herself on her tiptoes, so she could kiss Jen's cheeks, gently and quickly, then moved to her nose, and finally, her forehead.

Jen dropped her head into Amanda's kisses, allowing herself to receive her affection. Amanda's tender brushes soothed as well as ignited Jen's emotions. Seeking comfort and affection from the person she hoped Amanda could be, Jen fell into Amanda's embrace.

Instinctively, she wrapped her arms around Amanda's waist, holding on in a tempest of uncertainty and conflict. *Can I ever trust her again?* The familiar curve of Amanda's shape felt heavenly against her own, temporarily obliterating her reservations. Jen moaned, burying her face in Amanda's curls, her crying subsiding. The champagne buzz lubricated her need to touch and smell and taste Amanda.

When Amanda felt Jen's arms around her waist, her dreams came true. After six weeks of being apart, Amanda threw herself into Jen's solid curves, the familiar heat of Jen's body penetrating Amanda's dress, restoring her sense of what mattered in the universe—being with Jen. This minute. The two of them. Alone. Hopelessly in love.

"I've missed you so much," Amanda whispered. She ventured further by tilting her head, so she could find Jen's lips. When she nudged Jen's lips with her own, Jen was reluctant at first but inclined her head too, her lips still closed. They kissed tenderly, as new lovers might, testing the water.

How can I hate you and simultaneously want you? Jen thought. She wasn't ready to open for Amanda, still afraid of completely turning herself over.

Amanda initiated more by lightly biting Jen's lower lip, then sucking on it. She hungered for the full taste of Jen, kissing her as passionately as she could with their mouths still closed. She didn't want to push too hard too fast, but she had to have her. She gently nibbled on Jen's lower lip again, and when she released it, she heard a low moan emanate deep from within Jen's throat.

Jen's lips parted of their own accord, a fury of hormones pumping through her, clouding her thoughts. Her lips jumped into action, engulfing Amanda's eager mouth.

Amanda kissed Jen harder, and when Jen accepted Amanda's tender exploration, Amanda's legs turned to mush. *Mmm. Is that champagne I taste?* She felt Jen's hand move to the center of her back, then up to her neck, and finally into her hair, where she twined her fingers before cradling Amanda's head firmly, taking the kiss deeper.

Feeding her desire, Jen dove in with more force than she had intended.

Amanda's hands were on Jen's neck, feeling the pulse of her heart just beneath her skin, so hot from the sun. Jen's neck invited Amanda to kiss it while making love to her, as she had once cherished. Her body burned with desire, propelling her hips into Jen, sealing them together. The world spun around them like a merry-go-round.

Amanda's aggressiveness opened the floodgates of Jen's sexual frustration to a torrent of heat eddying between her legs—the place that had been ignored. Amanda was sinfully perfect. *I want you more than ever.* She glided her hand across Amanda's back again, then explored her neck—suddenly needing to touch all of her.

Reality came crashing down that they weren't alone in a bedroom when a group of women came bustling into the locker room to change out of their sailing attire and into their dinner clothes. The ladies were well into the center of the room, punching the combinations for their lockers, when Amanda and Jen registered their presence and reluctantly stopped.

"Don't let us interrupt," one of the women said playfully. They laughed, forcing Jen and Amanda to smile. They took a step back and looked at each other, raw hunger in their eyes.

"I want to be with you," Amanda said softly, so the others wouldn't hear. Sadness tinged the edges of her eyes.

"Me too, but," Jen said, wiping her mouth.

Amanda looked like Jen had stolen her soul. "Can I call you?

"I'd like that." Jen wanted Amanda as much as Amanda wanted her. She hadn't realized how powerful the sex had been with Amanda until she had come close to sleeping with Nicole. *This fucking chemistry.*

They stood staring at each other, their hands resting on each other's hips.

"We should leave," Jen said.

"I guess. I don't feel like returning to the campaign tent."

"Lane is waiting for me in the bar. I never even used the bathroom."

"Want me to wait outside while you do?" Amanda asked.

"No. Go ahead. I'm sure Jack and Chloe are wondering where you are."

Jen brushed her fingers across Amanda's cheek then passed by her toward the bathroom stalls.

24

Jen used the bathroom then stared at herself in the mirror above the sink. *Did we just share the hottest makeup kiss?* She touched her lips where Amanda's hungry mouth had been. *God, I need more of her. Please help me control myself, but I want her. With my entire being.*

She smoothed back her pony. Feeling deliciously tipsy and like she was walking on a cloud, she pushed through the door to Amanda leaning against the opposite wall, looking at her cell phone, her knee bent and one heel resting against the wall.

Jen's tummy zinged with sexual energy. She'd be damned if she let Amanda return to the fundraiser without making a plan.

"How'd I know you'd be standing here?" Jen asked.

Amanda dropped her cell in her clutch and opened her arms wide, inviting Jen to walk straight into them.

Jen collided with her, pushing Amanda into the wall, their faces only inches apart. "If you want more of me—"

"With my entire being," Amanda finished for her, turning Jen's thoughts into words. "I've never wanted anything more in my life."

Jen leaned down and brushed Amanda's lips with her own, re-igniting the lightning across the night sky. "I want you too."

Amanda raised herself onto her tiptoes and wrapped her arms around Jen's neck.

Like teenagers behind a stack in the library, they fell into a full-on French kiss, neither holding back.

Fireworks exploded behind Jen's eyes, obliterating her sense of time and place. She had the sensation of sailing again, her legs attempting to remain grounded. The only thing that mattered was Amanda. She could feel Amanda's tense body hum with excitement like her own, and she knew that they were meant for each other.

Jen moaned, further cracking the ice around her heart, now melting like a spring day and allowing her true feelings to bubble up without being trapped by anger. Her inhibitions fell one by one, motivating her to do what she finally wanted. Kiss Amanda. Taste her. Feel her. Give herself to her. *Maybe the champagne was a good idea.*

Miraculously, no one came down the hall as they ravaged each other's mouths. They slowly and reluctantly eased up on their deep kiss, but Amanda kept her grip on the back of Jen's head.

"I've gotta have you," she whispered against Jen's burning lips.

Amanda's words released another round of pheromones in Jen, creating a dizzying cloud.

Jen shivered, her hips curving into Amanda's body in an involuntary thrust. "I feel the same way."

"Wanna get outta of here?" Amanda asked, trying to be playful despite her professional exterior.

Sighing against Amanda's mouth, Jen still had the sense to listen to the caution pumping through her veins. "You know we can't."

"Like hell. Ten minutes to my house."

Jen was tempted by sexual spontaneity, but pride demanded that she not capitulate. *Amanda's house. Ugh. There has to be a better way. Something new. Can't fall into the same old routine.*

"I want to, but it wouldn't be fair to Lane or to your constituents out back. We have obligations."

"I feel like I've given them enough of me. I want to give myself to you."

Fire burned across Jen's skin, sticking like cotton candy between her legs. "Willing to walk out on a campaign fundraiser? I want you to win this election, and admit it, you do too."

"Fuck the election. I want *you*. Raising money means nothing to me. You know it never has."

Spoken like someone who has a lot of money. At least the formality had left Amanda's speech, assuring Jen that Amanda was still the Amanda she knew. Jen tilted her head and found Amanda's eyes. They burned with honest desire, and no promise of money could compete with Amanda's desire. Amanda had never been motivated by money. She did what she did because she *wanted* to, not because she *had* to. But she also had to be re-elected to DA for her mental health. Jen had learned what a broken Amanda looked like. She didn't want to be the cause of another downward spiral.

"We need to take the time. I want our reunion to be special. Maybe at my new place. Not at your place. Too many memories. I'm sorry, but I'm being honest," Jen said.

Amanda moved so she could whisper in Jen's ear. She ran the tip of her tongue over it then blew gently, her hot breath sending warm shivers down Jen's spine. "Uh-huh. I totally agree. You name the time and place."

Jen's body quivered and melted. The things Amanda knew how to do. Seduce the shit out of her. Toy with her. Drive her mad. Most importantly, Amanda knew how to deliver her to salvation. Jen groaned, shuddering with excitement. "You're very convincing when you do that."

"I hope so," Amanda said, nibbling on Jen's ear lobe. She moved to Jen's neck and found the light pulse there. She kissed her neck, sucking on the tanned skin with a feathery finish, further paralyzing Jen.

Standing was becoming a monumental task. "You're making me weak," Jen whispered.

"Good, because I really want to fuck you," Amanda whispered so softly against Jen's neck that she thought she was going to combust.

You're going to kill me with your dirty talk.

Jen felt a whoosh of air as the hallway door opened. She quickly pushed back, leaving a small space between them.

"There you are, beautiful!" Chance said, looking between Jen and Amanda. "Everything okay?"

Jen took a full step back, but still held Amanda's hand. "Hi, Chance."

"Dr. Dawson. So good to see you. How are you this evening?"

"Swell. You?"

"I'd be perfect if I had my leading lady back. Are you sweeping her off her feet?" he asked with knowing eyes.

Jen laughed at how theatrical he was. "I was sailing with a friend and ran into your leading lady. She needed a slow, sultry kiss. So I delivered."

He clapped his hands. "About time!"

"Boundaries, Chance," Amanda warned.

"I'm so happy for you, dear. You need to get laid, and you know it," he said.

"Outside, Chance." She pointed. "Wait for me outside."

Chance shrugged and winked at Jen. "I'll give you 60 seconds, District Attorney Hawthorne."

"I'll be right there," Amanda said to his back.

"He seems more fun with you than he was with me," Jen said after he left.

"Oh, trust me, he's a hoot when he's not creating messages and controlling my delivery. 'We have to stay on message,'" Amanda said, imitating him with air quotes.

"Admit it. You love every second," Jen said, smoothing back Amanda's curls where she had messed them.

Amanda leaned into Jen's touch, not giving any indication of returning to her fundraiser. "I love it when you touch me," she said breathlessly.

"Don't get me going again," Jen whispered. "I should return to Lane. He'll probably come looking for me."

"When will I see you again?" Amanda asked, a desperation to her voice that Jen had never heard.

"On election night?" Jen asked.

Amanda's eyes grew wide and her mouth fell open. "You wouldn't dare make me wait that long!"

Jen laughed. "It's only a week away. Be the master of your own domain, girl."

"You're torturing me."

"You need to focus on your job and the campaign. I'd be a distraction."

"But such a welcome one. So full of pleasure and satisfaction," Amanda said, hooking her finger under Jen's jaw. "Will you come to my election party? Win, lose, or draw, I want to share it with you."

"I'll think about it." Jen allowed Amanda to kiss her again, slowly moving her mouth from side-to-side, savoring the taste and feel. *Oh, how I want to get lost in you.*

Amanda pulled back. "If you're still here in an hour, I'm coming to find you. We don't have to go to my house. We could go anywhere you want. I just want to be with you."

Jen laughed. "Election night, sexy. Let's plan on getting together then. All night."

"If you insist," Amanda groaned, her brown eyes pleading.

"Text me," Jen said, wiping the smudged lipstick from the perimeter of Amanda's lips.

"Can I sext you?" Amanda tilted her face into Jen's hand.

"What if our phones are hacked? Would you want our dirty sexts to be in the news?"

"At this point, I'm not so sure I'd care. But I have a solution. I'll have a burner phone delivered to you at work."

"You can't be serious."

Amanda's face lit up at the possibility, her right brow arching. "Oh, but I am."

"How clandestine."

"It's a plan then. Until we can be together."

Chance opened the door and peeked his head inside. "It's time, Amanda." He sounded serious.

"Bye, Candidate Hawthorne." Jen broke away and walked backward toward the bar.

Amanda stood her ground, locking eyes, a hungry look on her face.

When Jen reached the end of the hall, she blew Amanda a kiss then turned and disappeared around the corner into the bar area.

25

The Next Day

Will you come to my election party? Win, lose or draw, I want to share it with you. Amanda's words haunted Jen, distracting her from focusing on her patients. Stethoscope draped around her neck, she hustled and bustled from one exam room to another, attentively listening, diagnosing, and treating, while the wings of a dove thumped in her chest.

If we got back together, would she be loyal to me? Or would reuniting enable her to have another affair five years from now? On the other hand, if I don't take a chance on her—trust her—what would my life look like without her? With someone like Nicole?

Jen's desk phone buzzed, cutting into her gossamer web of drama. It was Ginny.

"Yes?"

"There's a special delivery for you up here. He won't let me sign for it. Says you have to."

"I'll be right there." Jen hung up, curious as hell.

She arrived at the front desk and signed the electronic screen a courier held out to her. He gave her a bulging, padded-mailer.

Ginny watched, obviously expecting Jen to open it in front of her.

"Thanks Ginny." Jen disappeared behind the door and returned to her office, where she cut open the package. A burner phone. There was a Post-it note on it in Amanda's handwriting: "Turn me on and text Amanda!"

Just what the doctor ordered, Jen thought. When she turned it on, Amanda's name was the only one in the contacts list, so she sent a text. *My lips are still burning from your hot kiss.* Jen didn't know what was more fun—getting the phone or sending the first text.

Shannon, her nurse, stuck her head in Jen's office, disrupting her new game. "Your next patient is here."

"Right. Who again?" Jen asked.

"Mr. Tom Richgels. He's here for an annual medication refill on his Synthroid."

"How long has he been with the practice?"

"He and his wife joined a few years ago. He's a big wig with a tech company—lots of money. He knows Melissa's husband."

"Friends with Bruce, huh?"

"I think they work together. Personally, I don't care for him."

"Why?"

"Just something about the way he acts, like he's hiding something. Shifty, you know?"

"Okay. Good to know. Let me look him up in the new EMR to get some background." Jen turned to her computer screen. Melissa had just purchased a new electronic medical record— the same brand as the old—and the vendor's team had recovered 80% of the old medical record data, which was a miracle considering HELLFIRE had tried to destroy it.

"There isn't much in there. He comes in annually for a physical and a Synthroid refill," Shannon said, nodding at Jen's screen.

Shannon had already looked him up at the nurse's station.

"You're right as usual," Jen said, glancing through the scant info. She stood and automatically reached for her stethoscope, still draped around her neck.

She followed Shannon down the hall and knocked on the exam room door.

"Come in," a male voice said.

Jen walked in to find Mr. Richgels sitting in a chair next to the small desk. He stood and they shook hands. He waited for her to sit at the desk before returning to his seat. The computer screen was on, but Jen faced him, sitting knee-to-knee in the small room. He was a tall man whose legs filled up the small space.

"What can I do for you today?" she asked.

His eyes travelled the length of her body. "I could think of a lot of things, but I'm here for my annual choking test so I can get my Synthroid refilled."

She let the comment slide. "Has anything changed with your health in the last year?"

"Nope. This high-performance machine is still going strong. In fact, that was one thing I wanted to discuss with you. I'd like a prescription for some Viagra too."

"Tell me about that," she said, wondering if Viagra was the real reason for his visit.

"Well. Uh. The soldier stands at attention, but not always when I want him to and not for the same amount of time as he used to."

"So, when your wife is ready, your erection has already passed?" she asked, careful that her tone was neutral and not demeaning.

"Yeah, and I'm not as good for as long as I used to be."

"Any trouble urinating?"

"No. That department works just fine. Stream is strong, and I finish without dribbling like the old guys."

"Okay. I might suggest Cialis instead of Viagra because it will allow more flexibility for timing. You can take it before you go out to dinner and be ready for several hours.

"Whereas Viagra will give me a hard-on right away?"

"Pretty much. Let me enter Cialis into your medical record." She waved her badge over the recognition bar and updated his medication list, which populated quickly in the new system. "Do you have any history of heart disease?"

"No."

"How about any family members with heart disease"

"No."

She entered his responses. "Let's have you sit on the exam table, so I can listen to your heart and check your thyroid."

She waited until he was perched at the end of the table, his knees extending out further than most, his large dress shoes resting on the footrest. She stood at his side and placed the diaphragm of her stethoscope on his chest for a few beats, then she moved the diaphragm to his back. "Take a deep breath for me."

He did.

"Again."

He did.

"Heart and lungs sound good," she said, returning to his front. She removed the scope from her ears and draped it around her neck. "I'm going to check your thyroid now. It might be a little uncomfortable."

"I've had it done before. The choking test."

Jen stepped between his knees and placed her thumb and index finger on his throat to palpate his thyroid. As she began her exam, she felt his hands land firmly on her ass. He squeezed tightly, lodging her hips between his legs.

"Whoa!" she squealed.

He smiled. "Sorry. Automatic reaction when a woman steps between my legs. You have a nice ass." He didn't remove his hands.

Momentarily flustered, she couldn't believe that he was groping her. She placed her hands on his shoulders and pushed.

He tightened his grip.

"Get your hands off my ass, Mr. Richgels."

His eyes took on a lascivious glint. "Are you sure?"

"Very. I'm a doctor, and you're my patient. Let me go—now!"

"Fine. Your loss. I heard you play for the other team, so I guess it's true." He let go.

She slapped him across the face. "You think I must be gay because I won't let you sexually assault me? You're an ass. Get the hell out of my clinic."

The predatory look slid off his face, instantly replaced with anger. "With pleasure."

The door swung open and Shannon appeared. "I heard yelling. What's going on?"

"That," Jen said, pointing. "He just grabbed my ass!"

Shannon sized up the situation and extended her hand to Jen to guide her out of the room.

Richgels hopped off the table and stood, towering over the women. "Look at my fucking face! She slapped me! I'm gonna sue this place!"

"Come on, Dr. Dawson. Let's get out of here." Shannon grabbed Jen by the hand and led her out the door. "Mr. Richgels, you need to leave. Now!"

He bulldozed his way out the door, pushing them aside. "You haven't heard the last of me. That dyke bitch fucking hit me! I'm telling Bruce and Melissa." He stormed off, leaving a shocked staff in his wake.

"Go to your office and close the door," Shannon said to Jen. "I'm going to make sure he leaves." She followed him down the hall and into the waiting area. He paused like he was going to talk to Ginny but when he saw Shannon watching him, her cell phone in her hand, he thought better of it and stormed out the glass doors to the elevator.

"What's going on?" Ginny whispered.

Shannon leaned down so the waiting room full of patients wouldn't hear. "If he comes back, hit the panic button and call 911. He just assaulted Dr. Dawson."

"Oh, shit. Shouldn't we be calling the police anyway?"

"I don't know yet. I have to tell Dr. Cohen."

Jen paced in her office, her heart racing. *What a fucking monster. What will Melissa think? I slapped one of her patients, a colleague of Bruce's, no less. Will she be pissed?*

There was a light tap on her door. "Yes?"

"It's Shannon. I'm coming in."

When Shannon entered she held her arms wide for a hug. Jen appreciated the gesture, hugging her. "I'm sorry. I don't know why I'm crying."

"Because you're scared, that's why. Being violated is terrifying."

"I can't believe he did that. Will Melissa fire me for slapping a patient?"

"Don't be ridiculous. She'll fire *him* before she fires you. She's in with a patient, but her nurse will send her to your office as soon as she's finished."

"What about my next patient?"

"Relax. I'll take care of it."

There was a knock on the door. "Come in," Jen said.

Melissa entered. "What's going on? I heard you needed to see me."

Before Jen could talk, Shannon said, "Dr. Dawson was sexually assaulted by Tom Richgels. She slapped the asshole to set herself free. She's going to tell you all about it while I room the next patient." Having set the context and background, Shannon squeezed by Melissa and left.

"Is this true? Tell me what happened," Melissa said, closing the door.

"I'm so sorry. I feel like I'm bringing bad luck to your clinic," Jen said, her eyes welling up again.

"Nonsense. I've never liked Tom. Bruce told me he's cheated on his wife for years with several women at the office."

"Well, they might not be consenting." Jen told Melissa what he said and did to her during the thyroid exam. "If I weren't confident and strong, I think he would've taken it a lot further."

"The bastard. That pretty much sums it up for me. I'm terminating him from our clinic," Melissa said. "No one does that to one of us and comes back. He's out of here."

"Thank you. I'm so sorry," Jen said.

"Stop apologizing. It's not your fault. It's *his*. Don't let that asshole do this to you. He's a letch."

"You're right. I don't know why I feel like I did something wrong when I didn't."

"Do you think you can continue seeing patients?" Melissa asked.

"Of course."

"Darn, because I was hoping to get out of a meeting. I'd rather see your patients," she joked.

"Thank you, but I'm fine now."

"Do you want to call the police? Press charges?" Melissa asked.

"I don't know. That sounds like a contentious battle, and I was just in the news for a malpractice case that I have to fight. Then there's Amanda's campaign, and that's an epic battle too. I'm tired of fighting. I didn't go into medicine to fight, much less be in the public eye.

I just want to crawl under a rock and live my life, hoping never to see him again."

"I can see why some of the fight has left you today. Why don't you sleep on it? Maybe talk to Tommy too. He might have some advice about getting the police involved," Melissa said.

"I will, but as of right now, the fact that you're going to terminate him from the clinic is enough for me."

"I'll have Vicki draft a letter for me to sign right away. Let's talk tomorrow," Melissa said, patting Jen on the shoulder.

"Thanks Melissa."

Jen saw a few more patients then left for a pre-scheduled meeting with Guy Deluca, her lawyer, for a quick sandwich in a small deli across the street.

When she arrived, he stood from the table. They shook hands and ordered their sandwiches at the counter.

"Thanks for agreeing to see me on short notice," he said. "I don't trust texting or emailing anything to you in the current electronic environment."

Jen sat across from Guy at a tiny table while they waited for their sandwiches to be delivered. She let her eyes wander over his lawyerly appearance. His tailored suit and Jerry Garcia tie bespoke not only of sartorial acumen, but also of some rebel underneath.

"My private investigator, Rick Spinelli, got some video of the patient who's suing you," he said.

"Really? That was fast. Let's see."

He handed her his cell phone. "Hit Play. That's her flying a kite at Chrissy Field."

Jen knew the grassy field well. It was in the Marina District next to the Bay, a popular destination for people on Saturdays. She and Kristin had gone for strolls there and watched the kites many times. The video focused on a woman holding a spool, rolling her right wrist— the one with the fracture—over and over while letting out the line. Once the kite was up in the sky, the woman deftly used both of her wrists to control it.

"She makes that look easy," Jen said. "I don't see any limitation or disability in her wrist with those movements."

"Neither do I. But wait, there's more," he said, motioning for her to hand his phone back. "Rick went to a club where her band was playing last night and grabbed this video of her playing bass guitar. Check it out."

"She plays in a band?" Jen asked.

"Yep. We picked it up off her Facebook page." Guy handed Jen his phone again, and she watched in amazement at how the woman played without a care in the world, her right hand picking the bass notes while her left moved up and down the fret. "She isn't limited in any way."

"I have a third video. Here," Guy said, teeing it up for her.

Jen watched a short video of the woman riding a bicycle, standing up and leaning hard on the handle bars to pedal up a hill, putting lots of pressure on her wrists. "That's probably the best indication of full functionality of all the videos. My wrists take a beating biking. She's working hard."

"That's what we thought too."

Their sandwiches arrived.

"So what does all this video mean, aside from the fact that she's a liar and just trying to use the lawsuit for a big payoff?" Jen asked.

"Well, if I play my hand—no pun intended—too early, she and her lawyer might dream up excuses for what we just saw. I know him, and he's never been receptive to logic early in a case. The better course is for me to notice up her deposition and get her on the record describing her 'injuries and damages.' I'll walk her through all of her life activities— things she could do before the accident versus the things she alleges she can't do now. Hopefully, she'll fall into the trap of saying she can no longer fly kites, play bass, or bike, all under oath."

"What if she doesn't?" Jen asked around a bite.

"I'll be sure to work them into the conversation. No worries. Once I have her testimony locked in, a few days later, I'll show her lawyer the video that proves otherwise. I'll tell him to drop the case, or I'll file a motion for sanctions because she obviously perjured herself."

"Perfect. Can we countersue, so I can recover for the loss to my reputation this lawsuit has caused?"

"Sorry. Afraid not. As I explained last time, not even this video would be enough for us to prevail in state court. You'll just have to settle for the satisfaction of getting the case dismissed without making a payment."

"Not fair. Gavin Morales called me a quack on the evening news."

"That's a different issue. He was out of line."

"Maybe I should be suing him," she said.

"Or making a complaint to the Bar Association for unprofessional conduct."

"Would you help me do that?"

"How about we wait until both the election and this lawsuit are over?"

"Pretty shitty system that allows what happened to me."

"Most of the time, our system works very well, but I agree that both this patient and Morales tried to take advantage." His voice remained neutral, not a hint of anger or condescension.

Jen appreciated his equable nature. He definitely had a calming effect on her.

They finished their sandwiches and Jen thanked him for his excellent representation. They parted on an upbeat note, and she returned to clinic with a positive attitude, finally feeling like someone was truly in her corner.

26

The Hall of Justice

Lost in thought at her desk, work the furthest thing from her mind, Amanda was reliving every minute of kissing Jen at the Yacht Club. *We kissed last night,* she thought as she touched her lips where Jen had. *I told her I loved her and she didn't shut me down. She fixed my lipstick and told me she needed me.* Her heart filled with hope.

She had to win Jen back. Not just to get laid. Their relationship was never about just getting laid. Okay, maybe a little was about how good the sex was, but more importantly, Jen was her true soulmate. The only woman who ever understood her. All of her. The unvarnished truth inside of her. Amanda had safely and confidentially turned herself over to Jen.

And the best part was that Jen had never judged. Until Amanda blew it, of course. Then she deserved Jen's judgment. For how long, she wasn't sure. *Has enough time passed?* Actually, now that she thought about it, she was probably lucky that Jen hadn't pummeled her the way she had Roxy. *I got off easy.* Amanda couldn't help but smirk when she pictured Jen breaking Roxy's nose. *Why is that so funny? Probably because violence is so out of character for Jen, yet she resorted to it for me.*

Jen was everything in a woman that Amanda wanted. The way Jen's brain worked was sexy

311

as hell as Amanda remembered how quickly Jen had solved the password code that Jina Pak had left in her safe deposit box.

She was continuously impressed with Jen's knowledge of medicine, her dedication to being a good doctor, how she took care of everyone's needs—especially her patients'—before her own.

She thought about what a good mother Jen was. Her utter love of and devotion to Kristin.

She smiled as she thought about what a fantastic cook Jen was. Her delicious Italian dinners. How sweet the house had smelled when Jen had lived with Amanda in Sea Cliff— like basil, garlic, and wine in a red sauce, simmering in a pot on the stove.

She thought about the respect Jen showed to Tommy and her commitment to co-parenting with him.

Unlike the professionals in Amanda's world, Jen ran her life without gamesmanship or manipulation. She was earnest and straightforward, beautiful inside and out. She didn't harbor any guile, which was such a refreshing change.

Amanda came to rest on Jen's intense blue eyes. Her tanned skin. Her glow from sailing. How she smelled of sunblock and the sea the other night. Amanda ached to kiss her—from head to toe. *Did she get the burner phone yet?*

"Amanda. Knock, knock. Is anyone home?" Tommy asked from her doorway, Roxy standing next to him.

"What? Oh. Hi, guys. Please, come in," Amanda said, shaking off her obsession.

"Are we intruding?" he asked.

"No. Of course not. Just thinking through some things," she said, watching them enter and take the seats in front of her desk.

"Have time to talk about our investigation?"

"Always." She avoided eye contact with Roxy.

"Roxy and I have been discussing some things with Jeremy—"

Amanda raised her eyebrow.

"Hear me out. We had a good reason," Tommy said.

She nodded, glancing at Roxy, whose nose was still puffy. *Damn, Jen. You really lost it.* Amanda smiled apologetically, but Roxy didn't return it.

"To protect you from being placed in a conflict, therefore subject to criticism in your campaign, we sought Jeremy's counsel and help with getting search warrants," he said.

"For what and where?"

He ticked off a list on his fingers. "For the campaign headquarters, legal offices, and home of Gavin Morales; the home and office of the Treasurer of his campaign—Herb Whitehead; a business in Healdsburg called California Vintners; and the Facebook and Twitter advertising departments to see who paid for negative ads about you."

"Fascinating. What criminal evidence is the subject of the warrants?"

"Computer drives with financial records and other proof that Gavin Morales' team colluded with the North Korean government to hack into the Cohen Clinic computer system. With the help of a wiretap we got last week, we've obtained emails between California Vintners and Pacific Rim. The emails are full of conversations about digging for dirt on you at Cohen Clinic. Dirt that could be put on the Truth for Election website."

"So, basically, Herb Whitehead, on behalf of Morales, teamed up with Yon Song-Muk to smear me," Amanda said.

"Yes. Yon Song-Muk and HELLFIRE went apeshit after they figured out you were with me in New York and on Cape Cod," Roxy said, crossing her pencil-thin legs and swinging her Givenchy boot.

Don't fucking remind me, Amanda thought, but didn't say. "Is my life in danger again?"

"Probably not. Certainly not to the extent mine is," Roxy said.

"I'm sorry," Amanda said.

"I should be the one apologizing for putting you in that position."

Even though Roxy wore the trappings of a work face, Amanda couldn't help but wonder if she was talking about sex on the Cape. "Apology accepted."

Roxy shrugged, her patrician mask covering any emotion.

"Anyway," Tommy said, ignoring the communication between the two women, "We need solid proof of their conspiracy to break into the Cohen Clinic medical record to get your therapy note before we can make an arrest."

"And Chance's email to Jen," Amanda supplied, reminding him. Someone had to advocate for Jen.

314

"That too. HELLFIRE is very good at hacking and stealing," Tommy said.

"Morales and Whitehead must be impressed," Amanda gritted.

"Now you know why Jeremy's name, and not yours, was on the wiretap warrant and will be on the briefs accompanying the search warrants. We don't want to look like we're busting everyone to influence the election."

"Agreed. What's your timeline?" she asked.

"Tomorrow," he said.

Amanda sucked in a breath. "That's faster than I expected. Can I discuss this with Chance, so we can put together some talking points for the media?"

"Absolutely not," Tommy said. "You know that loose lips sink ships. We'd never do that in any other case."

"You're right." She tsked. "I got ahead of myself. I'll work on my own talking points. *After* you execute the search warrants, I'll discuss them with Chance."

"Good girl," Tommy said.

"I hope you uncover more intel on North Korea that helps your future efforts—whatever those might be after San Francisco," Amanda said to Roxy, speaking in the vague and evasive terms that spies loved.

"Me too."

"Back to New York?"

"Something like that, I suppose."

"I haven't seen any cigarettes floating under your nose lately."

"That's because the good Dr. Dawson slapped a nicotine patch on my arm." Roxy patted her right deltoid.

Amanda blanched but quickly recovered. She squinted at Roxy. *Jen? Roxy's doctor?* "You're joking."

"Actually not. When we were at the Cohen Clinic, I chatted with her about some…ah…miscellany…and she gave me the doctor speech about smoking causing cancer. Bloody boring, blah, blah. Then she hopped up and slapped a patch on me before I knew what was happening. She was as fast with the patch as she was with her left hook." Roxy pointed to her nose.

"I heard about that. So unfortunate. Must have been painful."

"Very," Roxy said, referring not only to the nose break, but also the Amanda break.

"We're powerless over matters of love and rage. There's nothing we can do, is there?" Amanda asked rhetorically.

Roxy nodded once, her eyes holding Amanda's, signaling she registered what was conveyed.

Having used all the spy craft-speak Amanda could think of to tell Roxy that: (a) she shouldn't have taken her to New York; (b) she unfairly seduced her; (c) Roxy deserved to get punched in the face by Jen; (d) there were no hard feelings; (e) she expected Roxy to leave town after the arrests were made; and (f) Amanda wasn't changing her mind about getting back together, Amanda was out of things to say.

Tommy looked from one woman to the other. "Good. Glad we got that cleared up. Roxy and I will be off. Just wanted to give you the heads up, so you didn't get caught flat-footed in front of the media."

"Thanks for thinking of me," Amanda said.

On their way out the door, Tommy turned and said, "Did you hear the good news?"

"About what?" Amanda asked.

"Ryan got the job for Chief of Police," Tommy said, referring to his cousin.

"Excellent! I was wondering how the interviews were going and when they were going to announce. I should go congratulate him."

"You should. He's in a good mood today," Tommy said, slapping the door frame.

"In that case, you should ask for a raise."

"Already did." He winked and left.

That went well, Amanda thought. *And I didn't feel a thing for her. What the hell had I been thinking six weeks ago?*

She checked her burner phone—her new intimate connection with Jen—for messages. A text had arrived while she had been meeting with Tommy and Roxy. *My lips are still burning from your hot kiss.*

Tingles spread down her arms. She replied, *Can't wait to set fire to other parts of your body. How's your day going? All I can think about is you.*

She returned the burner to her bag and grabbed her other cell phone. She took the stairwell to Ryan's floor, where she found him walking the halls, joshing around with his staff. "Hey, Ryan. Congratulations."

He ambled over to her and surprised her with a big bear hug. "Thanks Amanda."

"Have a minute to talk?" she asked.

"For you? Anything. Follow me." He led her to his office and closed the door. She sat, and he rested his butt against the front of his desk, facing her.

"When is the announcement?" she asked.

"Later today."

"I'm thrilled for you. You earned this position, fair and square."

"Thanks for your support. If you're wondering if it's going to be reciprocal, fear not. I support you, hands down, and I plan to say so when asked."

She sighed in relief. "Thank you. I owe you one."

"Actually, you owe me two. Remember the eyewitness accounts from China Beach when you shot Eddy Valentine?"

"I'd forgotten about that," she fibbed.

"Let me remind you because it's coming up again. Some people could've sworn you shot him *after* you disarmed and interrogated him." He leveled a stare at her.

"Well. I don't remember it that way. So many things happened at once, all in a matter of seconds." She tilted her head, studying his body language to see whether they could agree on that story.

"That's what I told the senior officer in charge of the reports. You did a service for the force, avenging the death of George Banks, and

318

stopping a known killer from further harming yourself or anyone else. I just want to make sure we know where we stand on the favor tally."

"Thanks for reminding me. Glad we see eye-to-eye on how that went down. You know I always have your back, right?"

"We have each other's backs. Now, get out there and win your election. I fucking hate Gavin Morales."

"Me too. Congrats again and have a good press conference this afternoon."

Amanda stood and Ryan pushed off from the edge of his desk to shake her hand.

She left his office and walked through his department, greeting several people who wished her good luck on her campaign.

God, I love this job, she thought as she headed back to her office to create some draft talking points about her opponent's home and office being searched. *And I love Tommy. He'd better fucking find something on Gavin Morales' computers.*

27

That evening

Jen picked up Kristin from daycare and drove to Tommy's house. They had about an hour to play, walk the dog, and finalize dinner before Tommy got home. As they drove up Vallejo Street, Jen saw Cy standing outside his house chatting with an elderly woman.

As she drove by, she slowed, rolled down her window, and waved. "Hey, Cy!"

He didn't hear her, but the woman he was talking to did and nudged him to look. He waved back then disengaged from their conversation and motored up the hill toward Tommy's house as fast as his elderly gait would allow.

He arrived in time to watch Jen park in a vacant spot close by. "How are my girls today?"

"Bumpa!" Kristin said from the back seat.

Cy stood patiently on the sidewalk while Jen removed Kristin from her car seat. As soon as Kristin's shoes hit the sidewalk, she ran to Cy and hugged him. He lifted her up for a kiss, and she grabbed the herringbone flat cap off his head to reveal his short-cropped, grey hair.

"Whee!" she screamed, waving his cap in the air.

"Kristin. Give Bumpa back his cap," Jen said as she grabbed their bags from the car.

Kristin plopped it askew on his head.

"Thank you," he said politely, setting her down, adjusting his cap, and reaching for her tiny hand.

As they walked hand-in-hand down the street, Jen slowed behind them, taking pics on her cell phone. Cy was bending over slightly, looking down at Kristin, who was bouncing along to keep pace, her ponytail bobbing up and down. She wore a powder blue jacket with pink leggings and white tennis shoes, a stark contrast to his gray slacks and tweed blazer.

Jen immediately knew she'd treasure this photo—grandfather and granddaughter walking together on the street where Cy had lived for over 50-plus years. "Are you available to join us for dinner tonight, Cy?"

"Only if you have enough," he said.

"We have more than enough. I put a pot roast, potatoes, and carrots in the slow cooker when we left this morning."

"It sure smelled good when I stopped by and took Zane for a walk this afternoon," he said.

"Aw. You walked Zane for us? Thank you so much," Jen said, thinking what a sly devil he was.

"It's the least I can do. You kids have busy jobs," he said.

Jen's heart squeezed. *If I move to the Sunset District, we won't see Cy on a daily basis. Or Tommy, for that matter. Everything will have to be scheduled. There's something to be said for bumping into Bumpa when we get home. He's an important part of Kristin's life. On the other hand, how am I going to get any privacy with Amanda if I rent an apartment in*

Tommy and Cy's neighborhood? Cy doesn't like Amanda, and he obviously disapproves of our relationship.

Jen unlocked the front door and they entered the living room to the smell of a homecooked meal. Zane greeted them, tail wagging. "Hi, Zaner!"

"Yaner," Kristin imitated, petting his head and giggling when he licked her face.

"I suppose he should go out again," Cy said.

"Probably," Jen said. "Do you want to take him, or should I?"

"I will. We have a route, don't we, boy?"

After Cy left with Zane, Jen fed Kristin a snack, got her situated in the living room where she could see her, and made the last-minute meal preparations. A while later, Tommy and Cy entered together while Jen was reducing the meat juice to a gravy in a sauce pan on the stove.

"Excellent. Another one of Jen's homemade dinners," Tommy said, coming to her in the kitchen and giving her a hug from behind.

"Thanks Tommy. How was your day?"

"Exciting. I'll tell you about it later." He leaned down and picked up the apple of his eye.

"Daddy!"

"How's the most beautiful girl in the whole wide world?" he asked.

"Good!" she said, making him smile.

They sat down to dinner as a family, Zane sitting next to Jen, his head on her lap, his expressive brown eyes hoping for a morsel.

Bumpa said grace and they dug in.

"How was clinic today?" Tommy asked. "Is your electronic medical record back online?"

"Yes," Jen said with relief. "Melissa had to buy a whole new system, but we're up and running. They recovered most of the data in the old system but not all of it. It's better than nothing, though. The paper world sucked. Of course, the electronic world doesn't stop the crazies and creeps from coming in."

"Crazies and creeps?" Tommy asked.

"A patient assaulted me in my exam room today. Really scared me."

Tommy's happy expression fell. "How?"

Jen explained what Tom Richgels did to her, not disclosing the name.

"I wish you would have called me. I would've taught him a lesson," Tommy said.

She rested her hand on his forearm. "I'm sure you would have, but my main goal was to kick him out and keep him out."

"Do you want to give a statement and file charges?"

"I'll think about it. My life is pretty full of legal battles and media coverage right now, so I'm not sure I want to add another layer."

"Well, think about it and let me know if you do."

"Speaking of calling you, can I get two hours of your time tonight?"

"Sure. For what?"

"To help me move some stuff over to my new apartment."

"Did you say, 'new apartment?'" Cy asked.

"Yes. Kristin and I have overstayed our welcome at Tommy's. I rented a nice place in the Sunset District overlooking the ocean. You should come with us tonight, Cy, so you can see it," she said.

"Then I won't see you when you get home from work with Kristin," he rasped.

"I'm sure you'll see plenty of us but no, we won't run into you as much." A surge of guilt hit her hard in the chest.

"I'll miss my little girl." He rubbed Kristin's cheek with the back of his knuckle.

Tommy looked at Jen with his puppy dog eyes. "I'll miss my girls too. Will you have us over to dinner at your new place?"

She laughed. "Of course. We're family."

While they were washing the dishes after dinner, the local news reported that Ryan Delmastro was promoted to the Chief of Police.

"Wait a minute," Tommy said. "I want to hear this." He turned up the volume, and they all watched.

At his press conference from the Hall of Justice, Ryan made a few remarks at the podium then opened it up for questions from the media. Kip Moynihan was front and center. "Are you endorsing either candidate for District Attorney?"

Ryan nodded confidently. "The SFPD Union has officially endorsed District Attorney Amanda Hawthorne. I've known DA Hawthorne for years and have worked side-by-side with her. She's done an excellent job and I fully support her for re-election."

"Follow-up question," Kip said. "Is it true that SFPD covered up eyewitness accounts at China Beach that DA Hawthorne shot Eddy

Valentine *after* she disarmed and interrogated him?"

"We don't disregard witness accounts during investigations, but sometimes shootings can cause people to remember things differently, especially if their own lives are in danger. From the time Valentine shot at Dr. Jen Dawson— who was swimming—then shot and killed Police Officer George Banks, to when DA Hawthorne shot and interrogated him, less than a minute transpired. A lot of things happened simultaneously. As I understood the full report, Valentine died as DA Hawthorne was talking to him. She did a commendable job protecting herself and others from an armed gunman who had just shot a police officer. We closed that file two years ago."

"So you're agreeing there were conflicting reports from the eyewitnesses?" Kip asked.

"Not to my knowledge," Ryan said, cutting off Kip and moving on to another reporter's question.

Tommy took a deep breath and made a note to discuss that situation with Ryan. He had been in Hawaii at the time but remembered how crazed Amanda was during her war with the mob. She was protecting Jen with her entire being, so caught up in their new relationship.

"I don't remember it that way," Jen said. "That MF was shooting at me in the ocean, and Amanda saved my life!"

"Did you see her shoot Valentine or interrogate him?" Tommy asked.

"No. I was out in the surf."

"Well, either way, she owes Ryan big time for the endorsement and defense of her character," Tommy said.

"That's my nephew—Chief of Police!" Cy said, pointing at the TV.

"Would you like to go to his swearing-in ceremony with me, Pops?" Tommy asked.

"Absolutely! When is it?"

"Next Thursday. I'll pick you up at ten in the morning."

"I'll be ready."

"Would you two like to help me move some stuff now?" Jen asked.

"If you insist on moving out, I'll help," Tommy said.

While Cy entertained Kristin, Jen and Tommy loaded their SUVs with several boxes, lamps, and furniture that she had been storing in his basement. She drove her truck, and Tommy, Cy, and Kristin followed in Tommy's old Jeep.

When they arrived, Cy and Kristin toured the apartment, especially focusing on Kristin's bedroom, while Jen and Tommy made quick work of bringing everything up to the second-floor space.

"I have to admit this is a beautiful view," Tommy said while standing in front of the picture window overlooking the beach beyond Highway 1.

"Isn't it? And, you know how much I love the beach. Kristin, Zane, and I can go for walks and swims," she said, standing next to him.

"I might have to sell my place and buy a house in this neighborhood, so I can be closer to my baby," he said.

"Me too," Cy said. "Maybe we can pool our resources and live together."

Tommy's eyebrows shot up and his eyes grew wide as sand dollars. "I'll think about it, Pops."

Jen laughed. "I'd love it if you both moved over here. You used to like spending time over here, didn't you Tommy?"

"Yeah. The commute to work isn't as convenient though."

"But you'd be next to us."

"Are you going to stay here for more than a year? Not moving back to Sea Cliff, are you?"

Ouch. How does he know Amanda and I are on good terms? "No. I don't plan on moving into Amanda's house ever again. Living here is part of my independence. For Kristin and me."

"Good to know. I won't rule out moving to the neighborhood then."

Tommy helped her unpack the boxes for Kristin's room and set up the crib. "She won't be needing this much longer. Good thing it converts to a toddler bed."

"It's a matter of months, I suppose. I'm kind of scared that she'll wake up and start wandering around the apartment, though, once she's not contained in a crib."

"Maybe we should add a bolt lock to the top of the door," he said.

"In addition to the one above the handle that she can't reach?"

"Yes." He went to the front door and inspected it, then made a short list of what he would need to buy at the hardware store. "I'll install it next time I come over."

"Thanks Tommy," Jen said, collapsing boxes that she needed to reuse. "We'll stay at your house for a few more nights. I want everything to be perfect before we move in."

"I get you for a few more days then."

"And I have several things at Amanda's that I need to pick up," she said, looking around at her sparse furnishings.

"I can help you move those too," he said.

"Thanks. There's actually a matching sofa and poofy chair that I really like. They're in her basement rec room."

"Of course they are."

She smiled, knowing exactly what he meant—that Amanda hadn't considered them nice enough to be in her upstairs living areas. "Maybe we can pick those up tomorrow night?"

"Unfortunately, I'll be late getting home tomorrow night," he said. "Have some stuff to do on a case."

"Maybe I'll call some movers for those. Time to leave?"

"Yeah. It's getting late."

Jen locked the door as they left, and Kristin got in the car with Tommy and Cy for the ride back to Tommy's place.

When Jen was seated in her car, about to slide it into gear, her phone chirped with an incoming text from Nicole.

Hey, are you free for dinner tmrw night? I plan to make lasagna.

Jen looked at the ceiling and sighed. *Here it is. The time of truth. Start a new relationship with Nicole or back off to see where things go with Amanda.*

She replied, *Sorry. This week is really crazy with work—for both Tommy and me—and I'm slowly moving into my new apartment each evening.*

She was tempted to ask for a raincheck but didn't want to lead Nicole on. Best to stop and see where things went with Amanda.

Are you still working out tmrw am? Nicole asked.

Yeah. See u there? Jen replied.

Nicole replied with the bicep emoji and a smiley face.

Jen couldn't help but feel like she had just avoided making a big mess of two potential relationships. *Not fair. Amanda fooled around on me, and I haven't even had a revenge fuck.*

Thinking of Amanda, Jen was reminded of her burner phone. She must have dropped it in her bag, but as she looked around the front seat of her car, her bag was nowhere in sight. *I must've left it in the apartment.* She quickly texted Tommy that she forgot her bag and was going back to her apartment to get it. *Go ahead without me*, she texted.

She raced up to the second floor and unlocked the door, making sure to lock it behind her. She found her bag on top of a box in the living room and foraged in the bottom for the burner phone. She re-read Amanda's last text, *Can't wait to set fire to other parts of your body.*

How's your day going? All I can think about is you.

Jen smiled, her heart rate accelerating. It was her turn to reply, and she had failed all day. *I'll make it up to you. I'll give you something to dream about,* she thought to herself.

She walked into the bathroom and flipped on the light. Stripping down to her matching bra and panties, she snapped several pics in front of the mirror in seductive poses. When she found the one she liked, she texted it to Amanda with the caption, *Start imagining what you'll do with this. Moved into my apartment today. My bedroom is waiting for you.*

She dressed, turned off the lights, and locked the apartment again. By the time she was sitting in her car, ready to drive back to Tommy's, Amanda had replied to her text.

What's your apartment number? I'm on my way over.

Jen replied, *Down girl. Not staying here tonight. Election night.*

Still torturing me, Amanda replied.

Torture me back, Jen replied, although she seriously doubted that Amanda had the gumption to text her a nude pic. Make no mistake, Amanda was proud of her body, never too shy to walk around the bedroom nude, but sending a pic was different. She was waaay too paranoid about her work reputation, being a high-profile public servant and all.

28

North Beach

"Did you say that today is a big day at work for you?" Jen asked Tommy the next morning over coffee.

"Yeah. You have to keep this confidential, but we're executing search warrants on Gavin Morales in the city and his campaign treasurer, Herb Whitehead, up in Healdsburg."

"Are you driving all the way up there yourself?" she asked, stirring yogurt into her granola.

"No. The Sonoma County Sheriff will execute the warrant on Whitehead's house and office and grab the computers for us. We're sending two uniforms up to retrieve the equipment."

"That will be a big deal when it hits the media," she said.

"No doubt." Tommy folded his toast and stuffed the entire piece in his mouth.

"Do you suppose he'll continue his campaign for DA?"

Chewing, he said, "We won't be arresting him, so I'm sure he'll say the raid is unfair and politically motivated to derail his campaign, but we have to do it."

"What are you looking for?"

He gulped coffee as his Adam's Apple moved. "Proof that he conspired with the North Koreans to hack into the Cohen Clinic medical record for Amanda's therapy note and the clinic email system for Chance's email to you."

"So it wasn't just HELLFIRE who was retaliating against Amanda? He actually connected with Gavin Morales and his campaign staff?"

"That's what Navarro and Roxy have pieced together. They also bought the negative ads on Facebook and Twitter against Amanda."

"But that isn't illegal, is it?" she asked.

"No, but it's further evidence of how they colluded through the corporation Truth for Election."

"I hope you find the evidence you're looking for, especially if it helps Amanda win. Wouldn't it be horrible if Morales were elected, only to be arrested?"

"We don't want that either. That's why we have to move fast."

"Do we have to take any precautions at home? Are we in danger?" she asked.

"Nothing we can't handle with some visible protection."

"What about you? You're in this up to your eyeballs now," she said, rubbing his shoulder.

"I'm not worried." He folded his second piece of toast.

"Well, I am. Watch yourself today."

"Just so you know, there will be a uniform at daycare again today, and the same guys who watched the house while I was in Cayman will be back today and tonight."

"Just make sure our daughter is protected," she said, giving him a peck on the cheek.

"The two women I love most in the world are protected." His soft brown eyes reinforced his words.

She smiled and hugged him, pulling back quickly.

He finished his coffee, grabbed his blazer and keys, and left before Kristin woke.

Later, after Jen fed Kristin breakfast, she dropped her at daycare and greeted the officer, thanking him for his service.

When she returned to her car to drive to the CrossFit box, she heard chiming in her bag, indicating an incoming text on the burner phone.

A surge of excitement bubbled through her as she entered the password and clicked on the text. To her surprise, there was a scandalously nude pic of Amanda on the screen.

Well fuck me.

Jen was shocked at her audacity but simultaneously over the moon. She enlarged the pic with her fingers. Just seeing Amanda in this licentious pose drained all the blood from her brain to the vee between her legs.

You win. I could devour you right now.

She rested her head against the seat and took a deep breath.

Why did I have to tell her to wait until election night? To be the master of her own domain? I won't be able to master my own with this image.

She thought for a minute then decided on her reply. She typed, *Fucking hot as hell. I could devour you right now.*

She tossed the phone back in her bag and started the car. Maybe lifting weights would keep her horniness at bay. *Nah. Probably not.*

When Jen entered the workout space, Nicole was there, stretching on a mat, her flawless body clad in a flimsy top and Lulu's. Despite the sumptuous curves, all Jen could see was the nude pic of Amanda. She was hopelessly turned on by Amanda, and no one else compared. The fire she felt inside when Amanda kissed her pushed out the thought of any other woman.

Jen sat down on a mat next to Nicole to stretch before their class began. "Hey."

"Hey, stranger," Nicole said, leaning in for a kiss.

Jen offered her cheek, which caused Nicole to do a doubletake and raise her eyebrow.

"Sorry. It's so public in here," Jen mumbled, struggling for an excuse.

Nicole frowned but didn't pursue it.

They partnered up during class for the workout, but Jen didn't flirt or linger to chat afterward. She hit the locker room, showering and dressing for work in record time. As she was stuffing her workout clothes in her bag, Nicole sidled up next to her, leaning against the locker. "Did I offend you?"

Jen closed her eyes and focused on adopting a compassionate face rather than an annoyed one. "Of course not. I'm just running late for work and have a lot of things on my mind. It's not you, it's me."

Nicole whispered so others wouldn't hear. "Okay. Because I could've sworn that we had something going the other day. You seemed really into it. Into me. And I want to make sure I didn't misread the situation."

"I was. You didn't misread anything. I'm just up to my eyeballs in work and stress this week..." Jen's voice trailed off.

"Are you getting sucked into the campaign stuff again?"

"No. Different stuff that I can't talk about. I'm sorry."

Nicole shoved off from the locker. "I get it. You have a busy life. When you break free, text me."

"Okay," Jen said with a shaky smile.

Nicole turned and left.

Fuck! Jen thought, staring at her locker. *Why can't I tell her the truth? I need to break it off with her.*

The rest of her day was equally uncomfortable, seeing patients, but thinking about Tommy and the search warrants, then worrying about Kristin, her mind overactive and on alert. She kept checking the news outlet websites, but nothing was on there yet about their raids.

After work, she hustled over to the daycare for Kristin. She thanked the uniformed officer for posting guard at the entrance, a woman instead of the man who was present that morning. She scanned the room for Kristin.

"Mama!" Kristin yelled when she saw her. Jen scooped her up, and they drove back to Tommy's place in North Beach. Her anxiety lowered when she saw Cy and Zane sitting on Tommy's front stoop waiting for them.

"Look, baby. There's Bumpa," Jen said to Kristin.

"And Yaner!" Kristin said enthusiastically.

Across the street, there was an unmarked cruiser with two officers in it. She noticed that they saw her right away, so she waved.

She found a parking spot across the street and up the hill from Tommy's—under a tree on Vallejo Street. She carefully parked in the tight space then got out and opened the back door for Kristin. The late sun warmed her back as she leaned in and unbuckled her baby.

Cy and Zane ambled up the hill and joined them on the sidewalk. Once Jen set Kristin down, Zane licked her face, and she hollered "Yaner top," batting at him while giggling.

Cy pulled Zane back with the leash and handed it off to Jen so he could hug Kristin. "Did you have a good day at school, my sweet?"

"Me paint!" she said, holding up her palms for him to see the red and purple stains from a job well done.

"You did? I hope I get to see your painting." They walked hand-in-hand to the curb, where Cy looked both ways, then proceeded into the street. There was hardly any traffic on the corner of Kearny and Vallejo since both streets dead-ended at this block. Cy still practiced good habits, though, because cars sometimes whipped around the corner without slowing down.

Poor Cy. He's really into our home routine, Jen thought, as they entered the intersection, kitty-corner from Tommy's house. When they were halfway across the street, she heard the screech of tires and looked up in time to see a small car with black-tinted windows barreling down Kearny Street at them.

"Cy! Car!" Jen yelled. She dropped Zane's leash and lunged for Kristin, grabbing her arm and jerking her into the air, pulling her along as she made a mad dash from the trajectory of the car, which was gaining speed instead of slowing down.

Jen felt as if she were moving in slow motion as she ran, glancing back to see the rear windows of the car roll down, and an arm with a pistol in hand pointing at them. *Noooo!*

Jen made it back to the opposite side of the street and dove—with Kristin in her arms—behind a parked car in time to hear the windows of the parked car shatter from bullets. She was obscured from the shooter's angle, crouched behind a tire, and prayed to God that Cy was carrying his gun. She and Kristin hit the sidewalk, Jen's shoulder taking the brunt of the impact. Jen heard the *pop pop* of more gun shots over Kristin's loud scream, so she covered Kristin's ears and hugged her tightly, scooting up against the tire of the car for protection. Jen lay over Kristin as their bodies shook with fear.

A cacophony of gunfire broke out and thundered around them. Jen's body went rigid, as she held Kristin with all her might, covering the top of her head with one arm and cradling her head from the sidewalk with the other.

Please let us live. Please let us live.

Jen envisioned the cops in the unmarked cruiser, hoping they had come to Cy's rescue.

The unmistakable sound of metal hitting metal told Jen a car had crashed into another. Men yelled. Then everything went silent—

except for the pounding in her chest, and the ringing in her ears.

"Mama?" Kristin asked in a shaky voice.

"I'm here, baby. Mama's here."

There were two more gunshots in quick succession, causing both Kristin and Jen's bodies to jerk to the *crack, crack*. Jen's veins popped with adrenaline and fear.

Lying on the sidewalk, totally exposed to a shooter, Jen prayed, *Dear Lord, please save my baby. Take me, but save my baby*. She covered Kristin with her own body as best she could. If Cy and the officers had been shot, she thought, Kristin and her destinies were fatally sealed.

Straining to hear through the ringing in her ears, the unmistakable sound of footsteps running on the sidewalk escalated her fear. If she were alone, she'd stand and defend herself, but with Kristin in her arms, all she could do was cover and protect. She was terrified to look up at who was approaching. A nightmare. While trying to keep Kristin tucked under her, Jen turned and squinted into the sun to see who was on the sidewalk.

To her shock and amazement, gun in hand, Roxy was kneeling to them. "Jen, are you and Kristin okay?"

Jen saw more than heard Roxy talking to her, adding to the surreality of the events. Her brain was still chugging along in slow motion. She was confused because she had heard Roxy's footsteps, but now had difficulty understanding what Roxy was asking her.

"What?" she heard herself say, looking at Roxy's calm face, the pupils in her smoky blues dilated.

"Are you okay? Is Kristin okay?" Roxy asked again, laying her hand on Jen's shoulder to have a look.

Jen propped herself on an elbow and looked down at Kristin, who appeared okay except for a scrape on her cheek. Kristin's blue eyes were as big as saucers as she looked from Roxy to her mother.

"Yes," Jen said. "What about Cy?"

Roxy nodded, but cautiously. "I think he will be. He was shot in the abdomen, but he returned fire like a pro, hitting the driver of the car."

"Who?" Jen asked.

"HELLFIRE himself was in the back seat shooting at you. Two other men were in the car. All dead now." She stopped, glancing in Kristin's direction.

"HELLFIRE? Here?"

"Yes. It was a longshot, but I suspected he might turn up here. I spent most of the day sitting in a car down the hill, so it took me a second to get out and run up to the shooters. The police in the unmarked car did a commendable job of returning gunfire right away to divert HELLFIRE'S attention away from Cy."

"Can we see Cy?" Jen asked.

Roxy again glanced at Kristin. "He's losing blood pretty fast. There's quite a bit on the street. I don't know if you want Kristin to see that."

"I have to stop the bleeding," Jen said, standing. "Can you hold Kristin while I tend to him?"

Jen jumped up and handed Kristin to Roxy, as she made a beeline for the middle of the street to examine Cy.

The officers were on their knees around him, and Jen heard sirens in the distance. She lowered herself, so she could speak into his ear. "Cy? Can you hear me?"

He looked at her, his large brown eyes full of fear and tears. "Is Kristin okay?"

She patted his arm. "Yes! She's fine. We're both okay. Thank you for defending us. We love you."

"Stomach," he said, wincing in pain and laying his head back on the pavement.

Jen turned her attention to his belly. She lifted his shirt to see a bullet hole by his bellybutton. There wasn't anything she could do other than put pressure on the wound to help stem the bleeding. While she was pressing firmly, she looked past Cy and saw Zane lying on the street, blood pooling around him. He had taken multiple bullets and was dead.

"Oh, Zane," she said, tears springing to her eyes and running down her cheeks. She caught Roxy's eye, tilted her head toward Zane, then shook her head, signaling to Roxy not to let Kristin see Zane.

Roxy turned the other direction and walked down the hill, rocking Kristin in her arms. She spoke to an officer who ran over and put Zane in a body bag. He carefully carried him to the sidewalk and set him down next to a squad car.

In a matter of minutes, which felt like hours to Jen, an ambulance arrived, and the EMTs took a report from Jen. She removed her hand, and the EMT placed his gloved hand on Cy's belly to put pressure where Jen had been applying it. "Take him to San Francisco Community Hospital," Jen said, then turned to Cy. "We'll meet you there, Bumpa."

In pain, he nodded, and kept his eyes on her until the back doors of the ambulance closed.

Jen knew she had to call Tommy, but she couldn't until she did one more thing. She went to the body bag on the sidewalk and unzipped it, so she could say goodbye to Zane. She leaned down and kissed his furry, butterscotch-colored face. "Goodbye, Zaner. See you on the other side."

She zipped the bag closed and stood, fighting back tears. Jen felt in her pocket for her phone as she walked toward Roxy and Kristin. She called Tommy and quickly told him what had happened. He had just hung up with the senior officer at the scene so had received a preliminary report.

"We're fine. Cy was shot in the abdomen. He's going to the hospital. Meet us there."

"I'm coming to get you and Kristin."

"Not necessary. We can drive."

"The hell you can!"

"I can drive you," Roxy offered, overhearing their conversation.

"Roxy will drive us," Jen told Tommy.

"She's there?"

"Yes. She shot HELLFIRE."

"Officer Chang didn't tell me that. I'll see you at the hospital."

They ended the call and Roxy handed Kristin back to Jen.

"We need to find my car keys," Jen said, looking around the street. "They should be in my bag."

Her bag was in the middle of the street, only a few feet from where Cy and Zane had been shot.

"I'll get your bag and I'll talk to the officer about disposition of the other thing," Roxy said, nodding her chin toward the body bag lying a few feet from them.

"There's a veterinary hospital close by, Westway Animal Hospital, if they could bring him there for cremation," Jen said.

"Got it," Roxy said, then hustled over and spoke to the officer standing by Zane's body.

Jen kept Kristin's face averted from the car crash and dead bodies as she walked back up Vallejo Street to her truck.

Mary, Mother of God, please let Cy live, Jen thought. She held back her own sobs, as she consoled Kristin.

Roxy returned and unlocked Jen's car, helping situate Kristin in her car seat. Jen's hands didn't seem to be working, now shaking uncontrollably. There was no way she could drive. *Fuck. I'm in shock. I can't believe it. I know what's happening to me, but I can't stop it.*

Roxy opened the passenger door for Jen then took her hands in hers. "You're suffering from shock. It's okay. You might not be able to think straight and your motor control will be

344

slow. As a doctor, I'm sure you know this, but it's different when you're the one going through it. Take deep breaths while we drive to the hospital. You're safe in the car with me. You and Kristin are safe. It's over." Roxy unexpectedly hugged her.

Jen found Roxy surprisingly reassuring in the moment. "Thank you…Thank you for saving our lives."

29

San Francisco Community Hospital

Jen, Roxy, and Kristin progressed slowly through the rigorous security system outside the Emergency Room, including walking through metal detectors and setting their bags on a conveyor belt for X-ray screening. Jen couldn't help but compare this visit to the last time they had arrived together at the ER in the heat of battle against each other. Roxy had become the hero, saving their lives, and Jen was grateful.

Jen noticed that Roxy didn't set her gun on the conveyer, instead showing security her special identification.

As soon as they pushed through the double doors, Jen spotted Cy on a gurney in the hallway. She got only two seconds with him, walking alongside as the staff rolled him to the operating room, maintaining his IV bags as they moved. She looked at him with an encouraging smile.

The surgeon peeled off from the group and turned to Jen. "Are you the family?"

"Yes," Jen said, even though she wasn't, but she wanted info to pass along to Tommy, and knew the surgeon wouldn't talk to her if she answered honestly.

"We'll take him to surgery to remove the bullet, which, on X-ray, appears to have missed his ribs and spine. I expect intestinal damage, though, so the surgery might take several hours. We won't know until we get in there."

"Thank you. Do what you need to do," Jen said.

With that brief exchange, Cy's fate was left in the confident hands of a young man wearing thick glasses and a green cap.

"I wish Tommy had been here to see Cy before surgery," Roxy said.

"I'll text him," Jen said, holding Kristin in one arm while texting Tommy with her other hand.

As Jen was texting, Tommy came rushing down the hallway.

"How's Kristin?" He crashed into Jen and wrapped Kristin into a bear hug, holding onto both of them so tight that Jen thought Kristin would protest but she didn't.

"Just a scrape on her cheek."

"Thank God." He kissed the top of Kristin's head and backed off a bit. "Should she be seen for that?"

"They could clean it, I suppose," Jen said. "I was more focused on Cy, who just went into surgery."

"Where was he hit?"

"In the abdomen, next to his bellybutton. The surgeon said the bullet missed his ribs and spine, but there might be damage to his intestine. He'll know more when he gets in there."

"Is he gonna live?" Tommy asked, his upper lip stiff with courage but his eyes welling over.

"At his age, it's harder to recover, but he's got a lot of fight in him. He was awake and talking to me on the street." She squeezed his shoulder, mindful that she hadn't answered his question because she didn't know.

"Those fuckers," he snarled.

"Tell me about it. Thank God Roxy and the cops killed them."

"Jen? Is that you?" Lane Wallace asked from down the hall.

"Lane! You wouldn't believe what happened," Jen said.

"I remember him," Roxy said. "He fixed my broken nose."

Jen smiled sheepishly. "Yeah. We're colleagues. I used to work here."

"Hello, Ms. MacNeil," Lane said, shaking Roxy's hand. He paid special attention to her nose, then nodded, pleased with his work.

"Hi, Doc. Thanks for the nose job."

Lane smiled then turned his attention to Kristin's cheek. "What do we have here?"

"I'll tell you about it. Can we clean it up?" Jen asked.

"Follow me." He led them into an empty exam room. Jen held Kristin on her lap, and Lane washed off Kristin's cheek then dabbed antibiotic ointment on it.

Jen told him the entire story, using some vague references, so Kristin wouldn't pick up all the gory details, allowing Tommy to hear the story for the first time as well.

"That's an insane experience. I'm so sorry you and Kristin had to go through that," Lane said.

"Thank you. Do you have time to join us for a bite in the cafeteria?"

"I'd like to, but business is picking up," he said, pointing with his thumb to the main part of the ER.

"I understand. Thanks for taking the time to clean Kristin's scrape. I should probably get her dinner before she starts crying," Jen said.

"Good plan. I'm sure she's in shock from what happened," Tommy said.

"I might step outside for a fag and meet you later," Roxy said from the doorway.

Jen and Lane looked at her, taking a sec to process what she meant.

"Can I join you?" Tommy asked. "I need to call my sister, and you and I need to talk about a few things."

"Be my guest," she said, motioning with her hand.

"You shouldn't smoke while on the patch," Jen reminded Roxy. She wasn't going to tell Tommy that he shouldn't be smoking *at all*.

"Ah, buggers. I forgot." Roxy shrugged off her leather jacket and hoodie then lifted the sleeve of her T-shirt to expose her right arm. "Will you kindly rip it off?"

Jen groaned but ripped it off for her. If the lady needed to smoke to get over killing, that was her business. Jen finally understood what Roxy had been trying to tell her the other day in her office. The ugliness of her job made her who she was, but there was still some love and compassion buried deep down inside. Jen patted her arm and tossed the patch in the waste basket. "All set. Come to the caf when you're finished."

Roxy shrugged into her hoodie and jacket and left with Tommy.

Lane kissed Jen on the cheek. "Bye, Jen. Talk to you soon, okay?"

"Thanks for a lovely day on your boat. I'd like to do it again sometime."

"Let's. I have to run."

She watched him disappear around a corner. "Guess it's just you and me, kid," she said to Kristin. As they walked down the hall, Jen heard her name and turned in time to see Amanda running toward them.

"Oh my God, are you okay?" Amanda collided with Jen and Kristin, kissing Kristin on the forehead.

"Mama Man!" Kristin said, leaning toward Amanda and squirming to get out of Jen's arms.

"A booboo on your cheek, baby?" Amanda asked, taking Kristin from Jen, then looking at Jen to see how she was.

"Owie," Kristin moaned, pointing to her cheek. Amanda kissed her above it.

Jen was surprised that Kristin wanted to leave her and go to Amanda since she had been clinging to Jen like Velcro. Kristin hadn't even done that when Tommy had arrived. *She really loves you,* Jen thought, the realization washing over her like a tidal wave. Then she felt relieved that she didn't have to provide all the emotional support to Kristin during this trauma. *I can't be strong all the time.* As the horrific scenes of the shooting flashed through her mind, her expression contorted into a pained cry.

"Ahh, baby. Come here." Amanda opened herself to Jen, inviting her into the other side of her body while holding Kristin.

Jen crumpled into Amanda, burying her face in her neck so no one would see her breaking down. She felt Amanda's solid arm curl around her back so eagerly took refuge in Amanda's warmth and strength. Her throat constricted with the overwhelming need to let go. Just let go and give up control of everything because nothing felt remotely normal anymore. Her love life. Her work life. Now her home life. *God, please help me deal with this and not go batshit crazy.*

The three of them huddled together, Jen letting the tears flow. She was surprised her crying didn't cause Kristin to cry too, but Kristin was so relieved to see Amanda that she probably hadn't noticed the extent to which Jen was breaking down. Amanda kissed the side of Jen's head, her affection easing her shock.

"We'll get through this together. Let me help you," Amanda said.

Jen realized she was saturating Amanda's neck with tears, so she looked up to find Amanda's empathetic brown eyes, so clear and understanding. "I think I'm in shock."

"I know the feeling. Is there a place we can sit and talk?"

"The cafeteria. Kristin will be hungry for dinner soon, and we don't want her to get hangry."

"Let's go."

Jen wiped her tears away with the sleeve of her sweater and grabbed Amanda's hand.

Once they were seated with their trays of food, she updated Amanda on Cy's condition.

"Does Tommy know yet?"

"Yeah. He's outside having a cigarette with Roxy," Jen said.

"She's here?" Amanda asked, but not in a judgmental way.

"She saved our lives. She was actually parked on the street, protecting Tommy's house—"

"I thought a couple of plainclothes guys were assigned to his house."

"They were there too, but Roxy said she had a hunch that HELLFIRE would make a play for Tommy at his house. Or us. I guess we were the targets." Jen was still shocked at the very notion of it, but carefully chose her words in front of Kristin. "Anyway, Roxy was amazing. She, Cy, and the officers you-know-what to the men in the car. Then she found Kristin and me hiding behind a parked car on the sidewalk."

"God. I'm so sorry you had to go through that. Poor Kristin. Did she see anything horrible?" Amanda asked.

"No. She just heard the gunfire and the car smashing into another one."

"Still. Very traumatic. Our poor baby." With a napkin, Amanda wiped food from Kristin's face and hands.

Jen noticed how Amanda had said *our baby,* and it re-enforced her hope that she didn't have to face so much of life alone. "And sad news. I had Z-A-N-E on a leash, but had to drop it to grab Kristin. He didn't make it."

Amanda's eyes grew wide and filled with tears. She covered them with her hands, so Kristin wouldn't see. "Who am I going to practice my legal arguments on? He was such a good listener and companion."

Jen frowned, unaware of how Amanda had been subjecting Zane to her boring legal arguments behind her back. *God, that poor dog.*

"Zumba doesn't give a shit about me," Amanda said. "He just walks away, twitching his tail. Zane, on the other hand, actually sought me out for attention. Did you know that he visited me during yoga almost every morning?"

"No. I didn't realize he went down to your studio."

"Well, he did, and we cuddled on the yoga mat. He'd scoot under me while I did downward-facing dog."

"I never knew—"

"Someone else is going to miss him very much." Amanda signaled to Kristin.

"I know. She's been chasing him around Tommy's house lately."

"Poor guy. Remember how Zumba used to attack him while he was sleeping, and Zane would just take it?"

"And how he was sucking on Kristin's pacifier that one time?" Jen smiled then teared up again. She dabbed at her cheeks with a napkin. "Damn. The business you guys are in really sucks. It's been the worst two weeks of my life."

Amanda lay her hand on Jen's arm, causing Jen to wince in a wee bit of pain from the fall. "I'm so sorry. You didn't deserve any of this. You know I love you, right? I'll do anything for you... Anything."

Jen had never seen Amanda so earnest. Desperate, even. "Yes. I know. Thank you for being here. For supporting us."

"You and Kristin are more important to me than anyone else in the world. I want us to be together so badly, I—"

Amanda was prevented from finishing her sentence, as Tommy and Roxy approached the table with their dinner trays.

Amanda didn't remove her hand from Jen's arm, though, gently caressing it.

"Hey," Tommy said.

"Hello, Amanda," Roxy said, her eyes traveling over Amanda's hand on Jen's arm.

"Hi. Thanks for protecting Jen and Kristin today," Amanda said to Roxy.

Roxy patted Jen's back as she passed, taking a seat opposite her. "It was the least I could do."

Jen met Roxy's eyes as soon as she sat. *Fine. We're even. The slate is wiped clean.*

What could have been the most contentious meal ever, considering the relationships around the table, was instead solemn and comforting as they picked at their food and talked about the significance and ramifications of HELLFIRE being killed. With the exception of Kristin, who ate a healthy amount of tator tot casserole, then demanded to be held by Tommy, none of them did a very good job of cleaning their plates.

Jen was struck by the irony of their dinner, recalling when Tommy had been in the hospital six weeks earlier from poisoning, and she,

Amanda, Kristin, and Roxy had eaten at a table close by. She sensed that Roxy wanted Amanda from the minute she had met her. And who could blame her? Amanda was all that and more.

Jen was relieved, however, that Amanda now seemed like she didn't even notice Roxy, focusing all of her love and attention on Jen and Kristin.

Jen had learned the hard way that getting shot at was distressing as hell, much less actually taking a bullet to the rib cage like Amanda had. If it weren't for Kristin, Jen would've welcomed a shot of whiskey and a few painkillers herself. The rush of emotions she was suddenly experiencing—concern for Tommy, worry for Cy, all-encompassing love for Kristin, enduring passion for Amanda, and gratefulness to Roxy—exposed her soul, leaving her raw, vulnerable, and exhausted, unable to process what had transpired and what everyone was now saying.

She sat there in a daze.

Amanda must have felt Jen's angst, as she scooted her chair closer and put her arm around her shoulders.

"Thank you. I…I'm feeling…very cold." Jen folded her arms over herself.

Amanda removed her Sweaty Betty hoodie from her bag and draped it around Jen.

"That's natural after what you've been through. It's part of the shock. We're here for you," Amanda said.

All Jen heard was *I'm here for you.* Amanda's hoodie was so warm, and it smelled heavenly—like Amanda and a field of lavender.

Jen leaned into Amanda's body, not feeling self-conscious in the least in front of Tommy and Roxy. Her near-death experience underscored the importance of love and seemed to have erased the spite that had been festering in her belly for the past six weeks. She realized just how much she needed Amanda. Tommy was great, Nicole was sexy, but—and this sealed the deal—Amanda completed her.

Roxy's phone chirped, so she turned her attention to reading and replying to messages. When she finished, she announced, "I've been summoned to Langley."

"Just like that, you're gone, huh?" Tommy clicked his fingers.

"Just like that, my battle with HELLFIRE is over. Score one for the good guys." She rattled the ice in her plastic glass and drank her soda just like she was drinking a Scotch.

"You're one of the best detectives I've ever worked with," Tommy said. "Thanks for saving Pops, Jen, and Kristin. I don't know how I'll ever repay you."

"No worries, mate. I hope we get the chance to work together again. And, likewise."

"Thank you for helping on this case, Roxy. I wish you the best," Amanda said.

A flash of regret crossed Roxy's face, but she quickly disguised it. "I'll never forget you, Jen, and Kristin. Take care." She shoved away from the table, and everyone stood to give her a hug.

When Jen hugged Roxy's skinny body, she leaned in and said, "I'm sorry I broke your nose. Thank you for saving us today."

Roxy didn't let go. "I deserved the broken nose. You're a fantastic physician and mother. Kristin is lucky to have you. So is Amanda."

Jen just about melted under the weight of Roxy's genuine compliment. Tears momentarily sprang to her eyes and her mouth went dry.

When Jen released Roxy, Amanda hung back, not stepping forward for a hug. She tilted up her chin once but didn't move from her spot. "Goodbye. Take care of yourself."

"You too," Roxy said, nodding.

Jen was flooded with relief that she didn't have to see them touch each other. *I have to hand it to Amanda for being sensitive at a time when I need it most.*

Roxy briefly hugged Tommy and gave him a peck on the cheek.

They watched her walk through the cafeteria like a humming bird disappearing into pine trees.

Jen was struck by how strange life was, having someone like Roxy in her life for only a brief time, experiencing such strong and conflicting emotions over Roxy's seduction of Amanda, then her rescue of herself and Kristin. How could she hate, then appreciate, someone that much? "And, just like that, she's gone."

Amanda pressed her body against Jen's back, hugging her. "That's a good thing."

Flooded with relief, Jen nodded as she felt Amanda's arms tighten around her. Seeking more, she turned her head to the side, inviting Amanda to kiss her on the cheek, which she did.

"I wonder when Pops will be out of surgery," Tommy said, picking up Kristin from her high chair.

"Probably in an hour or two," Jen said. "Did you call Tina?"

"Yeah. She said she'd come right over. We'll stay here together. You two can take Kristin home if you want," he said.

"I don't know," Jen said, feeling the graphic grime of trauma descend upon her.

"Kristin will be tired soon, and you look like you need a shower. I'll text as soon as I hear anything," he said.

"I'd like to go, but..." She was at a loss for how to complete her thoughts.

"But what?" he asked.

"I don't know where to go or what to do. No offense, Tommy, but I'm not ready to return to your street. That would be bad. Really bad. And my apartment isn't quite ready—"

"Come to my place," Amanda said over Jen's shoulder, still hugging her.

"I don't know...I'm just...so confused right now."

"Why not stay at my place? You took a nap there a few days ago, and Kristin's nursery is totally set up," Amanda said.

Tommy raised his eyebrows. Jen hadn't mentioned that they had napped together.

"I know. It's not you. It's me. I'm hung up on the fact that we once lived there, but that part of our life is over now. You know what I mean." Jen implored Amanda with her eyes not to make her explain in front of Tommy.

"Okay. I get that you don't want to live there, but at least let me put you up for the night. The place is crawling with security, and the familiarity of Kristin's room might be good for her right now," Amanda said.

"I think it sounds like a good idea," Tommy said. "Kristin needs some familiar surroundings."

"A shower and bed sound inviting," Jen said, her voice gravelly. And Kristin's room was, indeed, comforting and secure.

"Then come over. I promise it won't be long term," Amanda said, not letting go of Jen.

Jen turned in Amanda's arms and found her eyes. "For tonight only."

"It's your call," Amanda said.

"Thank you." Jen hugged Amanda tighter and longer than she had intended in front of Tommy, but she was in the reassuring arms of the woman she loved.

As they broke apart, Tommy's sister, Tina, came down the stairs and crashed into his arms for a hug. She still wore her white apron from the kitchen of her restaurant. "How's dad?"

30

Sea Cliff

"How about I give Kristin a bath while you shower?" Amanda suggested when they entered her kitchen.

"Are you sure?" Jen felt Zumba twining around her legs and she immediately missed Zane. She wanted to double over and cry but couldn't break down in front of Kristin. Her furry companion. Always loyal. Always true. Gone. She would miss him so much.

"Yes, I'm sure. I'll use the guest bath for Kristin's bath, and you can use our shower—sorry—the shower upstairs." Amanda bit her lower lip.

"That sounds nice. Thank you for offering." Jen's voice was a parched whisper.

"I've got this. Go on. Feel free to wear anything of mine when you're done."

Jen smiled and slowly dragged herself up the stairway. She heard Amanda talking to Kristin, her comforting words soothing to Jen too. At the top of the stairs, she turned in the opposite direction of Amanda's suite and went into Kristin's room. Flipping on the light, she saw that Kristin's room was tidied up and there were a few new outfits draped over the crib. *Just like Amanda to buy clothes for her. Ever the shopper,* Jen thought as she ran her fingers over the soft, pink fabric.

Gratitude for Amanda seeped into her heart from every angle as Jen returned to the master suite and shed her clothes, leaving a trail to the bathroom. She turned on the shower and regarded herself in the mirror while she waited for the water to warm. Her reflection bore the stress of what they'd just endured. Tiny lines appeared around her mouth and eyes, reminding her of what she used to look like after a night shift in the ER. *I can't take this shit anymore. Tommy and Amanda have to get out of this business.*

She entered Amanda's sizeable shower and let the hot spray pound her, washing away the tortured sights and sounds of the shootout. After shampooing her hair and washing her body, she sat on the floor, letting the spray hit her shoulders and neck. The shoulder that had cushioned their fall on the sidewalk was especially sore.

When she was finished, she borrowed Amanda's clothes, pulling on a tank, underwear, and yoga pants, topped off with a soft hoodie. They smelled like Amanda, which comforted her to an unquantifiable degree. *How quickly I've fallen back into her life.*

Hearing soft singing from the hallway, she went to Kristin's room, where she found Amanda rocking Kristin to sleep. She recognized the tune as *Clair de Lune*, but she didn't realize there were lyrics to it too.

The words sounded like they rhymed, but were in French, so Jen didn't have a clue what Amanda was singing. *Of course, Amanda's singing a French lullaby. Who is she, anyway?*

Some child prodigy who happened to go into law? Then fall in love with me?

Rather than interrupt, Jen observed from the doorway, allowing the sight of Kristin on Amanda's lap to warm her heart and settle her nerves. Amanda continued to sing oh-so-softly into Kristin's ear, following the tune that she had played on her cello. The sight of Kristin resting comfortably in Amanda's arms reassured Jen that everything would be okay. She smiled and quietly backed out.

She found herself in the kitchen, hoping Amanda had some alcohol—of any kind—stashed somewhere. Just when she needed a stiff drink, her lover had to be fresh out of rehab. Of all the dumb luck. A quick scan of Amanda's wine fridge revealed only bottles of water. *Shit. She's gotta have something here for entertaining.*

She opened the fridge. Nothing. She went to the cupboard above the fridge— Amanda's de facto liquor cabinet. One bottle of Cointreau for baking and a bottle of Scotch. *A bottle of Scotch? For Roxy? No, Amanda said Roxy had never been in her house.* Then she recalled that Jack liked Scotch. *He's probably been over a lot during the campaign. Scotch has never been Amanda's go-to drink.*

She poured herself a healthy amount over the rocks and brought her drink to the living room where she turned on the gas fireplace. Sitting on the floor and facing the fire, she tucked pillows behind her back and wrapped herself with a soft throw from the sofa. She sipped, the thick liquid burning her throat a little before it traveled to her head.

As her buzz took hold, relaxing her, she heard Amanda walk through the kitchen then felt her warm hands on her shoulders. A sigh escaped Jen.

"I see you found Jack's Scotch."

"Hope he doesn't mind."

"Are you kidding me? Drink as much as you want." Amanda gently massaged Jen's shoulders and neck.

"What was the song you were singing to Kristin?"

"The poem of *Clair de Lune*. The song was actually named after a French poem from the mid-1800's. Debussy wrote the music in the early 1900's. I learned it in music class—obviously," Amanda said.

"You sing beautifully. You're hiding all sorts of gems in that talented body of yours, aren't you?" Jen could barely form words under Amanda's commanding fingers. Only Amanda could do this to her—melt her while simultaneously starting a fire deep within. She wanted to kiss her. Take her in front of the fire like she had so many times.

"Let's focus on your needs." Amanda grabbed another blanket from the sofa and joined Jen on the floor, spooning up behind her. She continued to massage Jen's neck lightly with her right hand and moved her left arm across Jen's tummy. "I'm not trying to seduce you. I just want to help you any way I can. I totally understand what you've just been through. Can I hold you?"

"I'm not worried about you seducing me." Jen turned her face to Amanda. "I love you, you know."

Amanda smiled and hooked her finger under Jen's jaw, guiding her lips to her own. She planted a tender, light kiss on sad lips. Neither sought more, even though their mouths lingered, savoring the ripe fullness.

Jen felt the light tingle of minty toothpaste on Amanda's tongue, making her curious how her Scotch-tinged mouth tasted to Amanda.

She relaxed and leaned in as Amanda kissed her nose and forehead with feathery light brushes, full of tenderness and love. Amanda's mouth hovered over Jen's ear. "I love you too. I want you with every fiber of my being, but tonight isn't the right time."

"Mmm," Jen moaned, letting her hands skate over Amanda's skin.

She felt Amanda smile against her ear, kiss it and blow softly, sending delicious sensations over her, igniting goosebumps and shivers.

Jen set her drink down and collapsed into Amanda's embrace, moving on top of her and slowly pressing her back to the floor. She propped herself on one elbow as she studied Amanda's face. Exhausted from the rigors of her campaign, Amanda was still clear-eyed and happy, her own eyes never leaving Jen's. Jen smiled and lowered her body onto Amanda, kissing her passionately with everything she had, her tongue submerging into the depths of Amanda's heat.

The Scotch buzz mingled with fireworks as Jen welcomed losing herself in Amanda. The rest of the world didn't exist when she was inside her. It had been that way since the very first time they'd kissed— against the wall in the ladies' room at the Curtain Call. A comparison to her recent kiss with Nicole was inevitable, and she was happy as hell that Amanda's kiss surpassed it like a rocket.

Jen had the sensation of falling several stories when she was deep into Amanda. When Amanda made love to her, she soared back up and shot off into outer space. To be brought to orgasm by Amanda was to experience the rarest passion that life had to offer.

Jen moved her hands under Amanda's T-shirt and lifted it over her head, then covered Amanda's lacy bra with her hands as she kissed her neck, touring to the creamy white flesh above her lacy bra. Jen felt Amanda's nipples harden.

Amanda's hips came off the floor into Jen's body. "Oh God, I've missed you so much." She threaded her fingers through Jen's wet hair and pulled her mouth back to hers.

After a long, sensuous kiss, Jen started back down Amanda's neck, to her breasts, searching for the clasp to her bra behind her.

Amanda uncharacteristically pushed Jen's head off her breasts and stared into her surprised eyes. "I really don't think sex is a good idea for you right now. You're still in shock and you've had something to drink. I don't want to take advantage. Even though I want you, I don't want *you* to regret it later."

Jen's heart and heat throbbed so hard that she wasn't sure if she'd heard Amanda correctly. "What? You don't want sex?"

Amanda groaned. "I want to make love to you in the worst way, but I don't want to take advantage of you tonight. Look at what you went through today."

Jen realized Amanda was serious. She propped herself on her elbow. "Is this because Roxy took advantage of you after you were shot in New York?"

Amanda swallowed hard. "In part. I was high on painkillers and wine and had been traumatized beyond imagination. I felt like the bullet was still inside of me, and I didn't know what the fuck was happening. I can't do the same to you because I know I wouldn't have succumbed to Roxy under any other circumstance. I want you to want me when…umm…you're clear-headed. Under normal circumstances, you know?"

"That sounds confusing, but bringing up Roxy's name and how she seduced you makes me crazy with jealousy." Jen rolled off Amanda onto the floor.

"I didn't mean to make you angry because you have nothing to be jealous about. I could barely work with her, and you have no idea how happy I am that she's leaving. I love you like I've never loved anyone, Jen. I want you for the rest of my life, to marry you and have more kids with you. But I want you to want the same thing when you're not under the influence of shock." Amanda stroked Jen's arm.

"You're a real buzzkill, you know that?" Jen said, reaching for her drink.

"So I've been told. Maybe I can just hold you in front of the fire and we can talk."

Jen took a sip of Scotch and pulled the blanket over Amanda's scantily clad torso. She couldn't concentrate when Amanda's bare skin was staring her in the face. "Yeah, I suppose."

"Will you sleep with me tonight?" Amanda asked, searching Jen's face.

"Full of conflicting messages, aren't you? Do you think we can share the same bed and not make love?"

"Wasn't it *you* who told me a few days ago to 'be the master of your own domain, girl?'"

"Did I say that?" Jen laughed at herself, but it rang a little hysterical, even to her own ears.

"Indeed. And I listened to you because I love you." Amanda toyed with Jen's wet hair, smoothing it back.

"Yes, I'll sleep with you, but when do we get to have sex?"

"Someone—I can't remember who—told me we get to make love on election night."

"What if *you're* traumatized and in shock?" Jen mocked.

"Hmph. Nice try."

"Speaking of traumatized and in shock, I wonder how Cy is doing. Where's my phone? I should text Tommy." Jen felt around on the floor for her phone and found it under a pillow. After texting Tommy, she cuddled into Amanda.

"I'm sure Cy will pull through. He's a tough old goat," Amanda said, wrapping her arms around Jen.

"I hope so. It was bad enough losing Zane. I'm not sure I could take losing him too."

"I know," Amanda said, rubbing Jen's shoulder and back.

Jen's phone vibrated, so she read Tommy's reply aloud. *Out of surgery. The doctor said it went well. Tina and I r spending the night.*

"Good. I want to visit him before work tomorrow," Jen said.

"Me too. Maybe we can go together."

"Okay," Jen said with some trepidation. She remembered that Cy had said he didn't like how Amanda "controlled her." *He'll have to get used to us being a couple again,* she thought. *Maybe I'm being too hard on him. I like him in Kristin's life and really want Tommy and him to visit us often at our new place, but he needs to accept Amanda.*

"What are you thinking about?" Amanda asked, her powers of perception cunning as usual.

"Ah. Just that Cy is sooo old fashioned in his thinking. He was hoping for Tommy and me to get back together. Can you believe that?" Jen said.

"Yes. His generation can be that way."

"I know. I like him and want him in Kristin's life but I wish he'd drop the old thinking."

"He might come around. Let's give him some time."

"He was developing a new routine at Tommy's where he'd show up as soon as Kristin and I got home from work and daycare. He was actually helpful with walking Zane and stuff. And, well…Kristin is really fond of him."

"I'm sure she is," Amanda said.

"I'd like to keep Tommy and Cy in Kristin's life. You know, have them over for dinner and stuff. Especially in light of what happened today. Life is too short, you know?"

"Oh my gosh, of course, Jen. I wouldn't expect anything less." Amanda stroked Jen's hair and caressed her neck.

Jen allowed herself to relax into Amanda, finally coming down from the trauma. *God, I love you.*

31

Sunset District
A few days later

Alone in her new apartment, Jen finished eating a bite while she watched the news coverage of the statewide elections. KPIX reported that Amanda held a strong lead in the DA's race. The anchor at the news desk flipped to Kip Moynihan at the St. Francis Yacht Club, where Amanda's tribe was gathered.

A pan of the crowd showed people smiling, drinks in hand. Kip reported they were anticipating a celebratory dance with a live band, but that Amanda and her family hadn't arrived yet.

Jen did her dishes and went into her bedroom to prepare. Kristin was at Tommy's for the night so she was on her own. *Hopefully not for long.* She'd been unpacking boxes and creating a suitable home for the two of them and was pleased with her progress. She found herself staring blindly at her closet, wondering what to wear to an election-night gala. Even if her mind was ambivalent, her body knew what it wanted—Amanda. And, tonight was the night.

Her regular phone chirped. *Leaving my house now for the Yacht Club. Jack and Chloe are with me. Can we pick you up?*

Jen stared at the text from Amanda. Cinderella was far from ready for the ball, and besides, she didn't want to get there that early. All that glad-handing. Yuck.

Go ahead. I'll be along in a bit.

Can't wait to see you! Amanda texted back.

Jen smirked and tossed her phone on the bed then turned to the choices in her closet. Nothing jumped out at her. *Maybe I should do hair and makeup first. Where's Chance with his tinted chapstick when I need him?*

***

A few miles away, standing in her Sea Cliff kitchen, Amanda watched her phone for a reply from Jen, but when none came, she sighed and dropped her phone in her bag.

"Ready to go?" Jack asked.

"Ready as I'll ever be."

"Why the long face? The returns are looking great," he said.

"I know. I was just hoping—" She didn't know how to admit to her parents that her night wouldn't be complete until Jen arrived.

Their expressions full of empathy, they stood in the kitchen waiting for their beloved daughter to share her feelings.

"Never mind. It isn't important," Amanda said, grabbing her black and gold wrap. "Let's go."

Conditioned to Amanda's private nature and secret life, they shrugged on their coats, turned off the lights, and locked the door on their way out. Frank drove them in Amanda's Jaguar to the Yacht Club, where they were met at the entrance by Chance.

"Welcome," Chance said, his eyes dancing, his dark hair mussed with product, and his body radiating super-human energy.

"What's the mood like inside?" Amanda asked.

Chance smoothed a flyaway strand of her hair as he scrutinized her makeup. "Jubilant. They're waiting for their leader and now you're here, looking gorgeous as always. The media is inside on the left. They're hungry, girl. Do you have any tidbits to toss their way, or should I give you talking points?"

She smiled. "I'm all set, and don't call me 'girl.' Like. Ever."

"Wouldn't dream of it." He winked and opened the door for her then escorted her ahead of her parents. As soon as the media recognized Amanda, they swarmed her like five-year-old's around a soccer ball.

Kip was first to interview her, his cameraman pointing the large device in Amanda's face like it was a machine gun. "Welcome to your election party, DA Hawthorne. Do you have any comment on the returns thus far?"

"Thank you Kip. It's good to be here. I'm grateful for the tremendous show of support tonight. I'm pleased with the early returns but the polls are still open, so I don't want to get out in front of the voters."

"Ever the cautious candidate, do you have any comment on your opponents' repeated allegations that the SFPD covered up a shooting you were involved in at China Beach?"

Amanda gave him her remain-calm-and-carry-on smile. "I have great faith in the SFPD investigation of the shooting, which was concluded two years ago. I sleep well at night, knowing I defended myself and others on the beach when a mobster killed Police Officer George Banks, who was by my side, and was taking shots at Dr. Jen Dawson, who was swimming. The mobster even told me he was going to kill me after he shot me in the arm. Here." She tapped her deltoid. "There was nothing to cover up. I shot a man in the name of justice, and the beach was filled with people who were eyewitnesses."

"Gavin Morales said the police covered up witness accounts that you shot Eddy Valentine after disarming and interrogating him."

"That's nonsense. I'd say Mr. Morales' attack is a last-ditch attempt to deflect attention from being investigated and having search warrants executed at his home and campaign headquarters for colluding with the North Koreans. He's grasping at straws, and it won't work. The voters know my record and have heard my position on the real issues—issues that matter to our city. Thank you Kip. I'm going to mingle and thank the people in attendance tonight. You're welcome to stay if you like."

She nodded at Chance, who bulldozed a path through the media for her to enter the sea of supporters.

***

As Jen applied makeup, she listened to Amanda's remarks on the TV located in her bedroom. She rounded the corner and looked at the flat screen. Amanda looked confident, but she could see the stress lines around her mouth. Even though she handled the limelight well, it wore on her.

She looks kind of defeated even though she's winning. She needs me by her side. Someone who can make her smile. Light up her world. I need to get my ass in gear.

She returned to her closet to choose something sexy but supportive. Amanda was in an elegant dress with a wrap. *Should I wear a dress too? That would mean strappy heels. Ugh. Chance said I should embrace my tinted chapstick self and my natural beauty. Amanda is attracted to me the way I am, so I don't have to impress her. And I sure as hell don't want to compete with the princess.* Jen selected her stylish black slacks—her "ass pants"—and a slinky cold-shoulder top that flaunted the toned strands of muscle running over her shoulders.

She picked up the burner phone and looked at the nude pic of Amanda, her last text, and Jen's reply: *Fucking hot as hell. I could devour you right now.*

She wondered whether Amanda even had her burner phone with her, but took a chance, texting: *Guess what? Tonight is election night, and I'm going to give you a victory fuck that you'll never forget.*

She laughed to herself then raced down to her SUV that was parked on the street. She drove quickly to the Yacht Club and, as she entered, she could hear the party in full swing. The polls had officially closed, and the most recent tally indicated that Amanda had won by a landslide.

The place was packed, but Amanda was nowhere in sight. Jen had no idea how she was going to find her.

Kip Moynihan saw Jen immediately and pounced on her. "Dr. Jen Dawson. Don't you look lovely tonight? Have a minute for an interview?"

Jen felt ambushed and unprepared. She plastered a smile to her face but her insides clenched. She didn't have any talking points and didn't know what the hell her relationship was with Amanda, even though she knew what she *wanted* it to be. Moreover, she just wasn't in the mood for Kip-fucking-Moynihan. "Maybe later, Kip."

Fortunately, Chance emerged from the crowd and as soon as he saw Jen, he broke into a broad smile. "About time. Amanda's been waiting for you all night. Follow me, gorgeous."

"Does the good doctor have time for a short interview?" Kip asked Chance.

"Later," Chance said, brushing him off a second time.

"Count on it," Kip replied.

By the look of the T-shirt Chance wore over his white collared shirt and tie, they believed Amanda had officially won. The phrase on the front said, "**Fabulous as Fuck, DA Amanda**." Jen looked around and others were wearing it too. Amanda's victory T-shirt. *Talk about shaking up the old guard at the Yacht Club!*

She slipped her hand through Chance's arm, and he serpentined them through the crowd to the other side of the room where Amanda was holding a glass of something fizzy, talking to a group that included Melissa Cohen.

Jen was shocked to see Melissa since she had asked Amanda not to continue therapy at the clinic during the election. A surge of anxiety surfaced as they drew near.

"Melissa is here?" Jen whispered to Chance.

He smiled. "She and her husband, Bruce, are big donors."

"I'll be damned."

They approached the periphery of the group, somewhat behind Amanda. Chance stayed by Jen, so she wouldn't be left hanging.

Jen's presence must have triggered Amanda's sixth sense because she turned suddenly, her eyes finding Jen's. She stopped mid-sentence in her story and held out her hand for Jen. Amanda took a half-step back, so Jen could join the group.

"Everyone, this is my partner, Dr. Jen Dawson," Amanda said.

"Hi, Jen," Melissa said. "Good to see you here tonight."

"Likewise. Hello, Bruce," Jen said, shaking his hand. She had met him at a few work occasions and she liked him.

Amanda introduced Jen to two other people in the group.

Chance leaned in and said to Amanda, "I'm sure you have plenty to talk about. I'll be back in a few minutes with an update and the timing for your victory speech, District Attorney Hawthorne."

"Take your time," she said, talking to Chance, but focusing her adoring brown eyes on Jen.

Jen leaned in next to Amanda's ear. "You look hot in that dress."

"Can I kiss you?" Amanda whispered back.

Jen smiled and stayed close. Rather than a simple peck on Jen's cheek, Amanda planted a full kiss on Jen's lips. For Amanda, that was a risqué public display of affection, especially at an election party.

As they broke apart, Amanda said, "Thanks for coming."

"Wouldn't miss it." Jen's soft voice was barely audible above the talkative crowd.

"Looks like you're going to win this election, Amanda," Melissa said, drawing Amanda and Jen back into the conversation.

"With your help. Thank you for your generosity, Melissa. Did you get your clinic computer system running again?" Amanda asked.

"We did," Melissa said. "Everyone is so relieved that we're back in the 21st Century. The millennials in the office were initially dumbfounded about how to run a clinic without a computer, weren't they, Jen?"

Sure, easy to joke about it now. "Oh yes, but the older nurses remembered how to see patients in a paper world. I'm eternally grateful for Shannon. She helped me stay on schedule."

"Hurray for Shannon," Amanda said. "Listen, good seeing you both. I'm so happy you're here and let me know if there's anything I can do for you. You have my direct number."

378

Melissa nodded.

"Jen and I are off to make the rounds so we can properly thank everyone in attendance."

Amanda led Jen away, ducking into a hallway off the main ballroom. She pulled Jen behind a coat rack where they could have two seconds of privacy.

Unable to contain her excitement, Amanda reached for Jen's bare shoulders. "I got your latest text. Who knew you liked to talk so dirty?"

They looked at each other, the noisy crowd fading away, their private moment turning into a charged intimacy.

"I'm a 'cunnilinguist,' and I meant every word I said. Fuckin' hotter than hell." While holding Amanda's eyes, Jen brought Amanda's palm to her lips and delicately French-kissed the warm, soft skin there. She was rewarded with Amanda's eyes spitting fiery lust and an involuntary convulsion of pleasure.

"You're killing me," Amanda rasped.

"This is just the beginning." Jen moved to the inside of Amanda's wrist and tickled it with the tip of her tongue.

Amanda practically levitated. "You're full of naughty tricks behind those innocent blue eyes, aren't you?"

Jen smiled and lowered Amanda's hand.

Their lips collided, smudging lipstick, as Jen gave Amanda a taste of what she had in store for her.

"Wanna leave now?" Amanda asked when they eased back.

"We have to make the rounds," Jen said against Amanda's lips. She could feel Amanda quivering like a Chihuahua.

"If you say so. Where's Kristin tonight?" Amanda slid her hands down Jen's arms and grasped her hands.

"Staying with Tommy at his place." Jen knew how Amanda's mind worked. "Want to come back to my place after this?"

Amanda nodded. "I'd love to. I have an overnight bag. Not that I was expecting to—"

Jen's eyes twinkled, as she shushed Amanda by kissing her again.

Chance shattered the moment with his persistent presence. "There you are! Sorry for interrupting the school girls behind the book stacks but all the votes are in. You got 88% of the vote and your tribe wants to hear from you, dear."

"'Dear?' You may not call me 'dear.' Only 88%, huh?" Amanda asked.

"You're welcome," he said, bowing.

Jen laughed. "I'm sure that's the lowest score Amanda has ever received on a test."

Amanda squeezed Jen's hand.

"And see, that was my highest," Chance said. "I graduated *nada cum loud*! And I mean really loud."

The women guffawed.

"Here's your victory speech." He handed her a plastic sleeve with a few typewritten pages in it.

"Thank you for your hard work and masterful strategy." Amanda hugged him.

"It was my pleasure. Ready for the stage?"

"Only if Jen stands by my side," Amanda said.

"I'm not sure," Jen said. "I'm not one for the spotlight, you know."

"Please?" Amanda implored her with a lusty, possessive look. "I don't want to get separated in the crowd afterward. I can't stop touching you."

"Since you put it *that* way." Jen didn't want to surf the crowd either.

Chance led the way to the stage where a band was set to play after Amanda spoke. He introduced her as the next District Attorney, and everyone cheered as she took the microphone, all the while holding Jen's hand. After glancing over Chance's remarks, she returned them to him.

"Thank you all for re-electing me the District Attorney of San Francisco County!" Amanda raised their clasped hands in the air.

Everyone applauded for an extended time.

"We have much work to do, and I'm proud to be your representative to get it done. This was a grueling campaign, as you saw firsthand, and I'm indebted to you for standing by my side throughout." She looked at Jen then at her parents in the front row. "Specifically, I want to thank my parents, Jack and Chloe Hawthorne, and my partner, Dr. Jen Dawson." After another round of applause, Amanda said, "I'm proud that we ran a positive campaign, keeping the voters' issues our main priority and our eye on fighting crime for the benefit of the city. Thanks to Chance Greyson's oversight for getting our message out. I'd like to note that the victory Tshirts some of you are wearing tonight were not approved by me. Those are Chance's brainchild!" She looked directly at him and winked, then waited while everyone laughed. "I invite you to stay and dance to this awesome band that Chance tells me will rock you late into the night. The room is ours so enjoy yourselves. Thank you, everyone."

Everyone roared with applause. Amanda clapped in return at Chance and her parents, pointed to a few people in the crowd, including Melissa and Bruce, then led Jen to the stairway off the small stage. Chance followed, signaling the band to start. Jen and Amanda were met at the bottom of the stairway by Jack and Chloe, who hugged each of them.

"Hi, Jen. So good of you to come. How's Kristin?" Chloe asked.

"She's doing great. We should get together in the next few weeks if Amanda has any time off," Jen said.

"We'd love that. Do you want to drive down to our place for dinner? Kristin can play in the backyard," Jack said.

"We'd love to," Jen said, sliding her hand through Amanda's arm.

"That sounds relaxing. It's a date. Mom and dad, thanks for going all-out on this campaign." Tears welled in her eyes.

"We believe in you, dear," Chloe said, hugging her.

"Thanks Mom." Even while hugging Chloe, Amanda didn't let go of Jen's hand, which was looped through her arm.

"We love you and Kristin too," Chloe said directly to Jen.

"We love you too, Chloe," Jen said, her voice full of genuine warmth.

Chance interrupted them. "Amanda, you wanted me to tell you when Chief of Police Delmastro got here."

"On our way. Catch you later," she said to her parents, pulling Jen along.

Ryan was in the center of the crowd with his wife, a beautiful woman both Jen and Amanda had met on prior occasions.

"Ryan, thanks for coming," Amanda said, as they approached.

He leaned down and hugged her. "Wouldn't miss it." He turned to Jen. "How are you, Jen?"

"Fantastic. Thanks for asking. Hi, Rebecca, long time, no see. How are you?"

"Excellent. So good to see you again, Jen."

Jen hugged her. "Congratulations on your promotion to Chief of Police, Ryan. I think Tommy is planning to bring Cy to your swearing-in ceremony."

"Uncle Cy will be there? Awesome," Ryan said.

"He's so proud of you," Jen said.

"Is Tommy here tonight?" Ryan asked, scanning the crowd.

"No. He's babysitting Kristin."

"Right. That makes sense. How old is she now?" Ryan asked.

"Eighteen months already," Jen said, beaming.

"I'm so happy for you. What a fun age," Rebecca said, squeezing Jen's arm.

"She just started running around the house," Jen said, turning to Amanda, who smiled.

"The challenge is keeping up," Rebecca said.

"Uh-huh," Ryan said. "Big win, tonight, Amanda. Congrats."

"Thanks for your support. I owe you one for the way you handled the media at your press conference," she said.

He held up two fingers, reminding her she owed him two.

She laughed. "I haven't forgotten." She was more than comfortable trading in the currency of favors with Ryan.

After chatting more with the Delmastros, Jen and Amanda made the rounds for an hour, Chance guiding them, dutifully thanking everyone. Jen didn't know many people there, but she was amazed at how Amanda seemed to know just what to say to each of them.

When people started talking less and dancing more, Jen leaned into Amanda's curly hair and asked, "Do you want to dance or leave?"

Amanda visibly shivered in response to Jen's voice, so close and low in her ear. "Let's dance at your place."

"In that case, let's go. I drove, so we can take my car."

"Done. I'll tell Chance." Amanda turned to look for him. He was standing within arm's reach.

"We're going to leave now. Thanks for everything you've done. Talk tomorrow?" Amanda asked.

"Not going to dance?" Chance asked playfully, eyeing up Jen.

"Not here," Amanda said, smiling.

"Have fun." He gave them each a peck on the cheek.

They turned and Kip Moynihan was standing between them and the door. Jen stifled a groan. "Hi, Kip. You look nice tonight," she said, admiring his sharp suit.

"Thanks. Chance actually applied my makeup—" he said.

"And taught you a few subtle tricks," Chance said, moving to Kip's side.

"And taught me one subtlety," Kip said, casting an indulgent look at Chance.

"He has quite the touch," Jen said. "He applied mine before your interviews and I've never looked better."

"See?" Chance said to Kip, jutting out his hip and putting his hand on it.

"No arguments here," Kip said. "Time to dance?"

"Thought you'd never ask," Chance said.

As they made their way to the dance floor, Amanda whispered to Jen, "I knew Chance was a good hire. Daddy was very insightful about that move."

32

Sunset District

"I can't tell you how good this feels—to be back in your car," Amanda said as they drove through the fog to Jen's new neighborhood, Frank Degrugilliers trailing them in Amanda's car.

Is she speaking in metaphors again? Does "my car" really mean "my good graces?" Jen wondered. "I'm glad you're fond of my car because I like having you in it," she joked, then said in a more serious tone, "I actually enjoyed being by your side tonight, even on the stage."

"It was a good crowd, but it wouldn't have been half as fun without you." Amanda shifted in her seat and adjusted her seat belt so she could lay her hand in Jen's on the center console.

The good kind of chills ran up Jen's arm. "I was surprised to see Melissa there. Last I heard, she asked you to go to another clinic."

"She's a class act. Asked me to leave in one breath—to protect her business—and donated money in the next. I respect her decision. She told me tonight I can return for therapy now that the election is over."

"Excellent. I was worried about that."

"Me too. I don't want to fall off track. The personal attacks in this campaign just about derailed me. Worse than trying a high-profile homicide case, if you ask me. Thank God I have another five years in office before we have to start this ugly process again."

"How about we just enjoy tonight before we plan what we're going to do five years from now?" *Does this woman's brain never stop?*

Jen found a spot on the same block as her building and carefully parallel-parked her SUV in the tight space. She turned off the motor and felt Amanda grip her arm, stopping her from getting out. *First Nicole, now Amanda. They won't let me leave my car.* She turned and looked at Amanda in the sulphurous glow under the street lamp.

"I know you're taking a huge chance on me tonight. I promise I won't let you down," Amanda said, her serious tone just above a whisper.

Protecting her heart, Jen said, "No promises. Let's just keep it simple."

"That sounds a tad impersonal." Amanda ran her finger along the inside of Jen's wrist.

"Sorry it came out that way. I didn't mean it to. What I meant was—we don't have to make a bunch of promises. Let's just take it one day at a time, okay?" She shivered under Amanda's light tickle.

"I can do that, but fair warning, I want you back," Amanda said, leaning over for a quick brush of the lips.

That's what I'm afraid of. Big declarations of commitment.

Amanda's initial kiss was a gentle graze, reuniting lips that had once been close on a daily basis. The spark spread through Jen, popping off fireworks in her stomach. "We need to get out of here."

They broke apart and opened their doors, Jen coming around to the sidewalk to help Amanda down in her dress and heels. Once Amanda's Louboutins hit the sidewalk, Jen pulled her into her body. She leaned down and kissed Amanda properly, exploring the taste of her mouth.

Amanda was more nervous than she had been at her election party, afraid she would disappoint Jen. She wanted her so much that her tummy clenched in both agony and desire when Jen leaned down to kiss her. She didn't want to appear sex-starved, but her hands had a mind of their own, flying to Jen's back, caressing her muscles, admiring the sinewy bands that were more defined than six weeks ago. She traced the ridges around Jen's shoulder blades then moved to her ribcage, her thumbs exploring the ripped abs under her blouse. There wasn't an ounce of fat on her. Amanda had never been attracted to bodybuilders, but Jen's solid curves turned her on. She broke from the kiss long enough to say, "Wow. You've been hitting the gym."

Jen moaned in response, her skin searing under Amanda's touch. The wattage in Amanda's fingers was palpable. She returned to Amanda's mouth, pressing her tongue against Amanda's lips, demanding to be let in.

Amanda parted for her, welcoming her, pulling her in so deep that Jen felt like she was swimming in a pond of warm pudding. After a few minutes of blissful submersion, they broke apart, breathless and panting.

Jen turned to Amanda and draped her arm around Amanda's shoulders. "To my apartment." She kissed Amanda's temple as they stumbled along the sidewalk.

Amanda's fingers found the spot on Jen's ribcage that drove her wild. When Amanda circled her thumb over the blouse, Jen almost crumpled to her knees.

"Stop it! You know I can't breathe when you touch me there!"

"That's why I like to, but in the interest of making it to your apartment, I'll lay off," Amanda teased, kissing Jen's neck.

So accustomed to security detail now, Amanda didn't pay any attention to Frank trailing behind them, carrying her overnight bag. She had actually forgotten all about him.

Jen noticed him then remembered what it was like to live in Amanda's world. "Where is Frank going to sleep tonight?"

"I think he just wants to make sure we get into your place okay, have a look around, then leave," Amanda said.

When they entered the lobby of Jen's building, she froze.

Nicole was standing in the center of the lobby staring at them. While Jen didn't remove her arm from Amanda's shoulders, she stood stock-straight. "What are you doing here, Nicole? I didn't miss something, did I?"

"No. I, uh, was going to surprise you. I texted you, but I guess you were busy." Nicole nodded toward Amanda.

"Hi, Nicole. I'm sorry I disrupted your plans," Amanda said.

Frank sauntered to her side, his black hair slicked back like feathers on a crow. In a black suit and tie, he still cut a large, ominous figure.

"Thanks, but I doubt that," Nicole said, her voice flirting with menace.

"Second floor, 203," Jen said, pressing her keys into Amanda's hand. Jen didn't want a scene, and didn't know Nicole well enough to predict what she might say or do. In any event, Nicole deserved to have a few minutes alone with Jen to end their relationship, if you could call it that.

"See you in a few minutes," Amanda said, disappearing up the stairway, Frank right behind her.

"I'm sorry, Nicole. I went to Amanda's election party, and…well…I think we're getting back together. I apologize for not being able to tell you sooner, but I didn't know myself."

"Were you seeing her while dating me?" she asked, her voice cracking in anger.

"No. Of course not. I was available when we went on our one date. It's so hard to explain, and this isn't fair to you, finding out Amanda and I are back together by running into us." Jen shrugged with frustration.

"Were you just using me to make her jealous?" Nicole asked, her voice truculent.

"No, it wasn't like that at all." Jen tentatively took a step forward. "I like you and I was really into you on our date, but I'm no longer available. I told you my life is complicated, and my relationship with Amanda is part of that. I'm sorry if I misled you."

"You're kind of a fucking mess. It's best if we don't see each other again." Nicole pushed past Jen and stormed out the door.

Jen looked at the ceiling and groaned. "Why am I so bad at relationships?"

She went to the stairway and passed Frank on his way down.

"Need me to stick around?" he asked.

"No. She's gone. She won't make any trouble."

"Does she have a key to your apartment?"

Jen recoiled, her eyes flashing. "No. God no."

"Good. I'll stay in the car outside for a while to make sure she doesn't come back into your building."

"Thanks Frank."

"No problem. I prefer a locked building with a doorman, though."

Jen restrained herself from rolling her eyes, turned, and took the stairs two at a time. When she arrived at her apartment, she knocked on the door.

Dressed in only her bra and panties but still wearing her heels, Amanda swung the door wide. "I like your place."

Wow! Did seeing Nicole light a competitive flare? Jen quickly closed and locked the door behind her.

"It looks better with you in it." Jen admired Amanda's feminine physique, running her finger along the outline of Amanda's sexy bra, then resting her hands on Amanda's slim waist. She walked Amanda back against the wall where she could ravage her mouth while pressing her body against her.

Grateful that Amanda didn't want to discuss the Nicole drama, Jen kissed her hard. Deep into their kiss, she felt Amanda's leg curl around her waist, so she grabbed her ass and pinned her back to the wall. Amanda writhed against her, pressing into Jen's hips.

Jen leaned into Amanda and dove into her mouth. The look of shock in Amanda's eyes was immediately replaced with lust, driving Jen to do more. "Did you find the bedroom?" Jen asked against Amanda's lips.

"Show me." Amanda gently bit Jen's neck then licked it, making Jen moan.

We have to get horizontal. Jen let go of Amanda's ass and Amanda's feet slid to the floor. Jen led her through the living room, where Amanda's dress was draped over a chair, her big bag next to it, and into her spacious bedroom overlooking the beach.

"I'm a little nervous. How about you?" Amanda asked, resting her arms on Jen's shoulders and twining her hands through the hair at her nape, removing her ponytail holder.

Jen let her head fall back against Amanda's hand and shook out her hair. "A little. It's been so long that I'm almost desperate but don't know where to start."

"So long? I thought you and Nicole—" Amanda said.

"Let's not talk about her, huh?" Jen interjected, seeing the curious glint in Amanda's eyes. "She doesn't compare to the way I feel about you." If Amanda thought Jen had a short relationship with Nicole—including sex—so much the better. Even Steven.

Amanda's eyes turned a darker shade of brown and she took the initiative by grasping the hem of Jen's blouse and pulling it over her head. "God, your body is beautiful." She ran her fingers along Jen's collarbone, over her shoulders, and down her arms, squeezing her triceps along the way. She buried her face in Jen's chest while simultaneously unhooking her bra, then devoured Jen's breasts, licking and nibbling each nipple with the right blend of care and recklessness. Her hands glided over Jen's rib cage, down her abdomen, into her waistband and the blonde curls waiting there.

Her nipples on fire, Jen arched into Amanda, submitting to her. "Yes," she hissed, barely able to breathe.

Amanda returned to Jen's mouth, covering her wet breasts with her palms. "I want you so bad it hurts."

Jen reached around Amanda and lifted her up, holding her in the air while she kissed her. Amanda used the opportunity to kick off her heels and wrap her legs around Jen's waist again.

Capable of supporting Amanda's weight, Jen gracefully turned them and lowered Amanda to the bed, her back hitting first, and Jen landing on top of her. A maneuver she wouldn't have attempted a year ago, she now did easily after amping up her CrossFit routine.

Amanda's surprised shriek made Jen smile. "You like being tossed around?"

"Yes. Especially when you land on top of me."

Taking physical control made Jen feel like possessing Amanda in the most raw and preternatural way. She unclipped Amanda's bra and pressed her chest to hers, savoring the sizzling curves of her hot body. She propped herself on her elbows and kissed Amanda's neck while rubbing her foxy dive against Amanda's. When she scattered a frenzy of kisses down Amanda's neck to her breasts, she felt Amanda tremble beneath her.

"Oh, Jen. I—"

Jen shushed Amanda and traced her fingers around Amanda's breasts, watching her nipples grow taught. She bent and placed the tip of her tongue on the peak of the nipple closest to her while cradling Amanda's rib cage with her hands.

As Amanda watched Jen's tongue flirt with one nipple then move to the other, she whimpered. An involuntary wave trembled through her torso, setting off a long, slow hiss.

Jen put Amanda out of her misery by taking one breast in her mouth then the other, sending frissons of passion across Amanda's skin. As Jen sucked, she felt herself become wet, the blood in her body traveling to her pussy.

An even lower, guttural moan escaped Amanda as she twined her fingers in Jen's hair, gently holding her. When Amanda's hips rose off the bed, Jen left her breasts and licked a slow line down to Amanda's bellybutton, where she did a circle, then continued down to her black, lacy panties. After kissing her through the fabric, Jen peeled them off, pushing them past Amanda's ankles and tossing them.

"Show me all of you," Jen rasped.

Without hesitation, Amanda spread her legs for Jen.

Jen admired Amanda's pussy, inhaling her female scent, her mouth hovering within striking distance. She glanced up to find Amanda watching her. "Even more beautiful than the pic you texted me."

The gold flecks in Amanda's eyes burned so hot that Jen thought they were going to illuminate the room. "I want you so much."

"You'll get me," Jen said, lowering her mouth to the valleys and contours surrounding Amanda's Venus.

One hand on her breast and the other grabbing Amanda's tight ass, Jen's tongue did delicious things to Amanda, making her entire body gyrate in pleasure.

"Oh, Jen," Amanda said, her muscles contracting in sweet agony. "Yes. Oh, yes. God."

When Jen slipped a finger inside Amanda's tight heat, she felt Amanda clench around her.

Amanda leaned her chin down and looked into Jen's eyes as the tip of Jen's finger massaged with the right amount of pressure in just the right spot. Jen had never had any trouble finding Amanda's G-spot, its ridges almost as defined as the roof of her mouth.

Passion overtook Amanda, her nostrils flaring and her mouth falling open, as her stomach muscles shivered in tense anticipation.

Seeing her lover on the edge of ecstasy made Jen smile against Amanda's pussy. Amanda was so close, Jen knew she could take her there with a few delicate tongue strokes. As Jen moved her finger, Amanda's breathing became jagged, small gasps of pleasure punctuating her writhing body and filling the silence of the room.

"Please," she whimpered.

Jen opened her mouth wider and covered Amanda's clit again, her tongue flicking madly.

Amanda thrust her pelvis skyward, her body going hard on arrival to orgasm, then shaking violently as she screamed Jen's name.

Amanda clenched her thighs around Jen as her hands flew to the back of Jen's head, holding her in place while she came down from the intensity of release.

Reveling in the pleasure she delivered, Jen teased Amanda with a few more tongue darts, amplifying her aftershocks and making her spasm in delight.

"Oh, God. I can feel your tongue all the way to my heart when you do that."

Jen cradled Amanda's hips in her arms, keeping her face nestled in Amanda's sensuous valley, the scent and taste of Amanda's sex filling her senses, making her dizzy with desire. She was throbbing herself, wanting to be touched—needing to be touched—but she savored every second of being this intimate with Amanda, taking pride in setting her free.

She felt Amanda's fingers cajoling the back of her head, signaling her to make the trip from Amanda's pussy to her mouth. She kissed her way over the peach fuzz on Amanda's tummy and licked a small line from her bellybutton to one of her nipples, gently savoring the warmth of one breast in her mouth, then the other. Amanda held Jen's head, moaning with limp satisfaction.

"Come here," Amanda said, pulling Jen to her mouth, where Jen was consumed in a hungry kiss, Amanda's ardent tongue plundering her.

She felt Amanda's hands roam over her back, lingering lightly to scratch her shoulders, then move lower to her hard ass, where Amanda dug in, her palms rubbing frenetically.

"Bring your pussy to my face," Amanda commanded against Jen's mouth.

Jen propped herself up on her elbows and looked at Amanda. "Are you sure you want me on top of you?"

"More than anything," Amanda pleaded.

She always felt so selfish in this position, the focus on her own pleasure, but Amanda wanted her, so she was going for it. *I deserve this.* Jen slid her hips over Amanda's chest and rested her knees on either side of her neck.

Amanda placed her hands on Jen's breasts at the same time her tongue speared Jen's clit, too long neglected and yearning to bask in the sun. The force of Amanda's tongue-thrust made Jen double over the headboard. As Amanda teased and licked upward, Jen hung on for dear life while Amanda's fingers tormented Jen's nipples and her tongue worked magic over her hotspot.

Surrendering, longing for sweet release— *Oh fuck, her mouth is so talented*—Jen felt Amanda's tongue and fingers in her, then over her, probing and circling. Jen was reminded of how Amanda's deft fingers had worked the strings on the neck of her cello, then was jolted back to the reality of a crescendo building deep within her.

The rumble started in the vee between her thighs, sending waves outward to her limbs, rippling through her body as it built momentum and shattered her senses, resulting in her screaming, "*God. Yes. Amanda!*"

She came with force, her abdominal muscles rippling as she leaned down, cradling Amanda's head. Amanda teased some more, firing off convulsions, until Jen couldn't withstand the lashing any longer.

Drained and satisfied, Jen scooted down Amanda's body, so she could lay on her, her glistening body melding to Amanda's every curve. Amanda wrapped her arms around Jen, their wet skin fusing with heat.

"Thank you," Jen whispered in Amanda's ear. "I loved every second."

"I love you," Amanda whispered in return.

A few heartbeats later, Jen said, "I love you too."

Amanda answered by hugging Jen even tighter, then wrapping her leg over Jen's, securing her in place. "I'm never letting you go."

Her body and soul at home—adhered to Amanda and satisfied—Jen's mind was free from all thought as she drifted off to sleep.

33

In the middle of the night, Jen stirred, surprised to discover Amanda lying on top of her back like they had slept pre-pregnancy—over two years ago now. Oh, the feeling of being completely pinned to the bed, her soulmate's heartbeat drumming through her. Amanda's hot breath flowed across Jen's neck, the rhythmic flow steady and warm. A feeling of security consumed her, Amanda's curly hair falling around Jen's face like a warm cape.

My love. Jen fell back asleep.

When she awoke again later, her chest swelled with happiness at being spooned up to Amanda. She moved her hand down Amanda's arm and over her ribs to rest on her tummy. She scooted closer, pressing her chest into Amanda's back, holding her in a loving embrace, squeezing a little too hard, but she couldn't stop herself. She was hopelessly in love with this woman, whose presence in her bed filled her world with rare contentment. When she and Amanda were one, the rest of the world didn't matter.

Amanda was awakened by Jen's hand sliding down her arm. Momentarily confused, she let her eyes adjust to the glow from the streetlight outside. Her mind relaxed when she remembered she was at Jen's apartment. Her beloved Jen. They'd made love, fulfilling Amanda's deepest desires. She felt Jen conform to her back, the warmth of Jen's body spooning against hers, the tickle on her bottom from Jen's soft tendrils. Amanda pulled Jen's arm tight around her ribs, relishing her hand resting on her tummy. *I won my Jen back.* She fell into a state of bliss as she drifted off again, Jen's warm breath on her neck. She moaned but wasn't conscious to it.

At dawn, Jen awoke to sun filtering through the fog and the sound of muted keyboard tapping. Her eyelids fluttered open to find Amanda sitting next to her, an iPad on her knees, typing away. Jen's heart leapt at the sight of Amanda back in her bed. How was she going to contain her enthusiasm? She breathed in and smelled the musky scent of their sexually satisfied bodies. So poignant, she couldn't tell where Amanda's scent stopped and hers began. A proprietary mix. She closed her eyes and reached over to her lover, her hand nestling into the soft skin along Amanda's bikini line.

"Whoa! You're awake." Amanda folded the cover over her iPad and tossed it on the floor. She slid under the covers and rolled over to face Jen, her brown eyes dancing with energy. "Good morning, sexy."

"Mmm." Jen found Amanda's breast and gently cupped it, eliciting a hum.

"I emailed work and told them I'd be in around noon," Amanda said, kissing Jen's forehead.

"What time is it?" Jen moved her hand to Amanda's back, pulling her closer.

"A little before seven," Amanda said.

"We have an hour. I have to be to work at ten."

"I can do a lot of fun things to you in an hour," Amanda said, smothering Jen's mouth with her own.

Forty minutes later, Jen lay in a zombie state, incapable of forming words. All she could do was listen to the beating of Amanda's heart, which was slowing down after Jen had made it race to the finish line.

"I better get you a cup of coffee if you plan to shower and be to work on time," Amanda said, throwing off the sheets.

Jen closed her eyes, falling into a catnap while Amanda went to the kitchen. Not enough time passed before Amanda awakened her. "Hey, beautiful, here's your coffee."

"If you insist." Jen pushed herself up and leaned against a pillow. She held the cup under her nose and breathed in the aroma. "Thank you."

Amanda tucked in next to her, a mug in her hand and her iPad back on her lap. "I love you." She pecked Jen on the forehead.

By Jen's count, Amanda had said, "I love you," more in the last 12 hours than she had during their two-year relationship.

Rather than reply, Jen sipped her coffee, which she noticed had just the right amount of cream and sugar in it. "This is fantastic. I wish we could stay in bed all day."

Amanda ran her hand down Jen's thigh. "Your job is too important. Maybe we could plan an overnight this weekend?"

Jen nodded, not wanting to commit to anything too soon. Amanda seemed to understand her reluctance so didn't press the subject. She tipped her chin at the window overlooking the beach. "Great view."

"The benefit of being on the second floor. I get to look at my favorite beach."

"You like living in this neighborhood, don't you?"

"Always have. Not that I have anything against Sea Cliff. It's just that Ocean Beach sings to me. It's so vast and beautiful, the entire ocean before us."

"The sun suits you too," Amanda said, stroking Jen's long, blonde hair.

"And Kristin. We'll have a lot of fun playing out there."

"Picking up sand dollars," Amanda added.

"Yeah," Jen said wistfully, recalling the last time they had walked the beach as a family, Zane on a leash.

"I'll miss Zane on our next beach walk," Amanda said, reading Jen's mind.

"Me too. I loved that dog. I suppose I should call the vet today and make arrangements to pick up his ashes."

"Let me do it," Amanda offered. "You've been through enough."

"You'd do that for me?"

"Of course. I'm doing it for us. I loved him too."

"Thanks. I owe you."

"Nonsense."

"Guess I should hop in the shower." Jen dropped a kiss on the side of Amanda's head and got out the opposite side.

When Amanda heard the shower running, she called Jack. "Hi, Daddy."

"Hi, baby. Congratulations! Nice article in *The Chronicle* this morning."

"I saw it. Chance really earned his money, didn't he?"

"You earned those votes, kiddo. No one else."

Pride crept in around her heart. "Thanks. I saw that Mayor Woo was re-elected too."

"You'll have to deal with him for another term."

"Aw. He's sort of grown on me. I'm in my second term now. More powerful."

"That's my girl."

"Hey, I was wondering if you and mom might be interested in a new project. That is, if you have any money left."

"Very funny. Yes, our extra security precautions on all of our accounts prevented any more theft. In fact, Lieutenant Navarro and Agent MacNeil already recovered the $2 million for us."

"They're pretty amazing," Amanda said, not wanting to talk about Roxy. The less her parents knew, the better.

"I was just saying to your mother that I didn't know what we were going to do with all the time on our hands now that your campaign is over."

"I have the perfect solution. How about you and mom look for a nice house in the Sunset District overlooking the beach along the Great Highway? Buy an old one and renovate it for Jen, Kristin, and me."

"Does this mean you and Jen are back together?"

"Nothing permanent yet, but she likes living in the Sunset District, and her current apartment is too small for all three of us. We plan to take it slow, but I'm pretty sure she won't move back to Sea Cliff, so I want something first-class in her neighborhood."

"A lot of those beach houses are pretty run down. We'd have to gut something and rebuild it. Might take six months, or even longer."

"That sounds about right. Maybe your holding company could buy it, and we could pay rent. That way, Jen wouldn't have to know you own it."

"I could set aside her rental payments as a college fund for Kristin," he suggested.

"Maybe set them aside as a capital investment in the house, so we can buy it from the corporation."

"Then you'd have to pay taxes on it, which will be pretty steep."

"Oh, right." She let those thoughts go. "We'll figure all that out later. For now, just buy something and renovate it into home beautiful, will you?"

"Won't Jen want input on the decorating?"

"I really don't want her to know we own it. Let's just present it as a house for rent."

"Your mother and I can decorate it, but we'll need one of you to give us your ideas."

She sighed. "I will. Remember to design a yoga studio, and I'd like a garden terrace on the roof."

"See what I'm talking about? You have definite ideas."

"No worries. I'll work with you," Amanda said.

"We'll start looking today. Anything for you, Jen, and Kristin."

"Thank you Daddy."

"Love you."

"Love you too. Bye."

Amanda returned to her emails, her mind refocusing on the District Attorney docket.

Jen emerged from the bathroom and got dressed for work, humming a nameless tune as she dressed in front of her full-length mirror.

"Mind if I shower here too?" Amanda asked.

"Please do. If I'd known you wanted to, I would've invited you in with me."

Amanda stood and walked around the bed, fully nude. She leaned into Jen. "Next time."

Jen kissed her and watched her walk to the bathroom. *Perfection.*

She grabbed her phone from the bedside table and texted Tommy. *Everything good with you and Kristin this morning? Need my help with anything?*

A few minutes passed, and he replied, *Nope. All is well. I'm going to drop her off then visit Pops in the hospital.*

Jen replied, *Text me later and let me know if he's strong enough for Kristin and me to visit him after work.*

Tommy replied with the thumbs up emoji.

She dropped her phone in her bag and noticed her burner phone lying next to her wallet. It made her smile. She picked it up and texted Amanda. *Thanks for last night, sexy.*

While Jen sat at her kitchen table, eating a bowl of cereal and waiting for Amanda, she scratched out some phrases that were floating around in her mind:

My Recovering Heart

My heart rages to the sublime,
Infinitely courageous, it knows no crime.
Shedding tears of the past,
It screams to intertwine.

My heart defies reason,
Seeking love despite pain.
Combining with yours,
It finally beats again.

My heart rides the fire,
Hope deep within.
Consumed with desire,
No sinning again.

"What are you up to?" Amanda asked, as she entered the kitchen and poured a glass of orange juice. She was drying her hair with one towel and had another wrapped around her body.

"Eating breakfast and writing mediocre poetry. Do you need something to wear besides your cocktail dress from last night?"

"I love your poetry, and I brought some yoga pants. I'll swing by my house and change before I go to work. I have to feed Zumba too."

She likes my poetry. Jen smiled. "Hungry?"

"A banana sounds good." Amanda broke off one and leaned against the counter, watching Jen as she chewed.

Jen returned to her poem scribblings. "You're staring."

"I can't believe we made love and I'm standing in your kitchen." Amanda said. "Pinch me so I know it's real."

Jen laughed. "How am I supposed to write with you staring at me?"

Amanda ignored her question. "Have you heard from Tommy this morning? How's Kristin? How's Cy?"

"Both good. Kristin and I plan to visit Cy after work today."

"Good idea. I'll try to swing by there at some point today too. When do you think he'll be able to return home?"

"In a week. That was a big surgery. Hard to recover from when you're in your 70s."

"Poor guy. He's a fighter, though."

"That, he is." Jen stood and went to Amanda. Carefully lifting the towel over Amanda's hip, Jen lightly pinched Amanda's ass, then slapped it.

"Ouch. What was that for?" Amanda squealed, the pain rendered sweet by sexual excitement.

"You asked me to pinch you if it was real, and I'd say it's pretty real."

Amanda let the towel drop. "Kiss me and make it better."

"God, you're so high maintenance. Are you always going to be this needy?" Jen asked, as she dropped to her knees, kissing her way down Amanda's tummy. She blew over her damp, curly hair, making Amanda shiver in pleasure. Soon, her mouth was doing indecent things for a kitchen.

"I can't get enough of you," Amanda said, placing her hands on Jen's shoulders and doubling over.

"You taste spectacular, but I have to leave for work," Jen said against Amanda's pussy.

"When will I see you next, so I can ravish you?" Amanda said through a love-starved rasp.

"Tonight? Text me on our private phones. I already sent you a text this morning."

"That sounds exciting." Amanda scooped up her towel and wrapped it around herself again. She found her bag on a chair, but came up empty-handed for her phone. "That's weird. I can't find my burner phone."

"What?" Jen asked, looking up from loading the dishwasher.

"I can't find my burner phone. I had it last night at the election party, but I don't see it in my bag." She turned her bag upside down and dumped its contents out on the table. They both searched through the items, but the burner phone wasn't there.

"You had it at the party last night?" Jen asked.

"Yeah. I got your text last night about a victory fuck then dropped it in my small clutch, which is here, in my big bag," she said, showing Jen.

"There has to be an explanation. If it's not in your bag, maybe it fell out in my car. I'll run down and check." Jen grabbed her keys off the counter.

"One sec, let me check the pockets in my dress."

Jen hesitated by the door as she watched Amanda go to her dress where it was draped over the living room chair.

Amanda picked it up and felt inside the pockets. Nothing. She fell to her knees on the carpeting and checked in and around the chair. Nothing. She turned to Jen, her eyes filled with concern. "Not here."

Jen registered Amanda's panic. "I'll be right back." She rushed out the door of her apartment.

***

THE END

***

Message from the Author

If you enjoyed *Tinted Chapstick,* I'd be grateful for your review on Amazon and Goodreads.

***

If you want to stay in the loop and up-to-date on my novels and latest news, visit my website: https://www.alexivenice.com.

***

The next book in *The San Francisco Mystery Series* is *Sativa Strain.* Available now on Amazon and Kindle Unlimited. Look for this cover:

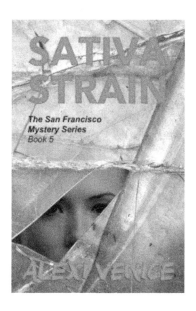

In *Sativa Strain*, Amanda carries with her the quiet confidence of a yogi, the unrelenting burden of a prosecutor, and the demons that torture the corners of her soul.

Newly re-elected as San Francisco's DA, Amanda faces her biggest internal and external foes yet when she and Detective Tommy Vietti investigate a high-profile murder implicating Kara Montiago, the CEO of a Silicon Valley tech company and candidate for President of the United States.

Navigating the shoals of SFPD corruption and hidden treasures, Tommy and Amanda learn that Kara Montiago is a Sativa-smoking dominatrix who preys on male subordinates.

Battling her desire to control everything around her, Amanda rekindles her relationship with Dr. Jen, the love of her life, pushing the boundaries of Jen's patience.

Acknowledgements

My friend and colleague, Erin Skold, continues to edit my books. She is steadfastly loyal to the character trajectories of Jen, Tommy and Amanda, as well as their individual voices.

My friend and colleague, Mik Burgraff, is a fantastic editor and mystery sleuth. She's a real Nancy Drew with a Fitbit, always pacing, pacing, pacing. I strive to make her proud and don't know what I'd do without her.

A friend and colleague, Susan McHugh, has been a delight to work with and pose next to for photo shoots in bars.

I thank Dr. Sue for letting me interrupt her busy days with questions about all things medical. Talk about kindhearted and patient, she's the real deal.

Many thanks to Reyka for proofreading services. I'm so happy she started wearing lipstick again! If I could influence one person to do one thing in my lifetime, that was it.

Rob Bignell's professional editing services rock.

Thank you to Melissa Levesque, Project Manager at eBookIt, Karen Carpenter, formatter, and Bo Bennett, founder of BookMarketingPro.

Erin, Sherry, Mik, Alexi, Susan and Reyka.
We mean business about *The San Francisco Mystery Series*

About the Author

Award-winning author Alexi Venice's legal and crime thrillers with sapphic leads serve up deadly appetizers, spicy main dishes, and HEA desserts.

Her bestselling spy thriller, *Lady Hawthorne, SFMS, Book 7*, received two 2022 Lesfic Bard Awards in Action & Adventure and Mystery.

Her bestselling legal thriller, *Standby Counsel, A Monica Spade Novel*, received the 2020 Lesfic Bard Award in Mystery and was named The Best Legal Thriller of 2021 by BestThrillers.com.

Venice is a member of International Thriller Writers, Golden Crown Literary Society, the Crime Writers' Association, and Romance Writers of America.

Thirty-four years of practicing law informs Venice's legal, medical, and crime fiction. Her heart, imagination, and life experience are the pesto on the pizza.

Instagram: alexivenice_author
Twitter: @VeniceAlexi
Website: www.alexivenice.com
Facebook: www.facebook.com/alexivenicenovels

Made in the USA
Monee, IL
12 October 2023

44488742R00234